Meeting of the Waters

KIM McLARIN

Meeting of the Waters

A NOVEL

WILLIAM MORROW · 75 YEARS OF PUBLISHING
An Imprint of HarperCollins*Publishers*

ISBN 0-688-16905-8

For Samantha and Isaac

Acknowledgments

Gratitude to Tibby, Tracey, Lindsay, Sam, Jennifer, Catherine, Hazel, the Ashmont Nursery School, and child-care providers everywhere, known and unknown. You are my heroes and heroines, always.

My thanks also to Claire Wachtel for her patience and to Suzanne Gluck for her persistence and to the talented members of the John Oliver Killens Writers Workshop. And to Kimmerly for title help.

And, finally, to God, my family, and to Matt.

Meeting of the Waters

Chapter 1

The first time he saw, in Philadelphia, the woman who had saved his life, Porter thought he might be hallucinating. What was it called—post-traumatic stress disorder? He knew the name of the condition because he had once written a story about it. Post-traumatic stress disorder, foxhole frenzy, battle fatigue, the clean-sounding phrase for freaking out after some hideous, life-shattering event. The story he'd written was about how the disorder manifested not just in war but in the everyday world. He built the story around a North Philadelphia kid whose four brothers and two uncles had been cut down, one by one, on the same block by the same combination of gangs and drugs over the course of two years. The kid, who was nine years old when his last remaining brother poured his blood into the street, spent nights pacing the living room of his house and went to school each morning dressed in his one good suit to save his mother the trouble of bringing it to the funeral home when he was killed. A psychologist at Temple told Porter he suspected there were more cases of PTSD walking the streets of urban America than had ever raised rifle against the Vietcong. "Philadelphia is choked with people waging their own private wars," the psychologist said.

Porter had looked for the woman in Los Angeles, had left his name and telephone number at the hospital where he was treated, and he checked at several more in case she herself had been hurt. But trying to track her that way, without a name, was ludicrous. A big, fat waste of time: "Uh, you don't have a beautiful black woman, midthirties, with big brown eyes, wearing some kind of greenish jacket in your hospital, do you?" He'd even gone back to South Central the day the curfew was lifted, back to the very same block where all hell had broken loose. That was difficult, and he was only able to do it because the area swarmed with news vans and reporters with cameras and cops. Still he stayed in his car and drove slowly through the streets, scanning the faces of black women, avoiding glaring into the eyes of black men. He was afraid of seeing again the men who had beaten him—not just because of what they would do but because of what he, in his humiliation and fear, might. After an hour or so he gave up.

And then, bang! Three weeks later, there she was! In Philadelphia! At least, he thought it was her.

He was outside the *Record* building at the time, having just returned from an interview ten blocks away through the suffocating late June heat. All Porter wanted was to get inside to air-conditioning and a cold soda from the fourth-floor machine, but he was waylaid by Karl Dullard, the transportation reporter. Karl had stationed himself on the sidewalk in a sliver of shade to smoke and moan about being passed over by the Publisher's Award committee. This was not the first time such a grievous oversight had happened. And, since Porter sat next to Karl in the news-room, this was not his first time hearing about it.

"You read my piece on federal transportation funds!" Karl whined through a puff of smoke. His wife would not allow a cigarette within a mile radius of their home, so Karl compensated by inhaling two packs a day between the hours of ten and six. He held his cigarette like a woman, between the first two fingers instead of pinching it between thumb and index finger. Porter, who hadn't smoked since college, always had the urge to snatch Karl's cigarette and show him how it was done.

"It was masterly," Karl whined. "That's what the undersecretary called it—masterly! I deserved that award."

The award in question was one hundred bucks and one's name tacked to a bulletin board near the elevator for a month. Porter was about to tell Karl he'd gladly give him the money and scrawl his name on the wall with a felt-tipped pen if he would just shut up, then she drove past. A black woman in a white car, a profile, a fragment of memory behind glass.

"Did you read that crap that won?" Karl was saying. "Hey! Porter! You listening to me?"

"No," Porter said. His eyes followed the receding car. Should he run after it? Maybe he could catch her at a light. But that was ridiculous. It couldn't have been her. There were three thousand miles of country between this place and that corner in L.A.

Karl looked over his shoulder. "What are you staring at?"

"I thought I saw someone," Porter said. "A woman."

"Ooh!" Karl turned around now. If there was one thing he enjoyed more than moaning about how underappreciated he was it was leering at women. "Which one? Oh, I see, that blonde in the miniskirt. Yowee! What I wouldn't give to be unchained like you, Porter boy. Yikes!"

"Shut up, Karl."

He went inside and had his soda and wrote the incident off as his imagination working overtime. It wasn't her, just someone who looked like her. That's what he told himself. But the next morning it happened again.

It was early this time. The sidewalks around the *Record* building still glistened from the daily dawn washing and the heat had yet to rise. Porter had stopped by the office to pick up his tape recorder; he was headed to Bucks County for the day to report a story about the tenth anniversary of the unsolved murder of a Bryn Mawr student–turned–working girl. Just as he stepped from the building a white car rolled past, reached the corner, turned from sight. Without thinking, he ran after it, but he tripped over the curb and fell and scraped his hand, and by the time he recovered and reached the corner the car was long gone from sight. Hands stinging, he walked slowly back to his car. Maybe he really should be worried about his state of mind. Seeing someone once could be a trick of the imagination. Twice meant she was really in Philadelphia, or he was going insane.

For a week Porter searched the face of every black woman he passed until one woman raised her umbrella and snarled, "What the fuck you looking at?" That was it. Enough was enough. It wasn't her. He hadn't seen her. Time to stop this lunacy before some woman washed his face with pepper spray.

And then, suddenly, there she was, standing in the middle of the newsroom, talking to an assistant metro editor named Suzanne. Later he would remember feeling, more than surprise or excitement, a drenching sense of relief. He reached into his desk for the earring he'd been holding on to, then forced himself to cross the newsroom floor and insert himself between her and Suzanne. "Excuse me," he said when their conversation faltered. "This might sound strange, but aren't you the woman who saved my life?"

It took him ten minutes to get her away from Suzanne, who found the idea of hiring a heroine of the Los Angeles riot tantalizing. "Does Max know? Why didn't you tell us? Maybe you can write some kind of first-person piece for the magazine. Maybe you two can do it together, victim and heroine: their own true tale!" But finally he got her upstairs to the cafeteria where a few sad souls sat huddled over their coffee, trying to convince themselves it was worthwhile to go downstairs and work. The sharp smell of lime filled the air, and cafeteria workers bustled quietly about the steam tables, preparing for lunch. They were expecting a crowd. Tuesday was Mexican Day.

He bought her a cup of coffee. They introduced themselves. Her name was Lenora Page and she was a journalist from Baltimore.

Baltimore! All the time he'd been imagining her across the country and she'd been hiding out just down the road. She had just been offered a job at the *Record* and she did not seem the least bit surprised to find him there.

"You were wearing a *Record* ID that day," she explained. "Peter Stockman."

"Porter." He couldn't believe it. All that time he'd spent searching and wondering about her and she had known where he was. "If you knew where I worked, why didn't you ever contact me?"

She sat down at one of the tables. "What for?"

That took him by surprise. He had assumed she would wonder about him, would want to know what had happened after they parted. "Well, for one thing I wanted to thank you," he said.

"You thanked me then."

"But I wanted to really thank you. I looked for you, but I didn't know your name or who you were or anything. I didn't realize you were a journalist. I don't remember seeing your ID."

"I sometimes leave my press identification at home on riot days," she said dryly. "I'm shy that way."

He smiled at the joke, appreciating her sense of humor. Appreciating too her full, bare lips, cheekbones to hang your hat on, and eyes large and saturated brown. Not doelike, though. Definitely not a doe.

"I have something for you," he told her. "I found it on the ground the next day when I went back to look for you."

"You do?"

A thrill ran through him at the excitement in her voice. He pulled the small gold rose from his pocket and presented it to her with a flourish, pleased with himself.

"Oh," she said, taking it.

"Isn't it your earring?"

"It is." She twirled the earring between her fingers. "I just thought, or hoped I guess, it was something else I lost. Something more important."

So much for minor heroics. "I'm sorry. What was it?"

"A gold chain with a small pin on it. Actually the chain is unimportant, but my father gave me the pin. It was from the first convention of the Universal Negro Improvement Association."

He must have looked blank because she said, with just the slightest hint of condescension, "Marcus Garvey? You know—back to Africa?"

"Of course." He barely knew who Marcus Garvey was and had never heard of the Universal Negro Improvement Association but hell if he was going to admit as much to her.

"The pin was a little gold ship with the letters *BSL* for Black Star Line. My father got it from an old man he knew once. Not very many like it left out there."

"And you lost that in the scuffle." He shook his head. "Now I really feel terrible."

She tried to smile, but he could tell it was an effort. "Oh, well," she said. *"C'est la vie."*

"Yeah. Well. I've thought about you a lot since that day, hoping you were okay. You were okay after we left, right? Obviously you were. I mean, look at you. I mean, here you are." He was babbling like an idiot. To shut himself up he bit the inside of his cheek.

"I was fine," she said. "Thanks for asking."

"I hated leaving you there."

"I was fine."

"Still, I wish you had come with us. I would have felt better."

"I was better off on my own." She smiled. "Frankly, I didn't know if you guys were going to make it out or not. I got in my car and drove straight through the crowd, unmolested."

"Good day to be black, I guess," Porter said, and instantly regretted it. He had broken one of the cardinal rules when dealing with someone black: never mention race unless they mention it first. He tried to recover from the fumble. "That was a joke."

"Yes." She began gathering the detritus of morning coffee: lid, stirrer, torn sugar packet, paper napkin stained brown like her skin. "Well, Peter, it was nice meeting you again."

"Porter."

"I have to get back downstairs. I have some paperwork to fill out."

"So you're taking the job?"

"I haven't decided."

"You probably have someone at home you need to consult," he said, glancing at her left hand. It was, thankfully, bare.

Still, she said, "Yes." And stood to go. "Take care."

He wanted to say, Don't go, please. Instead he said, "May I ask you something?" It had the same effect. She turned back to face him, those eyes breaking like a wave across his face.

"Go ahead."

He'd meant to ask something mundane like *What do you think of Philadelphia* or *What's your beat* or *How much vacation are they offering you?* Just something to keep her there a moment longer while he recovered himself, thought of something witty, which would leave a better impression than the one he'd made. But instead of sitting down again she stood over him, which meant he had to look up to see her face. From that angle she seemed taller than he knew she was, taller than himself and for a moment he saw her as he first had, back on that street with the smell of burning rubber acrid in his nose and the sound in his ears of someone cackling in the crowd and the feel of blows raining down upon his head. He was back there, being beaten and being saved, and the question which left his lips was this: "Why'd you do it? Back there, I mean."

She didn't answer right away. It was not, he supposed, any easy question. Not if you were serious. He'd read interviews with other riot heroes: the actor who rescued a Japanese man from a mob, the group of friends who saw televised scenes of Reginald Denny being dragged from his truck and rushed to Florence and Normandy to save his life. All these people, when asked why they had risked their lives to save others, answered essentially the same thing: somebody had to do something.

Lee sat down. "Before I answer your question, let me ask you something: I saw you early on, talking to that guy with the dreadlocks. I knew you were a reporter, of course. I'd already passed your photographer getting into his car."

"That asshole. He ran out on me."

Lee shrugged. "The instinct for self-preservation is a powerful one. Even the cops were fleeing town. But I saw you and you were listening to that guy and you were . . ." She paused, searching for the right word. "Enraptured. There's a mob forming around you and you're listening to this guy as if he were Moses returning from the mountaintop."

He had to smile at this image, a dreadlocked Moses, bringing down the law of God and finding his people in disarray. "So, what's your question?"

"What was he saying?" she asked. "Why did you stand there and listen to him so long?"

He hesitated, not because he didn't remember what the man had said but because he did, and so well. Which was strange, considering he lost his notebook in the chaos and wasn't able to use any of the interview. But it was as though the mugging had seared the man's words into his brain. They weren't particularly poignant or insightful words, as Porter remembered. Typical street-corner philosophy. Had he been enraptured? Why? *You think you know what's happening here but you don't. You don't even know yourselves and that's what will be the end of you.*

"He was explaining the riots," Porter said. "Nothing you haven't heard a million times by now."

She seemed to weigh this. Then she asked, "Weren't you afraid?"

This was a question he'd heard many times since his return. *Weren't you afraid?* He usually got the sense people wanted him to lie, to say no, he had not been afraid. Sometimes he did lie. But not this time.

"Yes. I was."

"Why didn't you leave?"

"Because I've been afraid before in situations like that, where I don't belong or where people think I don't belong. The thing I've learned is the value of staying put."

"Staying put?"

"Of not walking away because I'm offended or uncomfortable or afraid. If you stay put, if you listen, sometimes you can get something good."

"And sometimes you get beat up."

"And sometimes," he said, "you get saved just in time."

For the first time in the conversation she looked at him with something approaching interest, maybe even curiosity. At least he hoped that was the way she was looking at him.

"Well," she said. "I really do have to go. Nice seeing you again, Porter."

"You too."

It wasn't until she was gone that he realized she hadn't answered *his* question. He didn't go back to work right away but sat for a while in the cafeteria, listening to the taped salsa music, trying to regain his equilibrium. He felt oddly off center, the way he did when he didn't know what was going on. He felt just as he had once, when he fell asleep while covering a city council meeting after a night of partying. He had no idea how long he dozed, but he awoke to thunderous applause. People were cheering and jeering and shouting for order and it was clear something big had just happened, something important. But damn if he knew what it was.

Chapter 2

From the air that day Los Angeles looked peaceful, glittering in the sunlight like the cheap spangled dress of a prostitute. Flying in from San Francisco where he'd been on vacation, Porter could detect no signs of disturbance or chaos. All below seemed as placid and self-satisfied as the faces of the few other passengers around him on the plane. The only person even remotely upset was a woman in first class, agitated at being told the plane would not land on time. Porter couldn't see the woman—he was sitting in coach—but her high, querulous voice slid past the curtain separating the haves from the have-mores, haranguing and pestering the male flight attendant as if he were keeping the plane in the air out of spite. "I simply cannot be fifteen minutes late," the woman whined. "I have an appointment with Giorgio. He gets upset."

Giorgio must have been beside himself that day because by the time the plane landed they were half an hour late. Porter grabbed his bag and made his way through the chaos of LAX toward the exit where he was supposed to meet the photographer, a freelancer who lived in town. No sooner had he stepped out into the blinding sunshine and slipped on his sunglasses than a battered gray Toyota pulled up to the curb and a man climbed out, signaling with his arms. He wore a green army jacket despite the heat and had his thinning gray hair pulled back into a ponytail.

"Stockman? You were supposed to be here an hour ago!"

"Sorry." Porter tossed his bag into the car's backseat. "The plane was late."

"Yeah, man, I dig, but we got to make tracks," Coles said. He was a tall man, taller than Porter even but weighed probably forty pounds less. He looked as though food were of very little importance to him, as though he subsisted on adrenaline and other, less energetic drugs. He wore beneath his army jacket a plain white T-shirt and blue jeans so old they seemed more like a loose collection of strings than actual cloth, but his feet were shod with brand-new, blinding white designer sneakers that probably cost two hundred bucks. The overall effect was part aging hippie, part Michael Jordan wannabe.

"All of South Central is up in arms!" Coles rubbed his hands and grinned. "Tinseltown is going to rock tonight!"

If there was one thing Porter disliked in a photographer it was glee in the face of mayhem. Glee meant the photographer was a hotdogger and a hotdogging photographer was not only dangerous but also a pain in the butt. Porter wished mightily he'd been able to book his own rental car. He'd tried that morning when the national desk tracked him down on his vacation in San Francisco and begged him to fly down to L.A. But every rental agency he called was fresh out of cars; it was as if the world had decided to visit L.A. for the day. "Don't worry," the national editor said. "I'll have Coles pick you up. You guys can ride together. It's better that way anyway." Porter didn't ask better for whom. Editors always preferred to have reporters and photographers ride together; that way the names in the stories matched up with the people in the photographs. It made for a better piece. Porter could appreciate that but he nonetheless preferred to work alone. At the very least he liked to have his own transportation, his own method of getting into, and out of, a situation. He didn't like having to depend on anyone else or deal with their screwups.

Coles raced around to the trunk of his car and flung it open. Out came a black bulletproof vest. "Want one?" he asked, pulling it on. "I always carry a spare."

Porter was ambivalent about bulletproof vests. They could be invaluable when someone unsteady was shooting directly at you. But in the middle of a riot, in which your best hope was to be inconspicuous, a vest was like a big, flashing neon sign saying "Please, please shoot me in the head." He'd last worn one during his month in Kuwait. One slow day a fresh-faced army captain explained how certain bullets fired from certain guns at certain ranges would punch through the vest like a nail punching through an egg. "At Easter my mother always used to put two holes in the eggs and blow out the stuff inside before we dyed them," the soldier said glumly. "I saw somebody get hit while wearing a shell once and that was what I thought of: Easter eggs."

Now Porter shook his head at Coles's offer. "Thanks, but I'll pass."

"You sure?" Coles looked him up and down with surprise. "South Central can be a little rough, especially if you're not used to it. South Central is like no place else, man."

Porter smiled. Despite globalization, despite the eye-widening impact of television, people everywhere were still amazingly parochial. They believed their city was like no place else, their parks the prettiest, their politicians the dirtiest, their criminals the worst. The idea that South Central was any rougher than, say, the corner of American and Somerset Streets in North Philadelphia was amusing. Porter enjoyed it. He enjoyed it also that this Abbie Hoffman throwback assumed he was just another lard-assed tenderfoot who only saw the mean streets of a city from the plush seat of a suburban multiplex. People often assumed as much about him, partly because of the way he looked. There was, he knew, an air of the corn-fed about him with his milky skin, his strawberry blond hair, his freckles, which he had long ago given up trying to forge into a tan. People told him he was like an attractive Larry Bird, which was a painful compliment any way you looked at it.

So he was neither surprised nor injured when people assumed he spent his life hiding behind a desk. Sooner or later they learned better, and their surprise and admiration were either helpful or gratifying, depending on the case.

"I'm all right," he said to Coles.

"Okay, man." Coles slammed shut the trunk. "Suit yourself."

Like a good hotdogger, Coles had a police scanner mounted to the dashboard of his car. It sputtered and cackled as they drove, listening for signs of strain in the dispassionate dispatcher's voice. They left the highway and entered a neighborhood of small, tidy homes with small, manicured lawns. "Welcome to South Central!" Coles cried. "The anti–Beverly Hills!"

Abruptly, the sidewalks overflowed with teenage boys. They strutted or strolled, or gave up all pretense of cool and ran, gleefully, like children unloosed at a park. Something was happening. Just then the police radio crackled: officer needs help! We're taking rocks and bottles from Florence and Normandie."

"That's five blocks from here," Coles said. "I'm going to park here."

Porter fastened his press pass around his neck and checked his notebook and pens. He didn't expect to do much actual writing, but the notebook was important as a kind of signal of his nonpartisan, observer status. He wished briefly, as he often did when covering a riot or a war, for a television camera to strap upon his back. People would say and do things for Channel Eight they wouldn't consider saying or doing for a guy slinking around with a little white notebook in his palm. By the same token, people seemed to view a television camera, and the body holding it, as very nearly sacrosanct. Not to be touched. Porter had once watched a man being chased by the police for trying to stone the mayor pause before a cameraman long enough to shout, "Hey, Mom!" He ended up getting caught.

Coles was at the trunk, pulling out equipment. "Last chance for a vest, man!"

"No thanks. I don't want anybody thinking I'm a cop."

"Okay, kemo sabe." Coles slammed the trunk close and grinned. "Let's rock and roll!"

Up ahead, on the major street that turned out to be Florence, a white Cadillac raced past, its tires squealing. In the split second before it disappeared from view, Porter caught a glimpse of the driver's twisted, terrified face.

They turned the corner onto Florence and the world grew hysterical. The street before them lay littered in debris, rubble and paper and a layer of shattered glass. There were people everywhere, packed along the sidewalk, pushing into the streets. Porter couldn't get a good perspective, but there must have been at least several hundred people and more arriving by the minute. One man had climbed halfway up a streetlight to get a better view. Helicopters circled overhead, beating down noise with their blades, but nobody on the street paused to look skyward. The crowd had focused its attention on a handful of police cars parked haphazardly in the intersection. Porter wasn't sure whether to be relieved or worried about the police presence; at home in Philadelphia the cops had a dangerous habit of making bad situations worse.

"Let's head . . . ," he began, but stopped when he saw Coles had already pushed himself into the crowd, shutter snapping as he elbowed people out of his way. "Come on!" Coles called over his shoulder, oblivious to the trail of anger and irritation in his wake.

"You go ahead." Porter waved the photographer away and watched him be swallowed up by the crowd. He would either get some Pulitzer Prize–winning shots or be mauled to death. Hotdogging photographers.

He himself liked to make a gentler entry into neighborhoods like this. He'd learned from years of work the best approach was one of quiet, casual, and respectful persistence. Don't charge in like John Wayne on a horse and don't sneak in trying to be inconspicuous—one way might get you killed and the other will get you laughed back downtown. Don't treat black people like exhibits and don't treat them like victims. Just show up, shut up, listen, don't ask too many questions too soon, don't laugh at jokes that aren't funny, tell a few yourself. In that way the canyon could at least be temporarily crossed.

He found a spot on the sidewalk with a good view of the intersection and settled in to watch. The area was so mobbed he was jostled and shoved by people trying to get past, but no one paid him more than fleeting attention. Everybody was watching the cops.

There were about ten or twelve of them out there; they had retreated into crowd-control stance: shoulder to shoulder, arms down, faces set, a wall of blue-sheathed flesh against the crowd. They did not have riot gear, which surprised Porter. How could they be caught unprepared like that? Did they think they could control this mob with the sheer force of their personalities? While the crowd jeered and the cops stood their ground, two of their number handcuffed a black man and tried desperately to shove him into the backseat of a patrol car. The more the man resisted, the harder the cops shoved; the harder the cops pushed, the more the crowd rumbled and steamed, a volcano of anger. A woman standing behind Porter opened her mouth and screeched, "Leave him alone!" directly into his left ear.

"Leave him alone!"

"Yeah!" echoed the crowd. "Leave him alone!"

"Pigs!"

"Assholes!"

"Fuck the cops!"

"You motherfuckers better get out of here now!" A fusillade of bottles, bricks, jagged pieces of concrete flew toward the cops. "This one's for Latasha!" someone yelled, and the crowd took up the chant: "Latasha! Latasha!" The cops ducked and dodged. A man near Porter said casually, as though he were observing the weather, "Cops gonna die tonight." Porter wanted to ask him who Latasha was, but when he turned around the man was gone.

Among the cops was one woman, short and wide hipped, ruddy skinned and freckled, a thick braid of reddish brown hair spilling from beneath her policewoman's hat. Cops in general seemed to be getting shorter, and this, he thought, was a dangerous trend. Short male cops made him nervous—back in Philadelphia they strutted about with their thick necks and their inflated chests and their Napoleon complexes like hair triggers on their guns—but the sight of a small woman in uniform, wobbling down the street like a child dressed up for Halloween, downright frightened him. He often had the urge to run up to such a woman and toss her over his shoulder or tip her over onto the sidewalk or take her gun away, just to show her how easy it would be. Just to show her how ridiculous it was for her to be out there, a dot in the thin, blue line. He had that urge now, watching the woman duck and dodge. She reminded him of his sister, who as a child always insisted, to his mother's dismay, on bypassing the fairy princess outfits and dressing for Halloween in boy costumes—cowboy, fireman, cop. Just then, a gob of spit, nearly translucent in the waning sunlight, shot through the air and struck the policewoman just above her eye. She screamed as though she'd been shot—maybe she thought she had—and Porter's heart went out to her. It was one thing to dislike cops, but to pick on the only woman in the crowd was cowardly, and to spit on her was just disgusting and low. Two other cops heard the scream and came running, red-faced, hands on their weapons. Not everyone in the crowd was watching this particular scene, but those who were began to panic. "Ah, shit! Here it comes!" someone cried. Porter too felt fear crackling through the air.

But then the woman cop was holding up her hands, patting the air at her approaching colleagues, yelling, "I'm okay! I'm okay. Holster your weapons! I'm okay! It's okay! Holster your weapons now!"

Reluctantly, the two cops who had drawn their guns holstered them, then lined up with the others facing the crowd, as though searching for the culprit. Porter followed their eyes and saw, among the faces, a skinny black kid of eighteen or twenty with thick, black glasses and astonishingly white teeth and a black stocking cap tied down over his hair. It was the glasses that made him stand out in the crowd; they looked incongruously intellectual against his stocking cap and baggy clothes. And it was the look of amused triumph glistening on his skinny face that told Porter he was the one.

Asshole, Porter thought. Coward. The spitter stood firm, grinning at the cops, taunting them with every skinny inch of himself. But either the police didn't see him or they dared not wade into the crowd because after a few moments they retreated. The spitter wiggled his hips in glee. "Bitch! That's exactly what you deserve!"

Porter spotted Coles on the other side of the crowd, his camera clicking steadily. Porter hoped he'd gotten the shot of the policewoman grabbing her face in terror. It would make a compelling photograph.

"Coles!" he yelled. "Coles!" But his voice was drowned out by an earsplitting cheer from the crowd. The cops were pulling out. One by one they broke ranks and jogged toward their cruisers, dodging bottles and taunts as they ran, until only the policewoman was left. *Go!* he wanted to yell, but she just stood there, gazing at the foaming mob. He couldn't tell whether she was challenging them or trying to regain her pride or simply in shock. *Just go, just go.* Finally, still wiping her face, she turned and ran toward her frantic partner. The mob cackled with triumph and erupted with glee.

"Run, pigs!"

"Better get out of here!"

A man with dreadlocks shook his head at Porter. "Cops," he said with disgust. "Guard dogs of the oppressor. You ought to be ashamed."

"I'm not a cop," Porter said. This was always the first assumption and usually the hardest to overcome, even when he wasn't in the middle of a riot. "I'm a reporter for a newspaper in Philadelphia, the *Record*. I'm here to observe and to listen."

"You're here to make monkeys out of us."

"Why do you say that?"

The man narrowed his eyes. "That's what you always do. Piss on our heads and call it rain. Push a man against the wall, then when he reacts call him violent and animalistic and mow him down."

"Is that what's happening here?"

The man laughed softly. "I bet you think what you see before you is a riot. You look but you cannot see. This is no riot; this is a rebellion long overdue."

The cops were retreating. The crowd was swelling in size and the temperature where Porter stood seemed to have spiked ten degrees. Still the man kept talking and Porter kept writing in his notebook. "A rebellion against the courts or the LAPD?"

"The LAPD could not perpetrate its storm trooper tactics on us without the permission of society at large. Government, including that Negro sitting down there in City Hall, the courts, and yes, the media, they're all culpable. You're all responsible."

"All white people?"

The man looked him squarely in the eye. "You think you know what's going on here, but you don't. You don't even know yourselves and that's what will be the end of you. In the meantime, these children out here . . ." Porter lost the end of the man's sentence because the crowd around them was turning up the noise level. Someone picked up a brick and tossed it through the window of a check-cashing store whose owner had long since fled, smashing it to bits. Porter flinched, the crowd cheered and surged forward, pushing Porter and the man along. They fought their way to the outside of the group and watched it flow into the store. The man shook his head. "Time for you to go, reporter."

Porter glanced around, adrenaline bracing his blood. "Finish what you were saying."

The man looked at him. Then he said, "There will be lots of gnashing of teeth over this day. Bush and his pals will argue these kids suffer from a lack of morality. Liberal white folks will say its because they're poor and hopeless, locked out of the American Dream. But what's really wrong with these my unschooled young sisters and brothers is that they've swallowed your American Dream hook, line, and sinker. They've bought into the American idea of material goods, material wealth, being the true measure of freedom." He stopped and pointed to a teenager running past with an armload of clothes he'd grabbed from somewhere. "That's why they're running down the street with a bunch of shirts they don't need and can't wear. They think that by attacking stores they're hurting white folks, hurting you."

Porter was scribbling furiously, wishing he had a tape recorder. This was the kind of thing he lived for, finding intelligence and perception in the most unlikely places, getting it down, showing the world. He looked around for Coles, wanting a photograph, but the photographer was nowhere in sight. The police too were all gone. "One more question: who's Latasha?"

The man just stared, a response Porter mistook for incomprehension.

"The crowd was chanting her name a few minutes ago?"

The man stared.

"But I guess you don't know who she is."

"I know who she was," the man said. "The fact *you* don't says everything. Good-bye and good luck."

"Wait," Porter called. The guy hadn't given his name and a quote without a name was useless. "What's your name?"

But the man just called back over his shoulder. "You don't need my name! You won't even use what I said! The only things America will see tomorrow is pictures of black people running wild!"

Then the man was gone, swallowed up by a crowd that seemed suddenly to sense Porter's presence like a fly vibrating in its web. Somebody shoved him. Somebody else stuck an elbow in his back. He ignored both gestures and eased his way through the crush of bodies, fighting the constant jostling, trying to absorb as much of it himself as he could and not pass it along. Once out of the crush he began a kind of deliberate stroll back toward the car. It was important not to run. Mobs were like dogs: they could sense fear, and it made them crazy. He put on his street posture: shoulders back, head tilted but not down, eyes straight ahead. The goal was to look confident but not challenging; to make eye contact briefly and firmly but not to stare. He walked a few feet, a few yards, half a block. People kept running past him, back toward the crowd, and a few glared his way, but no one stopped. All he had to do was keep walking. He was almost there when he heard someone yell, "Better get your white ass out of here!"

Keep walking, he told himself. Keep walking and ignore the idiot.

"That's right, you better run!"

Despite himself he hesitated. It was that voice—jeering, taunting. Where had he heard it before?

"Yeah, that's right—I'm talking to you, bitch!"

Porter stopped. He turned around. It was the guy from the crowd, the one who spit on the cop, then dared the other cops to move in. He sat perched atop a *Los Angeles Times* newspaper box on the other side of the street. He must have moved away from the crowd to command a better view of the chaos to which he'd contributed and now sat with those white-white teeth bared in a grin, a prince atop his steed, surveying his domain. He saw Porter turn around and yelled, "What the fuck you looking at?"

Porter said nothing, but he didn't move. The spitter leapt from the newspaper box as if it had been electrified.

The guy was smaller than he'd seemed in the mob—at least three inches shorter than Porter—but young and agile and probably taut as piano strings beneath his Los Angeles Rams jersey and baggy jeans. He crossed the street toward Porter, hips rolling like ball bearings in the pimp-walking, cool-acting manner of black adolescents everywhere. The guy took his time, as if giving Porter a chance to reconsider the error of his ways, and all the time the spitter was ambling across the street, a voice inside Porter's head suggested now would be a good time to walk away. The voice was right, of course. This was insane. He'd had the occasional bar stare-down, the chest-thumping-friends-pull-you-back kind of thing on the softball field, but he had not fought anyone since high school, not really fought. Fighting was not something people like him did in the everyday world. And yet he stood rooted to the spot, seeing still that wide-wide grin and that gob of spit and the bloodless face of the policewoman as she raked her face.

The spitter arrived. Standing close like that Porter could see the guy was probably in his twenties at least, not a kid but still dressing like one. Still acting like one, puffed up and posturing, his manhood to prove. He stared at Porter with a kind of surprised outrage, as if a car or a television or some other inanimate object that had been giving him trouble suddenly spoke. People had been flowing past them, rushing to join the mob that raged on at the intersection a block away, a great, swelling beast, venting its lunatic rage on the hapless motorists who wandered into its lair. But now a few people stopped, sensing the irresistible entertainment of a fight.

"I asked you a question, cracker. What the fuck you think you looking at?"

The correct answer was no answer. The smart move was to back up slowly, maintaining respectful but fearless eye contact, and get the hell out of there. This asshole didn't want to fight; if he did he would have long since pounced. He was all bluster and no balls, a bully who preferred spitting at women from the safety of a crowd.

"Better take off, white boy."

The smart move was to turn around and walk away. But Porter kept seeing that girl's face and his sister's face and the degradation and fear, and before he knew it he heard his voice saying, "Fuck you, asshole." Out loud.

Oh, shit.

The next thing he knew the universe had gathered itself into a ball and smashed the side of his face. He heard someone scream, "Crazy motherfucker!" and wondered fleetingly, almost casually, what had happened to Coles. Then someone came up behind him and struck the back of his head. He doubled over. Everything fell away—the sky, the thumping of the helicopters overhead, the muffled cries of the crowd, even his anger at Coles for deserting him. Nothing mattered except the pain. The pain and the struggle to keep from dropping to his knees, which he lost.

He was going to die. The realization came to him clearly, and as soon as it settled, the pain fell away. He was going to die, there, on the sidewalk, with the concrete digging into his knees and the acrid smell of something—human piss?—rising up from the gutter to fill his nose and the helicopters circling overhead. Probably recording his death for the evening news. Which would be apropos. He waited for the required flashing of his life before his eyes but it didn't come. He tried to think of people he loved, of his mother and father and family, but he couldn't keep it straight, probably because his mind, his whole body was suddenly focused on the foul taste in his mouth. As if he had licked the gutter. And he was parched. He wanted something to drink, he needed water, desperately. He was going to die, but if he could just have a drink of water, clean water, it would be okay.

At that moment, thunder erupted from the intersection, followed by screams and the tinkling of shattered glass. Everyone flinched and ducked and ran. A woman shrieked, "What was that?"

Porter felt a hand on his shoulder and screamed as though trying to rip out his lungs. He was going to die loud.

"Stop it, you idiot!" It was a woman's voice. "You want to get us both killed? Walk!"

Something sticky and wet had trickled into his left eye, half-blinding him. He tried to wipe it away, to look at the woman, but it was hard. All he could see was that she was black. Then there was another explosion and he came back to himself. He knew the sound, had heard it dozens of times in the Kuwaiti desert; something had exploded, probably the gasoline tank on a car. This was his chance. He staggered to his feet, shaking off the hand, and tried to move away.

"No, no! This way! Come on!"

She was pulling him down the sidewalk, away from the momentarily distracted crowd. Porter wiped his eyes and looked at her. She was black and tall and strong—she was practically holding him up, and although he was still afraid, something told him not to fight. To go with her. They had made it maybe half a block before the spitter caught up to them. He ran in front of them, forcing them to stop.

"What the hell you doing, woman?"

"Please," she said. She sounded like she was fighting to keep her voice calm. "You don't want to do this."

"The hell I don't!"

"Calm down."

"Why you want to take that white man's side against mine?"

"I'm not taking his side!" She sounded indignant at the idea, but she didn't drop Porter's arm. "I'm trying to save this fool's life. And yours too. Look up, look up at the helicopters. They're filming us."

The helicopters whipped the air over their heads, but the spitter didn't seem to care. He moved in closer, fists raised. Porter thought: not only am I going to be beaten to death but I'm going to be responsible for this woman getting beaten too. They were drawing another crowd; a young black man with a yellow scarf on his head jogged determinedly toward them, probably coming to join in the beat-the-white-man fun. Well, if he was going to die he would at least go without this woman's blood on his hands. He pushed her away from him. "Stay out of this."

The spitter laughed. "Oh, now you Mr. Big!"

"Run!" he told the woman. He thought if he lowered his head and went for the balls he just might stand a chance. But before he could move, the man with the scarf was there, not striking but inserting his body between Porter and the spitter. "Calm down, brother," he said, then turned to Porter. "Go. This might be your last chance."

There was the squeal of tires behind him. Porter turned and saw Coles racing down the street toward him in a car that looked even more battered than before. The windshield was cracked and both headlights smashed. Coles screeched the car to a stop, leaned over to open the passenger door, and yelled, "Get in! Quick!"

"Yeah, get in and go!" the man with the scarf yelled.

The woman grabbed his arm and shoved him toward the car. "Get in!"

"Come with us!"

"No."

"You're not going to stay!"

She pushed frantically at the car door, trying to get it shut. "Just shut up and go!"

"Not without you. You'll be hurt!"

She looked up, for the first time meeting his eyes. "I have a better chance on foot than you do in this car," she said. And then she was gone, running at first, then walking, as if she were forcing herself to walk, to look calm. She reached the corner and disappeared. A soda bottle hit the roof above his head, shattering with the sound of little bells.

"We're moving!" Coles yelled.

They faced one more mob on the way out, but Coles showed his teeth and floored the accelerator, neatly bisecting the crowd. On the way to the hospital they passed at least five burning minimalls, many with Korean signs. Porter pressed his hand against the bleeding place above his eye and tried to breathe down the pain while Coles hooted and laughed. The maniac was jubilant. He began counting the fires they passed. ". . . six, seven, oh, my, that's a big one. Eight!" Coles shouted. Porter's head throbbed. "There goes the neighborhood!"

Chapter 3

The first time Lee saw Rodney King writhing in pain on the lonesome freeways of Los Angeles, she sat down on the couch and cried. Then she got up and yelled. She yelled and cursed and threw pillows at the television screen until her mother entered the room and calmly suggested the daughter was losing her mind.

"But did you see that?" Lee shrieked. "Did you see what they did?"

"I saw," said Eda in reply.

"I can't believe it! I cannot believe this crap! If they get away with this," Lee declared, "I'm moving to Canada!"

Said Eda in reply, "Pack your bags."

Not that Lee was naive. She knew cops, she knew black men, and she knew which subset of humanity usually found favor under the American judicial system. More than once she'd heard her brother complain bitterly about being stopped, frisked, and otherwise harassed for DWB or WWB—driving or walking while black. Nor was Lee particularly inclined to believe in the inherent goodness or righteousness of white folks. She couldn't be, not while being painfully aware of the plight of black folks in America. If, for some reason, she ever forgot, all she had to do was watch the news, read her own newspaper, drive along Pennsylvania Avenue to the heart of black Baltimore, and weep. She saw brothers aflame with despair and self-loathing, hanging on the streets. She saw sisters, fat with ill health, starving for love. She saw children hopeless at ten, bitter at twelve. She saw all around lives being lived without meaning or hope or love or self-respect. Lee did not blame the white people she knew for all this misery, but their ancestors had set the wheel in motion, and whether they wanted to believe it or not, most still profited from the roll. Whites were no longer the enemy, but they had, after all, begun the war. They were not allies. They remained dangerous, always dangerous nonetheless.

Still she could not believe any jury could let those four police officers off scot-free in light of that videotape, not even if they wanted to. She couldn't believe it until she was sent to Los Angeles near the end of the trial and looked into the jurors' faces, saw their fear and anger, saw them lapping up the defense argument that King seemed wild and beastly, drugged up and out of control, a man who brought upon himself even the blows delivered when he was facedown in the California dirt. That night she called her mother, her voice trembling with fury and with fear.

"They're going to let them off, Mom. I think they're going to let them off."

Eda shrugged. "You act like you're surprised."

Lee twisted the phone cord and said nothing. As skeptical as she was of white folks, compared to Eda she was Martin Luther King. Even Sammy Davis Jr.

Lee went to college with white people. There were white people in the *Sun* newsroom she respected and even liked. They labored together, lunched together, complained together about newsroom politics. Sometimes these people even invited her to their homes for dinner or parties, and although she almost never went, she was gracious in declining and usually took the time to come up with a viable excuse.

To Eda the idea of befriending a white person, even on a superficial level, was as incomprehensible as trying to befriend a rhinoceros. It might or might not try to hurt you but it always *could,* and anyway, what was the point? All of the ladies Eda worked with in the lunchroom at

Booker T. Washington Junior High School were black, except Luisa, who was Puerto Rican but who long ago had assimilated into the cafeteria mainstream. Eda's supervisor was black. The children were all black. Many of the teachers were white, as was the principal, but how much real human interaction did it take to toss a veal patty roll onto someone's tray?

When Lee was eleven, she asked her mother if all white people were evil. It was the late spring of 1968. Martin Luther King Jr. had been assassinated, and all around them black Baltimore was erupting in flames. Eda kept Lee and Marcus in the house for three days with the doors locked and the shades drawn. They watched King's funeral on television.

"Why do white people hate us so much? What's wrong with them?" Lee asked. Even then, at that young age, it never occurred to her to wonder what was wrong with black people that whites should hate them so. Her father had managed to inoculate her against the crushing self-hatred so many black people felt. He'd done that much.

"I don't know what's wrong with them," Eda sniffed. She'd been weeping for days. "Wish to God I did."

"Is every white person bad? Haven't you ever known a white man or lady you liked?"

Eda wiped her nose and considered. "I knew a white girl once, named Connie. We worked together at the school. She was sweet and I liked her. She even came to my house, once, for dinner. I think she thought we were friends."

"Weren't you?"

Eda looked Lee squarely in the eye. "I liked Connie, but I always knew, in my heart, if it came down to it she would stand me on that auction block and sell me down the river. I never forgot that. You better not forget it either."

On the day of the verdict Lee was sent to South Central to get "reaction" from the community. When the news hit she was in the basement of the Restoration Church of God in Christ, hearing the pastor preach about nonviolent rebellion and the power of love to a group of street-scarred boys who'd been expelled from school. "They used to call them juvenile delinquents," the pastor told her. "Now they're at-risk youth. Renaming things is easier than fixing them."

Then word of the verdict arrived, and the boys slipped one by one from the pastor's grasp and out the door. "Fight back by voting! Fight back by getting an education! Fight back by hitting them where they live, in the pocketbook!" the pastor called. But the boys went on. He turned to Lee. "What good am I? My words fall upon stone."

Running, praying and breathing hard, she reached the intersection just in time to see spit smack the policewoman's fresh and freckled little face. Good! she thought, and then, more rationally, God help us. Here we go. Spitting on a white male cop, especially the LAPD, was crazy. Spitting on a white female cop in front of her male colleagues was like challenging a bull. Lee's stomach turned over with fear. A girl standing nearby squealed with teenage glee. "No he didn't!" She wore a yellow tank top with skinny straps and tight blue jeans that showed the curve of her hips and those ridiculously large, rectangular hoop earrings of cheap gold, the latest fad among status-starved kids, the latest rip-off of urban youth. At first glance she looked to be about eighteen, but when she covered her mouth and giggled, Lee could see she was just a child.

"No, he didn't!" she squealed again, and clapped her hands with glee, as if the whole scene were a movie being screened for her entertainment. The male cops went rigid with rage as the policewoman wiped spittle from her face. Oh, God. Lee began trying to force her way out of the crowd, wanting to drag the girl along with her. Instead she yelled, "Go home! This is dangerous! Go home!" But the girl just looked at her and giggled again.

Lee cleared the mob. She was hurrying toward her car when she saw a white guy standing in the middle of the sidewalk, staring across the street. Instantly she pegged him as a journalist. For one thing, he wore the standard-issue uniform: khaki pants, penny loafers, blue oxford shirt with the sleeves rolled up. For another thing, he was the only white guy in sight except for the cops; only a reporter would be stupid enough to be caught, alone and on foot, in the middle of South Central as a race riot got under way. Plus, he held a notebook in his hand.

Without knowing why, she stopped to watch him. The guy was listening to a brother with dreadlocks, this look of complete and utter absorption on his face. Lee was amazed. She could not imagine what the dreadlocked brother must be saying to keep the white guy so enthralled, but it must have been something good because self-preservation demanded that the white guy hit the bricks. Immediately. Yet there he stood, nodding and scribbling, ignoring the coming riot, his face intent. He looked transfixed, and for some reason the image of him there transfixed her too. There was, about him, a durability that intrigued her. What the hell was keeping him there, anyway? Did he really want the story that bad? Did he think his press credentials would save him when things got rough? Or maybe he thought he could pass, thought the crowd wouldn't notice he was white. Or wouldn't mind. There was a guy at Lee's paper who spent six years covering Africa and came back thinking he knew more about being black than Lee. He took to lecturing her about the African roots of soul food and showing up uninvited at certain parties because he wanted to dance. One night he strutted into a hangout called Lacy's Lounge on Westwood Street, started talking some jive, and got the crap beat out of him.

Lee shook herself. Whatever the guy across the street thought, it wasn't her problem. She kept walking. Halfway down the block she passed a young brother perched atop a newspaper box. He was yelling something at the white guy, and as she passed he jumped down and began crossing the street. The white guy had to see him coming. Why was he just standing there? *Move!* Instead he waited for the brother to reach him and the next thing Lee knew they were fighting, scuffling along the sidewalk and people were running to join in the fun. "Get him!" somebody yelled. "Get him good!"

Her car was just around the corner. All she had to do was go to it, get in, drive away. "Get him good!" That idiot across the street wasn't her problem. He shouldn't have been out there in the first place, unprotected and alone. Who did he think he was, John Wayne? "One for me!" screamed the brother who had been sitting on the newspaper box. He punched the white guy in the gut, then put up his hands, as though he'd just sunk a three-pointer, and yelled "Swoosh!" with triumph. Exactly the way her brother used to do it. The white guy doubled over. If she got involved they might both end up bleeding on the sidewalk. Why should she risk her life for some arrogant white moron who probably cheered when the cops walked? Who said she was responsible?

The white guy was staggering, struggling not to fall when suddenly the air cracked and broke into pieces and everyone, including Lee, ducked. She didn't know what it was; maybe the cops were setting off tear gas canisters back at the intersection. She had to get out of there. Across the street the white guy was trying desperately to stagger away from his tormentors. He would never make it on his own; already the young brothers were recovering from the explosion and following him. She hesitated, then started across the street, praying all the way.

For some reason, the brother who'd been sitting on the newspaper box smiled as she ran toward them. He must have thought she was coming to help.

"What is it exactly they want you to do?" her mother asked.

They were in Lee's car, on the way home from their regular Saturday afternoon grocery run, Lee in the driver's seat and Eda complacently beside her, scanning her grocery list for items desired but forgotten or simply not found. It was her mother's habit, an infuriating one, to wait always until they were miles from the store to check her list or suddenly remember something she could not live without. Lee had long ago resigned herself to Sunday follow-up grocery runs.

"They're calling the beat 'urban agenda.'" Lee chuckled. "Which means they want me to write about black folks and why they keep trying to burn down the countryside. It's a response to the riots, of course. But that's fine. It's a new beat, which means I can make it my own. It's a bigger paper, a bigger canvas. And it's more money."

"Last but not least," her mother said.

"Last but certainly not least," Lee agreed.

"I think you should take it. Of course, I thought you should have taken that offer from the *San Francisco Chronicle* years ago. For the life of me I don't know why you've hung on here all these years."

Lee thought: yes, you do. But all she said was, "San Francisco was too far."

"Well, Philadelphia is just up the road. No more excuses."

They were passing the statue of Billie Holiday at Landale Street; as usual, Eda called out "Hey, girl" and waved in salute. Eda loved Lady Day. She played her music constantly, especially during the dark times, and she quoted from *Lady Sings the Blues* the way some people quoted Shakespeare. Whenever Lee complained about some problem at work Eda said, "You can be up to your boobies in white satin, with gardenias in your hair and no sugarcane for miles, but you can still be working on a plantation."

Now Lee said, "I thought we could go up next weekend, look around for a duplex for us, or maybe two small stand-alones on the same block."

"A duplex for us? I'm not moving to Philadelphia."

"Of course you are."

"Oh no I'm not." Her mother pursed her lips. "I'm staying right here, thank you very much."

"What? Alone?" Lee laughed. Her mother might as well have said she intended to levitate out of the car—that's how ridiculous the statement was. "You couldn't even get around without me driving you."

"They have this invention," Eda said. "It's called the bus."

"Funny."

"And there's always Marcus."

"Marcus is busy with his own life," she said. Her baby brother spent almost as much time chasing and being chased by women as he did working as a software programmer. He dropped by the house every Sunday without fail and performed what home maintenance needed to be done, but he left to Lee most of the day-to-day tasks of caring for their mother: ferrying her around, confirming her doctor's appointments, checking to make sure she took her medicine. It wasn't that he didn't care, but he was a guy and younger and didn't understand. He thought their mother could take care of herself.

"Marcus will come if I need him," Eda said.

They were driving down one of the treeless streets of West Baltimore, past a string of row homes. She'd grown up around streets like these, with the houses pushed up shoulder to shoulder against the sidewalk and the street, and yet she had never rested easy among them. From her mother the transplanted country girl she'd learned to yearn for grass, to believe people should not be forced to live with their front doors opening onto the sidewalk, to need at least a swatch of lawn through which to pass upon leaving the world and entering home. One of the first things she'd done as a working adult was to move her mother from these relentless streets to a duplex with a front yard planted with azaleas and a backyard shaded by maple trees. From her own kitchen window in the other half of the duplex Lee often watched on summer mornings as her mother went outside at daybreak and sank her toes into the grass.

Eda went back to checking her grocery list. "I think I got everything this time."

"Well, if you didn't, let me know," Lee said. "I can pick it up tomorrow after church."

Eda didn't answer, only folded the list and settled back against the seat with a satisfied sigh; all of her needs had been met at the Stop and Save. "I was thinking," she said. "I might even get a car."

Lee glanced apprehensively toward her mother, who sat calmly smiling in her seat. The last time Eda drove she had plowed directly into the back of a police cruiser, so mesmerized by a Staples Singers song on the radio she had forgotten she was behind the wheel of a car. Even after the accident, even as the police officer helped her from her car and put her in the rear of the cruiser and checked her license and drove her downtown, she kept repeating the lyrics, over and over, until the cop begged her to shut up. That was nine years ago; since that day Lee had driven her mother everywhere she needed or wanted to go.

"You can't get a car," she said now. "You don't have a license."

"Yes, I do."

"Since when?"

"Since a month ago. My suspension was up years ago and I decided there was no reason I shouldn't go down and take the test again. So I did." Eda reached into her purse and pulled out the card with a flourish. "I'm official."

If Lee hadn't been such a careful and responsible driver, she might have slammed into the back of something herself. Instead she eased the car to the side of the road and put the gearshift into park. They were in front of an ice cream parlor. A woman came out, holding the hand of a small child with an ice cream cone. She kept urging him to lick faster; the cone was melting, but the boy took his own sweet time.

"You can't drive," Lee said slowly. "You can't drive and you can't stay here in Baltimore alone. What if you get sick?"

Eda stiffened. "I haven't had an episode in six years."

"But you might." Her mother didn't like to talk about her illness, but this time Lee was going to make her. "You're not cured."

"I know that."

"You will never be cured. Manic depression is a chronic, lifelong disease. You could have an episode at any time."

Eda was silent, her shoulders squared, her face turned away. Lee steeled herself for whatever might come, but when Eda finally spoke, her voice was gentle. "I know that, baby. I know it better than you."

Lee was surprised. Her mother's temper could be fierce, especially when discussing her illness. Her denial had been the biggest problem for so long. "I'm . . . I'm scared to leave you here alone."

"But I'm not alone, Lee. I have Marcus. I have Mrs. Morris and Mother Wideman and Brother McDonnell. I have your Aunt Alice and Uncle Frank if I need them."

"Yeah," Lee said. Aunt Alice was her father's sister, a self-important, sanctimonious woman who blamed Eda for driving her brother away and who attributed Eda's illness to the presence of evil spirits. "I know how much you like asking them for help."

Eda laughed. "Baby, I had to get over that a long time ago. We wouldn't have made it without Alice and her snitty self. You do what you have to in this world."

"But—"

"You don't have to baby-sit me anymore. I keep telling you that."

Lee thought: yes, you keep telling me that. She remembered a time, years ago, when her mother had said those words or similar ones as she was headed out the front door to a job interview. "I don't need you to baby-sit me. I can do this." She was gone for three days and when she finally came home it was with a backseat full of shopping bags from stores they could not afford to walk past. Two months later the phone calls demanding payment began. During that time, Eda crawled into bed and stayed there, eating just enough to stay alive. Lee was fifteen then. By the time she paid off the last of the credit card bills she was twenty-four.

Now she put the car in gear and pulled back into traffic. The late spring sun poured through the windshield and warmed the air inside the car. They were passing the Lilac Lady's house; her forty-six documented bushes hung heavy with fat purple blooms. Lee rolled down her window and inhaled. The perfume was intoxicating.

"What about Howard?" Eda asked. "What's he got to say about this?"

"Let me worry about Howard," she said impatiently. "Look, it's as simple as this: this is the third time they've come after me, the third time they've offered me a job. If I don't accept it, it'll be the last."

Eda scoffed. "Please. Didn't they say that last time? It's a scare tactic."

Yeah, they said that last time, Lee thought with irritation. For a crazy woman you sure have a good memory. Immediately she was sorry. It was cruel and unfair even to think such a thing. She just needed Eda to understand, just to listen and understand. "This time is different." She wished she could write the words in the air before them and underscore them for emphasis. Before, turning down offers to leave Baltimore for bigger, more golden climes, she'd felt curiosity, a little longing, maybe mild regret. But this time was different; this time she knew something final was being decided. Some path was being erased.

"I'm not a kid anymore," Lee said. "I'm not a promising young thing they think they can hire for a song and mold into what they want. I'm a good journalist, but being good is never as good as having potential. Especially for us. This might be my last chance. No one else might ever ask."

"Then you should take it, Lee. If it's what you want."

"But I can't leave you here," Lee said. But before her mother could respond the car in front of them, a sky blue Cadillac, stopped short at a green light, and she had to stand on the brake to keep from slamming into its rear. Lee lurched forward, then was thrown back by the seat belt and Eda threw her left hand out sideways to keep her only daughter from flying through the windshield. As a child, Lee had teased her mother about the gesture. "Like that would stop me from flying through the glass," she'd say. And Eda would answer, "You'd be surprised."

Now the car jerked and bucked and stopped, meeting no metal. Lee turned, heart pounding, to look at her mother's face. "Are you okay? Are you hurt?"

"I'm fine."

"I wasn't paying attention. I didn't even see him."

"It's okay. We're okay."

"That was so stupid. I can't believe I did that. We could have been killed!"

"Lee!" Her mother's voice was sharp. "Calm down. We were going twenty miles an hour. We wouldn't have been killed, and anyway, it wasn't your fault. That idiot stopped short."

Her mother was partly right. The idiot in the hulking blue car before them had been switching radio stations or seen a pretty girl walking past or just forgotten he wasn't the only one on the planet that day. Had she slammed into him it would not have been her fault, but the law would have assigned responsibility to her nonetheless. That was the way it was. It was your job to watch out for the other guy.

A man's hand emerged from the Cadillac and gave them a one-finger salute.

"Look at that!" She couldn't believe this guy, flipping her off after he nearly caused an accident. The world was full of selfish, unthinking idiots driving around as though they alone owned the streets. She wanted to show him, to grind her foot into the gas pedal, to shove her modest Toyota right up the idiot's backside and she might have, had her mother not ordered, "Pull over."

"What?"

"Pull the car over. You're too upset to drive."

She did as ordered, inching the car over to the curb. The Cadillac turned the corner and disappeared. Eda reached across the seat to stroke Lee's back, and Lee leaned into the massage, surprised at the strength of it. These old folks. "Cotton-pickers," her mother sometimes called herself and her friends, long-ago immigrants from a world farther south. Cotton-picking people learned early how to bend and not to break.

Eda turned in her seat. "You never really told me what happened out there in California."

It was true. She had painted only the broadest outlines of the incident, not wanting to frighten her mother in retrospect. Plus, she didn't like to think about what could have happened.

"I told you most of it," Lee lied. "It all happened pretty fast."

"Hm," Eda murmured, which meant she didn't necessarily believe but would not push. "May I ask something else?"

"May I stop you?"

"No."

"Then, dear mother, go right ahead."

"What in the world possessed you to go running into a mob, risking your life?" Eda's voice took on a shrill note, which meant she was getting angry. Lee knew it was an anger born of fear. "I could see if it was somebody's child. But this wasn't a child. This was some fool stupid enough to think the color of his skin was some kind of magic shield. What was he doing out there anyway?"

"Same thing I was: his job."

"Well, you shouldn't have been out there either, but that's another issue. I'm talking about him. What did he think—a mob of outraged black folks would just part and let his white self pass on through?"

"I don't think he thought that."

Eda raised an eyebrow.

"How do you know what he thought?"

"I don't," Lee said quickly. She hadn't mentioned to her mother that Porter worked at the paper in Philadelphia—it hadn't seemed important compared to everything else. And for some reason, she didn't mention it now. "I just think . . . he wanted to stay. He was the kind of guy who stays, even when it might be smarter to go."

Eda didn't seem to hear this. She rolled her eyes with contempt. "White folks are amazing. They think they own the world."

"Don't they? Own the world, I mean." Lee smiled. She was teasing, but she knew what her mother meant. Leaving South Central that day, her palms damp on the wheel and her arms still tingly with fear, Lee had the same thought. What else would lead a guy like Porter to the midst of a riot except some crazy, distorted sense of his own invincibility? And where else did that sense come from except being white? Lee had an uncle, Uncle Frank, who, when complaining about his white boss, liked to say, "The man's pissing on my head and calling it rain." Sometimes Lee wondered if white people had been calling it rain for so long, they had begun believing it themselves. She wondered if they weren't all going out back into their gardens and pissing on their own tomato plants.

"They think they're invincible," Eda sniffed.

"Well," Lee said.

"They think they're Superman."

Lee gave a little laugh as if to say: what else is new? But then she remembered a conversation she once had with an old boyfriend, Jake. They'd rented a cottage in the Poconos one weekend. It was fall and the colors were brilliant and the cottage was rustic and sweet and tucked deep, deep into the woods. Just before dusk, Jake went out for a walk while she took a bath. When Jake returned and found both the front door and the bathroom door locked, he teased her. Called her a nervous Nellie. Said she was being silly. Who was going to bother her out there in the woods. Bigfoot? "Better safe than sorry," she told him. She was just making sure, just being safe. That was what women did. Women knew they were vulnerable; they always carried a pebble of worry, a pebble of danger around in the bottom of their shoe. Jake, a big, hulking guy who never got challenged about anything, didn't really understand. She tried to put it in his terms. "Women," she told him, "don't grow up playing Superman."

"Lee?" It was Eda, prodding her from her reverie. "Are you okay?"

"Just daydreaming."

"You still haven't told me why you did what you did."

"You raised me."

"I didn't raise you to risk your life for white people."

It was a strange thing to do something right—insane for certain but undoubtedly right—and be bombarded with angry questions about it. Howard, her girlfriends, her mother, Porter himself. Why was everyone so pissed? "White people are one thing; some idiot getting beat by hoodlums in front of your face is another. I didn't want to help him. I was terrified. But the cops weren't there and he was getting beaten. He was going to be killed right there in front of me. Somebody had to do something."

"And that somebody had to be you?"

"Apparently so." Lee reached across the seat to pat her mother's hand, amazed, as always, at how small and frail-boned her mother really was. Lee was tall herself and strong and her brother, Marcus, played football throughout his school career; there was no weakness in either of them. Their father gave them that much.

"You would have done the same thing," Lee said. "I know you would."

Eda crossed her arms. With a smile Lee started the car and turned toward home. After a few blocks Eda said, "You remember when you were little and we went to Noon's house in Mississippi and you found a mouse in a trap down in the basement? You got your finger stuck trying to get him out but you didn't cry about that. You cried only when I told you he was dead and not coming back."

She did remember: the dank, darkened basement, the stiff little body, the thick, purple feeling of loss clogging her throat as she tried to set the mouse free.

"You were always too tenderhearted for your own good," Eda said.

"Don't tell anyone."

Chapter 4

He heard through the grapevine that she was coming to Philadelphia. She was set to arrive in three weeks. He was so excited, he had to laugh at himself.

Since that day in the cafeteria he had not stopped thinking about her. She intrigued him, this Lenora Page. She intrigued the hell out of him. She intrigued him in a way he had not been intrigued by a woman in months, possibly years, possibly since Chira, when Chira was young and certain and charismatic, or pretending very, very hard to be.

He wondered if his tangled and slightly obsessive feelings for Lenora had to do with the circumstances under which they'd met. He wasn't stupid. He knew it was hard to forget the person who'd saved your bacon. Harder still to know exactly how to feel about that person, especially if she was a woman. What were you supposed to do? What were you supposed to say after thank you? Where, exactly, did you go from there?

And yes, he was intrigued by the skepticism and disinterest in her luminous eyes when they fell on his face. Porter knew this much about himself: he liked people to think well of him. It wasn't vanity or arrogance. Or perhaps it was a mild form of arrogance, but if so it was one every human being shared. He just admitted it. Porter had met few people he couldn't charm if he wanted to and even those, like certain politicians, who otherwise hated his guts displayed a kind of grudging respect for his work. But he could tell Lee did not think much of him, and it chafed a little. He was eager to change that impression. Given time and exposure he knew he could.

But there was more to it than gratitude or the need to impress. Lenora Page was brave, beautiful, intelligent, eye opening in every way and, as far as he knew, single. There was no reason not to at least examine the possibility of pursuit. Certainly her race made no difference. True, he'd never dated a black woman before, but that had everything to do with opportunity and nothing to do with his feelings on the subject. He had no feelings on the subject. To have feelings on the subject would be distasteful, would be close-minded, biased, suburban, and small. Porter, whatever his shortcomings, was none of these things. He was far larger than that; of that, he was certain. He was as bright and wide open as a Kmart on Saturday afternoon.

In the meantime, he had to suffer through a blind date. He was on his way when the subway stalled. He groaned, sighed, glanced around the train for confirmation of aggravation and noticed he was one of only three white people in the car. The other two were a young, hand-holding couple, obviously tourists, adventurers from some clean and God-kissed midwestern state. The boy wore glasses and a blue baseball cap, the kind with the back made out of mesh. The woman was big in a healthy, milk-queen kind of way. They looked recently married, not newlyweds but almost, no more than a year or two. Porter looked away from them, checked his own watch, looked back. Something about the couple's milky mildness irritated him. What were they doing on the subway anyway? Why weren't they on a double-decker bus somewhere, gawking at the Liberty Bell? Did they think this was Disneyland and they were riding the tram?

They were still smiling fifteen minutes later, when the engines roared back and the train lurched the ten blocks to City Hall. Porter

still had one more stop. So did the tourists. People poured on and off;
Porter stayed, taking his chances. The doors closed with an electronic
warning bell. Across from him, the tourist girl, delighted, mimicked the
sound. "Bing bong!" Her voice was clear and high, a voice for calling
children home across the plains while the sun sank. "Bing bong! Bing
bong!"

Porter disliked blind dates. He had dodged this one for months,
but Elena, his friend and former lover, could wear away stone with
her relentlessness. "Come on," she badgered. "She's beautiful, intelligent, warm, and she can't wait to meet you. You're not seeing anyone.
Why not?"

Why not? He had a million reasons why not. Blind dates were awkward and unnatural. They carried the whiff of desperation, and he could
never be certain it wasn't him who smelled. Not one of the handful of
blind dates he'd slogged through in his life had involved a woman as
beautiful or intelligent as promised. And Elena's friends were not always
the most stable. Take Rachel, as one obvious example. He'd liked Rachel
a lot at first; she was sexy and funny and unconventional, a waitress with
a master's degree in English romantic poetry. They dated a few weeks,
things were going nicely until he got sent to Chicago for a week to cover
a federal mob trial and came back to find she'd broken into his apartment and telephoned every woman in his address book, demanding to
speak to him.

But Elena pointed out she'd had nothing to do with that fiasco. Just
because he and Rachel met at her party did not mean she was to blame.
"If you'd told me you were interested I would have warned you," Elena
said. "I know who's good for you and who's not."

So everybody seemed to think.

He made it to the restaurant twenty minutes late and went straight to
the bar, scanning it for his date. She was the only unattached woman in
sight and stood near the end, wineglass in hand and a nervous smile
pasted on her face.

"Janine?" At the sound of her name the lady turned toward him with
obvious relief. "I'm Porter. I apologize for being so late."

"You should," she said, but she was smiling more naturally now. "I was just beginning to think I'd been stood up. I was thinking of leaving."

"I wouldn't have blamed you."

"Oh, but this way is much more fun," she said. "See? Already you owe me."

She smiled again, exposing small, white, expensive teeth. She was a pretty woman, prettier than he had expected. Elena had called her "stunning," but he knew enough to disregard the descriptions of friends. She had thick, honey-colored hair she wore pulled back from her face, pale blue eyes, a firm jaw, and firmer breasts. She wore a slip-like black dress that showed off both her tan and the single strand of pearls around her neck. The dress was pretty sexy but the pearls gave her away as clearly and as surely as a sorority pin.

"Let me see about our table," Porter said.

Unfortunately, the hostess was less forgiving than Janine; she had canceled their reservation and given their table away. She told Porter he'd have to wait another thirty minutes, maybe more. This was bad news. He felt deeply that first dates, especially blind dates, should be quick. No lingering. Hit and run. If things went well, it whetted the appetite for the next time. If they didn't, better for all concerned to end the torture as quickly as possible.

He went back to the bar. Janine had managed, despite the density of the crowd, to find seats for them both.

"Oh, I don't mind waiting," she said after he explained the situation. She smiled and reached out to flick a bit of lint from his tie. "Not now."

They ordered drinks—Scotch for him, a Kir Royale for her—and chatted with great animation about nothing in particular. He brought up Elena, asked how the two women had met. Old college buddies, Janine said. Freshman dorm mates who ended up pledging the same sorority. Oh, the times they used to have! She launched into a long, purportedly hilarious story about the time the whole gang piled into a car and tried to drive to New York, except they kept getting lost on the George Washington Bridge and ending up in New Jersey somewhere.

She was one of those people who loaded their anecdotes with so much superfluous detail they ended up sinking of their own weight. He smiled through the story, thinking: do I care what Suzy's last name was? Or, for that matter, her first name? Or how she surprised everyone by pledging the Dippy Dippy Dos? Porter had been a diehard independent in college, a pothead intellectual who considered sororities and fraternities the height of absurdity and their members all bubble-headed saps. He liked to think he'd outgrown such bias, but he couldn't help thinking that being a sorority girl was not something a grown woman should confess on a first date.

When the conversation flagged, Porter apologized again for being late, explaining that SEPTA had stalled.

"You take the train?"

"Sometimes." He hoped she wasn't going to be one of those oh-my-goodness-the-city-is-so-dark-and-dangerous types. "I live in Spring Garden. It's very easy from there and it saves the hassle with parking."

"Wow," Janine said. "I don't really know anyone who actually takes the train in Philadelphia. It's not like New York, where everyone takes the subway." She tilted her head in a way that was supposed to be wistful and appealing and, he had to admit, was, and started to say something else, but the hostess appeared and announced she had managed to find them a table.

At the table the conversation turned to the restaurant and its famous chef who had been lured, Janine said, from one of the best restaurants in Rome. His dishes were divine, people drove down from New York to sample them. But when the waiter appeared, and Porter ordered antipasto and some seafood dish that was the famous chef's famous specialty, Janine ordered a Caesar salad and another glass of wine.

"Are you sure that's all you want?"

"I ate a monstrous lunch," she said, patting the hollow beneath her breasts.

"The chef will be insulted."

Janine giggled and waved her hand at him in mock dismissal. With the Elena connection and current events already exhausted, all that remained was work, family history (as in, "Where did you grow up?"), or personal dreams. Porter chose work. A mistake. Janine was a market analyst for some downtown firm. He tried to feign interest as she spoke about her work, but it was a pitiful effort. Fortunately, he was saved by the arrival of the appetizer. She had instructed the waiter to bring her salad as an entrée, so while he sat there stuffing his face with tiny sausage balls she nibbled at a roll. He ate as fast as he could without appearing to.

"So." Janine smiled across at him. She had, he noticed, a habit of tilting her head slightly to the left whenever she spoke. As if she were posing for someone. "You from around here?"

"I grew up in King of Prussia."

"Really! I'm from Bala Cynwyd."

"Practically neighbors."

"I bet you went to Upper Merion? I went to Lower Merion. We used to play you guys in football all the time! What year were you?"

"Class of seventy-three."

"That's the same year my brother graduated! From Lower Merion, I mean. Brad Tottinger? He was captain of the football team, a real BMOC all through high school."

He did not, of course, know this Brad Tottinger, but he could guess what he had once been like. The kids from Lower Merion were all wealthy and usually did not associate with the middle-class likes of him. He saw them at band competitions, when they arrived with gold-plated saxophones in fur-lined cases and years of private lessons behind them and blew everybody else away.

"Sorry. I wasn't really a big football fan."

"Oh, me neither," she said quickly. "My brother . . . I mean, all that teenage adulation. Kind of made me sick."

The entrées arrived. His was some kind of elaborate seafood stew with shrimp and white fish and fat sea scallops served on a bed of golden rice and topped by what looked like a robin's nest. Her salad was big enough to graze two cows, but the kitchen had made a mistake and tossed the dressing in instead of putting it on the side. She stared at it for a moment, then gamely picked up her fork.

"But enough about me. I'd much rather hear about you. Is Porter one of those old family names?"

"Probably," he said. "Just not my family. I think my mother got it off the back of a cigarette package."

Another giggle. "You are so funny! Elena didn't tell me how funny you were."

Apparently he could do no wrong. She clucked admiringly over his work, adored his tie, laughed at every word that slipped from his mouth. The restaurant filled around them, buzzing with the frantic gaiety of Saturday night. Porter ate as quickly as he could without seeming to rush. Janine chatted and picked at her salad and seemed to believe the vague, forced patter he tossed back her way rated as conversation.

After the plates were cleared and the coffee was ordered, they fell into a lull. Porter wracked his brain for something to fill the yawning void. Work? Done. Upbringing? Done. Current events? Dare he broach the topic of politics?

"So what—," he began. But at the same time as she leaned across the table and said, "Can I ask you something?"

"Sure." He was relieved. She was going to take responsibility for steering the conversation for a while.

"Isn't it hard for you to take the subway?"

"Hard?" He shook his head. This would be easy; a meaningless conversation about the benefits of public transportation in a traffic-clogged city. Very civic-minded. "No, not really. I just walk over to the Broad Street line and—"

"No. I mean, after."

"After what?" he asked. But then he knew.

Janine leaned in, lowered her voice. "Elena told me what happened. In Los Angeles. It sounded terrible, just terrible."

Well, that's what he got for having women friends. A man would have known better. A man would never reveal, to a woman no less, that his friend had been pounded like a punching bag. Janine's face glistened with pity; women loved a man they could feel sorry for. "It wasn't that bad."

"She said they beat you up."

"They didn't *beat* me up. It was a fight."

"But Elena said—"

"Where is that waiter with the check?" He made a big show of look-ing around the restaurant. "This place has terrible service."

But Janine was not to be deterred. She shuddered luxuriously. "The whole thing was horrible! Horrible! I mean, of course, the police shouldn't have beaten that man, that Roger King, but—"

"Rodney King," he corrected.

Janine waved her hand through the air. Her eyes were bright and her face flushed and she looked quite pretty and slightly drunk. "Right. Rodney King. That's what I meant. Anyway, for them to react that way. I couldn't believe it! Pulling people from their cars and beat-ing them? We sat around my office all day, watching it on television, horrified."

Porter nodded, not because he agreed but because it was the easiest thing to do. He'd had the same conversation a dozen times over the past month, people telling him how senseless and bewildering they had found it all, how frightening. People asking him to explain. As if he were some kind of missionary who had been "there" and studied "them" and could therefore translate.

"What I don't understand," Janine was saying, "is why people would burn their own neighborhood?"

"Because transporting pipe bombs on the bus is so unwieldy?" This drew a puzzled half smile; she thought he was joking but she couldn't be sure. "Just kidding," he said.

"Oh." Full smile now, all teeth. "But seriously. I mean I understood why they were upset, of course. But if I was upset I wouldn't set my condo ablaze. That's just ridiculous."

"What would you do?"

"What?"

"What would you do?" It was terrible, this impulse to tease her, but he could not resist. "What would you do if you felt there had been a travesty of justice, the latest in a long, long line? What would you do?"

"I don't know . . . complain to somebody. Call a lawyer, I guess. I know that's easy for me to say." She blinked. Her face reddened, but she stuck out her sharp little chin. "But I still say violence isn't the answer! I mean, what is the point of all that beating and burning? That's what I don't understand."

She shrugged and glanced across the restaurant. "But I guess we never could understand, could we? Because we're . . . you know. And they're not. So they probably can't understand us, either, can they?"

He didn't know what to say, so he said nothing. He only wanted the moment to pass.

"I guess," said Janine, "in the end, nobody understands anyone else."

Porter looked across the table at Janine with her delicate gold earrings and her small, unblemished teeth and thought how wrong she was. Most people were all too understandable. They wore their fears and prejudices, their hopes and aspirations and the narrow or wide circumferences of their lives smack on their foreheads for all the world to read. Porter sometimes had the feeling he could sit down with a stranger for an hour and at the end of it write his or her psychological life. Not the details: not the name of his first girlfriend or the place she lost her virginity, but the broad, important strokes. His buddy Charlie, who covered state government, called this the reporter's disease, this belief that anything and anyone could be reduced to eight hundred words. It was a disease, and Porter was stricken, grievously.

"No, me neither," he said, to end the conversation. There was no sense attacking her. She wasn't to blame.

The waiter arrived with the check. Porter signed the slip and put his credit card back into his wallet. "Shall we go?"

Outside the sun had set and the temperature dropped with the breeze. Janine's car was in the lot across the street. He walked her there.

"Are you okay to drive? I don't have my car but I could get you a cab."

"I'm fine."

"Are you sure?" He searched her face. With a stranger it was so hard to know, but she hadn't eaten anything and she seemed a little dizzy. "Let me get you a cab."

"But how will I get my car?"

Porter hesitated. He really didn't want to drive her home. He wanted the date over now and he didn't want to send any more mixed signals than he had already sent. But he couldn't let her get in the car and drive herself into a tree. "Let me drive you," he said finally.

She smiled. "That's so sweet."

On the way she tried to restart the conversation about Los Angeles. "I hope you weren't offended," she said. "Sometimes my mouth runs ahead of my brain."

"Happens to the best of us," he said, and launched into a long story about a reporter he once knew who cursed out the mayor into a microphone he thought was off. The story got them to her doorstep, as he intended, and he handed her the keys.

"Good night."

"Would you like to come in? I could call you a cab."

"That's okay. I'd rather take the subway."

"Well. Then. Thank you, Porter. I had a wonderful time."

"So did I. I enjoyed myself." That was the small lie; to keep from uttering the bigger one, he bent quickly to kiss her on the cheek. The last thing she said, before stepping inside, was, "You have my number." But she didn't wait to hear him promise to use it soon. He liked her for that, too. She was, in the end, a nice enough woman. He never planned to see her again.

He rode the train back downtown and got off at City Hall, headed to the Pen & Pencil club for a drink. He passed a young black couple, holding hands and gazing into each other's eyes. Tomorrow he'd have to deal with Elena, who would probably get a full report from her friend tonight. When she asked if he planned to call Janine, he would have to tell her the truth. He did not.

"Why not?" Elena would bleat. "Just what, pray tell, was wrong with her?"

Nothing, nothing at all. Except he had known her from the moment he sat down, known the sunny high school classroom that produced her, known the stone house with the circular driveway and the giggly strolls through the mall and her expectation of being married by now. Nothing, except that her golden shell earrings, her glossy hair, and her big-ticket teeth filled him with an aching, braying loneliness. Janine was lovely, but she had no secrets Porter had not already discovered, no depths he didn't know.

"It's me," he would tell Elena. "She's wonderful." The girl next door. But the last thing in the world he wanted was to go home.

Chapter 5

Baltimore threw Lee not one but two going-away parties, distinct and separate. Her newsroom colleagues bought her lunch at the local crab palace, then took her back to the office for coffee and cake and a silver-plated cup embossed with *The Sun* and her dates of service. Somebody cracked, "Kind of like a headstone!" and everyone laughed. She was expected to make a speech and so she did, though she disliked making speeches. "Thank you all for everything. This newspaper has been my professional home for most of my life, and it's been a good one. I've learned so much about the noble practice of journalism. Thanks again." That was it: in and out, short and sweet. Everyone applauded. "Take us with you!" somebody cracked. "Good riddance," somebody mumbled, but that too was newsroom life. Lee shook hands all around and pretended not to hear.

The managing editor, still grumpy about her departure, stopped by her desk afterward to say again he hoped she'd be happy up there in Philadelphia, although he doubted she would. He himself had worked there once (for a summer) and found the experience cold and unfriendly.

The people were competitive and backbiting and not nearly as warm and fuzzy as the crew at the *Sun*.

Lee nodded somberly. "I'll probably rue the day I accepted," she said.

"Frankly, we're still surprised you decided to leave us," he went on, oblivious to her mocking tone. "After all, we gave you the City Hall beat and when you were tired of that we gave you the social services beat. Most people would kill for either one of them."

She loved the way he said they "gave" her the beats, as if she hadn't worked her ass off to get both of them, hadn't kicked butt on both beats until she was sick to death of pontificating, duplicitous politicians and sick to her soul of children tied to radiators and used as sex toys and beaten to death. But that was the way it was. Ted had told her all this before, when she first announced she was leaving. He acted as though he'd brought her in from the fields and shod her dusty feet and taught her how to read and write. Lee had to smile at him.

"I'll miss you too, Ted," she said.

The rest of the afternoon people filed past her desk to shake her hand or pat her on the back. At five o'clock Lee hugged Irene, a sweet, white editor with whom she'd probably lunched eight hundred times but whose house she had never seen. Then she packed her books, old notebooks, maps, interview tapes, and six dozen pens into a box and carried it out to her car.

The second party took place the following Saturday, a loud, boisterous, and joyful congregation of food and drink and colored folk crammed into her friend Pauline's brownstone. Food in the dining room, booze in the kitchen, windows thrown open to let the soft air of early June drift through the house. Eda showed up with a snowy white coconut cake and spent the evening downstairs in the basement, playing bid whist with Uncle Ty and Aunt Ella and some other old friends and a man Lee did not recognize.

At eight-thirty, just as Lee was in the kitchen whipping up the first batch of frozen margaritas, the telephone rang. Pauline, hands full with bowls of food, signaled for her to answer it.

"Hello?"

Even before he spoke she knew it was Howard. He had a way of hesitating, of taking an audible breath before launching into a conversation, even on the telephone. It wasn't anxiety or nerves; it was preparation. Howard always liked to be prepared.

"Hello," he said formally. "May I speak to Lenora, please."

So what if he didn't recognize her voice. She told herself it was the noise. "Hey, baby," she said. "It's me."

"Lenora. How's the party?" He was the only person other than her mother who now called her Lenora, and even her mother only did so occasionally. Howard did not like nicknames; he was the kind of man who, if he ever got married again, would refer to his wife as Mrs. Norton. Even sometimes to her.

"Just warming up. You on your way?"

Again the slight hesitation. He was preparing his words. "Unfortunately, no," he said carefully.

He went on with his explanation, but Pauline had come back into the kitchen and was staring at Lee with concern. "Anything wrong?" she mouthed. Lee picked up her face, forced her lips into a smile. She shook her head and mouthed "Howard" and rolled her eyes comically. Pauline nodded and left the room and as soon as she was out the door, Lee peeled off the smile and threw it away.

". . . hospital," Howard was saying.

She tried to focus. "I'm sorry. Who's in the hospital?"

"Rasheed's mother," Howard repeated. "That's why he can't work tonight."

"Is she all right? Is it serious?"

"Serious for the rest of the world, but not for her. She's having another kid. Tyrone had to stay home and take care of the fifteen she's already popped out."

Lee had no idea how many children the woman really had, but she knew fifteen was an exaggeration. Rasheed's mother and her ripe fertility and the subsequent pressures on Tyrone, the oldest and most responsible, were a source of long-standing complaint for Howard.

"Just stay until nine, then close the store and come on over. The party will be just getting started."

"I have inventory scheduled for tonight," Howard said. "Tyrone was supposed to oversee it."

"Can't you do that tomorrow?" Lee asked, but she knew better. If Howard had something scheduled it got done. Even if she managed to convince him to put it off, he would be jumpy and distracted all evening.

"I'm sorry but I can't. My supply man is coming first thing Monday morning, a third of my shelves are bare, and the storeroom's a mess. I should have known better than to let that Cameron handle it."

She was silent. How could he miss her party.

"Lenora, I'm sure you're disappointed, but this is important," Howard said. Then, "I know you understand."

He always said that. *I know you understand.* He was trying to build a business, it was important, black people needed to be entrepreneurs, and being an entrepreneur required sacrifice. That was one of the things holding black people back in this society; they weren't willing to risk and they weren't willing to sacrifice. He knew she understood, because she was smart and tough and clear thinking, not like so many women he had known. Not weak minded or sentimental, not focused on how much jewelry he gave. It was why Howard loved her. She understood.

She had stopped making drinks but now she slammed a handful of ice cubes into the blender and turned it on, high. "Fine," she said over the roar.

"What? I can't hear you!"

"I said, fine. I understand. Go back to work."

"Now, Lenora!" he called. "Can you please turn that off?"

She did, reluctantly. She imagined him in his little windowless office in the back of his pharmacy, leaning into the phone. "I'll work as hard as I can and try to get there later. The party will probably go on for a while."

"Fine," she said again. "I have to go, Howard."

There was a pause. Then Howard said, "Lenora—" But she didn't want to hear it, whatever it was. She cut him off.

"I said it's fine, Howard. I understand." She softened her voice. "I understand, but I have to go now. People are waiting for me."

"I am sorry," he said.

She hung up and poured herself a glass of the frothy liquid. He wouldn't make it later. She knew that, even if he did not. It wasn't the first time Howard had left her alone and it wouldn't be the last. It was always the same reason—the store. Pauline had asked her once if she was sure that's where Howard was spending all his time, and Lee just laughed. Howard barely had time for one woman, let alone two or three. He was not the kind of man to dog around. It might have been easier if he was. Lee took a long sip of her drink, put on a smile, and went out into the living room.

The party was gearing up nicely. Music played, people mingled. Pauline was in a corner with Cleo, grousing about how she'd wasted her Saturday afternoon trying to persuade a young brother, a superstar athlete of much local acclaim, to invest in the black-owned bank of which she was president. He was having none of it.

"I explained what our goals for aiding the community were, and how the community needed him to set an example. You know what that fool told me? He said, 'I'm putting my liquid assets into a Hard Rock Cafe.' Can you believe that? A Hard Rock Cafe!" Pauline threw up her hands in exasperation. She was wearing yellow, her favorite color, and it brought out the lemony undertones of her skin. "What is wrong with this community? Seven million dollars in spending power and we toss it away on trash and white folks who give not one damn about us?"

Cleo shook her head. Lee sipped her drink and tried to shake off her disappointment about Howard. She joined the conversation. "Some people are lost, Pauline. You know that."

"Brainwashed is more like it," Pauline said. "By the way, I know you're not planning on closing your account."

"Actually I was. My account isn't big enough to make a difference to you."

"Lee, our average checking account is five hundred dollars. Average savings is a hundred dollars." She paused, leaned over, and rubbed her foot. "These shoes are going to have to come off. Just bought them yesterday and I swear my feet expanded overnight." She took Lee's hand and led her to a couch. "That's better. Anyway, Lee, you know as well as I do, every account is important."

"Well, you'll still have the mortgage on the house. And I hear they're starting a black bank in Philadelphia," Lee said. "United Bank. I'm going to open an account there."

Cleo beamed at Lee. "Not even there yet and already hooked up to the community," she said. "How'd you find out about the bank?"

"I looked it up in the *Record* archives when I was there," Lee said. Cleo had a way of idealizing the things Lee did that was both flattering and enervating. Sometimes she felt like the relationship was a balloon the girl was constantly blowing up, and she was constantly trying to deflate a little so it wouldn't pop. "No big deal."

Pauline put her hand on Lee's arm. "It's not that we'll collapse without your account, but right now I'm fighting to hold on to every dollar we have. If this bank is going to succeed, the community has to support it, even if that means a certain level of sacrifice."

Sacrifice was right. Half the shops and businesses in Baltimore had not heard of Reliance Bank; Lee couldn't count the times she had stood waiting at the counter while some bubble gum–popping clerk eyed her check suspiciously. Trying to write checks on a Baltimore-based bank in Philadelphia would be like trying to pass Monopoly money at the grocery store. But the president would not be swayed.

"All I'm asking is that you check with your new employer to see if they offer direct deposit," she said. "I'm certain they do. Then your check can come right here without you having to lift a finger. And you can get cash from any ATM on the Galaxy system. And you can do your banking when you come home. And I know you—you'll be home every weekend, checking on your mother."

"Okay." Lee laughed. "You win."

"Pauline always wins," Cleo said. "I'm going in the kitchen for a drink? You guys want anything?"

They both shook their heads. When Cleo was gone, Pauline looked at Lee and asked, "So. What did Howard have to say for himself?"

Lee hesitated. Pauline was not one of Howard's biggest fans, and Lee didn't like giving her ammunition. Pauline claimed what she distrusted was the way Howard seemed to take absolutely no responsibility for the failure of his first marriage. He and his wife had married young, just out of high school, and struggled together for two years before giving up. Howard said he wanted to go on, offered to see a counselor, to do whatever it took. But his wife was just not interested. No matter how hard he worked to give her what she wanted, it wasn't enough. Eventually she ended up sleeping with his best friend, and he even tried to get over that. But she wasn't interested, he said.

Pauline didn't buy the story. "It's never all one person's fault," she said. "If he doesn't realize that, he's a child." But Lee thought Howard's friendship with a man who had broken Pauline's heart was the real reason for the enmity. *That* guy was a jerk; Lee hated him too. But people could not be blamed for the foibles of their friends.

"One of his clerks couldn't make it in to work so he's staying to do inventory," Lee said, careful to keep her voice neutral. Still, Pauline smirked.

"Don't tell me he's going to miss your party?"

"He said he'd get here as soon as he could."

"I see," Pauline said. "And what do you think about that?"

"I'm disappointed, of course. But I understand."

"Do you?"

"Yes," she said firmly.

Pauline just looked at her, then shrugged and bent down to scoop up her shoes. "Okay. I'm sure glad you don't feel abandoned."

"Go put something on your feet, please," Lee said to shut her up. Pauline stuck out her tongue but headed upstairs to her bedroom. Lee walked downstairs to the basement to check on her mother. Eda sat cheerfully playing cards, Marcus standing behind her, pretending to help play her hand while the others around the table booed and heckled in good-natured protest. Marcus's girlfriend—Sheryl or Sherry or something like that—kept ferrying food and drinks to Marcus and Eda, beaming as if this was the work God had placed her on earth to do. She was small and pretty and young, younger than Marcus, but clearly smart enough to know the way to a black man's heart was through Mom. Unlike his last girlfriend, who'd sulked around at family gatherings rolling her eyes and examining her fingernails. Eda made short work of that girl; she didn't last a month.

Now Lee smiled across the table at her brother and saw him nod slightly, signaling her above their mother's head. She nodded back, then drifted away from the table and into the hallway, Marcus following her.

"I have news," he said, then added, unnecessarily, "about Dad."

Lee glanced around to make sure their mother was not about. Eda didn't know about Marcus's search for their father, and Lee wanted to keep it that way. She was afraid her mother would be hurt, would feel betrayed by her son's need to know the whereabouts of the father who had abandoned them. Of course Marcus did not accept the theory that their father had, in fact, abandoned them. He believed there was some reason, death or imprisonment or mental disease, that had kept their father from making his way back home. Lee used to argue, angrily, the absurdity of this supposition, the absurdity of this desperate wishing, but now she just let Marcus believe. She didn't care. Not about her father; not anymore.

From the age of consciousness until seven, she worshipped her father. Then he left, and from the age of eight until eighteen, she idolized him and prayed for his return. From the age of eighteen until twenty-nine, she detested him, hated him, never let him pass through her thoughts unscorned. At thirty she grew up and gave up; now, at the age of thirty-four, she considered their father as good as dead. There was no sense being angry at someone who was dead, no sense hating him. And no sense awaiting his return. The only reasonable thing to do was to acknowledge his gifts (pride in herself and her race), admit his deficits (the ability to abandon his children to poverty and fear), and move along. Now Lee felt about her father the way she felt about her elementary school principal: he was a nice man who had once meant a lot to her, but so what? She'd been young then and it was a long, long time ago.

But that was her and this was Marcus. Marcus wasn't even a year old when their father left. Having never known their father, how could he be expected to let him go? She asked only that he not tell their mother.

"Why not?" Marcus wanted to know. "She's over it. It's been nearly thirty years." But Lee knew there was a difference between being over something and being through with it.

Now Marcus told Lee he'd heard from a woman in Chicago there was a Clayton Page living on the South Side.

"What woman?" asked Lee.

"A friend of a friend. I asked her to look up some things for me."

"Marcus, how many Clayton Pages do you think there are in the world?"

"Not that many."

"Hundreds. Thousands, probably. You're grasping at straws."

"But it's an important straw. You said he always used to talk about going to Chicago."

She sighed. As a child Marcus had pestered her for tidbits about their father: how tall was he? what did his laugh sound like? what songs did he sing? Maybe she shouldn't have told him. Maybe it would have been better that way.

"Can you fly to Chicago and check it out?" he asked her. "You have some time before you have to be in Philadelphia, don't you?"

"You're not serious?" She laughed. "I have other things to do, Marcus. It's your search; why don't you go?"

"You know the company's going public in two weeks. I'm working fourteen-hour days. I can't leave town right now."

Lee looked at Marcus. He was a big man, her baby brother, six feet three, broad of chest and broad of neck, the kind of powerful-looking black man who had to step carefully through the world so as to appear neither too threatening nor too meek.

"This woman could be scamming you. How much did you pay her? What makes you even think he's in Chicago. Why not Detroit? Or L.A.? Or Borneo for that matter? Or the grave?"

Marcus winced, and she was sorry. She didn't mean to torture him with the possibility of their father being dead. "Let it go, Marcus. Focus on more important things, like your mother."

"My mother is fine."

"She is now. But you need to keep a close eye on her after I'm gone. I'll still be down on most weekends, but you need to make sure you're checking on her throughout the week."

"You act like she's an invalid." He gestured through the doorway; Eda had just come from the kitchen and was making her way back toward the basement. She carried two drinks in her hand and was smiling. "She looks fine to me. Better than fine."

Lee had to admit her mother looked good these days, with her stylish little Afro going silver in streaks. Eda smiled as she walked, and there was nothing tense in the smile, nothing frantic or wild in her eyes. She looked almost serene.

"You just need to keep an eye on her," Lee said.

"You don't have to tell me to take care of my mother," Marcus said, walking away.

Lee sighed. She'd find him later, apologize. But she was not flying out to Chicago on some wild-goose chase. That was his search. That was his dream.

What she needed now, she decided, was a drink. She was on her way to the kitchen when a hand grabbed her and pulled her into the part of the living room where people were dancing. When the crowd saw them coming it whooped, not for her, but for her dancing partner. Everybody loved to see Luther dance because he was so painfully, painfully bad. He acknowledged the crowd with a grand wave of his hand, then turned to Lee and began flailing away. She laughed and began to dance.

If Luther was rhythmically challenged, it was only fair; everything else about him was perfect. He was tall and ebony dark with even white teeth and a smile to make you stutter in bafflement. He spoke French and Portuguese and played the piano. He'd been a journalist at one time—that was how he and Lee met—but had quit early on in favor of business school and was now, as head of his own brokerage firm in New York City, worth more than everyone else in the room combined. His wife, Monique, pregnant with their first child, perched on the living room couch in her designer maternity dress, smiling placidly at her man and at Lee. Lee smiled back at her. Pauline liked to joke that Monique had stolen Luther away from Lee, but the truth was Luther had never been hers. She'd made her interest known, he'd replied with his disinterest, and so they'd long ago settled into being friends.

"You need to get this man some lessons!" Lee called to Monique over the music. "This is truly pitiful!"

Monique rolled her eyes. "I've been working on him for five years! You should have seen him before!" she said. Apparently forgetting that Lee had.

When the music changed, Lee begged off a second, determined to get a drink. In the kitchen, Pauline and Cleo stood near the sink, making margaritas. Pauline was laughing uproariously and Cleo had her arms crossed, looking irked but amused. They seemed to be in their comedy team routine, which fit them because they were, on the outside, such opposites: Pauline with her statuesque body, her silky page boy hairdo, her serious, professional air, and Cleo who was as thin as a pencil, who wore her hair cut short and natural about her pointed face, and who still had about her a bit of the fresh-mouthed, homegirl she used to be. Over the whirring of the blender she called out, "How was I supposed to know?"

Pauline was still laughing. "Ignorance of the brothers is no excuse!" she called out, then saw Lee and winked.

Lee thought how much she would miss the two of them. She and Pauline had been friends since high school; the girl knew more of Lee's secrets than anyone, and Lee knew more of hers. This would be only the second time in years they had not lived within get-over-here-now distance of each other. It would be strange to feel that hole.

As for Cleo: Lee had watched the girl grow from a sullen teenager bent on self-destruction into a poised and accomplished young woman, and she knew herself to be partly responsible for that. Of all the girls Lee had mentored in her life, Cleo was the one who affected her most deeply, the one she fought hardest for, the one she refused, under any circumstances, to lose. And she had not lost. She'd won, and that bound her to Cleo in a way that was different from the bond with Pauline but no less significant. They had long ceased being mentor and teacher and become simply friends.

"Supposed to know what?" Lee asked when the blender stopped.

"Supposed to know better than to throw away a perfectly good man," Pauline said. "Margarita?"

"Please." Lee held out a glass. The mixture was so tart and icy it furrowed her tongue, but it was delicious going down. "Back up, please, and tell me what you're talking about."

"Okay. There's this woman at work," Cleo began, and Lee understood the woman in question was white. Cleo worked as a reporter for a local all-news radio station and was one of the few black people on staff. If the woman were black Cleo would have said "this sister" or "this black woman" because when discussing the workplace, the default was white. Had they been discussing their social worlds, their churches, or Pauline's sorority or Cleo's little activist group of sister-friends, the default would be different, but at work a white person could still be assumed. There was no need to specify.

"This woman wants me to meet some brother her husband knows," Cleo said. "She keeps telling me how wonderful he is, smart and funny and articulate. Especially articulate."

"That means she had a conversation with him and he managed proper noun-verb agreement," Pauline said dryly.

Lee affected an earnest voice: "He used no profanity *and* he properly conjugated the verb 'to be'! He's so articulate!"

They laughed. From the living room Lee heard the front door open and close, followed by the whoop of new arrivals being greeted by the crowd. Someone turned up the stereo. The invitations said eight; now it was just after nine and people were arriving in droves. Cleo said, "Anyway, without my approval she told him to call me. And he did, he called the station and left a message for me to call him back."

"Which, of course, you promptly did," Lee said with a smile. She knew better.

Cleo gave her a look. "What do you think? I didn't want anything to do with this brother. If they like you that much, you must be doing something wrong!"

Lee laughed. It was sad but true: she had never met a black person beloved by white people she would want to befriend. Not that all black people had to be Mau Mau for Lee to appreciate them, scowling around their workplaces in Afros and black turtlenecks, fists in the air. Lee wasn't like that exactly, neither was Pauline nor was Cleo. Well, maybe Cleo was like that, though her Afro was close cropped and she preferred tailored suits.

Still, Lee got along with, and was liked by, most of her white newsroom colleagues and Pauline had no trouble dealing with white investors, businessmen, and bank regulators when she needed to. But Lee doubted if any of those people would rave unsolicited about how wonderful she or Pauline was.

"So this brother has the good whitefolks seal of approval, huh?" Lee said. "Kiss of death. I'd run as fast as I could."

"Don't think I didn't."

"Normally, so would I," Pauline said. "Except in this case, I happen to know the brother and he's cool. He's an attorney. I worked with him in the public defender's office, though I think he's in private practice now. He's serious and dignified and very sharp."

Cleo looked skeptical. "If he's so wonderful, why aren't you dating him?"

"He's a little young for me. More your speed."

"I don't know," Cleo said doubtfully. "I still wonder why this woman is bragging on him so much?"

Pauline shrugged. "He's probably the only other black person she knows. That happened to me once, a woman in my office kept trying to fix me up with this guy. Said he was a mechanic. I thought, okay, I can deal with a blue-collar brother, why not? Turned out he worked at Spiffy Lube. Spiffy Lube! His job was to vacuum out the cars after the oil was changed. He was ten years younger than me and already had three kids by three different women and when I asked this woman if she knew about all that, she said, 'Yes. But he seemed so nice and articulate.' "

Cleo shook her head. "Unbelievable."

"Actually it's pretty much par for the course. You wait a few years."

"A few?" Lee interjected. Teasing Cleo about her relative youth was standard practice among them. "More like ten. You forget the child is barely out of diapers."

Cleo put her fingers in her ears and stuck out her tongue.

"All right, ten," Pauline said. "But you wait. Once you pass thirty, and certainly thirty-five, people think you're desperate. They'll try to set you up with anybody. Four-time divorcés. Octogenarians. Imprisoned felons. White guys."

Lee gave a mock shudder. "Horrors! Not white guys!" She laughed, and in the midst of laughing, for some reason, thought of Porter Stockman. She pushed the thought away.

"Oh yes. I've had people try to set me up with white men more than once. I had to tell them I don't go that way." Pauline cocked her eye at Lee. "But if you're interested, Lee, I can arrange something."

"Yeah, maybe Howard and I could have a threesome," Lee said with a smile. But it felt like an obligatory comment, a statement of claiming and being claimed delivered without joy or pride or even relief.

"Anyway, Lee wouldn't date a white guy if somebody forced her to move to Switzerland for the rest of her life!" Cleo declared.

Pauline tried to pour more margarita into her glass but the blender pitcher was empty. She signaled Cleo, who was standing closer to the tequila, to hand it over. "Oh, no. She might do something stupid like save one of them during a riot, but she sure as hell wouldn't date one."

At eleven Lee gave up hoping Howard would show. At midnight Pauline suggested the neighbors had had enough, and turned down the music. The people with children at home left, as did Eda and Aunt Ella and Uncle Ty and anyone else over fifty. The party mellowed. Those remaining gravitated to couches and chairs and fell into deep and quiet conversations. At three Pauline kicked the last two stragglers out and surveyed the mess. "Tomorrow is soon enough," she said. "Let's go to bed." Lee dragged herself upstairs to the guest room and was out before Pauline finished brushing her teeth.

At eight the alarm clock screamed like a banshee; Lee knocked over a vase trying to shut it off. Her tongue felt woolly and her head pounded, but she forced herself out of bed and into the shower. She had to go to church. They were having a special good-bye for her during the service. She could not miss it. The little church had been her haven since she was ten. She would never forget getting dressed on Sunday morning, dressing her wiggling brother and taking his hand, and walking the five blocks to where people stood smiling in the doorway, their white-gloved hands out to guide her in.

On Lee's final Sunday the entire congregation surrounded her at the pulpit and called on Jesus to take this child safely up the road. Sister Jamison sang a special song. Reverend Murphy anointed her head with holy oil. Mother Little slipped Lee five dollars wrapped in a rose-scented handkerchief she had embroidered herself, and said, "The first thing you do up in Philadelphia is find a church. You need a church family, child, to make it in this world." Mother Little was an epic-size woman, squeezed into a suit of purple and gold, capacious and stern with love. The first time they met she admonished the adolescent Lee for appearing bare-legged and hatless in church, then took her out shopping and bought her lunch. Now Lee wrapped her arms all the way around her waist and hugged. "Amen, Mother," she said. "Amen."

Chapter 6

He had to visit his parents. He'd delayed his monthly visit as long as possible, but now that the swelling from his bruises had subsided, he had no excuse. He hadn't told his parents about the mob, the beating, the escape. He did not want to worry them, but mostly he wanted even less to hand his mother a howitzer in her long-running battle to restructure his career and his life. Porter's mother despised his being a reporter. Bad enough to have chosen journalism as a profession—as opposed to law or business or some other arena in which a man could attain power and wealth—but to still, at the late age of thirty-seven, be merely a reporter she found incomprehensible, and she told him so. Frequently. All those years of relentless pushing, and still her only son turned out to be nothing but a paycheck-collecting, pencil-pushing hack. "Well, there's always the possibility I'll be another William Randolph Hearst," he'd joked once. "He started life as a journalist."

"I believe Mr. Hearst had a father who taught him to aspire to greatness," she replied in that honey-dipped voice of hers. "And I believe by the time he was your age he was well on his way to building an empire."

Thus managing to skewer Porter and his father in one magnolia-scented and venomous breath.

He left work and drove west along the highway, leaving the city behind, headed toward the dreary little suburb of his birth. As soon as he left the highway he hit traffic: cars lined up to enter what had once been the world's largest mall. The designation had lasted fewer than five years, until some larger, more garish shopping monstrosity was built somewhere in Minnesota, but the town of Porter's youth was still defined, and defined itself, as much by the mall as anything else.

His mother hated the mall and refused to step foot inside. She drove instead to Bryn Mawr or Haverford or even into the city itself to shop the velvet-curtained boutiques around Rittenhouse Square. Such shops, she said, offered superior service and quality and, most important, catered to the right kind of people. Being around the right kind of people was very high on his mother's list of daily requirements.

By the right kind of people his mother meant class. His mother was the single biggest social snob Porter had ever known, and her great disappointment in life was that the Main Line society crowd somehow failed to recognize her as one of their own. She was forever lecturing him about her family, the Hobgoods of Mississippi. The Hobgoods were descended from prosperous landowners. The Hobgoods had governors and senators in their lineage, and although they had fallen on hard times during the Depression—why else would she have ever left the Delta state—they never forgot who they were. "We are not common people, Porter," she told him. "We are not average." On this point she was especially adamant. "Whatever you do, Porter, don't be average. You might as well be dead."

By average his mother meant all that surrounded them in their little corner of suburbia: split-ranch houses and card parties and modest summer rentals along the Jersey shore and bleached and bored wives and fat-bellied husbands, people who had only just climbed out of the laboring class. By average, she meant, most of all, his father, an intelligent but wildly passive, wildly unambitious man.

Porter was not average, but neither was he what his mother would have hoped. His mother wanted for her only son what his father would not, or could not, achieve: prominence, power, wealth. Unfortunately for her, Porter cared about none of those things. He didn't want power; he wanted to hound the power brokers of the world. He didn't want wealth; he wanted to afflict the rich. He did desire a measure of prominence, but as a watchdog, a whistle-blower, a relentless seeker of truth, a man who exposed the malfeasance, corruption, and greed of the so-called ruling class. That he'd succeeded in this regard, that in certain Philadelphia circles his name was known and widely loathed (every journalist's dream), frustrated his mother no end. "If you must act this way, can't you at least go to New York?" she asked. "California? Don't they have people who need harassing out there?"

He felt sorry for his mother with her aspirations to wealth and social status, but not sorry enough to leave town. He had fielded his share of offers from bigger newspapers, especially after he nearly won the Pulitzer for a series on state campaign financing. But in the end he chose to remain in Philadelphia. He liked the city, he liked the paper, he liked his editors. He was respected, effective, and relatively content. His mother would have to deal with it.

He got past the mall traffic and decided to stop at the local minimart for a pack of gum. If his mother was cooking he might need something to get the taste out of his mouth later on. Once inside he decided he might as well do his shopping for the week. Considering how often he ate at his apartment, this place was as good as any to pick up the necessities.

He was making his way to the counter with an armful of food when he heard someone call his name.

"Porter? Porter Stockman?"

"Yes?" He turned around. This happened to him sometimes, people he had interviewed once and forgotten appearing out of the crowd.

"You old son of a bitch!" The guy stuck out his hand for a shake. "You don't remember me, do you?"

Porter tried not to look blank.

"Brian Hansen. We went to high school together," the man said graciously. "Remember? I was Roger Stone's friend?"

"Brian! Good to see you." It came back, in chunks: Brian Hansen.

MEETING OF THE WATERS   67

Skinny kid, curly black hair. Angry red acne scarring his face until senior year. Played the saxophone and walked around in an old army jacket no matter how hot or how cold the temperature was. Brian Hansen.

But this wasn't Brian Hansen. Some pallid middle-aged man had swallowed Brian whole.

Porter shook hands as heartily as he could. "How the hell are you? What are you up to these days?"

"I can't complain. I have one wife, two kids, and three locations," Brian said. It was clearly a well-used line.

"Three locations?" Porter asked politely.

"I took over the business from my father. We've expanded. We have services in Haverford and Bucks County."

"Oh," Porter said, trying not to sound surprised. Brian's father was, or had been, a mortician, proprietor of Clifford Hansen's Funeral Home. Porter remembered Brian calling his father Cliff the Stiff with utter disdain and vowing not to follow him into the family business no matter what happened. "I'd rather be dead," he used to say. Apparently things had changed.

"That's great," Porter said. "Congratulations."

"What about you?"

"I'm a reporter for the *Philadelphia Record*."

"Oh." Brian glanced away, then back at Porter. "Well, I don't really read the paper much anymore."

"Really."

"Guess I find it too pessimistic. I don't understand why reporters have to be so negative about everything. What was it Reagan called you guys?" Brian squinted in concentration.

" 'Nattering nabobs of negativism,' " Porter offered. He'd had that phrase tossed at him a hundred times.

"Exactly." Brian grinned. "Reagan really knew how to turn a phrase. The greatest president this country has ever known."

It still surprised Porter to hear someone his age and general background gushing over Reagan. He always thought of the people who put Ronny into office as being old or southern or at least rich. Then again, maybe Brian was rich. Three locations, after all.

"Actually, Reagan didn't turn that particular phase," Porter said.

"Sure he did," Brian said. "I remember him saying it."

"I mean he didn't originate it. Spiro Agnew did. Reagan was just borrowing the quote."

Brian's eyes narrowed and his smile grew strained. "You always were a know-it-all, weren't you, Stockman? Guess you went into the right profession."

"I guess we both did."

There was a split second when the air around them threatened to grow dangerous and Porter's palms began to itch. Then Brian smiled thinly and the moment passed. "Old Porter boy. What a kidder," Brian said with what was clearly meant to be heartiness but came out somewhere between a condolence and a threat. "I should be getting home. The kid needs his diapers or he'll be pissing all over the house."

"You still live around here?" Porter asked, although it was clear Brian did. Probably lived in his parents' house.

"In my parents' house. They moved into Quaker Village a few years back. What about you? Moving back to the old neighborhood?"

"Me?" Porter laughed. "Just visiting my parents. I don't think I could live here now."

Brian lowered his voice. "I know what you mean. Actually my wife and I have put the old house up for sale. The neighborhood's not what it used to be."

"Really?"

"Yeah. We already have our new place. Remember where the baseball field used to be?"

Porter smiled. It was all of six or eight miles from the old neighborhood, but six or eight miles farther away from the city. "Sure do."

"They're building a group of new homes there now, beautiful homes. You should see the models. We picked the two-story one with family room, two-car garage, a pool, and a master bathroom half the size of this store. Great neighborhood too." Brian leaned in close. "It's going to be quite exclusive."

"Great," Porter said, trying to make the step back he took seem unintentional. He had zero interest in Brian and his neighborhood for the rich. But Brian seemed to want to press the point.

"Not everyone will be able to get in."

"Sure," Porter said.

"We won't have to worry about bad elements."

"Bad elements?"

"There aren't that many but they're coming," Brian said. "There's one on my street now. Once it starts you can't turn it back."

Understanding dawned. Brian wasn't talking about money, he was talking about race. He was shepherding his family into a newly built enclave to escape the dirty hordes of black people beating their way into the old neighborhood. Porter felt embarrassed, as though he had walked into Brian's house and caught him humping his dog or something equally obscene. "Well, if you'll excuse me, I have to get going," Porter said, turning to go. He made his voice chilly with disapproval, but Brian either failed to notice or failed to care. He handed Porter a card.

"When the need arises," he said.

Porter tossed the card into the sand-filled ashtray just outside the minimarket door. He hoped Brian would see it, the narrow-minded little prick. Amazing. How had he ever been friends with a guy like that? Of course, Brian hadn't been like that back in high school; at least, Porter didn't think so. They'd never talked much about black people back then. There were no black kids in their high school, and even though the civil rights movement was in full swing it seemed still far removed from their world of sports and girls and cars. Still, he would have known if Brian was a bigot back then. How could a person change so much in twenty years?

What had happened to his other friends? Russell went off to Penn State and then to medical school. Keith had become an alcoholic, sobered up through A.A., and married some wide-hipped, church-going girl. The last he heard they'd both come back to town. They probably lived within a mile of where he was now, probably voted for Reagan, probably never set foot in Philadelphia for fear of black people. What an astonishing waste.

They'd had fun in those days, sneaking down to the school basement during study hall, crouching in the dark, slithering into the dank crawl space beneath the pool where they kept their stash. Three of them could fit in there if they all curled up like the fetal pigs in biology class. They'd smoke pot and listen to the water, imagining themselves beneath the sea. Nobody, not even the janitors, even ventured into the crawl space, and the bitter white smell of chlorine drowned out the marijuana. They congratulated themselves daily on finding it. They used to sit around, fantasizing about girls and dreaming of the big things they'd do once they escaped the tedious limitations of their suburban life. They would become writers in Paris, gigolos in Hollywood, bandits in Mexico. What they would not do was stay in King of Prussia, become insurance salesmen or caretakers to the dead. One day someone raised the topic of fear, and they all went around in the soul-penetrating seriousness of people stoned out of their minds and talked about what frightened them the most. At first they said things like a shortage of pot, not enough sex, typical adolescent macho bravado. Then, as the smoke thickened and their heads expanded with the pot, they talked about their fear of not getting into college and being shipped off to Vietnam. Curled up, surrounded by the swim team's eager noise, stoned out of his mind, Porter said, "My greatest fear is never discovering my categorical imperative and instead living out my life in the existential despair that is my father's small, average, and pathetic life." Floating there in their ambient womb, his friends nodded in faraway unison. As if they understood just what the fuck he was talking about.

There were only two ways into the neighborhood where his parents lived; all other possible paths had been blocked by construction of the highway and the new high school. People considered such limited access a neighborhood selling point. Real estate agents called it "safe" and "enclosed" and "great for kids." In the city neighborhoods flowed one into another, making it impossible, except in the minds of local teenage boys, to tell where one ended and another began. But out here you had to turn into a neighborhood to enter it. No one wandered through this subdivision by accident. Everybody who came here came for a purpose.

In the gloaming the old neighborhood looked dormant. By this time of the evening, dinnertime, every boy had long been called home and each family lurked tucked away behind their own split-level facade with the shades lowered three-quarters of the way. The dead silence of the neighborhood hadn't seemed strange growing up, but now Porter found it slightly sinister. Where he lived now, in Center City Philadelphia, it was never quiet, not even at 4 A.M. Some car was always racing down the street, drunken suburbanites were always staggering back to their cars after a big Saturday night on the town. The one time his mother had visited his apartment—a few months after he first moved in—she had seized on the noise as an acceptable stand-in for everything about the neighborhood that frightened her. She'd stood near the window, gloves in hand, unconsciously checking and rechecking the lock. "You'll never sleep," she warned. But she was wrong. After a few months he slept fine.

His father greeted him at the door, glass in hand. He wore his usual starched white shirt and a royal blue tie with small yellow flowers scattered about the surface.

"Just get home?" Porter asked.

"No, no. I got home at six, just as I always do. Unlike you, son, my schedule is carved in granite. Much like a tombstone." His father held up a crystal glass darkly full. "Drink?"

"Why not?"

On the way to the living room he glanced into the dining room and noticed it had been completely redecorated. Not only was there a new cherry table, new matching chairs, and an enormous matching china cabinet that overpowered the modest-size room, but the blue walls had been covered in a shimmery wallpaper of palest gold, and a new rug lay on the floor. Porter wasn't surprised. His mother was forever renovating and redecorating some part of the house. It was, Porter believed, her frustrated attempt to turn the modest colonial into the grand mansion in which she believed she should live.

In the living room, Porter's father went straight to the liquor cabinet. His mother had asked him long ago not to drink around his father, and usually he acquiesced, but tonight he felt a little grumpier than usual at being home—probably a lingering effect of the riot—and he needed something to get him through the floor show. Anyway, it was a ridiculous request, as if in being surrounded by sober people his father would somehow pick up the habit. Porter took the glass of bourbon from his father and sipped. "Why the tie? Are we dressing for dinner now?"

"Only when I'm told to," his father said. "We were to have company tonight."

"Company?"

"Of the young and single female kind."

"Don't tell me," Porter groaned. "She promised no more surprise dates!"

His father chuckled, as if this statement was too naive to be addressed, and handed Porter his soda. "Fortunately for you, the guest of honor had to cancel. She's a judge and got held up in court."

"A judge. You mean this one actually has a career?"

"She's a judge of traffic court in Hagerstown," his father said. "An appointed position, probably by her father. Don't get too impressed."

Even before his mother spoke, Porter felt her presence fall like a shadow upon the room. His father must not have sensed it, because he jumped when she spoke. "No, dear, don't get too impressed. Heaven knows what might happen if Porter got too impressed with a fine young woman like Catherine. He might actually make something of his life."

He turned and saw her in the doorway, waiting to be recognized and complimented. It was a habit he'd noticed in other beautiful women, and his mother was still beautiful, although her complexion was less creamy than it once had been and her once abundant raven hair was now cut short about her face, as befitted a woman her age.

"You look nice, Mother," he said. "And thanks for the compliment."

She was coming toward him, arms outstretched. He had, as he often did around his mother, the sensation of being engulfed. "I didn't mean anything by it, darling," she said, embracing him. But they both knew that was untrue. She had meant something by it, just not something against him. Porter felt her glaring over his shoulder at his father, just as he could feel his father sinking deep into his chair and into his drink. Porter shifted his weight, blocking his mother's view.

"No more blind dates." He pulled back from the embrace. "I mean it."

She smelled overwhelmingly floral, of roses and lilacs and jasmine, a garden at dusk. "Catherine is a friend of mine. I am allowed, am I not, to have friends?"

"A friend? How old is she?"

His mother wiggled her finger at him. "You know a lady never tells her weight or her age. She's a beautiful young woman, a girl in spring."

"Well, it's a good thing this spring chicken isn't here because I would have walked out."

His mother smiled. "Oh, you'd never embarrass me like that," his mother said, patting his arm. "But next time you come to dinner, please do wear a tie."

In deference to Catherine the great, Porter's mother had asked the once-a-week cleaning lady, Camellia, to put on a maid's uniform and serve the meal of duck breast, spring potatoes, an elaborate salad with corn and peaches and some kind of dark fan-shaped salad greens. "Japanese tatsoi," his mother explained. "I requested them specifically for Catherine. Very popular this season."

Camellia paraded between the dining room and kitchen, her stiff black uniform swishing; she moved as if her shoes were pinching her feet. Porter suggested they let her go, since it was, after all, just the three of them. But his mother refused. "I'll have to pay her whether she serves or not," she said.

It was the usual family dinner. His mother discussed her latest attempts to infiltrate the inner circle at the Main Line Country Club, to which she and Porter's father belonged but did not really belong. His father sat and drank, speaking only occasionally. He would drink throughout the meal, contributing cheerfully to the conversation until the barbs flying from Porter's mother got to be too much or until he reached cruising altitude. At that point, high above the turbulence, his father would head to the basement to listen to his jazz records for an hour before again climbing the stairs, checking the doors, turning off the lights, setting the alarm, downing two aspirin and as much water as his belly could hold, before climbing into bed. His father was a drunk, but a precise and organized one.

"Guess who I just saw at the minimart," Porter said during a lull in the conversation. "Brian Hansen."

"Who, dear?" his mother asked.

"Brian Hansen. One of my friends from high school? His father owns the funeral home. Or, I guess, he owns them now. He told me he's moving into some new subdivision being built behind the playing fields. The jerk is fleeing the big, black invasion."

His mother smiled uncomprehendingly. "The what?"

"The black invasion. Apparently a black family moved onto his street and he's freaking out. Can you believe that?"

"That reminds me," his mother said, and launched into a complaint about the *Record*'s coverage of a battle against a halfway house for the mentally ill the neighborhood had just waged and won. His mother was expert at changing uncomfortable subjects.

"And your paper was completely unfair in the matter," his mother said. Whenever the *Record* wrote something with which she disagreed it became *his* paper.

"That little reporter twisted my words around. She tried to make me look like a monster, as if I didn't care about those people at all. She didn't even mention the four thousand dollars my garden club raised for that Camp Thunderhook last year."

"Camp Thunderhook is for special-needs children," Porter said. "It has nothing to do with the mentally ill."

"She should have mentioned it," his mother insisted. "Can't you do something? Talk to her superior? Have her reprimanded in some way?"

He shook his head in astonishment. "I can't do that! I wouldn't even if I could."

Too late he saw he had walked straight into her trap. His lack of authority, his absence of position or power, was precisely what she wished to remind him of. He felt the familiar hot hand of irritation upon his neck, but he was determined not to let his mother get to him. He would get through dinner without rising to her bait. Porter turned to his father. "So, Dad. How's work?"

His father came out of his glass with a grin. "Fine, fine! We won district-of-the-month. Know what for? Selling more baby policies than anyone else! Life insurance for babies. Never underestimate the intelligence of the American public. Next we'll be insuring goldfish."

"Your father finds the idea of winning district-of-the-month amusing," his mother said sweetly. Although she had not been south of Washington, D.C., in more than forty years, his mother maintained the gracious airs of a southern belle. She put on makeup before coming to breakfast. She flattered people to get her way. She smiled all the time, even when cutting his father to shreds. "Which perhaps explains why this is the first time his district has won in four years."

"Actually, Emma, it's been five."

Porter put down his fork. The duck was cold and fat and greasy in his mouth. He pushed away his plate, took a sip of water. "Can we change the topic?"

"Of course!" His mother put her hands together prettily and pretended to think. "Let's see. We could talk about Catherine. She's such a lovely girl. A graduate of Smith, I believe."

He was having a hard time controlling his irritation. "I don't want to talk about Catherine. I'm not interested in her."

His mother too, apparently, had reached her limit. "Well, what are you interested in, darling?" she asked. "Besides your little paper, of course."

He had a nasty urge to punish her and so he said, "I'm interested in Peg. I received a postcard from her last week. She said to say hello to you, Dad."

He regretted it instantly. If there was one subject on which his mother was vulnerable, it was Peg. She had driven his sister away, had nearly driven her to destroy her own life, and if given the chance, would probably do the same thing again, not from malice, but from a twisted kind of love.

The card from Peg had been postmarked Chicago. Apparently she had managed to swing a job as an "art therapist" in some downtrodden inner-city middle school, though she had no education degree and no formal training in either art or therapy save her own years on the couch. But if there was one thing Peg could do, it was land a job; she could talk the head of University Hospital into letting her perform brain surgery if

she wanted to. In the few sentences scrawled across the postcard she
sounded happy and fulfilled. Maybe this was the calling she'd sought for
so long. She signed the card, "Miss you, brother. Give my love to Dad.
Say hi to Leona Helmsley." It was a joking reference to their mother
never being satisfied, but Porter sensed in it a softening: for years, Peg,
in their spotty correspondence, never mentioned their mother at all.

Now he tried to soften his punch. "She's fine. She's working in a
school in Chicago."

"My kind of town!" His father smiled dazedly. "I've always wanted
to see Chicago. I've always wanted to drive across the vast midsection of
this great land."

"Why don't you do it this summer?" Porter asked, though he knew
it was useless. His father was full of small, pathetic dreams he would
never realize. It was depressing.

"Chicago?" His mother laughed scornfully.

"This summer's no good," his father said.

Porter persisted. "Why not? When else are you going to do it? What
else do you have to do?"

"Why, your father has to stay here and support the liquor industry!"
his mother said.

Porter turned to his father. "I could go with you."

"Go where?" Already his father had forgotten his dream.

"Chicago," Porter said.

"Oh, yes. Perhaps next summer. I would like to see the great Mid-
west and the still-untamed heart of this great land. Next summer, perhaps."

Camellia entered the room, carrying a silver tray with coffee and a
blueberry tart for dessert. She trudged to the sideboard, as though making her way through a foot of snow, sighing as she went. His mother was
still talking about summer vacation, joking scornfully about his father's
inability to take her anyplace more grand than the Jersey shore, which
she detested. Porter sat listening to her, watching her words fall like
stones upon his father's head, and to stop her he said, "Camellia, why
don't you sit down and join us for dessert."

Camellia, who had been slicing the pie, came to a standstill. His mother stopped midsentence. His father came out of his glass again and chuckled.

"Darling," his mother said, smiling carefully, "I'm sure Camellia has things to do in the kitchen."

"Whatever she has to do can wait until she has some pie." He rose and pulled out a chair. Camellia, not moving, looked from him to his mother and back.

"Porter." His mother's voice rose an octave in warning.

"Why not? After all, there's an extra place already set, since Catherine couldn't make it." He walked to Camellia, put his hands on her shoulders, and guided her back to the table. Her body was stiff beneath his hands, and she moved like a prisoner being taken to death row. "Sit down, sit down. I'll serve."

"Me first!" his father called. Of all the people at the table, he alone was enjoying himself. "I'll take a nice, fat slice!"

They ate in silence. Camellia swallowed two bites of pie, then excused herself and fled to the kitchen and probably out the back door. His mother waited until Camellia had gone, then rose from the table and left the room without a word, her pie untouched.

Porter put down his fork, realizing too late what a terrible position he'd put Camellia in. His stomach contracted into a knot.

His father rose from his chair with drunken dignity, then came around the table to shake Porter's hand. "Good night, son. Keep up the good work, son. I read you every day."

Porter sat and watched his father go out of the room like a warning. He got up and went into the deserted kitchen and poured out the last of his drink.

Chapter 7

She arrived at the cocktail party for new employees alone, wearing a white top beneath a long, dark blue jumper with a slit up the side. He noticed the absence of a boyfriend and the way the snowy white shirt made her dark skin seem to glow.

In general, the new employee cocktail party was an embarrassment, a hazing line through which new people were put. Unlike most people, she handled it with aplomb. She neither smiled sheepishly nor grinned smugly while her credits were read and the acquiring editor bragged about all he had done to lure her from Baltimore. Lee just stood there, arms loosely folded across her chest, eyes straight ahead, owning not the scene but herself in it. She seemed deeply absorbed in some question, something other than what the editor was babbling about. When the editor finished, it was time for Lee to make the required remarks.

"Thank you," she said. "That was a very gracious introduction. I hope I can live up to myself."

And that was it. No gushing about how thrilled she was to be working for the *Record* or self-aggrandizing statements about her plans for routing out corruption and restoring democracy to the city. Just "thank you" and that sly little comment, which seemed to be self-mocking but which, in fact, gently painted the editor as the blowhard everyone knew he was. She really was brave; either that, or she just didn't give a damn, which amounted to the same thing. Porter applauded along with everyone else, but his clapping was more than polite. As the applause died down, he watched her make her way quietly from the room while the other new employees hovered, talking too loudly, laughing too hard. Just before the door Lee stopped to acknowledge someone's outstretched hand and caught him watching her. He smiled. She hesitated, a half smile on her face, as though deciding whether to keep going or not. Just hold her eyes, he told himself, keep looking, don't be the first to turn away. But then someone tapped him on the shoulder and instinctively he turned around. It was Karl, the transportation reporter, grinning like the idiot he was. "Get any of the shrimp?" Karl asked. When Porter turned back toward the doorway, she was gone.

For the insecure—and they were legion—among the newsroom staff, fresh blood was not cause for celebration. A new person, an eager new face, just meant one more shark in an already crowded tank. Much grumbling often ensued, and any weakness was quickly seized upon. This was one reason a newcomer's first byline carried such importance, and why the acquiring editor made sure said story was not only factually clean but stunningly written, a symphony in newsprint. Anything less was sending Bambi to the wolves.

Porter usually paid little attention to newcomers or the grumbling they caused, but he found himself anxiously awaiting Lee's first byline. He wanted her to report strong and write well; he wanted her to blast the naysayers with her talent. He didn't want to have to listen to any crap about Lee.

Her first piece was a story about a black family of five that made the mistake of thinking it could live where it chose in the City of Brotherly Love. According to Lee's story, the family fled its old decaying and drug-ridden North Philadelphia neighborhood for Kensington—also part of North Philadelphia, also poor and job starved but considered a safer place to live. But not for the Millers.

Three days after the nation celebrated its Independence the Millers woke to the falsely festive sound of shattering glass. Outside their new home they found bottles and rocks and smeared feces and a spray-painted message from the neighborhood welcoming committee: Niggers get out.

"I was ready to go right then," said Stacy Miller, who purchased the house with her mother, Eleanor Hampton Fox. "But Mama said she wasn't going to let a bunch of . . . cowards drive her outta her house. She thought maybe they'd gotten it out of their system and things would calm down."

Things did not calm down. That night five bat-wielding men surrounded the house, chanting obscenities while the family armed themselves with carving knives and soda bottles and huddled in the master bedroom, awaiting the police. Mrs. Fox, trembling with rage, wanted to go outside and confront the men but was stayed by the cries of her daughter and grandchildren. "My sisters were crying 'cause they didn't want Nana to go," said Benjamin Franklin Miller Jr., age ten.

By the time the police arrived the men had disappeared, faded back into the darkness from which they came. They left behind them several pickle jars of urine and more ugly messages scrawled across the front of the house: Niggers. Monkeys. Back to your own kind.

"My sisters were scared," said Benjamin.

"Were you scared?" a reporter asked. Benjamin sucked his teeth and scoffed. "I was wishing I had a piece," he said.

"Have you ever seen a gun?"

Benjamin didn't answer. "They grow up hard where we used to live," said Mrs. Fox. "Benjy's a good boy and we're fighting to keep him that way."

"That's why we moved," said Ms. Miller. "But we're moving back. I'd rather deal with drug dealers than live with these hateful, evil folk."

Porter was impressed. Not only had Lee managed to extract a gut-wrenching interview from the Millers, who turned down all other requests and refused, even, to meet with the mayor, but she also managed to convince several white Kensington residents to spill their own dark thoughts for the city to read. She quoted one man who attributed the incident to a bunch of drunken kids who got a little out of hand, them blacks was making way too much of it. A woman suggested the incident was really a plot by the "N and A and CP" to take over Kensington.

"It ain't fair," Lee quoted one man as saying. He was a former carpet maker who had lived in Kensington all his life. "They're trying to paint the whole neighborhood as a bunch of racists. We're not racists. We're average, everyday people who just want to make sure our neighborhood stays clean." He might have been easily dismissed as a kind of caricature racist, except during the middle of the interview he had to stop and retrieve his wife, an Alzheimer patient, who had wandered, half-dressed, into the middle of the street. Lee put that in, put in how the proudest day in the man's life had been the day he burned his mortgage. But now, ten years later, he was about to lose his house because of the cost of caring for his wife. "But I don't complain. I don't like whiners," he said. "I don't like people who complain all the time and try to get something for free."

Getting people to expose themselves in print, especially across racial lines like that, wasn't easy. Few reporters could pull it off. Porter could. Apparently so could Lee.

The newsroom buzzed with appreciation. Karl, who sat across from Porter, said grudgingly, "You read this Kensington piece, the one by that new girl? Not bad."

"No, it's not," Porter said. "And we don't call them girls anymore, Karl."

"Excuse the hell out of me, Gloria Steinem."

"Oh, that I could excuse you, Karl," Porter said, getting up to take a spin around the newsroom. He wanted to happen past Lee's desk and congratulate her on her triumph. But she wasn't in. Three times that afternoon he checked her desk, until Gerry, who sat at a desk facing Lee's, said, "Leave a note, why don't ya? You're wearing a hole in the rug."

He slunk back to his desk, feeling foolish, feeling as though he were fourteen again, sitting in the bleachers, gawking at Cheerleader Cindy during the donkey basketball game. What was wrong with him? If he was attracted to this woman he should do something about it. He should act on that attraction like a man. He should send flowers. He would say, "Congratulations on the success of your first byline," and if she read something more into the gesture, that was okay too.

That evening, on the way home, he stopped by a florist and spent fifteen minutes picking out a bouquet. "You're not like most guys," cooed the florist. She had jangly silver earrings, long, stringy black hair, and dirt under all ten fingernails. She looked a bit like Cher, if Cher had bad skin and worked in a flower shop. "Most guys come in here all in a rush and say, 'What you got for thirty bucks?' They never think about the language of flowers."

"The language of flowers?"

"Oh yes." The florist spread her hands through the air. "Each flower has a message all its own. Gardenia means 'I love you in secret.' Violets mean faithfulness. Carnations mean admiration."

"Forget-me-nots mean 'Forget me not,' " he offered.

Cher beamed. "And red roses, of course, mean passion and love," she said. "Everyone knows that."

"Fascinating. How about, 'Thanks for saving my life.' Do you have a flower that says that?"

Cher took the question seriously, though he had not meant it that way. She consulted various books and pamphlets before finally suggesting a single calla lily surrounded by a dozen purple gladioli. Gladioli meant strength of character, while the purple represented valor and white stood for beauty and innocence. He thanked her but turned down the bouquet as too showy. He didn't want to announce his intentions with a bugle call. He wasn't even sure what his intentions were. He just wanted to drop a handkerchief in Lee's path.

In the end he chose a bouquet of jonquils and daisies because he thought they were pretty. Cher informed him jonquils meant "I desire a return of your affection," but he took the chance Lee wouldn't be current on her flower talk.

He had the flowers sent to the newsroom and was there the next morning when the delivery man arrived. Unfortunately, he couldn't see Lee's desk from his own. Porter sat on the west side of the newsroom, behind a line of peeling gray columns that presumably held up the floor above. It was in the back, away from the windows but away also from the roving eyes of the editors and near the door to the back stairway, and thus a highly prized spot. Lee, being the new kid on the block, had been assigned a desk up front, just inches away from the metro desk. When somebody telephoned about a stray dog on the highway and the editor glanced around for a warm body, hers would be the first in sight.

He watched the delivery man arrive. Five minutes later he watched the delivery man reemerge empty-handed and rubbing his back. Porter waited fifteen minutes, thirty, forty-five, for her to telephone, to walk over and thank him or something. When he couldn't wait any longer he got up and sauntered, or tried to saunter, toward the other side of the room. He half-expected to find her desk deserted, but there Lee sat, clicking furiously on the keyboard. She paused when she spotted him, hands held over the keyboard like a pianist. "Oh. Hi."

"Hello."

She hesitated a moment, then stood. "I was just headed up to the cafeteria for a soda. Want to come along?"

"Of course."

They walked through the newsroom in silence and well apart, as though they just happened to be headed in the same direction. He wanted to speak, to say something to break the ice, but she moved with such intense purpose he didn't have the chance until they reached the elevator and stepped inside.

"I wanted to thank you for the flowers," Lee said.

"You're welcome."

"You really shouldn't have," she said.

"Just wanted to offer my congratulations on your story. You might also consider it a very belated thank-you."

"I told you: you don't owe me anything."

"Not much. Only my life." He said this lightly, not wanting her to think he really thought it was true.

"Yeah, but you bought me coffee my first day here. We'll call it even."

Not knowing what to say to this, he simply laughed.

It was omelet day in the cafeteria. In a corner of the room a flushed cook stood over a hot plate, ladling eggs into a pan. A dozen people stood in line before him, fanning themselves with their plates. "Omelet?" he asked Lee. "We've got onions, peppers, whatever you like. Nothing's too good for *Record* employees. Except a raise."

She smiled but he couldn't tell whether it was one of amusement or indulgence. "I'm just grabbing some coffee and fruit for now. I have to get back. My phone's been ringing off the hook."

They got their food and paid the cashier. "Sit a moment," he said. "Come on, you deserve a break today."

She smiled again, this time clearly not amused, and he winced. What was wrong with him, spouting all these stupid phrases? He must be more nervous than he realized. Still she sat.

"Just for a second. I have to get back."

"The story is causing a stir, huh?"

She sipped her coffee. "The mayor's office wants me to get Mrs. Miller to meet with them. The NAACP. The Human Rights Commission. A few people offering money. And one old woman who cried in my ear for ten minutes. She wanted someone to know how terrible she felt about the episode."

"You sound like you didn't believe her."

Lee shrugged. "I believed her. I just wasn't sure what she wanted me to do."

"Probably just to hear her and believe. It was a good story; you struck a nerve, and when people get struck they have to tell someone."

"It wasn't me. Well, I suppose it was my writing," she corrected, and again he was impressed. He hated false modesty in women. "But it was primarily the Millers. They have a kind of . . . dignity you don't often find. All I had to do was capture it."

"You captured it," he said. "Very well."

"I was on the phone with the copy desk for an hour last night. The copy editor wanted to cut most of the white neighbor comments. He said they were inflammatory and off-point."

"That's insane."

"I know."

"They made the story," he said.

"I thought they were important."

"They were very important," he insisted. He felt himself trying to impress her. "They made the piece, I think. They balanced it. Those comments are why the story got on the front page. It was a great first splash for you. Everybody's talking about it."

There was a pause, and just the slightest shift in the way her body sat in the chair. But he felt it, felt it as though he had been sleeping sweetly and someone pulled the blanket off. One minute they were talking, really engaging each other, and the next she had shut him out. Clearly he'd misstepped somehow, said something wrong. He had no idea what it was. He could keep going, hope she'd forget whatever it was he said that she didn't like. But one of the first lessons he'd learned as a journalist was that it was better to confront your mistakes head-on than to ignore them. If politicians ever learned that lesson he'd be out of a job.

"What did I say?"

"Excuse me?"

"I said something you didn't like. What was it?"

She shrugged and looked around the cafeteria, as if she could not care less. Maybe she couldn't. "You just make it sound as though I wrote the story to impress the people in the newsroom. As if that were the purpose. The goal."

He felt stung, which was a surprise. God knew he'd been accused of far worse things in his life, but he wanted to impress this woman and so far he was doing a lousy job. He decided to take off the schmoozing mask and just be himself. "Let's be honest: as journalists we write as much for one another as anyone else. We write to impress our editors. We write to impress our peers. We write to impress the people on the Pulitzer jury. There's nothing wrong with that. The public still gets informed, the corrupt still get exposed. But those anonymous thousands reading our words don't make us feel as good as getting a slap on the back from our colleagues."

"Not me."

"You don't care what people in the newsroom think about you?"

"Not particularly."

"That's noble. Not to mention astonishingly self-confident."

"It's neither," she said, still glancing around. "I just come at this game from a different perspective."

"And what perspective is that?"

She looked briefly his way, and he saw the screen had come down. "It's hard to explain."

"Oh." He leaned back in his chair and crossed his arms over his chest. "So it's a black thing and I wouldn't understand. Is that it?"

Her smile was cool. "Bingo." Then she stood to go, dismissing him. But he refused to be dismissed and followed her into the hall. "You know, I hate that phrase. It's not true and it's so destructive to race relations."

She pushed the button for the elevator, not even bothering to turn his way. "It's always amusing when white people say black people are hurting race relations."

"But you are!" He heard the strain in his voice and controlled it. "You're saying you and I can't possibly connect as human beings because we're different colors. You're saying race matters above all else. You don't call that destructive?"

She shrugged. "I didn't make the world." The implication was, of course, that *he* did, him and his filthy, evil, limp-dicked, and oppressive white kind. This was nothing new to him. He'd heard it all before in various incarnations: white men were the villains of the twentieth century. It was the mantra of the 1970s and 1980s and it had given Ronny R. and his cronies the ammunition they needed to gun their way into control, and still people had not learned. But it never bothered him because he didn't buy into it. He had no use for Ronny's army of angry white males, but neither did he subscribe to the magazine of liberal white guilt. Usually evil-white-man diatribes rolled off his back, but coming from her it was different. It was somehow freshly horrible and infuriating and shameful and, above all, personal. And yet not personal. She hadn't looked at him since the middle of their conversation. She seemed, in fact, barely able to see him at all.

"What's the difference," he asked her, "between what you're saying and what David Duke preaches? Aren't you being just as racist as he is?"

He expected anger, but instead she laughed. "Black people can be prejudiced but they can't be racist! And as for David Duke, I wouldn't invite him to dinner but at least he's honest."

He was so astonished he sputtered. "Meaning I'm not? Meaning I'm a racist?"

"I didn't say that."

"That's what you implied." He was trying to glare at her, but the elevator opened and people began streaming out, making their way to the cafeteria for omelet day. She stepped off to the left to let them pass; he was pushed to the right. He couldn't believe she was just going to get on that elevator and go on back to the newsroom as if nothing had happened there, as if she'd been passing the time of day with the cafeteria man. "Hey!" he called to her over the heads of the crowd. "Hey!"

"Hey, what?"

Hey what? He had no idea. He raked his brain, trying to uncover something to shake her up, to crack that terrible mask of indifference on that face. She stood across from him like a piece of marble, cool and smooth and beautiful and utterly impervious. He couldn't even make a scratch.

"Hey, let me ask you something. About the riots."

The elevator was almost empty. She looked at her watch. "Go ahead."

Without planning, the question came out. "Do you know who Latasha Harlins was?" He didn't know why that question. He hadn't thought about Latasha Harlins since the week after he got back to Philadelphia from the riots, when he remembered the chants of the crowd and looked her up in the *Los Angeles Times* database. But there it was, and he went with it; sometimes the subconscious knows better than the conscious. "Do you?"

It worked, for a minute. The elevator emptied but she didn't step in. "Why are you asking about her?"

"I want to see if you know," he said, but even as he said it he realized that of course she did. And that it proved nothing other than how ridiculous he was being.

Lee let the elevator door close and looked at him a long moment. Then she said, "Latasha Harlins was the fifteen-year-old girl shot and killed by a Korean store owner named Soon Ja Du in Los Angeles around the time Rodney King first made national news. The store owner was found guilty of voluntary manslaughter, but a few months before the King verdict a judge named Joyce Karlin let the Korean woman off with five years' probation and a five-hundred-dollar fine, saying there was no need to send her to prison and ruin her life. Ignoring the fact that she'd murdered a child. Some people think the anger in the black community over the killing helped contribute to the riots."

He felt like an idiot. "Did you know all that before you went to L.A. to cover the riots?"

"Yes." She pushed the elevator button and the doors sprang open, as if even machinery bent to her will.

"I guess that's a black thing too? That you knew, although you were living in Baltimore?"

"Maybe." She stepped into the elevator. "Or maybe I'm just a better reporter than you."

Chapter 8

She took the flowers home with her that night. Had they been from Howard—had Howard been the flower-sending type—she would have left them on her desk for all the newsroom to see, evidence of her desirability. But they weren't from Howard, they were from Porter, and she didn't want him getting the wrong idea. Or rather, he seemed to already have the wrong idea and she needed to correct it. She wasn't interested in him. She wasn't attracted to him. She didn't date fellow journalists, and most important, she didn't date white men and that was that.

But Porter wasn't in the newsroom the following morning, or the next or the next. She wondered, idly, if he might be avoiding her, but decided he must have been out on assignment. Which was fine. Maybe the whole thing would just go away. Maybe she wouldn't have to say anything after all.

Her new beat had advantages and disadvantages. On the upside, a beat without history was undefined. Lee could carve out her own territory, finding stories that fell between the neat categories of police, politics, education, social welfare, or business and making them her own. But on the downside, a beat without history was unbounded. Anyone could wander into her space, and every editor who saw her wanted to rope her into his corral.

The education editor wanted help covering high school graduations. This was mind-numbing, eye-glazing tedious work usually inflicted upon the rawest, most pliant members of the staff, but the newsroom that spring was low on young recruits.

"It's not really my beat," Lee explained.

"Well, graduation rates among blacks are falling," the education editor argued. "You could write a story about that. Pick two or three schools, cover their ceremonies for me, and then write your piece for the weekend."

"When? In my spare time?"

"I only need six hundred words each."

"I'm tied up on this other project."

"This is more pressing."

"Ben asked me about this other project yesterday." This was only a partial lie. She'd run into the managing editor in the elevator and he'd asked, casually, what she was working on. That he had never heard of the story meant it was not being heavily promoted among the top brass, but the education editor was so far removed from the golden circle she would have no idea.

"Well in that case," she said, "never mind."

The political editor was shepherding a huge, preelection series on the angry and volatile American electorate and wanted Lee to do a sidebar on the growing number of black conservatives.

"What makes you think it's growing?" Lee asked.

"My neighbor was just made chairman of the local Republican party," the political editor said.

"So?"

"He told me there's a growing movement in the area."

"Movement of what?"

"Of people like him."

There was a pause, then Lee asked, "Your neighbor is black?"

The political editor nodded and smiled. He seemed relieved she'd said the word instead of him. The political editor was one of those over-compensating white people who sometimes feigned color blindness to the point of lunacy.

"I guess this story Ben wants could wait," Lee said.

"Oh. I didn't realize you were working on something," the political editor said. She smiled through her teeth. He didn't realize she was working on something? What did he think she did all day, sit around picking nits from her hair?

"I'll look around for someone else," the political editor said. "But I might need you to do it anyway."

When she complained to Lou, the national editor, who was supposed to protect her from these raids, he said he had five correspondents spread across the nation covering important issues and he couldn't stop to hold her hand all day long. When she went for advice to the sole black manager in the newsroom, an assistant metro editor named Warner, he told her to run, not walk, back to the political editor and beg for the black Republican story.

"The political editor is the heir apparent," he said. "If he wants you to scrub his bathtub, do it."

Lee looked at him. She didn't know much about Warner, only that he was one of only a handful of black people in management. The sports editor was black, but sports was on another floor and in another world. There was a sister who helped run the features department, but features too was a distant planet far removed from the politically cutthroat world of news. There had been, before Lee arrived, a dynamic black projects editor, but he was lured away by the *New York Times*.

"The important thing in this place is to figure out who's ascendant and then get on their radar screen," Warner said.

They were upstairs in the cafeteria eating cardboard sandwiches because Warner said he never went out for lunch, it took too long. He advised her not to either, but to stay in and work at her desk to demonstrate industriousness. About the fact that the metro editor often took two hours for lunch, and that it had not affected his career, Warner said not a word.

"I'm not interested in being on the radar screen," Lee said.

"You better be." Warner shoved the rest of his sandwich into his mouth and looked at his watch.

"I'm not some twenty-two-year-old ingenue, trying to make a name for myself," Lee said. "I'm interested in writing stories about issues that affect black folks. I want to be given the time and the resources to do them. That's what they promised me when I came here."

Warner slurped at his soda and looked at his watch. "I doubt if they said you'd only be writing about black folks. Even if they did, I'd be careful. That's a good way to get yourself categorized as a black reporter."

"I am a black reporter."

He looked at her. "You know what I mean."

She smiled. This guy was still an editor. She had to watch her mouth.

"Anyway," Warner continued, "this *is* a story about black people. And it's a political story, and politics is where the big boys play. You should jump at it."

"Writing about black Republicans is not exactly what I had in mind."

"I see." Warner stood. "You mean because black Republicans aren't real enough for you, right? They're not real black people."

"I didn't say that," Lee said, though, in fact, that was what she meant. Black folks who declared themselves Republicans were as real as anybody else, of course, and they had the right to their opinions. She didn't argue that. But it seemed crystal clear to Lee that twelve years of Reagan-Bush Republicanism had been painful to the majority of black people in the country, painful and hard. Any black person who ignored that pain and aligned himself with the Republicans was traitorous as far as she was concerned.

"I'm not saying don't do the story," Lee said. "I just don't want to be the one to write it. The issues I want to explore—the ones that affect the people I care about—nobody down there wants to touch them. But half the newsroom would jump at that black elephant story. Let somebody else do it."

Warner looked at his watch and wiped his face. "You have a very narrow definition of what it means to be black," he said. "Better be careful: someday you might have to change it."

Lee didn't say anything as he walked away, but she thought plenty, including this: and someday, Warner, you might have to look in the mirror and figure out who you are.

As a last-ditch measure Lee went to Joyce Hawthorne, a woman she'd met during the interview process and liked. Joyce was editor of the idea desk, which was, in some respects, the newsroom dumping ground. It was supposed to be a high-profile desk, a thinking-reporter's repose but in reality it lacked any sort of cachet. The idea desk was the place for reporters who had been shoved off, or leapt off, the ladder to the top; other reporters called it the desk where ideas went to die. But the reporters working for Joyce were left alone by the other editors. They could spend a month on a story if that was what it took, digging deep into the heart of the subject matter. And if the story was good, Joyce would fight to get it in the paper, fight to have it placed prominently. She usually won the first battle, if not the second, but Lee decided she'd rather have a serious piece about the crippling effects of long-term foster care on a growing number of black children on page twelve than a piece about black Republicans on page one.

"Can you get me on your desk?" Lee asked.

They were lunching at a joyfully chaotic Greek restaurant on South Street. Lee had to raise her voice to be heard above the din of pans clanging and glasses clattering and music blaring and customers laughing and waiters calling out to one another in Greek. It was Joyce's choice of restaurant. She went out to lunch every day, usually with members of her staff.

"People will think you're nuts, jumping from the national desk to the idea desk," Joyce growled. She took a sip of wine, cleared her throat so loud several people turned around, then took another sip of wine. Her voice was raspy from years of smoking and a brush with precancerous polyps on her vocal cords. She had the polyps scraped away, quit smoking, and now chewed incessantly on breath mints so strong they made Lee's eyes water whenever Joyce opened the box. "It's just not done."

"I don't care what people think."

"No slave to public opinion?" Joyce smiled. "Everyone likes to think they're independent-minded, but few people truly are. Especially journalists."

She knew Joyce was right. Journalists were as competitive and status conscious as anyone else, and the newsroom was far from a classless society. In Baltimore, she'd finally clawed her way into the select circle of reporters who were treated well, given time to write important stories, and not edited to death. But she had never been a star, never a member of the golden inner circle. She was respected but not envied, admired but not aspired to. Which was fine with Lee. She was more interested in doing meaningful work than gaining the envy of other reporters. She considered them her colleagues, not peers. They were not, by and large, the people she was trying to impress.

"If I can write the kind of stories I want to write, and get them in the paper somewhere, I'll be content," Lee said.

"Well, that's the dirty little secret of the idea desk," Joyce said. "We are content. We have no juice, no power, no cachet whatsoever. Ben doesn't come around very often, slapping us publicly on the back. My reporters don't get nominated for awards, although they should. People look at us with pity, not envy. But on a day-to-day basis, the people on my desk are the happiest, least anxious, least gnawed-at people in the room."

"Does that include you?"

Joyce coughed out a laugh. "Let me tell you something. I used to be national editor, did you know that? Yeah, I was hot shit. I was going to be the first female M.E. if it killed me."

"What happened?"

Joyce made a fist and knocked on her neck. "It nearly killed me. I was smoking four packs a day from the stress and it almost had my ass. Sitting in the doctor's office, waiting for the results of my tests, it dawned on me that I didn't really want to be managing editor. Hell, I didn't even like being national editor! Dealing with all those prima donnas on the national staff. I just thought that's what I should want to be.

But I finally figured out that if I was doing what everyone else thought I should be doing, but was miserable, then I was the imbecile. And if there's one thing I detest, it's an imbecile."

Lee laughed. She liked this crazy, independent woman who knew what she wanted from life. "Me too."

"Then welcome aboard," Joyce said, raising her glass of wine.

The switch was made. The national editor kicked up an obligatory fuss, but Lee knew he was secretly glad to be rid of her. Joyce further mollified the man by promising to send Lee straight to his desk in the event of natural disaster, major uprising, or any other extraordinary circumstance.

Lee's first story for Joyce was a continuation of one she'd already been working on. It did not, strictly speaking, fit into the categories of "race" or "urban issues," but it was a story she was deeply interested in. It was a long, complicated piece about the scourge of drugs and the feminization of crime and the effects of putting mothers in jail. She was focusing the piece on one particular family, in which the twenty-three-year-old daughter had been convicted of murder for shooting the Korean owner of a convenience store during a botched robbery.

Lee was still waiting to interview the daughter, locked away in prison, but she persuaded the girl's mother to talk, and so one morning she met her at the daughter's home, a one-bedroom apartment on the top floor of a ramshackle West Philadelphia row house. The place was dim and warm and chaotic with mess: piles of clothes, stacks of dishes encrusted with food, heap upon heap of plastic toys colored bright yellow and red and blue.

The first thing the mother said after opening the door was "I apologize for the way this place looks. I know I raised her better than this."

The mother had been reluctant to grant the interview, but now she seemed eager to talk. The words tumbled from her lips as she moved to sit down on the couch.

"I don't live here. I came this morning to clean up and get some of the children's things, but I just took one look and I had to sit down. I hardly know where to start. I didn't raise her like this. When she was eleven her uncle started messing with her. I didn't know about it. I was working, working hard to feed her and the rest. She didn't tell me about it until he'd left town. I put the law on him, but they didn't work too hard trying to find him and eventually he got in a fight out in Las Vegas and got knifed to death. Good riddance, I said. But Sheila started acting out. Pretty soon I couldn't do nothing with her. I tried to tell her to forget it, to go on. Everybody has something. Everybody has pain, everybody gets messed over at some point in this life. You think you the only one?" The woman gave a harsh laugh. "Girl, I could tell you stories! I told her you just got to pick up and go on. You can't just throw up your hands. But she wouldn't listen. She got involved with this worthless piece of trash and he got her started with them drugs and the babies started coming and it was a mess. I knew sooner or later she'd end up doing something bad."

For the first time the mother turned her eyes toward Lee. "God help her, she killed that man."

"Maybe you shouldn't say that." Lee's tape recorder lay on the table. She picked it up and turned it off.

"No, I believe she did it," the mother insisted. "The drugs have destroyed her mind. At one point I thought she might hurt me, she was so out of her head. I feared she'd hurt them children. I feared that all the time but I didn't want to call child welfare. I didn't want them going into foster care."

"Is that where they are now?"

The mother nodded. "My grandbabies. Course, they want me to take them . . ." Silence fell between them. The mother turned toward the room's only window, as though it looked out over a field or an ocean instead of an alleyway. Lee said nothing. It was a rookie mistake to jump in too soon, to trample the silence because you were uncomfortable. Better to wait, to let the person make her way back to the conversation on her own. After a while the mother shook her head, like a sleepy driver.

"Went back to school, you know. I got my GED last month."

"That's wonderful," Lee said.

"Took me more than a year. I just couldn't pass the English section. I was never any good with writing and words. But I stuck with it and I did it! I did." The woman stuck out her chin in astonished pride. "I didn't think I could but I did."

"Good for you!"

"The day it came in the mail I went right down to the community college and signed up for classes. Supposed to begin this summer. I want to get my A.B."

"Your grandchildren will be proud of you. It'll be good for them to see their grandmother in college."

"Yes," the mother said, and looked away again.

"What do you want to major in?" This line of conversation, this mother's dreams, was not, strictly speaking, relevant to the story. But a good reporter was like a psychologist: you listened to whatever the person had to say because you never knew. And Lee was interested.

"Something in finance. When I was young I used to dream of working in a bank."

"You can still do it now."

After a long moment the mother said, "Not if I take those children."

"You could get help."

"No." There was a stillness to her voice.

"You could go to school while they're in school," Lee offered, though she wasn't sure why she was saying these things. It was her job to listen, no more. "Or on the weekends. You could work it out."

The mother leaned forward and grabbed Lee's hand. Though she was startled, Lee managed not to jump or recoil. She felt no fear, only sadness. This could be Eda if things had gone differently. This could be her.

The woman's hair was trimmed and her bare nails buffed and she wore small gold earrings shaped like stars in her ears. She smelled delicately of jasmine. She looked like a woman who should be sitting behind a desk at the bank instead of in this apartment with its stained furniture and filthy kitchen and broken children's toys.

"I raised mine," the mother pleaded. "It nearly killed me, but I raised mine, and if I have to raise these, I'll never do anything else."

The mother's hands were incongruously moist. Beads of sweat formed where their skins touched, but Lee did not let go. "You could get help. I know some agencies—"

The mother tossed Lee's hand away with a harsh laugh. "Nobody helped me with mine. Nobody will help me with these."

"You'll still have time."

"I'm fifty-nine years old."

"That's not old."

The woman looked hard at her. "How the hell do you know?"

Lee said nothing. For some reason the woman wanted her to say it was all right, that she could give up the grandchildren and go on with her life blame-free. But it wasn't her place to say anything, to hand out advice. And anyway, she didn't believe it. Those children needed her; that was the simple truth. Black kids had a hard enough time in this hostile world. Without at least one caring adult, without some steady connection to family and love, they were almost certainly lost. The woman had an obligation that was bigger than herself.

The mother walked toward a corner of the room where toys lay scattered about the floor. Getting down on her knees, she picked up a toy fire engine and held it in her hands. Next to her sat two boxes. One was marked TRASH. The other was marked ANTHONY AND THERESA CUMMINS: TOYS.

"You know," the mother said, "I took civics class as part of my GED. I remember taking a civics class when I was a girl, but I was too stupid to pay attention then. This time, though, I listened. It was fascinating. The teacher talked about the Declaration of Independence, the rights of life, liberty, and the pursuit of happiness. How this country was founded on the principle of rugged individualism. All that."

Lee thought: we weren't part of that. None of those rugged individuals gave a damn about our rights of liberty. But she said nothing.

"Those kids will blame me," the mother went on. Lee nodded sympathetically but it was wasted effort; the mother was no longer looking at her. She was looking at the toys. They all seemed broken or hobbled in some way: the fire engine's ladder had disappeared; a jack-in-the-box had no crank; a doll, round-faced and pale, closed one green eye against her missing leg. Still the mother placed nothing in the box marked TRASH.

"It's a betrayal," the mother said. "I'm not kidding myself about that. Anytime you choose what you want over what's best for everybody else, it's a betrayal. It might be necessary. It might be absolutely the only thing you can do, but it's a betrayal nonetheless."

Chapter 9

He knew he was in trouble when he got to work one day and saw her cleared desk and a wave of panic rose up and clobbered him. Was she gone? Had she quit in the middle of the night and hightailed it back to Baltimore? Porter sat down and turned on the computer, but the whine of the warming machine seemed deafening and the letters on the screen kept leaping up and down until he realized it was his knee shaking the desk, and he stopped. Why would she leave like that? Did something happen? Did somebody come and sweep her away?

By eleven o'clock he had her married and on the way to Paris for the honeymoon and he couldn't take it anymore, so he saddled up to the national desk clerk, trying to keep his question casual.

"Oh, she went over to the idea desk," said the bored clerk. "They're on the fifth floor."

Porter had the urge to lean over and kiss the guy on his pimply little cheek. "Thanks," he said. He went back to his desk and sat down in sweet relief.

"Testosterone surge," said Joe. They sat at a black cast-iron table on the sidewalk outside a restaurant in Society Hill, awaiting their drinks. "When was the last time you loosed the reins?"

Porter's chair was warm from absorbing the sun all day, but it was early evening now and the relentless July heat had eased. Joe mopped his broad, red face with a napkin, grinning because he'd managed to secure one of the few tables outside the little hotel-restaurant. The town was crawling with tourists from Iowa come to run up the art museum steps like Rocky, gawk at Independence Hall, and tap the Liberty Bell. Getting a table anywhere in that part of town at that time of day was worth your wallet, but Joe was known at the little restaurant. He was known at bars all over town.

If it had taken time for Porter to recognize his attraction to Lee, it took even longer to admit it to Joe. Joe was unpredictable. You never knew when he would say something disarmingly sage and when he'd come out with something so stupid you wanted to haul off and punch him in the mouth. Something like "loosed the reins."

"Why is it southerners always feel the need to speak in metaphor?" Porter asked. "An unwillingness to face reality?"

"An appreciation for the exquisite utility of the English language. And you, son, dodged that question faster than a squirrel dodges a hound."

"That's because I have no intention of answering it," Porter said. "Anyway, it's not that. At least, it's not only that."

"What is it, then?"

"I don't know." He shrugged. "She's different."

"No shit, Sherlock."

"No, I mean she's really different. Special."

Joe looked at him over the wet rim of his glass. "Perhaps it has something to do with the little fact of her saving your life? That could make a fella grateful."

The waiter brought their drinks. Porter took a pull, felt the sweet heat of the Scotch loosening his gut. "She didn't . . . ," he began, then dropped it. "Anyway, it's not gratitude making me sweat in my bed at night."

"Please," said Joe, "I'm trying to drink here."

"She's fascinating and infuriating. The kind of woman who gets under your skin. I don't agree with half of what she says, but at least she has something to say." He laughed. "And, who knows? She might actually make me see things in ways I haven't seen them before. Not many people can do that. Present company excluded, of course."

Joe nodded his head slowly, and Porter thought: He understands. He's getting it.

"Let me ask you something, son," Joe said. "You ever dated a black woman before?"

Porter didn't answer right away. He had hoped Joe wouldn't ask the question, had hoped Lee's race would not be an issue for Joe. Joe was a southerner, a Mississippi native no less. But for all his traveling and despite his own mother's oft-claimed proud heritage, Porter himself had spent little time in the Deep South. It was still a land of perplexing mystery to him, a land of fat-bellied and red-faced sheriffs turning the hose on people trying to cross a bridge. He would not admit this feeling to Joe, who often raged against the way Yankees condescended to the South. It was one of his grand peeves, one of the things about which he loved to stand before his history students at the University of Pennsylvania and declaim. Joe was a larger-than-life character who rambled in class, engaged in occasional weeklong drinking binges, and slept with at least two graduate students a year. Only his reputation as a brilliant historian—and tenure—kept him employed.

"No, I haven't," Porter answered. "Have you?"

"No."

"Is that because you have a problem with the idea?"

Joe laughed. "Possibly. But not the one you might imagine. You Yankees love to pile the racial guilt of a nation upon our backs. You think it removes the burden from your own."

"Did you just make up that tortured metaphor or do they teach it in all the Mississippi schools?"

Joe ignored this. "I am simply asking whether you understand all the complexities involved in pursuing this woman? There are complexities—whether you care to admit them or not."

Porter laughed and shook his head. Poor Joe, trapped in a dynamic a hundred years old. "You make it sound as though we'll have to run away from the overseer and live a life on the lam." It was ridiculous. Sure, he knew racists still roamed the streets of Philadelphia. He'd sat in enough bars and heard enough uncensored opinions to know hatred never died. If he and Lee went out, he expected some dirty looks, some whispered comments from the knuckle-dragging set. But he was fairly brave about that kind of thing; he had never in his life kowtowed to public opinion. And no one he knew, none of his friends—with the possible exception of Joe—would give it a second thought. They'd be as impressed with Lee as he was. They wouldn't care that she was black.

"I understand the world is not some big Benetton ad," Porter said. "I know some people still think race is important. But we know better. Don't we, Joe."

Joe smiled and raised his drink. "I wonder if the lady knows?"

"It might be a slight issue for her," Porter conceded. "But I'm sure I could overcome that. If I could just get her to realize I'm alive."

Joe signaled the waitress for another round. "I probably shouldn't do this," he said. "It might not even be smart. But I can see you're smitten and I know you're a determined son of a bitch, so I shall help you out."

"Do, Don Juan."

"A simple bit of advice about winning a lady's heart. Two words: woo her."

Porter laughed. "Well, thank you, Romeo. But I don't think this particular woman can be snowed with a few flowers or chocolates or love poems. She doesn't seem like the wooing type."

Joe tipped back his chair and crossed his arms. "All women are the wooing type," he said. "You just have to figure out her particular woo."

Chapter 10

Lee loved her birthday. Any other holiday she could take or leave, but her birthday she wanted special. She wanted the day marking her arrival upon the earth to be always a day of enchantment, a day different from the hazy, ordinary other days of the year. That didn't mean a bland white cake and some waiters in a restaurant singing off-key; that meant something else. Or it should. On her birthday Lee was always unapologetically self-focused. She took off from work, ate what she wanted, did what she wanted, spoke only to people with whom she wanted to converse, and sent herself flowers if no one was around to do so. If all this effort produced a day that fell short of transcendence, at least she tried.

It was her father who ruined her this way. Even in the early years, even before he left them for good, he would come and go, come and go in their lives, but she always knew he'd be home for her birthday. Birthdays he liked. He always made a big production of them; they were the only holidays he celebrated with gusto. He allowed her mother to drag Lee and Marcus to church at Easter and Christmas, but only because she insisted. He himself had no use for "the blue-eyed Jesus of yore." He tolerated whatever scrawny, half-priced tree her mother dragged in on

Christmas Eve but would not tolerate Santa Claus. "Baby, no fat, red-nosed cracker is ever going to *give* you nothing," he told her when she was three. "Nothing good, anyway. And I don't want you waiting on Mr. Charlie for what you want!" Four months later, in response to a question about the Easter Bunny he replied, "Any six-foot rabbit I see hopping around here is mine." She didn't have to even ask about the Fourth of July; her father grew apoplectic whenever it rolled around. If he could work, he would. If he couldn't, he'd drink, then roll through the neighborhood lecturing anyone who dared hang out an American flag. "Nigger, this ain't your holiday! All men are created equal? Ha! They had your ass picking cotton when they wrote that!"

But birthdays were different. Birthdays, her father taught, were all your own, a salute to yourself and your beginning, a moment of which no white man had a part. Her father had made sure of that, insisting a black doctor deliver his children. "I wanted the first pair of hands you touched to be Negro hands. I wanted the first face you saw to be big and black and as beautiful as the night."

On birthdays her father didn't have to fight his inherent extravagance, the grab-it-all, screw-it-all exuberance that had first attracted her mother but that Eda came to hate and try to squash. On her mother's birthday he would bring Eda breakfast and champagne in bed, call in sick if he was working, disappear, then come home with a new dress or jewelry and his arms full of flowers and sweep her mother off for an evening of dinner and dancing at the Savoy. On Lee's birthday it was cake and ice cream for breakfast and a stroll through the fanciest downtown department store. "Pick out anything you like!" he'd tell her. Then she and he and her new stuffed lion would take a trip someplace they'd never been. Sometimes it was a museum in Washington, sometimes the shore. Sometimes they'd just get in the car and drive until they found someplace that looked interesting. "Be careful," her mother would warn. "Don't take her to the wrong place." But her father was fearless in that regard; he was not afraid to take risks. "She can go anyplace she wants," he said. "She needs to learn that."

On her sixth birthday, her father awakened her by singing "Happy Birthday to You," then "Lift Ev'ry Voice and Sing." He had a beautiful voice, a soaring alto he could make tremble and cry like Sam Cooke, but he sang so rarely that every song she managed to wring from him was like a gift. Because it was her birthday she knew this time he would not shake his head or brush her off, so she sat up in bed and smiled and asked in her prettiest voice, "Sing something else, Daddy. Please?"

"Little flirt," he said, chuckling. "Just like your mamma. Okay, one more. Then you and me, little Sheba, we're going someplace special."

"Where?"

"To see a prince. A black prince. His name is Malcolm."

He sang "Change Gonna Come," and she felt like crying because he sounded so sad, so mournful and full of longing. But then he lifted her from bed and carried her into a living room filled with balloons and she screamed with delight and forgot how sad her father had seemed.

It was a glorious day, hot but not humid, the sky a cloudless blue. After breakfast he took her to a part of Baltimore she didn't know, to a storefront gymnasium filled by women dressed all in white and men in dark suits and bow ties. The women sat on one side, the men on the other. She and her father sat in back with the other people dressed like them, the ones clearly apart from this glorious collection of princesses and kings. "Look at those brothers!" her father kept saying. "Just look at them!" The speaker, when he arrived, was like one of these men, dressed in a dark suit and a nimble bow tie. But there was something different about him, an inner light, a fierceness that shone through his bronze-colored skin and sparks that shot from his eyes. Lee wondered which country was it where he was a prince. She sat next to her father, holding his hand, and listened as the speaker told them all that the white man was a devil, a cold, calculating, blue-eyed fiend intent on destroying the black man. Alcohol and drugs were his weapons, integrationists his Uncle-Tomming coons or unwitting dupes. The only way for the black man to claim his identity, restore his culture, and create a full and productive community was to pull together, to unite, and then to separate.

"Any of you who believe this, who know what I'm talking about, stand up!" the prince called. The room exploded with the sound of chairs being pushed back, with shouting and stomping of feet. "Amen!" "You tell 'em, brother!" Her father leapt to his feet, clapping and roar-

ing and punching his fist into the air. Terrified and thrilled, she climbed
on her chair and screamed into the ocean of noise, no words at first, just
pure noise, just release. Then, recalling something the prince had said,
she yelled, "The white man is a lie!" and was rewarded with a grin from
her father so broad and loving she wanted to climb into it and sleep.
"The white man is a lie! The white man is a lie!" she yelled, over and
over, not knowing or caring what it meant, knowing only that saying it
made her father smile.

Eventually the crowd settled down and everyone sat. Then the
prince asked those who wanted to follow somebody—she couldn't
understand the name—to stand again. She waited for her father to rise
but he did not. Not more than a handful did. This time, instead of roaring, her father lowered his eyes to the floor.

Afterward he took her to dinner and bought her pork chops smoth-
ered with gravy, her favorite meal. Her birthday was the only day they
ever went out to dinner, and even then her mother did not come along.
While she ate her father drank something dark and sweet smelling and
nibbled at the side of okra she did not want. He didn't order any food
himself, saying he wasn't hungry. "Just thirsty," he said, looking into his
glass. "Muslims don't understand a man's thirst."

"What are Muslims, Daddy?"

"Those people we just saw, they were Black Muslims."

"And the man who spoke, he was the prince of the Black Muslims?"

Her father smiled proudly. "Yeah, Little Sheba. That man is the
prince."

After dinner he bought her ice cream and chocolate cake and carried
her home on his shoulders, singing all the way. It was the last birthday
she would spend with her father. On her seventh birthday her father
would be too entranced with his newborn son to take her out. By her
eighth birthday the prince would be dead and her father gone.

And now it was June again and her birthday bearing down. This year she
would reach the not particularly pleasant age of thirty-five years, but
what was the use of focusing on that? She focused instead on the new
job, new city, new house. Especially the house. It was a large Tudor with

faded elegance on a quiet street in the struggling Germantown section of the city. She'd gone through two real estate agents—both white, both provided by her new employer—before finding one who would even show her homes in the area. The first agent, a big, frosted blonde with enough gold on her neck and fingers to mold a graven image, wouldn't even drive Lee into the neighborhood. She was too frightened. "You're a professional lady," the agent said repeatedly, as if Lee had somehow failed to recognize her own economic status. "With your income, why would you want to live there?"

"Because it's important for the black middle class not to abandon our neighborhoods," Lee said. The woman stared openmouthed, as if Lee had suddenly burst into Swahili.

"Come again?"

"I have an obligation," Lee said.

"Excuse me?"

Lee pushed on. "Black children need to see black professionals living among them, so they will understand they can achieve," she explained. "It's important they know success is possible despite the obstacles in their path." The woman still looked blank, so Lee added, "I want to be a role model."

"Oh! Oh, sure, honey. My son did that. He was a big brother one year to this kid, cutest little thing you ever did see. But you don't have to live here to do that—I can set you up with an agency."

Lee gave up. "Just show me some houses around here, please."

But the agent kept driving her up Germantown Avenue toward "nicer"—and more expensive and whiter—Chestnut Hill. In a way it was heartening; at least Lee could not accuse the woman of racial steering. She wanted Lee to buy the most expensive house in the most expensive neighborhood Lee could afford, preferably one on which she was the listing broker. Racism conquered by good old American greed.

In the end Lee found her own broker, a sister with her own small but thriving agency who said, "If you want to live in Germantown, more power to you. I'll find you a house. I live in Gulph Mills." This sister found Lee her house on a one-way street on the border between the

Germantown and Mt. Airy neighborhoods. The house was stone and had once belonged to the estate of a textile millionaire, before the estate was divided into parcels and sold. It was a great block, lined by redbrick duplexes and triplexes and the occasional small wooden house, all tidily maintained. "White people look at North Philadelphia and German- town and see one huge, violent black hole," the agent said. "But the truth is, there are really a hundred little towns within these neighbor- hoods. One town is owner-occupied, clean, well cared for, friendly neighbors who look out for one another. And the next town, two blocks over, is a drug supermarket." The sister shrugged and started the engine on her gray Mercedes-Benz. "That's city life."

Lee's "town" was three blocks from a trash-strewn commercial strip of dollar stores and fast-food joints and layaway furniture marts where the window signs always promised 50 percent off. It was also eight blocks from the corner at which a small-time drug operation conducted nightly business. This proximity did not bother Lee. As the sister said, eight blocks and one major avenue was at least a continent away, and, at any rate, she was no stranger to urban life. She'd finally moved Eda and herself to a quieter neighborhood eight years ago, but before that her mother had lived in the same Druid Heights house in which Lee grew up.

Still, the proximity of Lee's new house to a struggling slice of Philadelphia did concern Eda, who would wag her finger at any Balti- more drug dealer but considered any other city's criminals unapproach- ably ruthless. And Howard hated both house and 'hood.

"Why do you want something this old?" he said about the house as they strolled through the empty rooms. The Realtor had retired to her car to give them time alone.

"I like the character."

Howard grunted, flicking a bit of peeling paint from a windowsill. "Lead paint. You know how dangerous this stuff is?"

She almost said, "Only for children," but she didn't want to raise that topic again. Instead she said, "I don't intend to make a meal of it, Howard. I'll paint over it or have it removed."

"Removing it will cost you a fortune. And look at this." He led her through the kitchen and downstairs to the unfinished basement. It was cavernous down there and cool, and Lee imagined a floor-to-ceiling wine rack against the coarse, white walls. "It's dry," she pointed out. "And they're leaving the washing machine."

Howard snorted. "That's generous of them. Look at this." He threw open the fuse box.

She looked. "What?"

"Fuses? Not circuit breakers? This system is at least eighty years old! You don't have enough amperage here to run a hair dryer."

"You're exaggerating."

"Plug in an air conditioner and you'll see." He began stomping around the basement like a two-year-old. "And the pipes are rusty and the hot-water heater looks dead and that old oil tank back there might be hazardous. You know how much all this would cost you to repair? This house is a piece of garbage."

"The house inspector said it needed work but was structurally sound."

Howard scoffed. "What does he care if you buy this rat trap? What does he care if you make a huge mistake?"

"It's not a mistake."

Howard shook his head. "I'm surprised at you."

She knew he was only looking out for her. But the scorn in his voice, the disappointment, both irritated and frightened her. She liked the house. She loved it, and Howard seemed to be saying that love indicated some flaw in her decision making, in her personality. She got defensive. "You just don't want me to buy any house," she said.

He was far away from her, at the deepest part of the basement near an old oil tank, and she could not see his face clearly for the shadows or hear what was in his voice. "You should buy whatever house you want," he said. "I just don't understand why you'd want this one." He paused, then added, as if it were an afterthought, "Especially if you're only planning to stay here a few years."

She walked to the washing machine, lifted the lid, pretended to peer inside. She'd told Howard she *might* not like the *Record, might* not like

Philadelphia, *might* very well decide to come home in a year or two, but he'd heard it as a declaration that she only intended to stay a few years. She could straighten him out now, make it clear she hoped to stay in Philadelphia, to make the new job work. But if she told him that, what would he do? Howard was a man of method, a mule who plowed ahead along whatever path he'd laid for himself, rarely deviating. He didn't like surprises and he didn't like change. On their first date he'd told her he always had a five- and ten-year plan; it was imperative, he said, to always have both a short- and a long-term goal. His goal upon retiring from the army had been to open his own pharmacy, and he'd done that. Now his long-term goal was to expand into a chain of pharmacies. His short-term goal was to marry again as soon as possible and begin a family in Baltimore.

"If it works out for me here, you could move to Philadelphia," Lee suggested. "You could open a store here."

"You want me to follow you?" he asked. "I don't know this city."

"You could learn it."

"I couldn't leave my mother alone."

"You could bring her," Lee suggested, though the last thing she wanted as a new bride was a mother-in-law in tow. Howard came out of the shadows, shaking his head. "She wouldn't want to leave Baltimore," he said.

"And neither do you."

He didn't hesitate. "No," he said. "I don't."

And so, there it was. He claimed to love her, to want to marry her, but he would not leave Baltimore for her, would not deviate from his lifetime plan. He wouldn't even consider it. Was that really love or was she just being plugged into the equation he'd established for himself: store + home + wife = happiness?

But maybe she was asking too much, judging too harshly. That was the problem with Howard; she didn't know if the relationship was wrong or her expectations were. She wanted to be realistic. She didn't want to be another fool throwing away a chance at a stable life because she'd bought into the silly, false—worse than that, destructive—myth of perfect romantic love force-fed to people by Hollywood. She didn't want to be her mother, who'd fallen, in her own words, crazy in love with her father and ended up abandoned and alone.

"I just don't like the idea of paying rent," she said. "Even if it is only for a few years." It was the truth. If not the whole truth, close enough.

Howard nodded deliberately, processing the information. Then he cleared his voice. "You should at least buy a newer house that'll need less maintenance. And you should find a better neighborhood. Out a ways."

"You mean in the suburbs?" She laughed, remembering how surprised she'd been when she first found out Howard lived out in Glen Burnie. She'd assumed he lived somewhere in the city because his pharmacy was in the heart of Druid Heights. It was there they met. She'd sought out a black pharmacist and been impressed not only with his credentials and the way he seemed to have all day for the little old ladies who asked his medical advice but also with his smile. She'd assumed he was a kindred spirit, a man who saw the importance of staying in the community and shoring it up. Then again, she also assumed a man who'd spent twenty years in the army, traveling the world, would be open to new adventures and to taking the occasional risk. She'd been wrong on both accounts.

Howard turned out to be cautious and set in his ways. And his feelings on community and responsibility were mixed. Yes, he'd chose to open his business in Druid Heights because the people in the neighborhood needed local businesses they could trust, places that wouldn't gouge them or sell them inferior goods. But he'd also chosen the area because the property was cheap and because of the lack of competition; at the time, none of the super drugstores would venture into the neighborhood. And in the four years he'd been open he'd been robbed eight times, all by young black brothers pointing guns. After the most recent robbery, in which he lost three days' revenue and a clerk so traumatized she quit, he stormed around Lee's house yelling about how fed up he was with his own people. He was thinking of closing his shop, moving out to a strip mall somewhere. He didn't want to hear anything about the crippling effects of poverty and racism and oppression, and he didn't want to hear anything about obligations or race loyalty. His obligation, he told Lee, was to the mother who raised him, to himself, and to the family he hoped to have someday.

Now, standing in the basement, he said, "I mean away from those niggers we passed on the way over here."

Lee stiffened. "You know I hate that word. I hate it when white people say it and I hate it when black people say it."

He began pacing. "There's a difference. White—"

She waved her hand through the air, cutting him off. "Yeah, yeah, I know: we can use it among ourselves as a term of affection. That's garbage. It's a contemptuous word and when black people use it it just means we've bought into that same contempt for ourselves."

Howard stopped in front of her. "You think I have contempt for myself?" His tone was suddenly so mild and removed he might have been making conversation with a stranger on the bus. "You think I dislike being black?"

She knew he did not. Howard was no self-hating Negro, no Uncle Tom. He was largely indifferent to white people, seeming to notice them only when one appeared as an obstacle in his path. There had been plenty of obstacles in the army, which, he said, was not the color-blind utopia Uncle Sam liked to pretend; on the other hand it was probably as close as any institution in America. Howard had ordered around, and been ordered around by, dozens of white men, and whenever one tried to render him less than human he simply dealt with the situation and moved on without looking back.

"The difference is, white people cannot distinguish between black people and niggers," Howard said in his careful, lecturing pharmacist's voice. It was the way he spoke when he explained drug interactions, standing high behind his counter, looking down at the afflicted and the weak. "They think we're all the same."

"We are," she said. They were back upstairs now, in the empty living room, before the fireplace. All her life she'd wanted to live in a house where she could build a fire in the winter and sit before it, reading a book. She was going to buy this house whether Howard liked it or not.

"We are not," he said. "I'm not the same as that nappy-headed asswipe who knocked down Mrs. Oates last month and stole her Social Security check. I am not the same as that vermin out on the corner, putting poison into children's blood. And I am not the same as those foul-mouthed punks who come into my store with their pants hanging down around their knees and stick guns in the faces of my clerks!"

"Calm down," Lee said, because the agent had left her car and was coming up the walk. But Howard always finished whatever he began. "Those people," he said, lowering his voice a fraction, "those people are niggers and I want nothing to do with them!" At the same moment the agent stuck her head inside the front door and smiled. "How are we doing in here?"

Lee put in a bid on the house and had it accepted straight out. Howard said nothing. Because the house was empty, and because her credit was spotless, she was able to close in less than a month. Howard helped her move, changed the locks, and paid to have a security system installed. He gave her a two-year subscription to the company's services. "No sense taking unnecessary risks," he said.

The Saturday before the Sunday of her birthday Lee spent ripping up the kitchen's lime green linoleum to expose a floor of golden pine. A gritty layer of dirt soon covered her jeans and dust containing what was probably poisonous adhesives flew into the air as she pulled and pried and broke the flooring. It was good, hard, physical work and she loved it for the sense of accomplishment it gave. Much as she loved journalism, it was often less-than-fulfilling work. No matter how passionately she wrote about a topic, no matter how many hundreds of words she filed or how many damning documents she dug up, injustice remained. The system might shift momentarily or even sway, but it always righted itself in the end. Black men were still harassed by the cops, still received harsher prison sentences than whites for the same crimes. Politicians still won elections by using racial code words. Black people were still economically deprived and politically powerless. She had gone into the field hoping to change the world and it was depressing sometimes to realize how little progress had been made.

The doorbell rang. It was a Federal Express deliveryman. She took the package back into the living room and began opening it, not even bothering to check the return address. It had to be from Howard. Pauline had already sent her a gift, and Eda had given her's the week before. No one else except Howard would be sending a birthday gift, though it was strange he would send one overnight mail, since she would see him later on.

Inside the envelope was a gold jewelry box. And inside the box was her lost pin. No, not her pin but one just like it, pierced with a small hole and strung through a thin, gold chain, just as hers had been. She picked it up and held it to her throat. It was cool against her skin.

She laughed out loud. Howard! Amazing Howard! Every doubt about him, every hesitation, every nitpicking little grudge melted in the heat of this one gesture, this proof of his thoughtfulness and passion and knowledge of her. She had to call him, call him right now. On the way to the telephone she snatched up the card.

She dialed the area code, opened the card, read the message. She dropped the telephone.

I know this can't replace your father's pin but I hope it lessens the loss. And makes you smile. Porter Stockman.

She sank onto the couch.

Porter Stockman. She looked at the pin and back to the card. The pin and its chain fit perfectly inside her palm, and the cool weight of it reminded her of something, a childhood game she used to play. How could Porter have even known about her pin? Had she mentioned it to him? She had. She remembered now, that first day in the cafeteria. But it was just a mention, a passing conversation with a man she barely knew. But he had listened, and then gone to what must have been a considerable amount of trouble to find a replacement. Of course, he was grateful for what she did in Los Angeles. Of course, he probably wanted to sleep with her. Still. She held the pin in her hand. Regardless of his motivations, it was an amazing gesture, still.

The telephone made her jump.

"Hello?"

"How's my big-city woman?"

This had become Howard's ritual greeting since her move to Philadelphia, his attempt at lightheartedness about the situation. He was trying so hard. Lee shook her head to clear it of Porter and tried right back. "She's looking forward to a wonderful night out with her handsome man. I hope you're calling from the interstate."

"Actually, Lenora . . . ," he began. Her father used to call her Lenora when he was angry or when telling her something she would not like. *Lenora, don't let me catch you spending money in that white man's store! Lenora, find me a switch! Lenora, we can't go anywhere today, your baby brother needs us to stay home, but I promise we'll celebrate your birthday next week.*

"Actually, Lenora, I'm afraid I can't make it to Philadelphia today. Dwayne came in high as a kite this morning. I'm surprised he managed to find the store. I don't know what's wrong with these children. Dwayne had more going on than most, but he's throwing it in the garbage can. Anyway, I had to fire him. Which leaves me shorthanded tonight."

"Can't you call someone else?"

Howard chuckled. "It's hard enough getting these knuckleheads to come in on their regular days," he said. "Nobody wants to work on Saturday."

She knew his laugh was one of frustration; still it infuriated her. "Close the store, then," she said. "Can't you for once just close the damn store?"

But she knew it was futile. Howard never closed early. It was a point of pride as much as a business decision; closing early was a sign of weakness, and any sign of weakness could get you killed in the free-enterprise jungle.

"I would, Lenora. But you know with that new SuperDrug opening up around the corner I can't afford to. I have to hold on to my customers, show them I'm not backing down an inch."

"I thought you were leaving the neighborhood anyway."

"I thought you wanted me to stay." His voice was light. He was trying to tease her out of being furious. "I really am sorry, baby. But why don't you come down here? I'll close at the regular time, leave the paper-work and restocking for tomorrow. We can still have a late dinner."

She wondered if the whole story was a lie to get her back down to Baltimore in some crazy hope she'd miss the city and see the error of her ways. He'd spent the weekend of her move picking Philadelphia apart and had not returned since, although some of that was her fault. She'd been back to Baltimore three weekends in a row to check on Eda and so had not asked Howard to make the drive. Now that she had, he came up with this. There was probably some truth in the story; Howard, as a rule, did not lie. Still, she could feel him digging in his heels in their little tug-of-war, trying to drag her back over the line onto his side.

"You want me to drive all the way down there on my birthday?"

"Since when is Baltimore all the way 'down there'?"

"Since I moved to Philadelphia, Howard. Remember? I live here now."

There was a pause. She had irritated him and Howard did not like to be irritated. It might mean losing control. "If you come to Baltimore, I'll get us a table at Creation."

"Right." Creation was the hottest new restaurant in Baltimore. No way would he be able to get reservations. But Howard said, "I know a guy there. He'll get us in, I know he will. Come on, baby. I miss you and want to see you. And you don't want to spend your birthday alone."

Lee looked around the kitchen at the partially denuded floor, the boxes she had yet to unpack pushed against the wall. She didn't want to spend her birthday alone. If Howard knew her, he knew that.

"Okay. I'll come."

"You won't regret it."

She hung up the phone and tried on the chain from Porter. It fit perfectly.

To save time they met at the restaurant. Howard arrived dressed impec-cably in a dark blue suit and waltzed them right past the long line to the host, who sat them at a table with a good view of the waterfront. Lee had nursed her anger all the way down Interstate 95, but under the influence of the shimmering harbor lights and the soft music and a glass of champagne, the anger began to melt. Howard droned on and on about his problems at the store; she sipped and smiled and tried to listen.

"But I guess you don't want to hear about all that," he said after a while.

"Oh, no, I do."

"No, you don't." He reached into his pocket and her heart skipped. She realized she was both hoping for and dreading a ring. But what he pulled out was a white envelope. "Happy Birthday."

She opened the envelope. Inside was a piece of paper with a cartoon of a smiling car in one corner, a grinning garage in the other, and the words "gift certificate." She stared across the table at him.

"It's a gift certificate for an automatic garage door opener," he said, grinning. "They'll be out to install it on Monday."

"Oh."

"Now you don't have to worry about security when you come home late at night. You can just drive straight into your garage without getting out of your car." He grinned at her, so clearly pleased with himself. She made herself smile and lean across the table to kiss his lips.

"It's something you'll use every day," Howard was saying. "You can never be too safe."

"Thank you. It's very . . . thoughtful," she said. And it was, in its way, a very thoughtful gift. Thoughtful, utterly impersonal, slightly paranoid, and oh, so practical. Howard was nothing if not practical.

She ran her fingers lightly across her neck, thinking of the weight of that gold chain.

"Is something wrong?" Howard asked. "Something wrong with your neck?"

She laughed. She couldn't help it. It must have been the champagne. Howard looked perplexed. "What's so funny?"

"I don't know, I . . ." She tried to think of a graceful lie and gave up. "It's just funny because I thought it was a ring. But I love it. I do."

Still, she couldn't stop laughing, even though she saw the crestfallen look on his face and felt terrible. "I do like it, Howard. It's very thoughtful."

Howard said, "I didn't think you wanted a ring from me."

She stopped laughing. "What?"

"I didn't think you wanted a ring from me."

She stared at him, shocked. He met her gaze. "Why would you think that?" she whispered.

Howard shrugged. "You have your own life, your job. You moved two states away."

"It's a ninety-minute drive, Howard. And it's for my career. I have a career, not a job."

"That you do." He picked up his champagne and gulped it. Again, she was surprised. He had ordered the champagne for her and had a glass poured for himself just to keep her company, but he did not like it. Too pale and fizzy, he said. He didn't even like wine. When Howard drank, which was not often, he drank whiskey.

"What does that mean?" Lee asked.

"It means if you wanted to be with me you would have stayed in Baltimore. If you wanted a ring from me you wouldn't have run up the road to Philadelphia and bought a house I told you not to buy."

She stared at him and she knew there was shock in her face but she couldn't mask it. "I can't believe this," she said. "So you're punishing me? Is that it. Punishing me for not doing as I'm told?"

"I'm not punishing you, Lenora." He sounded pained but she didn't want to hear it.

"The hell you aren't."

He looked away. "My mother always told me to marry a woman who needed me."

Lee reached for her water glass and took a sip. Something—the champagne, the conversation—was making her breathless, as if she was running uphill. "Needed you? What does that mean?"

"It means what it means," Howard said.

"Silly me." She tried to laugh. "I thought people married for love."

Howard looked out the window to the dark water. "You don't love me, either."

She was too stunned to respond. Howard looked back and said,

"That's okay. You do care about me, and I love you. That would be enough if you needed me, but you don't. My mother always told me a woman who doesn't need you is dangerous."

He was devastating them, saying terrible things in his careful, modulated voice. She wanted to reach across the table and slap him until he yelled or cried or slapped her back, anything. "Do you always do what Mommy tells you?"

He looked at her. "Not always. But maybe I should."

They went silent. All around them in the dining room were couples, the warm sound of laughter and conversation, and the cool sound of tinkling glasses and forks to plates. She didn't know what to say. Howard was still looking at her, his eyes wide. He was waiting for something. She didn't know what it was.

His beeper shattered the hush between them. Howard looked at the number and sighed. "It's the store," he said. "Excuse me."

He was gone a long time, or for what seemed like a long time, and at first she was glad. She needed time to recover, to think. But after a few minutes she grew uncomfortable. She didn't have on her watch and the champagne and the emotion of the evening wrecked all sense of time. Had Howard been gone two minutes or ten? She hated sitting alone in restaurants, hated being left behind like that, adrift. Had he walked out? Would he actually leave her sitting there like that? She looked toward the back of the restaurant where the telephones were. Nothing. The waiter came to refill her water glass. Was he smirking at her? She felt instantly sober. Two couples at the table next to hers laughed gaily. One of the women glanced Lee's way. Howard did not return.

She took her purse from the table. Sipped some water. Patted her mouth with the napkin and glanced around. Wait until the waiter is in the kitchen. Look like you're going to the rest room. Smile absentmindedly. Walk slow.

Somehow she made it to the door and then she was outside in the night and the fresh air and to her car. Trying to open the door, she dropped her keys, but that was from shaking, not drunkenness. Once inside she sat for a moment, calming herself. She blinked her eyes once, twice, three times, to see if the parking space before her would shimmer and move. It did not, and when she opened her eyes the final time, she saw Howard running from the restaurant.

"Lee!" he called.

He was waving his hands as he ran. She tried to remember if she had ever seen Howard run before. He looked strangely boyish in the cool blue light of the parking lot and she had an urge to yell at him to be careful, to look out for cars, but she didn't. Howard could take care of himself. That's what men did; they took care of themselves. She put the car into gear and drove away.

Looking up at the darkened windows of her mother's house, Lee realized Eda was probably in bed. She wasn't expecting Lee until tomorrow. The sound of the front door opening might frighten her. If Lee had been thinking clearly, she would have done the right thing, the careful, caretaking daughter thing, and telephoned from the restaurant first.

Lee rested her head against the steering wheel and tried to think, but her brain felt stiff and mildewy, a rag wrung dry and tossed onto the floor. She could go to a neighbor's house, Mrs. Thornton across the way perhaps, and ask to use the telephone, but that would only be transferring the fright. Mrs. Thornton's house was dark too. So were most of the others. Anyway, no one on that street would eagerly open their door at that time of night. She could drive the half mile to the little Asian convenience store where there was a pay phone outside, but she wouldn't feel safe using that phone at night, even if it wasn't broken, which it usually was. She could drive to the nearest open gas station, two miles away, or back downtown, but the idea of starting the car, of concentrating enough to make it off the block was exhausting. She felt as though she had to get out and *push* the car, push it all the way, and she just couldn't. She just could not.

She opened the front door noisily, flipped on the light, and called, "It's me, Mom! It's Lee!" There was no response. Eda must be deeply asleep. She would go up to her bedroom and let her know she was there. But passing through the living room Lee felt something was wrong. Her mother's shoes lay carelessly sprawled near the stairway. Her purse had been tossed onto the couch instead of hung on the doorknob where Eda always kept it. And there was a strange, unfamiliar smell, something musky and red. It came to Lee in a flash—the smell was wine. But Eda rarely drank and never alone. Unless . . .

A jolt of fear sent Lee running. "Mom!" she cried, running but not seeming to get anywhere, like in a dream. "Mom! Where are you??" She ran through the living room into the dining room, prepared to find her mother cowering in every corner she passed, locked in another depressive episode. It wasn't until she'd scanned the kitchen and was headed upstairs that real terror struck. What if this wasn't just another episode? What if something really horrible had occurred? Her mother could be dead in a pool of blood somewhere and it would be her fault for having left her all alone.

She reached the landing and was assaulted by another smell, woodsy and dark. The smell of a stranger. It was like a slap, that sharp and startling, and it stopped her for a second. Fear and self-preservation clutched at her feet, tried to drag her backward. But she shook them off and cried aloud, "Mom!" and ran toward her mother's bedroom. "Mom!"

Just before she reached the door, it opened. Eda stood in the doorway, looking rumpled.

"Lee? Baby! What are you doing here?"

"Thank God!" Relief washed over her as she hugged Eda. "I thought something had happened to you!"

"Calm down, girl!" Her mother hugged her back. "I'm fine."

"Why didn't . . . ," Lee began, but stopped when she noticed the slippery silk material beneath her hands. Eda was wearing a black and red silk kimono Marcus had given her for her birthday five or six years ago, one she'd ohhed and ahhed over and stuck in the back of her closet. Lee stepped back to look at her mother. Eda's hair was mussed and she was wearing makeup, not only lipstick and eyebrow liner but foundation and eye shadow. Something was definitely off. It must be a manic episode.

"Mom." Lee kept her voice low. "Are you sick?"

Eda laughed nervously. "I didn't expect you tonight. Where's Howard?"

"It's a long story. I don't want to talk about it. Are you okay?"

"Me?" Eda laughed again. Lee decided her mother must be hysterical. "I'm fine, baby! Fine."

But she didn't sound fine. Her voice was flustered and breathless. And Eda Page never wore makeup to bed or dressed in silk or drank alone. Lee felt the tears stinging her eyes. Her mother had been well for so long they both had begun to believe she was actually cured. But of course there was no cure for bipolar disorder and it was never over. That much was clear.

Lee took a deep breath and brushed past her mother into the bedroom. "Have you been taking your meds?"

"Lee!"

"Where's your pillbox?" Lee demanded over her shoulder. "Let me check."

"You must be Lenora," said a masculine voice.

Lee stopped short. He stood by the bed, tying the sash on his robe with such immaculate care and unflappability he didn't pause even as Lee began to scream.

"Lee! Be quiet!" Eda grabbed Lee by the arm and shook her. "Baby, stop screaming before somebody calls the police!"

Lee stopped screaming. She'd been ready to shut up two seconds after she began, when she recognized the man's face from her going-away party and realized the horrifying truth. But she kept screaming, because as long as she was screaming she could forestall being mortified.

"That's better." Eda cinched her robe and ran her hand through her hair. "Well. I guess some introductions are in order. Lee, this is Mr. Carter. My friend. Albert, this is my daughter, Lee."

Mr. Carter produced a hand with such refined movement she almost expected him to follow the gesture with a bow. "It's a pleasure. Your mother has told me so many wonderful things about you, Lee."

"I am so, so sorry." She was trying desperately to back out of the room, but her feet didn't seem to want to work. She kept tripping over things: shoes, the carpet, air.

"Your concern for your mother is admirable, but she is, as you can see, quite well."

"Yes." She was never going to get out of this room. She was going to die there, gaping like an idiot.

"She has been taking her medications faithfully," Mr. Carter said. He was fully dressed now and talking to her as though they were two parishioners taking the air after church. "I see to that."

"You?" She didn't mean to speak, speaking just delayed her exit from this bad dream, but she couldn't help it. Had Eda actually told this man about her illness? Lee couldn't believe it. There were lifelong friends, relatives, who didn't know the truth. Finally she bumped into the doorway, turned, and fled.

"Lee, wait," Eda called, following her down the stairs. By the time they reached the living room Lee was breathing steadily again. She turned on her mother.

"What the hell are you doing?"

"Now, wait a second. I know this is a surprise to you, but—"

"Surprise? I almost had a heart attack up there!"

"I'm sorry," Eda said. "I'm sorry I didn't tell you. I'm sorry you walked in on this. But right now you need to calm down."

"Have you lost your mind?" Lee cried. That's how upset she was; she never used phrases like that with her mother. It was too close to home. "You can't do this! This is . . . dangerous! I won't let you!"

Eda folded her arms and narrowed her eyes, giving Lee the look that had terrified her as a child. She was amazed her mother could pull it off so well standing there in a bathrobe, smelling of sex. "I have news for you, Lenora Price Page: I don't need your permission to drive and I don't need your permission to have a man in my life! I am not a child. I am not a child and you are not my nanny and you don't talk to me like this!"

In the stunned silence Lee looked at Eda as though seeing her for the first time. Her mother's eyebrows had been professionally shaped and her skin, beneath the dusting of makeup, had a kind of fierce glow. And her eyes. Eda's eyes, vacant for long after their father left, then filled with Marcus and Lee, brimmed now with something new, something beyond motherly love and dull satisfaction at having made it through. Lee looked into her mother's eyes and felt shocked and exhilarated and lost. The next thing she knew, she was crying.

With a sigh Eda pulled her into her arms. "Baby. Baby, what happened? Where's Howard?"

"We broke up."

Eda shushed her a minute, then said, "I'm sorry. Listen. Let's go up to your room and talk. I'll make some tea."

She wanted to. She wanted to crawl up the stairs to her old bedroom and into bed, to have her mother sit nearby and stroke her hair and explain why love was so hard to find and harder to hold. But then she remembered Mr. Carter. "Oh, God," she said, pulling away. "No, I'll go to Pauline's."

"Don't be silly. This is still your home."

"No, really. I was going there anyway," she lied. "I just stopped by to check on you."

It was clear Eda didn't believe her, but Lee grabbed her purse and moved toward the door. "I'll call you tomorrow."

"Lee!"

"I'm fine, Mom." She wiped her face with her hands, forced herself to smile. "Pauline isn't that far. I'll call you when I get there."

Eda followed her onto the porch, still protesting. But Lee just smiled and got into her car and pulled away. When she was halfway down the street she realized she should have telephoned Pauline. Maybe she wasn't at home. Maybe she was out somewhere having group sex or baying at the moon or participating in an S/M marathon. Lee began to laugh and realized she was slightly hysterical. Who knew? Anything was possible. Her mother had a boyfriend. Her mother had a man.

To Lee's knowledge, he was the first man in her mother's life since her father left—the first man Eda even *considered* allowing near enough to shake her hand. But maybe that wasn't true. Clearly Lee had missed all kinds of things with Eda: the driver's license, the growing confidence. She'd missed the slow dissolve of her mother's anger toward men. Eda had slipped into a funk after Lee's father left, and the only way she was able to drag herself out was by stepping on his head. Even as a child Lee knew the anger wasn't directed at her, or at Marcus. But she felt it nonetheless. It was like living next door to a military base: you weren't the target but the ground beneath your feet still trembled when the shells hit.

Still, Eda had seemed happy. She had to admit that. But what if this Mr. Carter was just messing with her? What if he made her fall in love and then left? He had to be sixty years old if he was a day, but did men ever grow too old for abandonment? Pain like that would plunge Eda right into another episode and she couldn't take that. Lee couldn't take that either.

When she got to Pauline's house the living room light was still on and she could see, through the curtain, the blue flicker of the television. She rang the doorbell and called at the same time, "It's Lee!" Pauline peeked through the curtained window, then opened the door. She was dressed in the monogrammed silk men's pajamas Lee gave her last Christmas and she was holding the VCR remote. She looked, as Pauline always did, completely unsurprised.

"Call your mother," she said.

Chapter 11

He received a nice note from her thanking him for the pin. Figuring to strike while the iron's hot, he asked her to lunch. "Sorry, can't," she said. A few days later he asked again. "Sorry, can't," she repeated, leaving him to wonder what it was exactly she couldn't do. Couldn't lunch with him that day? Couldn't lunch with him at all? Couldn't stand the sight of him? Her signals were unclear, but then so were his. That was the problem with lunch, especially among office colleagues—it could mean anything. He would have to be more direct. He began plotting an alternative means of attack, but before he could come up with anything Mother Nature intervened.

A hurricane named Andrew roared up out of the depths of the Atlantic, strafed the Bahamas, and set a menacing course for Florida. "All hands on deck!" cried the national editor, but it was lunchtime on a Friday and the newsroom echoed hollowly. "Where the hell is everyone? I need bodies!" Lou cried, pacing the floor. From across the room Porter watched, debating whether to volunteer or slip out the fire door. Just then, Lee walked into the room, a gazelle wandering straight into the thicket where the lion waits.

"You!" Lou screamed, thrusting his bony finger toward her beauti-ful face. "You! Get on a plane!"

Twenty seconds later Porter was standing before the vibrating national editor. "Hey, Lou. Need some help?" Ten minutes after that he was on his way home to throw some clothes in a suitcase. He reached the airport in a record-setting twenty-two minutes and found Lee at the gate munching on an apple and reading a book. The flight had been delayed.

"Hi," he said. "Any news on the flight?"

Lee looked up from her book, placing her finger between the pages to hold her place. It was a universal sign. It meant: one minute from now I'm going back to my book. "They're predicting about an hour delay. It's on its way from Boston."

"Oh." He dropped his duffel bag on the floor and sat beside her. "Anybody else get the finger?"

"Jack Warren. He's in the bar."

Porter laughed. Jack was one of the paper's veteran reporters, a holdover from the pre-Woodward-and-Bernstein days, when newsmen were chain-smoking, blue-collar family men trying to make a buck instead of college-educated, self-important adolescents trying to bring down the government. He once told Porter he detested being called a journalist almost as much as he hated having reporting referred to as a profession. "Medicine is a profession," he'd growled. "Law is a profes-sion. Reporting is just a damn job."

"They also sent Clive Young," Lee said. "He's running around here somewhere. And apparently two photographers caught an earlier plane. Six people seems like overkill."

Porter laughed. "Lou loves natural disasters. Gets his heart pump-ing. Besides, the paper got creamed when Hugo hit three years ago. We only had one person on the ground in North Carolina and couldn't get anyone else in for two days. The *Daily News* had three people there. Lou's still rubbing his behind."

Lee smiled and it was lovely, but it wasn't the kind of smile he wanted from her. It was the kind of smile you give to some old woman who sits down next to you in the airport and interrupts your reading with details about her sciatica. Already Lee was making signs of wanting to get back to her book. Porter looked at the title: *Jazz,* by Toni Morrison. Hardcover. He knew just enough about Toni Morrison to know she was considered serious fiction—hadn't she won the Pulitzer? He thought about Chira, who read books with titles like *Parent Yourself* when she was feeling ambitious and who, when she was not, read Jackie Collins paperbacks.

"Excellent choice," he said, gesturing toward Lee's book.

She had reopened her book but now she closed it on her finger again. "You like Morrison?"

"I haven't actually read that one yet. Is it good?"

"I must admit I'm struggling with it a bit. The language is beautiful of course, stunning, but the story hasn't gripped me the way her first five novels did, especially *Beloved.* Wasn't that an incredible piece of art?"

Too late he saw the hole he had dug for himself. Having read no Morrison, he was in trouble if she asked for specifics. He might be able to fake it, but if she got into details he would end up looking like not only a fool but a liar as well.

"I haven't read that one yet either," he said, then lied. "It's been sitting on my nightstand for months, waiting for me to get to it."

"So which of her books have you gotten to?"

Porter was saved by a voice clearing its throat over the public address system. *Let it be our flight, let it be our flight,* he prayed. As soon as they got to Miami he'd sneak off to the bookstore and beg for anything by Toni Morrison. He would.

But it was only a temporary reprieve. The voice announced a flight to Los Angeles, boarding at the gate next door. Travelers began pressing the door. Porter turned back to Lee. "I haven't actually read any of her novels, but I understand she's very, very good."

"Yes," Lee said, going back to her book. "She is."

Strike one.

They reached Miami in the late afternoon, eight hours ahead of the storm. Once off the plane Jack went to telephone the national desk, then came back rubbing his hands.

"Lou wants us to scout the city, check out the preparations, see whether people are panicked. Probably won't get much in for tomorrow's paper, unless the storm comes ahead of schedule. Let's meet at the hotel by seven. We'll send Lou what we have, then assess whether it's safe to go back out on the streets."

Everyone nodded but Clive. "But I thought the deadline for final edition wasn't until nine."

"Ten," growled Jack. "So?"

"Then shouldn't we stay out? If we're lucky, the hurricane will have hit by then."

Porter exchanged glances with Lee. Clive was the youngest among them, a reporter trainee fresh out of college. The editors always sent at least one brash, eager body along to do all the work the older reporters didn't want to. This was Clive's first big natural disaster. He was practically vibrating with excitement and eagerness. He thought it was going to be fun, like something out of the movies, the intrepid reporter scrambling around to interview grateful survivors standing among their broken teacups. He had no idea.

"Yeah," said Lee. "And if we're really lucky maybe the hurricane will devastate the entire state. Maybe thousands will die."

"Don't be an idiot, kid," Jack growled. "Hard to report the news from a coffin."

They rented two cars and headed out. Despite his best efforts at subtle maneuvering, Porter got stuck with Clive. They drove straight into the heart of Miami and found a city frantic with people hurrying home before the storm. Together he and Clive hit the usual spots: grocery stores where people were stocking up on bread and water, hardware stores where people loaded plywood and flashlights and went squealing off into the wind.

They reached the hotel just after seven to find it nearly deserted. Most of the regular tourists had already fled, leaving only a few, insane weather tourists and journalists. Porter and Clive were given rooms but advised to gather with everyone else in a windowless basement ballroom to ride out the storm. "Mattresses, sheets, blankets, and water and non-perishable foods have been provided," the clerk said, looking at his computer. He might have been asking whether Porter preferred a smoking or nonsmoking room.

By nine there were about thirty people in the ballroom, and the place took on a festive air. Some people played cards, some read. An elderly couple danced to big band music from a portable radio. The hotel set up a buffet table in one corner of the room and served drinks. "Give me a hurricane!" one red-faced tourist in a pink shirt kept exclaiming, as if it were the wittiest joke in the world. When the winds began, people went upstairs to peek outside at the walls of rain and bending trees. "Wow!" said Clive.

Jack spoke by telephone with the national desk off and on until ten, then dragged his mattress to a corner and went to sleep. Clive wandered the room, extracting quotes he would probably never use. Lee sat at a table reading again. Porter watched in admiration; she might have been stretched out by the pool on a hot summer day. But then this was the woman who had rushed through a riot to save him. Her bravery struck him as wildly sexy, a black silk negligee she wore lightly and easily and, in his fantasies, just for him.

By midnight the caterwauling winds and the sound of shattering glass could be heard even in the ballroom and no one was sneaking upstairs for a peek. They heard a loud crash and the ballroom snapped into darkness. Someone cried out in fearful surprise.

"It's okay! It's okay," cried the night manager. Porter felt sorry for the guy, forced to baby-sit a bunch of tourists and journalists through the storm. "The backup generator will kick in." And sure enough, a few minutes later emergency lights flickered on, casting the ballroom into shadows and lights.

"What do we do now?" Clive asked.

"Sleep," Porter said, watching Lee. She had curled up on a mattress beneath the table. Her eyes were closed, her breathing soft and steady. He wanted to crawl over and whisper himself into her dreams.

Jack woke them just after dawn the following morning. "Hotel's still in one piece and electricity's back on. You can get to your room and shower, grab something to eat. Then we hit the streets."

Porter pulled himself to his feet, stiff from sleeping on the floor. Lee was sitting groggily on her mattress, smoothing down her hair, which had mashed up on one side during the night. He walked over and offered his hand to help her up. "How can anyone look so beautiful after spending the night beneath a table?" he asked, thinking to appeal to her vanity. He had learned long ago that even beautiful women—sometimes especially beautiful women—needed to have their beauty ratified. Maybe that was Lee's particular woo. If she stroked her hair or blushed—did black women blush?—or giggled "Stop!" prettily, he would know he'd hit the mark.

But instead she just yawned and shrugged and followed Jack out of the ballroom. Strike two.

He didn't see much of Lee the rest of that day. Jack kept her in Miami while Porter and a photographer named Ed spent the day trolling the southern suburbs and small farming towns south of the city, some of which the hurricane had nearly wiped off the map. The air force base there, evacuated at the last second, had taken a hit. Porter couldn't get past the armed guard at the gate, but a spic-and-span major was sent out with a two-line press release: two thousand buildings damaged, no personnel injuries.

The town itself was just as bad. Porter had covered the aftermath of natural disasters before, primarily tornadoes, but a tornado was a precision instrument of destruction, a scalpel that excised one house and left the house next door untouched. A tornado's destruction was usually localized. But this, this was something else. Porter and Ed drove through destroyed neighborhoods, one after the next, mile after sprawling mile of roofless, windowless, crumbling houses, as if a bomb had detonated inside each one. Roof shingles, broken street signs, pulverized tree limbs littered the streets that weren't plain flooded out—he almost got stranded twice. In some neighborhoods people stumbled around the rubble of their homes, dazedly plucking at crushed and water-soaked objects that only the day before had been treasured parts of their lives.

"It's horrible," one crying woman told him. "It's like something out of the Apocalypse."

But there was also a palpable sense of relief: that the warning had come early enough, that people had listened, that more people had not died. "At least we're alive," said a man who had spent six hours huddled with his family in the hallway of their modest home, a mattress held over their heads to protect them from flying glass. "Thank God for that."

That night, back at the hotel, Porter sat in the bar with Jack and Clive and several other reporters and photographers from other newspapers. While the others told war stories, their voices growing louder with each drink, Porter waited for Lee to come downstairs. It had been a long, trying day and he was exhausted from all the driving, all the climbing through rubble, all the physical and emotional havoc he'd dutifully recorded and passed back to Philadelphia for people to read over their morning plate of scrapple and eggs. He felt an almost physical need to see her, but she didn't come down.

"Hugo was worse," said some guy from New York. "Easy."

The comment drew loud protests. "The hell it was!"

"Where'd you spend the day—inside this bar?"

"This is going to turn out to be the worst natural disaster of this century. Mark my words."

"Who'd you get to say that?"

"Anyway it doesn't matter," said the guy from New York. "L.A.'s already got the spot news Pulitzer sewn up for the riots. This is a no-prize disaster."

On the way to bed, Porter walked by Lee's room, although it was on a different floor. A room-service tray sat just outside her door, the plate covered with a silver lid.

The next morning, over breakfast, Jack said to him, "Lou wants you and Lee to do a story on the federal emergency response. People are complaining it's been too slow, even though Bush was here yesterday promising everybody the sun and the moon." Jack chuckled. "Election year."

"Great." Porter turned to Lee. "Want to ride together?"

"Probably be better if we split up. We can cover more territory that way."

He nodded, trying not to let his disappointment show. "Okay, but let's meet at the high school, the one in South Miami where they set up an emergency shelter. We can compare notes, see what still needs to be covered. Say about three? That'll leave us time to get back here and write before deadline."

"Three o'clock," she agreed. "Don't be late."

And alone he went back into the nuclear winter landscape of South Florida, searching for signs of a federal response. The air of exuberant relief at simple survival that had permeated the air the day before was gone. Now people were sorrowful, frustrated, angry, and full of fear. They came out of their ruined houses carrying rifles, telling stories of holding off looters in the night and a morning spent scavenging among obliterated grocery shelves for food. "Where are the troops?" one man complained. "Where's the damn government when you need them? If it was tax time you can bet your sweet ass they'd be here!"

He made it to the high school around two-fifty. Lee wasn't there yet, so he decided to walk around a bit. It was an older neighborhood, the houses made out of brick or stone, which may have explained why the damage wasn't as bad as in some other places. A few people were out, picking through rubble or sweeping debris into piles. The neighborhood reminded Porter of the one where he'd grown up, the one where his parents still lived. There were the same rolling lawns, the same gabled homes, the same long driveways, perfect for roller-skating down. Only the color of the sky was different, and the trees growing up from the sidewalk were not maples but palms.

He was about to turn around and head back toward the school when he heard a scuffling noise, followed by someone shouting, "Hey!" Porter turned to see two figures running down the driveway of a house on the other side of the street. One figure clutched some kind of black box, probably a stereo receiver or a tape player, its cord dangling in the wind. The other one held what looked like a silver teapot beneath one arm and a red box in the other; as he ran something shiny spilled from the box and clattered on the sidewalk. Then something else and something else, a fork, a spoon, a knife. The guy was spilling silverware, leaving a trail of utensils beneath the hot Florida sun. The two figures crossed the lawn and took off down the street in the direction from which Porter had just come. As they did, an old man hurried around the corner behind them, stumbling over broken branches and shattered glass, his arms scissoring the air.

"Stop!" the old man cried. "Stop!"

Porter watched in amazement. Just blocks from a designated emergency shelter and this helpless old man was being looted in broad daylight with no police, no federal troops in sight. It was the perfect anecdote to begin his story. Porter took out his notebook and began making notes, wishing for a photographer. He was just about to cross the street to interview the old man when he heard a strange, high-pitched howling noise, a terrible, soul-wrenching sound that nearly made him drop his pen.

He looked up from his notebook. It was the old man. He had sat down in the middle of his driveway amidst the scattered debris of his possessions and begun to sob. An old woman in pink shorts down to her knees and a pink sun visor and those huge, wraparound plastic sunglasses came out of the house next door and began inching her way across the lawn. As she walked she waved a mobile phone through the air like a sword. "Mr. Crouch! Mr. Crouch! I called the police!"

But the old man seemed not to hear her or notice her at all; he just sat in the driveway, rocking and clutching his knees to his chest and howling, as though the world were approaching its end. "Nancy's teapot!"

"Mr. Crouch!" screeched his neighbor. It was astonishing how much noise two old people could make.

"Nancy, Nancy!"

"Mr. Crouch! Are you hurt?"

"Oh, God! Oh, God!"

"Somebody do something!" the old woman squawked. "Somebody help!"

She was not looking at Porter as she said it; she seemed not to have noticed him at all there across the street, as though he were just another palm tree, another plastic flamingo in pink. Still he experienced the cry like a hand on his shoulders, like a shove. *Somebody do something!* He thought of Lee, of Los Angeles, of that day. *Somebody had to do something.* Heart thumping, he looked around. A few more old people had come out of their houses, blinking in the sun, but what could they do? The looters were already a block away and moving fast; by the time the police got there—if they got there—it would be too late. Dropping his notebook with a curse, Porter began to run.

He felt more irritated than afraid, more put out than anything. He didn't have time for this; it was almost three o'clock and he had to meet Lee at the school, then get back to the hotel and write his story before deadline. These kids were going to make him late. And they were just kids, he could tell from the long, greasy hair flying behind them and baggy, hip-hop–wannabe clothes and the loose-jointed way they ran. Just kids out screwing around, not realizing how much they were hurting that old guy.

Then one of the looters, the one carrying the teapot, glanced over his shoulder and cursed Porter with the casual malevolence of a psychopath. "Better quit, old man!" he called, a grin lighting up his pimply face. "Better quit before I fuck you up real good."

Porter felt a sharp pain beneath his rib cage at the place where he'd been bruised in L.A. He kept running, but now, suddenly, fear flapped about his feet like loose shoelaces, threatening to trip him with every step. What the hell was he doing? What the hell was he going to do if he actually caught up with them? Okay so what, they were just kids. Okay so this wasn't Los Angeles and the looters ahead of him weren't . . . like those other kids. Still. No matter how pleasant the neighborhood, how many pink flamingos or white picket fences they passed, this wasn't Mayberry and these kids in front of him weren't misguided Opies out for a stunt. They might very well be armed.

"Just drop the silver!" he yelled, making it clear he wasn't after them, didn't give a damn about them, was just trying to help an old man. "Come on! Leave the old man his fucking silverware!"

He didn't know if they heard him; he didn't know why they should listen if they had. He would never catch them; his heart was pounding and his right knee had begun to ache. They were pulling away from him, as fleet-footed and corrupt as any young Grecian god. But just as Porter was about to give up, the kid turned around, running backward now, and flung the teapot straight at Porter's head.

He ducked to avoid the silver missile, stumbled, skidded across the sidewalk on his forearms. As he went down he heard a dull thud—the teapot coming in to land—and the receding laughter of the looters as they danced off down the street.

It took forever to breathe; his whole body had to focus on the task. After a while it succeeded and his mind came back on line and began a mental inventory of injuries. Porter lay with his forehead against the sun-warmed concrete, thinking he might reconsider becoming an editor.

"You okay? Let me help you."

Porter rolled over on his back and opened his eyes. It was the old man, bending over him so closely Porter could smell his old-man smell of degeneration and Poligrip and Aqua Velva and loneliness. Porter noticed he'd already retrieved the teapot and clutched it under one arm. Teapot first, hero second, he guessed.

"I'm okay," Porter said, sitting up carefully. "Nothing broken, I don't think."

"You don't know how much this teapot means to me."

"It's okay," Porter said. All at once his left forearm began to sting. He looked down at it; the skin had been scraped raw by his little break dance across the concrete and was just starting to bleed.

"This teapot belonged to my late wife. I had a fire last year and this is the only thing that survived, the only thing I have to remind me of her." The old man was tearing up. "She was the only woman I ever loved."

Suddenly he remembered Lee. He glanced at his watch—three minutes to three o'clock. Porter climbed to his feet, helped by the old man and his neighbor who had just scuttled up. "You're bleeding!" she screeched. Either this was her natural tone of voice or she was still pumped up.

"Come back to my house. I'll get a bandage," the old man said.

"I'm fine. I have to go."

"But you're bleeding. Let me help, please."

The old lady wagged her mobile telephone at him. "And the police will want to talk to you. They're on their way!"

"I'll come back," Porter said, already pulling out of their little circle. "I promise. I just have to meet someone and let her know I'm okay."

She was standing outside the gym interviewing a woman with one child in her arms and another wrapped around her leg when he limped up. The woman glanced at him with utter disinterest. *Join the crowd,* her eyes said. *My house is gone. Get in line.* But Lee gasped, a breathy, surprisingly sexy sound.

"You're bleeding!"

"I'm fine," he said.

"What happened to you?"

As he told his tale the woman with the children wandered off toward an approaching army truck. The truck parked in the lot, a crowd formed around it, soldiers sprang out and began handing out boxes of food. Except for all the cars and the glossy stadium and the goal posts rising behind the building and the fact that most people there were white, they might have been standing in some African refugee camp. He finished his story. Lee was staring wide-eyed at him, her lovely lips parted in shock.

"When did all this happen?"

"Just now. Five minutes ago."

"Shouldn't you be at the hospital or something?"

The scrape on his elbow had leapfrogged from stinging to excruciating pain. He blew on it, fanned it with his other hand. "It's just an abrasion. All I need is some ointment and a bandage. The old man offered to fix me up and I'm going back there now to check on him. I just wanted to get here first, to let you know what happened."

She eyed him speculatively. "Why would you even worry about that?"

"I don't know. I just . . . didn't like the thought of you standing here, waiting for me, all alone." He looked toward the crowd of people spilling out of the gym and racing toward the army truck and felt like an idiot. What was he saying? He was probably ruining any chance he had with her. "Of course, there's only about a thousand people around here. Obviously, the fall rattled my brain. Ouch!" The sleeve of his shirt, which he'd been holding up, had fallen against the raw part of his elbow, igniting the fire in his tender skin. "Yikes!"

"Wait a second," Lee said. She disappeared into the gym and returned a few minutes later holding a wad of wet paper towels. She handed it to him; he took it and pressed it against his elbow, momentarily easing the pain.

"Thanks."

"Thank you," she said. "For thinking of me. Think you can make it back to the hotel without some kind of criminal incident?"

He stopped tending his injury and looked at her. She was smiling at him.

A hit. First base at least.

Chapter 12

It was late afternoon on their sixth day in Florida. Lee had finished her story and was waiting to hear back from the national desk. She washed her underwear in the bathroom sink, hung it over the shower curtain, recapped the tiny shampoo bottle with the tiny cap, and lined it up with all the other miniature toiletries on the miniature vanity. She hated hotels. She hated sleeping in beds where hundreds of other people had slept, using a shower hundreds of others had used. More than anything she hated the disconnection, the fact that no one in the building—not on the floor, not even, really, at the desk—knew who she was.

She dialed her home telephone number and checked her answering machine. No messages from anyone, especially not Howard. Not a surprise. He had called her only once since that night in the restaurant, to tell her he was dropping off some of her stuff. She arranged not to be home at the time.

Along with some clothes, her toothbrush, and a Temptations album, he left her a note saying "We could try to talk." It made her cry, and then it made her laugh. It was vintage Howard to leave a statement of fact instead of a request. Still, she was tempted, very tempted. She missed him, missed his arms around her body, missed his comforting presence beside her in bed. But every time she picked up the telephone, she made herself hang up because she knew the two of them together had been cracked. And once something was cracked it would eventually shatter; watching her parents' marriage dissolve had taught her that much. And, though her heart still felt hollow, it was better to be the one doing the tossing than the one being tossed aside. Of that much she was certain. She wasn't certain of very much else.

Including her feelings for Porter Stockman. From that moment in the airport with him, she'd been buzzing with a strange, low-level excitement, a kind of inner crackling. It felt, heaven forbid, like attraction, but maybe it was just the pump of being in a strange city, chasing the story of the week. Okay, so Porter was smart. She liked reading his stories; she learned from them. Okay, so he wasn't bad looking, in a whiteboy kind of way. Okay, so he risked injury to help an old man and then disregarded pain and blood to make it to the gym and ensure she wasn't left standing alone, waiting. She was impressed. She could admit that. But it didn't mean anything. She had to be careful. There was something about traveling, about being far from home and floating about the artificial world of hotel rooms and lobby bars that made people do crazy things, things they would later regret. She had to be careful. Lou had said they could fly home the next morning. At home things would probably look quite different.

She was packing her things when the telephone rang. It was her editor, Joyce. "How are things going down there?"

"Oh, fine." Lee propped the telephone on her shoulder and resumed her packing. "You ever covered a hurricane?"

"Can't say I have."

"Well, it's like any other big story, only messier and without electricity," Lee said.

Joyce laughed. "You've done some nice work. I think everyone here is pleased."

"That's good." Lee got down on her knees beside the bed to look for a missing shoe. "Lou's bringing us home tomorrow," she offered. She figured that was the reason for Joyce's call, wanting to know when she'd be back in the newsroom and back to her regular beat.

But Joyce said, "I know. That's great. I'm sure you'll be glad to get back home. Look, Lee, I'm calling because I think we have a little problem."

"A problem?" Lee sat back on her heels. "With the child abuse story?"

"Oh no, not that," Joyce said. "Actually it's about the obit you wrote the other day."

She'd been working on an obituary when Lou stormed up to her desk and ordered her to Florida. Writing obits was not part of her normal assignment, but the obituary writer was out sick and she was asked to pitch in. Five hundred words on an eighty-five-year-old man from South Philly, a retired barber and former Democratic ward leader, one of those mayor-of-the-neighborhood kind of guys. No big deal.

Her knees were beginning to hurt so she stood up. Then she noticed her mouth felt a little dry, and she glanced toward the bathroom, where the little plastic cups in their plastic sheaths stood sentry on the vanity. But the telephone cord was too short to reach in there. "What's the problem?"

"You wrote the guy was awarded the Purple Heart."

"So?"

"He was awarded the Silver Star. The wife says you made a mistake."

"I wrote what she told me," Lee said, trying not to sound defensive. She was holding the telephone cord, and now she wrapped it around her finger, just to have something to do. "I wrote what she said."

"She says she told you the Silver Star." Joyce coughed delicately. "She's pretty upset about it."

Lee twisted the phone cord around her hand. For some reason the inside of her mouth suddenly tasted like cardboard. She kept sucking at her cheek, trying to work up some saliva, but that made little squeaking noises and she was afraid Joyce would think she was crying.

"I'm pretty sure she told me the Purple Heart," Lee said again. She remembered it all quite clearly: being handed the death notice, checking the clips, calling the mortuary, the way you were supposed to, to make sure the guy was, in fact, dead. Then she telephoned the house and got first the daughter and then the wife. She'd been polite and sympathetic but not overly somber—people generally didn't expect somberness when the deceased was eighty-five—and as she went through her list of questions the wife responded with relative cheer.

Lee tried to clear her throat; it was as dry as dust. "Can you excuse me one second, Joyce?" She ran to the bathroom and tore the plastic from the cup with her teeth. The water—tepid, flat, hotel stale—tasted like a sip from a mountain stream.

"Sorry about that," she said when she returned to the phone. She pulled herself up tall, took a deep breath. There was no sense panicking about this. "I'm sure that's what she told me. I don't have that notebook here with me, so I can't check it, but I'm sure that's what she said." But even as she spoke Lee knew she wasn't really that sure. She had been rushing at the end; that much was true. The whole newsroom was cracking with excitement about the hurricane and Lou was breathing down her neck, telling her to get home and get packed and get on the plane before all the Florida airports shut down. It was just a five-hundred-word obit on some guy nobody cared about and those were the ones that always got you in deep.

"It's possible the lady got it wrong in her grief," Joyce said, but Lee knew she was only being nice. "The thing is, the Silver Star is a pretty big medal. You get it for meritorious service."

Lee swallowed. "And the Purple Heart?"

"Any guy who takes a bullet gets a Purple Heart," Joyce said.

"Shit." That was the bad part about print journalism: when you made a mistake, it was there in bold print, for all the world to see. Not as bad as being a doctor or a pilot, of course, and killing someone. But bad enough, especially for someone like Lee. She hated making mistakes.

"Excuse me?" Joyce said.

"Nothing. Why don't we just run a correction?"

"We already did," Joyce said. "But she's not satisfied. She says everybody reads the obit, nobody reads the correction. She's saying her husband was well known as being a war hero, he'd spent his entire life telling people he was awarded the Silver Star," Joyce said. "Now his obit says he got the Purple Heart. She says it makes him look like a liar. Plus, she can't put the obit in the family album. She says we ruined his death."

"Ruined his death?" Lee was horrified to hear herself laugh. It was tight and high-pitched, the bark she made when she was anxious, but Joyce wouldn't know that. She would think Lee was laughing at this old woman and her husband's ruined death.

"I'm sorry. I didn't mean to laugh."

"Look, the old lady is grieving. People get crazy in grief. Normally I'd say not to worry about it. But she called Max."

"Shit." Managing editors didn't always mind complaints about their star reporters; they took it as a sign the reporter was doing her job. But Lee was not a star reporter, not yet. She was still new, still relatively untested. She didn't want this to become Max's impression of her.

"Apparently the guy knew Max's father."

"Oh, great."

"She's threatening to sue, and her son is some ambulance-chasing lawyer in town. Max is taking it seriously."

Lee looked at the hotel pillows mounded like little hills at the top of the bed. She wanted to stick her head in the valley between. "I can write the second obit."

"Oh, Scotty's on that," Joyce said with deliberate breeziness. Lee blinked. Scotty was the obit writer, the guy who'd gotten her into this in the first place. He should be writing it, of course. But it also meant they didn't trust her to write the second piece. "Listen, don't get upset by this. You've done great work down there and everyone here knows it. Just fix this little thing and forget it. Move on."

"How can I fix it?"

"Max wants you to call and apologize. I have the phone number. Got a pen?"

Lee took down the number, hung up the phone. She could hear, out in the hallway, the maid going slowly up and down with her cart. Still knocking on doors at four in the afternoon, still cleaning up other people's messy remains. Lee went into the bathroom for more water. This time it tasted of lint.

The wife, when Lee reached her, was not polite. She raised her shrill, old woman's voice and hurled it at Lee, then she put her daughter on the telephone to rave some more. Lee took it all, took every word, apologizing over and over until she was in tears. "I'm sorry," she said.

"You should be," the daughter said, and hung up.

An hour later Jack called from his room. He, Porter, and Clive were headed out for a farewell dinner on the company dime. Did she want to join them? She did not. "I'm not feeling well," she said. "Think I'll order room service. But thanks."

"Order something expensive," Jack said.

She hung up, wondering if he knew, then realized how ridiculous the idea was. Did she think Max had telephoned the whole staff? There were mistakes in the paper every day. The correction box was never empty. Still, she thought about the grieving widow and felt small. She hated making mistakes.

There was a knock on the door. She peeked through the keyhole and saw Porter standing in the hallway, smoothing his hair.

Her heart, sluggish with guilt and self-disgust, sped up a little. She glanced into the mirror and saw her puffy eyes, her reddened face. She looked like crap.

He knocked again. "Lee? Are you in there? It's Porter."

What could she do? Slowly, she opened the door. He looked at her and smiled with such amazing tenderness she felt a little faint.

"Jack said you weren't feeling well. Just wanted to stop by and see if I could get you anything?"

"Oh, no. I'm fine. Just an upset stomach. I just need to rest."

"You sure? I'd be happy to go to the drugstore and get you something? Pepto-Bismol?"

"No. Thanks."

For a long moment he searched her face. She didn't look away and then he said, "You've been crying."

She laughed, embarrassed, and put her face down. "That bad, huh?"

"Not bad at all," he said with a smile. "What happened?"

"Oh, nothing important. Nobody died or anything."

"Tell me."

"It's silly."

"Tell me anyway," he said.

"I really don't want to."

"You'll feel better," he pressed. "Come on."

Lee watched a white woman in a business suit come down the hallway. She was carrying a garment bag and a purse and, strangely, a small birdcage to which she clucked and cooed. She opened a door and went inside. Lee looked back at Porter, who was still staring at her.

"Tell me," he said again.

"You're persistent, aren't you?"

"Persistence pays," he said. "Tell me."

She felt him yearning toward her, his whole body straining for space, but it wasn't threatening or suggestive or aggressive, though it was decidedly sexual. Whatever it was, she heard herself telling him about the wrong medal right there in the doorway. She couldn't invite him in. He didn't ask, just stood there, nodding, listening.

"It was a stupid mistake. I remember I had an editor once who told me most libel suits came from stupid, careless mistakes like this."

"You're human. You're allowed to make mistakes."

"I should have double-checked."

She had been leaning against the door to keep it open but now she stood up straight and stretched her back. Porter reached over her head and caught the door. "It's good to be a little hard on yourself," he said. "But don't draw blood."

She didn't say anything to that because she didn't know what to say. She was suddenly acutely aware of how quiet it was in that hotel hallway, how perfectly still. She moved back a little.

"Come to dinner," Porter said. "Come on."

"No. I'm tired. I'm going to stay in and go to sleep."

"Are you sure?" he asked. She could tell he was awaiting some signal from her and it scared her. She stepped backward into the room. "Thanks for stopping by. I'm just going to go to sleep."

But she didn't sleep. She telephoned her mother to check on her, then called Pauline. She wanted to talk to someone, but Pauline wasn't home, which was probably just as well. Lee left her a message, then lay awake with the television on but the sound muted, the hotel bedspread heavy at her feet, listening for him. At one o'clock someone knocked tentatively on her door. She didn't move, did not even rustle the sheets, just held her breath. After a few minutes whoever it was went away.

She woke up thinking about him. She thought about him while she showered and dressed and applied, very carefully, her makeup. She thought about him as she went down to the lobby in the elevator and met Clive, who told her Porter was staying through the morning to help Jack and would be catching a later flight home. She thought about him during the flight, despite her best effort to concentrate on Clive and his bringing-down-the-president dreams. She thought about Porter—about his voice and his eyes and the smell of him close—until she felt her mind was like some kind of rat and Porter the maze she kept running through, running without getting anywhere. Back in Philadelphia, she drove home from the airport with the windows down despite the suffocating August heat, hoping the hot wind would drive him from her mind. But later that evening, as she sat on her stoop with the rest of the neighborhood, she was thinking of him. And when the telephone rang, she knew who it was.

"Hey," he said, not even identifying himself. "Eat yet?"

"Where are you?"

"The airport."

"How was the flight?" she asked. She was stalling.

"I can be at your house in an hour," he said.

She felt breathless, as though she had run a marathon instead of just to the phone. "Here's the thing, the thing you should know. I don't usually date people with whom I work. I don't date journalists. And I don't date white men."

She couldn't see his physical response to this proclamation. What he said, without missing a beat, was "I don't blame you. Most journalists are jerks."

She laughed. "You think I'm kidding," he said. "I wouldn't let my sister marry one."

"You're a nut," she said. "But at least you didn't say 'But I'm not your average white guy.' That's the going line."

"I didn't say it because I am the average white guy. I eat hamburgers every night. I read *USA Today* for the international coverage and *Playboy* for the interviews. I think Ronald Reagan was the greatest president this country has ever seen."

"Now you're scaring me."

"I think Michael Jordan is god. I listen to Garth Brooks on my car radio. If you saw me dance you'd take pity on me. On Saturday nights I sneak out to this country-and-western place in South Jersey. They have twelve different kinds of American mass-produced beer. Everybody gets drunk and sings 'Sweet Home Alabama' and throws up on the floor. It's great. You been there yet?"

"That's a lot of detail," she said. "I'm starting to believe you."

"Okay, I got a little carried away there. Here's the point: call it a date or a meeting or whatever you want. I'm not asking you to renounce the throne here, just that you let me take you out, buy you a steak. Two people sharing a meal. That's not against the rules, is it?"

"Depends on which game you're playing," she said, but just to keep the banter going. She knew she was going to have dinner with him and so did he. "I can't make it tonight, but how about tomorrow? Pick me up at eight."

He picked her up at her house and took her to a restaurant in West Philadelphia she did not know, a big, airy place with deep blue walls and a parachute dangling from the ceiling in white, silken folds and a giant fish tank gurgling behind the bar. No sooner had they stepped in the door than a girl with flowing blond ringlets bounded over and kissed Porter on the cheek. "Porty! How are you? You look great!" She spoke in exclamation points and seemed to have trouble holding herself stationary, as if her earth was spinning faster than the one on which everyone else stood.

"Hi, Sandy," Porter said. Lee was amused to see him flush at the girl's greeting. "Working on a Saturday?"

"I need the money for my dog! Did you know I got a dog? I got a dog! Found her limping along the side of the highway! She only has three legs and needs an operation on her kidneys! Did you know dogs had kidneys?"

"Yes," Porter said. "Is our table ready?"

"Oh, wow, we had this couple that just wouldn't leave! But they have their check and I'm scooting them on out of here! Five minutes, okay?"

"That's fine."

"Have a drink at the bar! On the house!" The girl pecked Porter's cheek again and bounced away.

"She acts like that with everybody," Porter said apologetically. He seemed embarrassed.

"Don't be modest, Porty," Lee said, and laughed when Porter groaned.

She was in a giddy mood. At the bar she ordered a sea breeze, took a sip, and felt the alcohol hit her bloodstream almost instantly. It was hot and she hadn't eaten much all day because of the heat. She'd better slow down.

"So," she said, turning in her seat to look at Porter.

"So," he said. Then, after clearing his throat, "Nice house. Renting it?"

"Nope. Buying." She took another long sip of the drink and chuckled, suddenly, inexplicably amused. "I mean, what kind of loser would I be to still be renting at my . . ." Then the look on Porter's face broke through the sweet buzz of alcohol and she wished the glass in her hand was ten times bigger so she could hide behind it.

Porter crossed his arms and smiled. "Go on."

"No. It was nothing."

"You were going to say what kind of loser would you be to still be renting at your age."

"No."

"Yes, you were. Come on," he urged. But he was laughing and after a moment she began laughing too.

"You're not still renting, are you?"

"Oh yeah," he said. "Still renting the same one-bedroom dump I rented when I first moved to Philadelphia. When I was making about thirty thousand dollars less than I do now. Every year my accountant begs me to buy something."

"Why don't you?" Lee asked.

"Just haven't gotten around to it. Is that sad or what?"

"How old are you?"

"Thirty-seven." He made it sound as if he were confessing a crime.

"That's not just sad," Lee said. "That's pathetic." They both laughed.

She could imagine his apartment, decorated in early-frat-boy furnishings—cheap bookcases, milk crates for his albums and CDs, a nice stereo system. The plain linen curtains were a gift from an old girlfriend who got tired of stripping free for the neighbors each night, but now that she was gone they remained forever in the pinned-back position. Three chipped water glasses, a set, of sorts, of mix-matched plates. Probably a nice bed and the golden oak dresser from his childhood, the only thing he brought from home.

By the time Sandy bounced them to their table Lee felt nearly starved. Something had brought her appetite roaring back. She ordered chilled gazpacho to start, a salad of wild greens, crab cakes with roasted potatoes and green beans. *Making him pay,* said a voice inside. But more than that, it was strangely exhilarating to be out with a man and to order freely, not to worry whether her appetite seemed waifish enough or whether the onions on the salad would linger unpleasantly on her breath.

Porter said the crab cakes sounded so good he'd order them too. If that was all right with her.

Lee smiled. "You don't have to check your order with me."

Porter nodded to the waiter and handed him the menus. "I once knew a woman who considered it a minor crime for two people to order the same thing in a restaurant. Took all the fun out of picking off my plate, I guess."

"I never pick off other people's plates."

"I might have guessed that," Porter said. "It's always the people you wouldn't mind doing something who never do it. Another drink?"

They talked about work, about beats covered and stories missed, about the traveling they'd done. He told her about his two months in Kuwait covering the Persian Gulf War. She told him about her two trips to Africa: to Nigeria in 1982 to cover what was the world's fourth-largest democracy, and to Kenya and East Africa later out of personal curiosity.

"I was offered the Africa post six years ago," Porter said. "I turned it down."

"Why?" Lee asked, but she knew. It was amazing how even the most intelligent, educated white folks could be so frightened of Africa. Heart of darkness, lurking savages, all that crap. She felt a stab of disappointment. But then Porter shrugged and said, "Just chicken, I guess," and something about the self-effacing grace of the gesture made her realize, as clearly as if he had said it, that it was a woman. A woman with whom he'd been in love and it was *she* who hadn't wanted to go. Not fear.

"Do you regret it? Not going?"

"A bit, yes."

"Isn't the post coming open again soon?"

"I'm too old now," Porter said. "What about you? The desk would love to send you to Africa. You're so talented."

She waved the compliment off but he persisted. "Of course, those of us on the homefront would hate to see you go."

Fortunately, the waiter appeared just then with their entrées, sparing her the necessity of responding. And she couldn't respond, because what could you say to something like that, with a man sitting across the table caressing your face with his eyes? Lee stuck her face into the steam rising from her potatoes, which gave her an excuse for the moistness on her upper lip. Casting about for safer ground, she said, "Nice work on the conventions. What did you think of Clinton anyway?"

"I didn't get that close to him—the campaign reporters did most of that. But from what I saw he seemed polished, savvy, and smart. Do you think he's impressive?"

"Decidedly," she said. "And also scheming and manipulative."

"Aren't those requirements for the job?"

"Maybe." Lee picked up her fork and dug into the crab cakes. They were all meat, and the rich, buttery flesh nearly melted on her tongue.

"Still, I don't like the way he orchestrated that whole Sister Souljah deal. It was a message."

"So I've heard," Porter said with a smile. "But it's just politics. He has to court the middle-class male vote."

"The white middle-class male, you mean," she said. "Clinton isn't courting the black middle-class male vote with that message." Lee found it amusing too how white people, white liberals especially, would go to ridiculous lengths to avoid the mention of race. Her freshman year in college there were two girls named Maggie—one white, one black—who lived in the same dorm suite as Lee. Both girls were popular; both got a lot of telephone calls from white guys wanting to ask them out. "Which one you want?" Lee would ask, and since half the time the guy didn't know the last name of his lust object he would end up having to describe her. "She's tall," they'd say. Or "short hair" or "big eyes" or anything else but the very real and very definite separating factor of race. With the white Maggie it wouldn't occur to them to describe her as white. With the black Maggie, they thought it was somehow wrong to say.

"Yes," Porter said now, wiping his mouth. The waiter appeared, refreshed their water glasses, floated noiselessly away. "The white middle-class male vote. It's all politics. It's not personal."

"I love it when people say that. That's like a rapist telling his victim, 'Don't feel bad. I just picked you out of a crowd. It wasn't personal.' "

"Whoa!" Porter raised his hands as if in surrender. "Okay, I give up! Guess that's why they say you're not supposed to talk politics on a date."

"That's okay," Lee said. "This isn't a date, remember? Just two people sharing a meal."

"In that case—what are you, a Commie pinko or something?"

They had coffee afterward, then stepped outside into air electrified by an approaching storm. Up and down the block trees danced expectantly in the wind and people hurried to get inside, to get someplace they believed would keep them dry and safe. Lee wrapped her arms around herself and lifted her face to the wind. "I love summer storms."

Three white girls, college age, hurried past, miniskirted and giggling, smelling of youth. Lee watched them go, not thinking anything, then glanced at Porter to see if his eyes too had followed the girls. He was staring at her and his look was electric; Lee felt it like a charge to her flesh. They stood like that for a moment, then Porter cleared his throat and looked away.

"So. There's a great little jazz club just up the street. I think we could just catch the second set."

"Are you a jazz connoisseur?"

"Connoisseur might be too strong of a word. Let's say I'm a fan."

"My mother loves jazz. She always said music was one of God's greatest gifts."

"My father used to say the Irish created music."

"But black people perfected it," she said. "Are you Irish?"

"I think my great-grandfather on my father's side came from Ireland, so he clung to that as a shred of identity. But in truth we're about as Irish as green beer. Shall we, then?"

"Actually, Porter, I think I'll have to take a rain check."

"Are you sure? We could have a nightcap."

Lee smiled but shook her head firmly. "Thanks, but I think I better call it a night."

"Are you all right? Are you cold?"

"Fine," she said, but she wasn't. She felt the wind was blowing inside her, rushing thoughts and feelings past before she could identify them. She wanted to be home, to be in her bed with the window open to the sound of the rain on the leaves. She wanted to be alone so she could think. He must have sensed her mood because he didn't press her anymore and he didn't speak on the drive to her house, only tuned the radio to a station playing John Coltrane and opened the windows to the wind. The first, fat drops of rain struck her face and shoulders as he walked her to her darkened porch. She had forgotten to turn her porch light on before she left. She opened the door by feel.

"Need an umbrella?"

"What for?"

"For the rain?"

"Is it raining? I didn't notice."

"Good night, Porter. Thank you for dinner." She waited for him to kiss her but instead he took her hand and brushed it with his lips. It was astonishingly sensual. Her knees loosened and her nipples tensed and she felt a warmth gathering inside. She took back her hand. "Chivalry will get you nowhere."

"That's flattery," he said, turning away into the rain.

Storms rolled through the city, cracking the purple sky. Outside Lee's window the rain fell in sheets, fell like a curtain between her and the possibility of sleep. At 2 A.M. she gave up trying and went downstairs and turned on the television. For some strange reason a cable station was showing a rerun of an old *60 Minutes* episode. Mike Wallace came on, growling about a group of overfed and underfit business executives who paid $75,000 each to climb Mount Everest for their kicks. They got up there, got caught in a blizzard, ended up with most of them frozen like icicles, including the two poor suckers who had been paid to take them up Mount Suicide. One of the survivors, his face still purple-black with dead and frozen skin, laid out for Wallace and the nation the grisly tale. He was broken, but Wallace had no mercy, grilling the man like a three-inch steak about what he thought would happen when he tried to climb the highest and most dangerous peak in the world with a month's experience.

"Listen," the guy finally squeaked in exasperation. Clearly he'd expected something different from the interview—sympathy, maybe. A nodding head, a few tears in the eyes. Instead he got this constipated, choleric old man who implied it was his own damn fault he nearly ended up with frozen custard inside his veins. "Obviously if I had known, if I had even suspected it would end in disaster, I wouldn't have gone."

"Obviously," Wallace smirked.

But Lee didn't think it was obvious at all. She'd seen enough in her job and in her life to know people often ran headlong into adventures they suspected would devastate them in the end.

Chapter 13

Lee was getting dressed for church the next morning when the telephone rang. She thought it might be Pauline; they were supposed to hook up the day before, but Lee had left a message saying she wasn't up for the long drive to Baltimore. She didn't, of course, say why.

But it wasn't Pauline on the line when she picked up. "I miss you," Porter said.

Lee laughed. "It's only been about twelve hours."

"That's eleven hours too much. Want to go to a jazz festival at Penn's Landing this afternoon?"

Feeling the way she did after she'd just eaten a second helping of ice cream, Lee said, "Why not?"

He picked her up at two. The temperature was up but the humidity down and a steady breeze off the Delaware cooled the riverfront and fluttered flags along the crowded promenade. While the musicians for the first band tuned their instruments, Lee and Porter wandered the booths on the promenade and stopped at one selling Cajun food. Lee bit into a sausage so spicy it felt as if her tongue was blistering. "Water!" she croaked. "Well, I promised you a hot date," Porter said dryly after she'd gulped down three cups of icy lemonade, the first cold liquid he could find.

"Be quiet," she said. But she felt her mouth smiling at him and she remembered, suddenly, Eda telling her once what it was about her father that had first attracted her. "He was good-looking, but a lot of boys were good-looking back then. I liked him because he was passionate and unafraid and he made me laugh."

After the fire in Lee's mouth was quenched they wandered around until the first band struck up a song.

"Let's find a seat," Porter called. She nodded and gave him her hand. He led her up the broad white steps of the amphitheater and she followed, feeling that the heat radiating from the stone and the breeze from the river were both just right. When they were about halfway up, Porter stopped and pointed above and to the right. "How about there?"

"Fine," she said. But then she saw three black men sitting together near the space Porter had pointed out. They were, as a group, astonishingly good-looking, all with close-cropped hair and strong chins and long, long legs and wearing neatly pressed shorts with tucked-in shirts. Two of them were about her age and one man was older, his hair mostly gray. Stretched out there in the sun, they looked like a cover for some magazine, *Essence* maybe, for an issue entitled "Men We Love." The easy, glowing, long-legged beauty of them made her stomach muscles contract. Too bad Pauline wasn't there. Nobody appreciated male beauty like Pauline.

"Lee?" Porter's voice broke into her thoughts. She'd almost forgotten about him. "Ready?"

And then she realized they would have to pass the guys to get to their seats.

"Wait a second."

"Something wrong?"

"No. But maybe we should find someplace else. We'll have to crawl over those guys to get in there."

Porter looked up toward the men. "I'm sure they won't mind."

But suddenly she saw herself as the men must have, a black woman, dressed to attract in loose, cotton pants and a sleeveless black top that showed off her throat and arms, being led up the stairs by this big, world-claiming, air-sucking white guy. Being led like a child or a dog. Wouldn't they mind? She always minded seeing a brother with a white woman on his arm. It had nothing to do with her state of relationship bliss—even when she was with someone, with Howard, even when she was happy and in love, the sight of a black man with a white woman still raised her hackles. She remembered once being out with Howard and running into a friend of his and his white girlfriend. She and Howard were still in the throes of new love; they'd just come out of a movie during which they had kissed and caressed each other into a state of high distraction. She was high with possibility and arousal, and running into the friend was like running into a spike: the air in her high immediately began to leak. She didn't even know this man. His decision to date white had nothing in the world to do with her and yet it felt like a slap. An affront. The woman was only marginally attractive and, from the way she spoke, only marginally educated. Had Lee been asked to guess the woman's occupation she would have said secretary, shop girl, reception- ist at the DMV. Because that was almost always the case: black profes- sional men who would turn up their noses at intelligent, powerful sisters fell all over themselves trying to get to a white waitress. They always dated down. Anything to get that white skin.

Lee looked down at Porter's hand. It looked glaringly white, like some hairless newborn animal. She tried to ease her hand away but Porter was dragging her along and she had to go or make a scene. They reached the aisle. "Excuse us, please," Porter said.

All eyes swung their way. Lee caught her breath. "We're going over there," Porter said, oblivious to her slow and painful death there beneath the sun. After an eternity of moments, the men stood and cleared the path. "Thanks," Porter said, dragging her along.

"No problem," said the older man.

"Thank you," Lee mumbled as they passed.

"No problem, sister," said one of the younger ones. His voice was compact and unreadable. Lee glanced at him, but his eyes were covered by sunglasses, and he had already turned his attention back to the stage. Lionel Hampton was coming on. The crowd roared its approval.

On the drive home they listened to the Temple University station, which was having a Sam Cooke retrospective. Looking out the window, Lee hummed along with that sweet, angelic voice crooning about love and loss.

She asked, "Have you ever dated a black woman before?"

"Oh, was this a date?" Porter joked. When she didn't respond he fiddled with the radio dial—the DJ was taking a break, asking for contributions—and finally said, "No. I have not."

"You had to think about it?"

"I just got the feeling there was a wrong answer and I didn't want to give it."

"Ah." She got the feeling there was a wrong answer to that question also, but she didn't know herself what it was. Would it have been better, would she trust him more easily, if he'd been the kind of whiteboy with a fever for the flavor? Or just the opposite, a mature white man who had never considered crossing the line before?

"I don't have to ask you if you've ever dated a white guy before, I guess."

"No," she said. "No, you don't."

"No, I don't."

At the door he bent to kiss her hand, she stopped him with a touch and pulled his face toward hers. His lips were warm—what had she expected?—and fleshy beneath her own. His tongue sought hers; she allowed it to be found. Then it occurred to her she was kissing a white man, there on her porch in front of the neighbors and God. And anybody else. She thought about a friend of hers, Andrea, who preached loud and often her belief that the ancestors floated about them, watching, guiding, clearing the path. Lee didn't necessarily believe in watchful ancestors, but she didn't rule it out. And so now she imagined the spirit of Harriet Tubman hovering over the porch, finger wagging, scowl on her face.

"That's okay," Porter said. "You aren't the first woman to laugh while I'm kissing her."

She laughed harder, and pulled Porter's lips down to hers, and this time there were no ancestors or ghosts beating their chains against the railings.

Porter touched her face. "God, you're beautiful."

"Yeah, yeah."

"No, you are. Your face is like some jewel, like a diamond that's been cut and polished." When she didn't respond, he said, "That's not a line, you know."

No, she didn't know, but standing there with his arms wrapped around her, Lee wondered what difference it really made. The truth was, she wanted Porter. She wanted to take him inside and let him make love to her. She wanted to feel hands caressing her, feel lips against her neck, the hollow between her breasts.

She was tired of fighting this attraction; tired too of the suspicion in which she'd held him from day one. She was like a driver on a road alone late at night who wanted only to close her eyes. All the guarding of her long-misplaced virtue seemed suddenly ridiculous, a laughable waste of time. All right, maybe all Porter wanted was an exotic fuck. Okay. She was a big girl. She'd slept with more than a few men in her life, more than a few of whom had turned out not to be so much interested in her as in what lay between her legs. Black men. So what? She had survived them and she would survive this whiteboy too, if it came to that. Tonight all she wanted was to be loved. Afterward, they could both get on with their lives.

Porter had said good night and started down the steps, but at her call he paused and looked back.

"Leaving so soon?" she asked.

Chapter 14

The day Porter knew he was an adult was the day he admitted to himself how much first-time sex really sucked. First sex with a new partner was so self-conscious and awkward, so flush with peril it more than offset the extra edge of excitement that came from being with a woman for the first time. Porter much preferred times two, three, four—ad infinitum. First-time sex was something to be gotten through.

Which was not to say he'd had complaints. His most recent woman friend, Alice, had screeched and clawed with such feline ferocity that first time he half expected to find a fur ball among the bedclothes. And more than one woman had remarked, even after the first time, on what a considerate lover he was. "You actually seem to remember that I'm in the bed too," gushed Daisy. "So many men don't. You have no idea!" She spoke with such vehemence, he wondered: What exactly were those other guys doing anyway? Turning on ESPN? Spreading the sports page over the woman's face?

The first time he had sex was at seventeen, just before he left for college, with a volatile, green-eyed girl named Laura who took up with him during that last wild month of school to make her ex-boyfriend jealous.

It didn't work. The boyfriend, a drama type who played Jesus in *Jesus Christ Superstar,* was oblivious to their public displays. Porter knew he was being used but didn't care. He was a Molotov cocktail of adolescent desire, lit and burning, ready to shatter and explode. Laura offered the only possibility of safe release. For a few weeks they staggered the corridors arm in arm and kissed their lips raw behind the stairwell, until one Saturday night they got stoned and snuck into Porter's basement and did it on a pile of laundry while his parents entertained upstairs. "Well, that sucked," Laura said afterward, wiping tears from her eyes. Porter knew she just missed Superstar; nonetheless, it was hard not to take such criticism personally. He sulked amid the dirty socks while Laura slunk out the basement door.

It was two years before Porter had sex again—this time in a bed, in a dorm room at college, and afterward the girl resolved his dilemma of whether to stay or not by kicking him out. Things went on like that for a while; his twenties were a wasteland of awkward groping, half penetrations, last-minute changes of mind. Things improved dramatically as he neared thirty and became both more eligible and, more important, comfortable with himself. Still, he disliked first-time sex, maybe because it always reminded him of that green-eyed, lovesick girl.

Lee's bathroom, Porter was glad to see, was not one of those superfeminine creations where the soaps were so intricately carved it seemed crass to soil them. Alice—and as soon as he saw this he knew it wouldn't last—not only decorated her bathroom with floral-patterned seat and lid covers, but had actually draped a pink, ruffled skirt around the bowl. The bowl.

Lee's bathroom was more like something in a design magazine: muted earth tones, a wicker basket full of towels in the corner, and on the toilet back, a small vase of fresh eucalyptus leaves with their pleasant, winter-pine smell. On the wall above the toilet hung three small photographs of someplace that—by the color of the grass and the slant of the light—had to be in Africa. He wondered if Lee had purchased the photographs somewhere or taken them herself.

Porter conducted his business, then stood for a moment looking down at himself. Ten minutes before, on the porch with Lee, he'd been so hard it was nearly painful; had, in fact, been eager to end the good-bye so he could get home and get to bed and think about her. Then she invited him inside and it was a bicycle tire going over a nail in the road. Pfffft.

It wasn't that he didn't want to sleep with her. Lord knew, he did; he'd been fantasizing about it for weeks. Lee had an impressive body. There was no missing the banner breasts, the succulent hips, the round, high ass (he had never been an ass man, but then he had never seen, personally, an ass like hers), though she dressed in tailored pants and loose silk blouses and at-the-knee skirts. He got the feeling she was trying neither to hide her body nor to use it as a weapon the way some of the younger women in the newsroom did. He wanted her bad, but she'd caught him unprepared.

Lee had been like a fortress with him, defenses fully manned. To suddenly have the battlements dropped was alarming. His body sensed a trap, and no amount of urging, even there in the bathroom surrounded by the soft, damp scent of her, could draw the soldiers out.

They had not talked much about past relationships, but Porter was not naive. Lee was over thirty. She was a beautiful and intelligent woman. She'd probably slept with at least ten guys in her life, maybe twelve or twenty or thirty—he didn't know—and every one of them black. That much he knew. She'd never dated a white guy before him, much less slept with one. What if he couldn't handle her? What if he couldn't keep up? He had a sudden image of Lee on a bed, naked and glistening, laughing at him as he lay panting and gasping for breath, unable to move. An inept, out-of-shape flabby piece of flesh.

He'd be climbing into bed between Lee and the memory of all her past boyfriends. Porter knew that all the myths and stereotypes about the sexual prowess of black men was just that: myth. Black men did not, as a whole, have bigger, thicker penises than white men. They weren't hung like horses; they weren't lustful, passionate beasts in bed, at least no more than any other man. All of that, Porter knew, was hysterical garbage, lies spawned by the fears and repressed sexuality of white men, an excuse for slavery and segregation. He had nothing to worry about. Nothing at all. Except . . .

Porter loved basketball. And anyone who loved basketball, who watched it with the eye of a connoisseur, had to admit black men were, in truth, physically superior. It was in the arms—the arms more than anything else. Watching college ball, Porter would look at some eighteen-year-old man-child lined up at the free-throw line and think: how in the hell did he get those arms? They were sculptured muscle, those limbs like polished black marble, some kind of god carved out of stone. A white kid might haul his butt up and down the court a hundred times without tiring; he might play smart and understand the game. He might thread the lane and hit the jump, and he might, might even be able to dunk, but in the end he would never have the grace, the liquid moves of the average black player. And he sure as hell wouldn't have those arms.

Porter imagined those arms wrapped around Lee's shuddering body, brown on glistening brown, and whatever alcoholic buzz he had going evaporated into the bathroom's blue-white light. "Great," he said out loud. He had never been so painfully sober in all his life. He zipped his pants, washed his hands, splashed cold water on his face and neck. His heart pounded and he hoped half-seriously for an attack.

There was a knock on the door. "Porter? You okay in there?"

"Fine," he said. "Be right out."

How embarrassing to be caught lingering in the bathroom. He felt fourteen years old, discovered in the laundry room with his father's *Playboy* magazine. But he was closer to forty than fourteen, and the last thing he needed to think about was his mother. What he needed was to grow up, calm down, and get a plan. He would have one more drink, a short one, for his nerves. And he'd get her one. And if they started out on the couch, he'd suggest moving to the bedroom. And he'd make certain the lights were off. He hoped that wouldn't be a problem, having sex in the dark; it wasn't with most women over thirty. The thing to do was to get through this first time without embarrassing himself. He'd concentrate on her needs, follow her lead, do what she wanted, bring her to climax if it took every ounce of will and strength. That at least would guarantee him a second chance.

The streetlight outside Lee's window spilled its glow into the room, illuminating them. Porter was glad. The lights were off—she'd seen to that. He wished they weren't.

Things had begun well in the living room—wine, kissing, caressing, both of them nibbling and gasping and making all kinds of sexy, ridiculous noise. Then the hand-holding walk upstairs, him wanting both to crawl and to race, wanting that feeling of anticipation to go on forever and feeling as if in another second he would surely burst. It was wonderful, wonderful. Until they reached the bedroom. She led him through the darkness to the bedside and he bent to turn on the lamp because he wanted to see all of her, but she stopped him. She put her hand over his on the lamp switch and drew it away. He felt it then, a slip, a scratch in the groove, but he told himself it was nothing because he couldn't stop. He didn't want to stop. He undressed her. She let him. He undressed himself. She watched, her hands moving expertly over his chest as he pulled down his pants. She didn't speak and so he didn't speak. He held his breath and plunged ahead. He knew he should stop; he wanted to stop. But the sight of her was overwhelming. He lost control and pulled them both down into the feathery nest of her bed. He wanted to kiss her everywhere at once, wanted to inhale her through his mouth. He heard himself moaning like a wounded animal while she stroked his hair as though he were a child.

Shuddering, he rolled onto his back, pulling her atop him. He tried to claim her with his hands. "Lee," he said frantically. "Lee, look at me."

For a moment she opened her eyes. They were dark, bottomless; he couldn't read whatever was there. Then she fell back onto the bed, pulling him along. Eyes closed, she began moving beneath him, urging him, shoving him relentlessly along like a bull being prodded toward the slaughterhouse. He dug in, held back. He would not go alone.

Again, he said her name, but this time his voice was calm. "Lee."

Startled, she opened her eyes.

"Be here," he said. "Be with me."

He slipped inside her, she arched against him. He felt himself coming apart. He wanted her to say his name and he knew if she did he would die and he didn't care. He moved and she moved with him and together they tumbled into the dark.

After a breath and a lifetime, he came back to himself. Lee was beside him on the bed, trembling. He pulled her toward him, wanting to feel the length of her body against his. She kissed him, stroking his hair.

"You're amazing," he said. She did not respond. After a while he felt his arm being moved. Lee slipped from the bed and went into the bathroom, closing the door behind her before turning on the light. He heard the toilet flush and the shower hiss on. He heard the hole in sound where her body broke the wall of water, and it frightened him awake. Shit, Porter thought. Showering in the middle of the night could not be a good sign. Twenty minutes later she came out, pausing in the bathroom doorway, backlit and surrounded by steam, a thick, blue robe cinched around her waist and a towel wrapped about her head like an African queen. Even in a terry cloth robe she was the most desirable woman he had ever known. Beneath the sheets he felt himself getting hard. If he didn't have this woman he would certainly die.

"Still here?" Lee said casually. Porter's heart skittered. Was that a joke or not?

She had not planned to shower. Showering in the middle of the night after sex was something she used to do in her twenties, when she was still operating under Eda's sex-is-dirty influence. "Nothing nastier than a woman who lays up in the bed and doesn't wash," Eda said once. Later, Lee realized her mother believed douching immediately after sex would prevent pregnancy. Like many older black women, Eda was a complicated mix of intelligence, practicality, and absurd superstitions and beliefs. Even at twelve Lee knew better than that. Her sex ed teacher at school said, "You can't outrun a sperm." Still, as a young woman, after sex, Lee got up and washed.

But she'd long since relieved herself of that particular inhibition. Thank goodness! Now Eda was acting frisky in the middle of the afternoon. Lee shook her head, not wanting to think about that. She had gone into the bathroom to check her diaphragm and to calm down and to think. And once inside she didn't know what else to do, so she turned on the hot water and climbed into the tub.

Looking down at herself through the water, Lee thought, Whose body is this? She felt electric and loose-limbed and rubbery. Whose body had that been out there, on the bed, popping open like a cheap suitcase? She stuck her face under the water and told herself to calm down. It was just sex. Good sex. Very good sex and the fact that it happened with a white guy said nothing at all about her. It didn't mean she was a sellout or a slut. It did not mean she harbored some subconscious wish to be raped by the oppressor. It didn't mean anything at all.

It occurred to her Porter might take the opportunity of her shower to depart, which would solve a lot of problems. She found herself straining to hear through the roar of the water. Leave, she thought. If he left he would be a prick, a white prick who wanted only an exotic lay and she wouldn't have to deal with what had happened back there in bed. Leave, she thought, and held her breath as she opened the bathroom door. He lay in bed, blinking at the sudden light.

"Still here?" It doesn't mean anything, she told herself. Only a real prick would sneak out in the middle of the night. Whatever else he may be, he's not a prick.

"I'd like to stay." He sat up. "I'd planned on staying, if that's all right."

Lee shrugged and snapped on a lamp, then moved to her dresser, trying not to tremble. She removed the towel from her head and picked up a brush. He wanted to stay. Did she want him to stay? Did she want to wake up in the morning with him there beside her? Maybe he was only hoping for another go-around.

"For one thing," Porter said, "I'd never get a parking space on my block this time of night."

Was that a joke? Was he joking? Did he think this was funny? She was suddenly, abruptly furious with him and with herself. What was she doing, sitting there in the middle of the night brushing her hair with a white man in her bed? A white man! How could she call Pauline and share this little adventure over a glass of wine? She hadn't just consorted with the enemy, she'd slept with him.

She turned around, brush in hand. "Let me ask you something."

"Go ahead." He was smiling.

"Have you ever slept with a black woman before? Before me, I mean."

"No. I told you I hadn't."

"You said you'd never dated anyone black. That doesn't mean you haven't slept with a black woman."

"I'm not that kind of guy," he said, still trying to joke it off. But she wasn't about to be joked.

"You're almost forty. Still single, good-looking."

"Thank you."

"I'm quite sure you've had your share of one-night stands."

And now at last he grew wary. "Lee. What's wrong?"

"Nothing." She crossed her arms over her chest and stared at him, hoping she looked formidable.

"Come here."

"Answer my question, please."

He sat in bed, naked save for the sheet. She thought he might get up and pull on his pants—men didn't like to fight with their pants down—but he didn't move. "I have never slept with a black woman before tonight."

"Ah," she said.

"Is that the right answer?"

"Is it the truth?"

"Yes," he said. "But you keep asking it as though you don't believe me. Or don't want to believe me. I'm trying to figure out what it is you want to hear."

So am I, Lee thought. If he had dated other black women, if he had slept with them, he was a chocolate lover, a whiteboy with a fever for the flavor, and his attraction to her had more to do with that than with her. Once you've gone black . . . On the other hand, if he really had reached such an advanced bachelor age without sleeping with a black woman, why now? Some last-minute fantasy of around-the-world conquests before he got serious and settled down with the local Barbie doll. Men were complicated enough. Did she need this extra aggravation?

"So you're a virgin, so to speak," she said. "What's the verdict?"

"Don't do that. Come here."

She turned away so he wouldn't see her trembling, and kept brushing her hair.

"Please."

"Maybe you should leave."

The bed creaked. He was getting up. She imagined him pulling on his shorts, his pants, buttoning his shirt, searching furtively for his shoes beneath the bed. He's leaving, she thought. Happy now? Then she felt arms encircling her waist and stiffened in surprise.

"Tell me what's wrong? What did I do?"

"Nothing . . . I . . . I'd rather be alone." She was fighting to keep her voice level, to keep her body stiff. "I'm tired."

"You need to sleep."

"Go home, Porter."

He shushed her like a child, moving them slowly toward the bed. "Come to bed."

"Listen to me," she said. But she let herself be pulled.

"Come to bed."

"The bar's closed. You're not getting another round."

"Sh." They were on the bed now. He was whispering and stroking her hair. "Just go to sleep. I'll hold you while you sleep."

Chapter 15

Summer ended, fall arrived. Philadelphia shrugged itself from its warm-weather slumber and buzzed with the frenzy of fall. Lee was no stranger to Philly; a girl could not grow up in Baltimore and never hike up Interstate 95 to visit the City of Brotherly Love. How many class trips to the Liberty Bell had she taken as a schoolgirl? How many times as an adult had she passed through on the way to New York? She'd formed an early image of Philadelphia as run-down, crowded, and culturally flat—Baltimore without intimacy or decent seafood, New York without glitz. There were the same Italian and Irish and black neighborhoods as Baltimore, the same row houses shoved shoulder to shoulder along the same trash-strewn streets.

But now, exploring with Porter, Lee found herself newly enchanted with Philadelphia, as if the true city was only now being revealed. Taken from the inside, Philadelphia seemed not less intimate than Baltimore but less claustrophobic. Not dowdier than New York but simply more sane. Philadelphia was human in scale, modest in offering. It was massive, but like the statue of William Penn atop City Hall, it didn't *seem* that way. It seemed manageable and quirky and nice. Philadelphia was self-critical without flagellation, self-content without being smug. Philadelphia offered the good if not the greatest, the bad but not the worst, the strange but not the most bizarre. It was seductive in its own, comfortable way, and Lee relaxed into it, gladly seduced.

Porter wooed her strenuously. He fed her brunch at dives where he was known and dinner at places where he was not. He took her to the Rodin Museum, to the Academy of Music to hear Bach, and to the Mann Music Center to hear Joan Armatrading sing beneath the stars. He prepared coq au vin for her at his apartment and it was delicious, and he knew how to clean the kitchen as he cooked. They had long conversations about everything. He seemed to love listening to her opinions, especially when they differed from his own. They discussed politics and religion, human nature and literature. He argued *The Great Gatsby* was the greatest novel ever written. She told him he was nuts and made him reread *Invisible Man*.

When they were out together, he took her arm, pressed her hand, opened doors. When they were alone he held her face in his hands and explored her mouth, the hollow of her neck and the inside of her wrist for great, long minutes, as if these were the destinations he'd labored long and hard to reach. It was, all of it, exhilarating.

She asked him to keep the relationship private in the newsroom. He agreed, and she didn't know whether to be grateful or hurt. But it was for the best. She was still the new kid on the block, and newsrooms were like any other office: what you actually did was only half as important as what other people thought of you. Porter was one of the golden boys in the newsroom; she didn't want people to think she was sleeping with him to raise her own profile. And she didn't want the other black reporters and editors to know she was sleeping with a whiteboy at all.

Porter agreed not to ask her to lunch repeatedly, not to hang around her desk, not to message her over the computer newsroom system, which was monitored by the editors, though they claimed otherwise. He said he found the secrecy exciting. When he wanted to talk to her during the day, he'd telephone from his desk. "This is Porter Stockman from the *Record* calling. I was wondering if you could meet me on Seventh

Avenue," he'd say, referring to a storage room on the seventh floor they'd discovered.

"I might be able to arrange that."

"I'd appreciate it so. The matter is pressing."

She'd grab her purse and jacket so anyone paying attention would think she was headed out for an interview, and take the stairs instead of the elevator, arriving breathless in that storeroom, feeling for him in the dark. They would hold hands and kiss and press their bodies together and her racing pulse would race more at the sound of voices falling up and down the hallway outside. Meeting that way *was* exciting and addicting and glorious and when one of them, usually her, would finally pull away saying, "We'd better stop," she would sneak down the hallway to the rest room and sit in a stall until she was composed. She felt seventeen and reckless and happy and rawly open to him. Then she'd splash water on her face and look into the mirror. *Yes, but remember: you are only having fun.*

Because it could never be serious.

Still, it was difficult seeing a man and not telling anyone. She longed for someone to gush with, to laugh with and sit around with analyzing everything Porter said and did. Normally by this time in a relationship, Pauline would know as much about the man Lee was dating as Lee. And she did try to tell Pauline—twice. Both times fate stepped in. The first was just bad timing—just as she was about to speak, Pauline got buzzed on the other line and had to go. The second time, just as Lee opened her mouth to confess, Pauline launched into a story about an auditor who'd been in the bank that week, a bull-necked, hard-assed, ex-jock whiteboy who tried to intimidate everyone until a male customer walked into a bathroom stall one morning and caught him jerking off with a pair of panty hose around his head.

Lee screamed, "You are kidding me!"

"Of course Mr. Jones came right out and told me—he's a good friend and he knew this asshole was riding us hard! He said the man was in there just getting down!" Pauline laughed wickedly.

"Oh, my God."

"He probably got careless. You know we don't have any men in the bank, so I guess he thought he was safe in there." Pauline chuckled. "Girl, white folks is a mess!"

It was their standard summation, the line they'd used between themselves a thousand times, the line their mothers and mothers' mothers had used. They weren't prejudiced; they only really believed it a little bit. No big deal. Only this time, an agreement was a betrayal of the man sharing her bed. This time, Lee didn't know what to say. So she said nothing. She sure as hell couldn't tell Pauline after that.

Lee found herself avoiding her best friend. She let her answering machine pick up the phone, then returned Pauline's calls when she knew she wouldn't be home. If Pauline called her at work, Lee would chat breezily for a minute, then claim deadline pressure and get off the phone. When Pauline informed her, via answering machine, that she had decided to take a long-delayed vacation to Brazil and wanted Lee to come along, Lee declined. She liked traveling with Pauline; she was companionable without being clingy, and they both preferred an afternoon on the beach to a ride on a tourist bus. But Lee didn't want to leave Porter, not when the fling was in full swing. And she could not spend two weeks on the road with Pauline and not tell all.

A few days after she declined Pauline's invitation, Lee picked up the telephone at work and heard her friend's voice.

"What the hell is going on with you? You don't return phone calls, you won't talk to anybody when you do, and now you're turning down a trip to Brazil?"

"I'm sorry," Lee said. "I've been so busy."

"Too busy to go to Brazil? You know—Rio, the beach, beautiful men? What about that list does not appeal?"

"Sounds great, but I can't take vacation anytime soon," Lee said. This was a lie. She could take vacation anytime she wanted; it was one of the perks she had negotiated. "You should go."

"I intend to," Pauline said. "I desperately need a couple of weeks on the beach."

"Maybe Cleo would like to go," Lee suggested. "Or Andrea."

"Andrea, maybe. Cleo, no," Pauline said. Then, "So what, exactly, is keeping you so busy up there?"

She couldn't tell if there was anything behind this question or not. Pauline could be inscrutable when she wanted to be, even to someone who knew her as well as Lee. "Oh, just this project," Lee said. "It's an examination of the racial makeup of people stopped for traffic violations on I-95."

"Let me guess: most of them are black?" Pauline chuckled. "Didn't you try to do this story years ago? Down here? I seem to remember you talking about it after your brother got stopped driving somewhere."

"Yep. The editors were not interested," Lee said. "But this is a new place and a new day."

"A new day, all right," Pauline scoffed. "Girl, I'm telling you, you need to call up Rodney King and give him a cut of your salary. Him getting beat nearly to death was the best thing that ever happened to your career!"

Lee laughed, knowing she missed her friend. Nobody could make her laugh like Pauline.

"Well, have fun," Pauline said. "But if you don't get your butt down here soon, I'll have to get on I-95 and drive up there myself. And I can't be held accountable for what might happen if I get stopped by the cops."

"When are you going to Brazil?"

"Three weeks," Pauline said. "Call if you change your mind and can take some time away from your glamorous new life."

One night at 2 A.M. the telephone rang. Lee answered before the first ring ended, though she'd been sound asleep. But it wasn't her brother, as she'd feared, and it wasn't her mother. And it wasn't Porter, who, for once, was not sleeping over that night. It was Howard.

He was calling from someplace noisy, a bar or a restaurant. In the background she could hear a woman singing the blues.

"Howard?" Lee asked groggily.

"The one and the same. What's going on?" Howard asked, as if they'd seen each other yesterday when in fact it had been months.

She peered at her clock. "Howard, it's after midnight. Why are you calling now?"

"Is he there?"

"Who?"

"Your new man. I called you last week. I wanted to talk. He picked up the phone."

She came fully awake. Porter. Why was he picking up the telephone in her house? What if her mother had called?

"Hey, no problem," Howard said. He slurred the word *problem* and she realized with a start that he was drunk. She might have realized it earlier with anyone else, but Howard rarely drank and never to excess. "I don't want to cause trouble. I just want to ask you something."

She felt a sudden wrench for the feigned casualness of Howard's voice. She didn't want to know what he would ask. "Howard, I have to go. Call me—"

But he wouldn't wait. "Why didn't you love me?" he asked. "Just curious."

She had the urge to slip the phone back onto the hook, to look away. It was shameful, shameful, shameful, and she didn't know if the shame was Howard's or was hers.

"Was it because you thought I only cared about work?" Howard's voice began to rise. He was dropping all pretense. "Was that it?"

"No," she whispered.

"Yes, it is. And you think I'm a mama's boy. Damn it! I have to take care of her. I have a responsibility."

"I know, Howard. I admire your sense of responsibility."

He laughed harshly. "Bullshit!"

Howard rarely cursed either, but she was no longer stunned. "Why didn't you love me?"

"Howard . . ."

"Why? Tell me."

"Howard, this—"

"Tell me, damn it!" he yelled. Behind him, the music stopped but the noise of people talking continued on. Nobody seemed bothered by a man screaming into a phone. "That's the least you can do, you heartless bitch! Tell me! Tell me, now!"

"You scared me!"

There was a pause, then Howard's voice, bewildered. "Scared you?"

It was like seeing her father cry; too painful. She wanted to finish this and be done. "Not physically. Emotionally. Part of it was that you seemed more interested in your store and part of it was your devotion to your mother. But part of it was I always felt scared with you. As though I were going to let you down. As though you were going to find out the truth about me, that I'm not so tough or so smart, and then you'd be disappointed and . . ." She let her voice trail off.

Howard exhaled but said nothing.

"I guess . . . I never felt like I could be vulnerable with you," she said weakly. Even as she spoke she wondered if that was just an excuse.

There was a long pause. The woman in the background started up another song. Then Howard said, "You never tried." He hung up so quietly the only way she knew he was gone was the music stopped. She couldn't hear the blues anymore.

A few days later, her friend Luther came to town for a conference of some sort and invited her to dinner. His hotel happened to be two blocks from the restaurant where Porter had taken her, and so when Luther asked for dining suggestions she named that place. They met there at seven, embraced. Luther looked as good as always, polished and glowing in his wealth.

"How's Howard?" he asked.

She winced and sipped her drink. "Howard and I broke up."

Luther looked startled. "When?"

"Few weeks ago."

"Huh." Luther shook his head. "I always thought that brother had his head on straight. Want me to kick his ass for you?"

Lee laughed, first at the image of Luther mussing his Armani suits and Gucci shoes kicking Howard's butt in some back alleyway, then at Luther's assumption Howard had been the one to call it quits. The man, after all, the prize. "No need for ass kicking," she said. "I'm the one who ended things."

"You did? But why? What happened?"

But Lee didn't like to think about what had happened with Howard, let alone discuss it. Certainly not with Luther—a friend, but a peripheral one. They had never really breached that wall of intimacy; once it became clear he didn't want to date her the progression toward closeness stopped. Plus, she was having second thoughts about Howard. Or, not second thoughts, precisely, but guilt. Regrets. It had been a revelation to hear pain in Howard's voice. It had never occurred to her that men could be hurt; women were the ones who needed love. But she realized now that Howard had been vulnerable too. He'd seen her job and her life and feared she would not need him, not in the way he understood. So he distanced himself, acted otherwise occupied. And she misread that as aloofness and potential disappointment. He misread her and she misread him and possibility crashed and burned.

She didn't want to discuss this with Luther, so instead of answering she just smiled and shook her head. Let him assume what he wanted.

"So, tell me what's going on with you?" she said. "How's that baby of yours? Got any pictures?"

Luther did, of course, enough to mount a show at the Museum of Art: Isaiah (Lee and Pauline called him the Heir Apparent) in his car seat in the back of the Legend, Isaiah on the plush, white carpet in the living room, Isaiah in someone's blue and silky lap. At three months he was already holding up his head, could track the black-and-white mobile strung over his crib, was soothed to sleep by Beethoven but cried at Schubert. Clearly a genius.

Luther rattled on and on and Lee smiled and nodded and tried to appear interested. But her thoughts kept finding Porter. He was out with friends that night but undoubtedly calling her, leaving her sexy messages at home. He'd pretended to be jealous that she was having dinner with some other guy. She'd pretended not to be turned on.

"So who is he?" Luther asked.

The waiter was clearing their plates, scraping invisible bread crumbs from the table with his little silver trowel. Lee shook her head and focused on Luther's face. "What? Who is who?"

"The man you're with," Luther said, eyeing her. "The one you left Howard for. Who is he?"

For a moment she was startled. Had Luther heard something from someone? But no, nobody knew. Had he somehow read her mind? Or was he just assuming she would not have left Howard unless there was another fish on the line.

"What makes you think there's someone else?" Lee asked.

"Why else would you leave Howard?" Luther said, poker-faced. Then, "Just kidding. No, there's a certain glow."

"Oh, please."

"Well?" Luther asked, leaning back in his chair.

The waiter returned, brandishing the dessert menu. Lee took one and pretended to study it. Here it was, opportunity. She'd spent the past few weeks wanting to tell Pauline about Porter, to share this moment of life with her friend. Now here was Luther, asking. She could tell him, could gauge his reaction, plan the moment with Pauline. Luther was a man, after all. Though they were friends, their relationship was different from the one she shared with Pauline, less intense, less intimate. Plus Luther lived in New York, not Baltimore. Though they knew many of the same people he was not in constant touch with her crowd. He would not be likely to share news she wasn't sure she wanted shared.

Taking a breath, she said, "He's a journalist. Works at the newspaper here, but we met in Los Angeles during the riots." She made herself stop. No need to go into more detail about *that*.

"Thought you didn't date reporters."

Lee shrugged. "There's an exception to every rule."

"I see." Luther nodded. "Older? Younger?"

"About the same age."

"Where's he from?"

"Philadelphia," she said, leaving out the "outside of" part.

"Name?" Luther persisted, as was his way in everything.

"Porter. Porter Stockman."

She watched Luther's face. He figured it out almost instantly. Maybe from Porter's name, which wasn't exactly lingua franca of the 'hood.

Maybe from something in her voice as she spoke, some telltale quiver of admission. Confession. Guilt.

"So he's white," Luther said. A statement.

She tried a tone that was neither apologetic nor challenging. "He is."

Luther nodded, not saying anything. The waiter slipped a cappuccino before her, its frothy white head sprinkled with brown specks of cinnamon. Luther tucked into a chocolate torte and chewed each bite thoroughly. Eda would have said he looked like a cow working on her cud.

"So what do you think?" she asked at last, when she couldn't stand it any longer.

"Think?" he responded, all innocence.

"About the price of tea in Tibet. Come on, Luther. What do you think?

"I'd just like to know," she said.

"Well. Okay. I'll admit I'm . . . surprised," Luther said.

"No more than I am," she grinned. Trying to joke.

Luther lifted his napkin to his face, then returned it to his lap. "If I'd heard it through the grapevine I would have said, 'Not Lee.' I just never saw it from you. I mean, you never dated white before. Have you?"

He might have been asking whether she ever pillaged and raped and neglected to inform him. "Of course not," she said. Then added, "It's not like I'm marrying David Duke, Luther. I'm just hanging out with this white man for a while, that's all."

"Well. Certainly it's your life," he said, speaking formally now, speaking businessman. Speaking to her forehead, her right ear, the wall behind her chair. She imagined this was the look he used when upbraiding a manager or firing someone, this look of disappointment, of cold disdain. "It's none of my concern. I'm simply surprised. Just because things with Howard didn't gel."

"This has nothing to do with me and Howard," she said.

"I would have thought you'd keep the faith, not give up on the brothers like that."

She was astonished. "Give up on the brothers?"

"I would have thought you'd keep the faith all the way to the end."

She was so flabbergasted she didn't even know where to begin. She picked up her cappuccino, put it down, picked it up again, and drained it. It was cold and made her want to gag. *Give up on the brothers?* She hadn't given up on anyone! She loved black men! Just because she was dating Porter didn't change that fact. She started to say all this to Luther, then changed her mind. She wasn't going to be dragged into justifying herself. Not to him.

"And I would have thought you were my friend," she said. "Apparently we were both wrong. Apparently I'm only your friend as long as my actions meet with your approval."

"I didn't say all that."

"Guess I've just been lucky these past ten years."

"Okay," Luther said. "Calm down."

"Fuck you!" She stood and glared down at Luther, noticing with satisfaction the thinning of his hair at the topmost point of his brown head. Pretty soon he'd have to do the Michael Jordan thing. "You can't insult me like that and then tell me to calm down. It doesn't work that way."

"Okay, okay. You're right."

"Who, precisely, do you think you are, Luther? Just because you have a fat bank account doesn't mean you have the right—or the intellect or the perceptiveness—to analyze people's lives and pass judgment. You want me to make a list of all the rich idiots in this world?"

Luther glanced around the restaurant. "I take your point. Now, will you please sit down?"

People were looking at them and she'd lost her steam anyway. But before she sat she wanted to make one more point. "Don't patronize me, Luther. I knew your ass when you went to JCPenney and checked out the sales rack!"

"Okay, okay, okay!" He held his hands up, palms out, surrendering. "I'm sorry! I'm sorry! Please, sit down."

He got up and pulled out her chair. After a minute, she sat, reluctantly.

"Damn!" Luther said, retaking his seat. "I hope this whiteboy knows what he's getting himself into."

He smiled that megawatt ice-melter he was so famous for, and she had to give in. "I am sorry," Luther said, still chuckling. "But you asked me."

He had her there. She had asked. She'd sought his approval in a way she had not about Howard or anyone else before. In a way it never would have even occurred to her to seek had Porter been black.

"My mistake," she said.

"It's not that I don't understand the possible attraction. I dated a white woman once."

Lee smiled. "Thanks for the admission, but it's not the same thing. A lot of brothers feel it necessary to stamp their tickets with that one. It's not the same thing at all."

"Maybe not," Luther said, looking down at his manicured hands. "But I almost married her."

This was a shock. Luther dating a white woman, no surprise there, but almost marrying her? Lee stared across the table at him. "What happened?"

"Guess you could say I came to my senses." He grinned, aiming for hearty but falling flat. "No offense."

She refused to let him off the hook that easily. "Tell me." And so he did.

It happened in North Carolina, of all places, while he was in business school at Duke. She was there too, a beautiful, curly-headed, level-minded law student from Chapel Hill. They were together for more than a year. All the other graduate students knew about them, but he never told any of his friends. They were deeply in love. Then the end of school loomed near and she began talking about marriage.

"And you didn't want to marry her?"

Luther seemed dimmed, though he was still trying for breezy remembrance. "I couldn't marry her."

She had to ask why not—although she knew the answer and did not particularly want to hear it.

"We don't live in this world by ourselves, Lee. I had an obligation— have an obligation—to do the right thing. All those black basketball players and football players and entertainers running around with white girls. What does that say to the world? That as soon as one of us gets anything we have to run after some white women, because secretly that's what we all want?"

The waiter approached, saw the expressions on their faces, retreated. Lee, feeling slightly desperate, said, "But didn't you love her?"

Luther shook his head, shaking the question off. Irrelevant. "There are too many of us shucking our responsibilities, too many brothers in jail or strung out or simply refusing to marry the mothers of their children. We need strong, black families. We need to expand the black middle class." He shook his head again, his mouth a determined line.

"Bottom line? It wouldn't have been fair to either one of us. And everyone I know would have considered it a betrayal. Including you. Or so I thought at the time."

Lee winced because she knew he was right. Had he invited her to the wedding she would have gone, but she would not have been pleased. She would have considered his choice a sign of contempt, for himself, for her, for everything black. She'd been jealous when he married Monique, jealous and lonely and a little afraid of being left alone. She was jealous when Luther chose Monique, but had Monique been white she would have hated both of them.

Across from them a table of businessmen pushed back their chairs and stood, shaking hands and slapping backs. One of them walked over to chat with Luther. When he was gone, she asked Luther, "Why didn't you ever ask me out?"

Clearly not the question he expected. He fumbled the golden credit card he'd pulled from his calfskin wallet, dropping it onto the floor beneath his seat.

"Why do you ask?"

She wasn't sure. Sleeping with Porter was not a betrayal of black men, not a giving up, as Luther had suggested. It wasn't, no matter what he said. But even if it was . . . could she be blamed? Hadn't brothers like Luther given up on her first? How many black men had she known who tripped climbing over women like her and Pauline to get to . . .

Lee stopped herself. She wasn't going down that street. "Never mind," she said. "Forget it."

He walked her to her car, passing an electronics store along the way. There was a television in the window showing a tennis match. Boris Becker heaved and danced his way across a green slash of tennis court. Luther paused in front of the store, stared at the television. "He's married to a black woman, you know."

"Is this going to be the gist of every conversation from now on? Are you going to keep a running tab of interracial relationships for my benefit?"

Luther laughed and put his arm around her waist. "No. But I admire Becker. I mean, he's German, he's one of their national heroes, and he married a black woman. Think about the courage that took!"

"Yeah, right."

"I'm serious."

She looked at him in amazement. He was serious. They walked on, and Luther turned the conversation to something else. She let it go. She was too tired for another round, and anyway, what was the point? He admired Becker but not her. Becker was a hero and she was a traitor and a whore. What about Becker's wife, who was, presumably, also German (they had some blacks in Germany, right?) or European of some kind. What was she, heroine or whore? A whore to black men and white women, a heroine to black women and white men? Or vice versa or some other combination? The possible permutations were endless, but one thing was becoming clear: where you stood on the issue depended upon with whom you lay.

The next night she and Porter fought for the first time. The fight was about Ronald Reagan, ostensibly, but really it was about race. Whenever they discussed race Porter was a good journalist: empathetic but uninvolved, removed, an observer but not a participant. He knew the face of racism; he'd covered one or two neo-Klan rallies where the protesters outnumbered the sheets, heard his share of invective spewing from small-minded cops and mob guys and skinhead 'hood boys in the north. He'd unearthed his parents' smoothed-over suburban prejudice and rid himself of it. He took people one by one as they came.

At first Lee thought this was all standard issue, the line white people used with black people to declare themselves. But as she got to know Porter better she realized he really believed it. He genuinely thought himself free of preconceptions, which was much more dangerous.

Porter considered himself liberal. He disliked Bush, scoffed at people who considered Ronald Reagan the savior of mighty America. But it was theoretical to him, a game he enjoyed playing because he could not lose. He didn't understand why she wanted Clinton to win the presidency so much she prayed for it.

"Politicians are all the same," he said.

"That's so cynical."

"It's not cynical. It's skeptical," he said. "There's a difference."

He was using his cool, lecturing journalist's voice, and it infuriated her. "Some of us don't have the luxury of being what you call skeptical," she said. "Twelve years of Reagan-Bush has been a nightmare for us. We have to believe Clinton would be better."

"We?"

She was agitated and so, for a moment, she'd forgotten herself and spoken to the lover instead of the man. But the man would always require explanation; she had to remember that. "For black people," she said slowly. "Reagan and Bush have waged a war against black folks."

They were at his apartment, having a dinner of delivered Chinese food: sesame chicken for him, moo shu chicken for her. It was only the third time she'd been in his place; they spent most of their time together at her house. From her seat at his wobbly, cast-iron table, the kind usually used as patio furniture, she could see the two bookcases in his living room. She ran her eyes over the titles crowding the shelves: Cormac McCarthy, Robert Penn Warren, many journalism books, Hemingway, of course. Not a single black author in the bunch, except for the Toni Morrison book she'd given him.

Porter dropped a chunk of breaded chicken into his mouth and asked, "Do you really believe that? A war?"

"Reagan demonizing black women as welfare queens, Bush using Willie Horton as his campaign manager. What would you call it?"

"I'd call it politics. The Republicans played on the fears of the average white voter because they knew it would work. But if they thought they could win by telling Joe Six-Pack the Martians would land and eat them all unless Republicans control the White House, they'd have done that. Democrats too. It's political, not racial. Not everything is about race."

He said it oh, so casually. She looked at him. The contortions white people would put themselves through to avoid acknowledging the obvious. "So Reagan didn't really believe affirmative action was the other great Satan? He was just saying that to get elected, which is okay."

"I don't think Reagan thought much of anything," Porter said. He seemed not to have heard the last part of her question. "But I believe his advisors thought affirmative action was mostly a good political tool."

"Mostly?"

"Well, I'm sure at least some of them partially believe affirmative action is undemocratic and harmful to both whites and blacks. There is some small nugget of legitimacy to that argument."

"Really?" She smiled. "And you agree with it, I suppose?"

"No, not necessarily," he said. "I'm just saying not everyone who opposes affirmative action is a racist. You have to admit that."

"Do I? Why is it black people always have to give white people the benefit of the doubt? I'm sure not every Nazi really believed the Jews were evil and inferior, but they killed them anyway."

"It's not the same thing."

She was so abruptly furious with him she wanted to hurl her plate. Not the same thing? How dare he sit there in his snug and impervious little white suit and minimize the suffering her people had faced. "The hell it isn't! If somebody's standing over me with a club, I don't have time to give them the benefit of the doubt."

"Don't make this personal."

She stood up. "Oh, right. It's not personal and it's not about race. God forbid! Not everything is about race. Especially if you're white."

He looked startled. Had he even been paying attention before this? She wanted to laugh.

"I don't want to fight with you about this," Porter said.

"I bet you don't. I bet you wish it would all just go away."

"Come on, Lee."

"Because you don't know what you're talking about. You don't have to live with it. You haven't had to work twice as hard to be given half the credit. Did your high school biology teacher tell you white people's brains were smaller than black people's, hmmm?"

"Okay."

"Did your guidance counselor tell you not to bother applying to college, you'd never finish anyway? Did your brother get accused of stealing by some white woman when he was thirteen, and nearly get sent to jail, even though the guy who actually did it was a foot shorter and two shades darker, but the only thing the woman saw was black? Hmm? Did that ever happen to you, Porter, dear?"

"Okay, okay."

He held up his hand in surrender, but she was rolling now, not even thinking about what she was saying, reaching not only into her own life, blurring the line because the larger truth was more important than the small. "Did your parents get chased out with bats when they tried to buy a house in the wrong neighborhood? Was your grandmother raped by a white man and everybody knew about it but nobody did anything and your grandfather had to leave town simmering, emasculated, because if he stayed and looked at the white man's face he'd have to kill him and then he'd be dead?"

Porter was standing now, trying to reach her. "Lee. Stop."

"Fuck you!"

On the way out of the room she stumbled over a stack of books on the floor, nearly blinded as she was by rage and tears. He caught her just as she was trying to open the front door.

"Lee!" He grabbed her arm, spun her to face him. "Wait."

She made her voice still and cold. "Let me go."

"I'm sorry."

"Let me go."

"You're right. I know you're right. I don't even know why I was arguing."

"I do. The truth always comes out when we're drunk or pissed off." She threw open the door and went into the hallway, half hoping he would follow her. He did.

"I wasn't pissed and it's not the truth. I was arguing the point. I didn't realize you were taking it so seriously."

She jabbed at the elevator button. "Leave me alone."

One of Porter's neighbors came out of her apartment with a poodle in her arms and joined them at the elevator. "Beautiful day," she said. They ignored her.

"You want me to beg?" Porter dropped to his knees. "I'm sorry. Please forgive me."

The dog went into a frenzy, barking and yelping as though hurt. The neighbor, clutching wildly, began backing away.

"Get up," Lee whispered to Porter, embarrassed. But he would not.

"I'm an idiot! I'm sorry."

"Fiji! Calm down!" The neighbor smiled awkwardly. "We really should take the stairs."

"Get up!"

"Not until you forgive me."

"Lord knows I certainly could use the exercise!" The woman reached the stairwell door and fled.

In spite of herself Lee began to laugh. "They're going to kick you out of this building!"

Porter got to his feet, dragging her into his arms. "I don't care."

She let him pull her back into his apartment, through the living room, to the unmade surface of his bed. His tongue found the hollow of her neck, the honey pot he called it. But even as she lay there, surrendered to the sensation, Lee thought about what had just taken place. It was their first fight. She'd picked it. She'd picked it and she'd won. As Porter kissed her, victory's weight pressed down upon her chest. The first fight established the power grid in a relationship; it set the tone for every fight to come. Lee won their first fight not because she was persuasive or insistent or even right, but because the battle had been about race.

She saw she would always win battles about race because she possessed the more powerful weapon: three hundred years of genocide, oppression, and immoral injury. If Porter was the man she hoped, if he was miraculously uninfected by America's racism, he was too lightly armed against her. She would crush him every time. And when a black woman dated a white man every fight had the potential to devolve into a battle about race. She wouldn't even have to do it deliberately or manipulatively; it could just happen. You never knew.

If, on the other hand, Porter was the man she feared he was, then he was well prepared to defend himself. The unforgivable word was his bomb, and in any loose moment of fury or disgust he might easily, carelessly, drop it upon her. She would have to remain forever alert, waiting, listening, holding her breath. *Nigger! Spade! Black bitch!* With these words Porter might not win the war but he would end it. Once released, his bomb would level the city and poison the landscape. Nothing could live there again.

Chapter 16

He woke up grinning. He grinned in the shower and on his way to work and at his desk, thinking of her. Even once while interviewing a city councilman about election reform—deadly dull stuff—he began day-dreaming and grinned despite himself. "I'm glad to see I'm amusing you," the councilman said huffily.

He couldn't help it. He was dazed with Lee, dizzy with her, full and fat and shiny with her. He was infatuated, completely. She occupied every thought and every pore and every cell of him. He loved seeing her and kissing her and stroking her and finding her in his bed at dawn. He loved talking to her and making her laugh and watching her as she drove her car.

He found himself looking forward to that part of being in a relation-ship that he had mostly tolerated before meeting her: the slow spilling of secrets, the unveiling of selves, the recitation of childhood hurts and dreams. In this, though, Lee was less forthcoming than many women he'd dated, less eager to spill. She told him about her life since college, about the newspapers where she'd worked and the beats she'd held and the battles she'd fought, but when he asked about her childhood the words slowed. All she would say was that her mother had gone through a difficult period when her father left but recovered and raised Lee and her brother alone.

"She sounds like a very strong woman," he said.

"Of course," she said, with something, some tone in her voice, he could not identify. "Aren't we all?"

He loved the way she challenged him, the way she never let him get away with a lazy thought or an assumption, the way she made him open his mind and think differently. At work he was pulled off his regular assignments to spend a month writing a long, insightful piece about the Los Angeles riots and their implications and aftermath. "Who better than you?" the editors asked. And so he spent a week in L.A. walking the streets where he'd been beaten six months before. He interviewed black community leaders, gang members, Korean store owners, city councilmen, sociologists and psychologists at UCLA. He went to the homes of people who'd been beaten, and listened while they talked bitterly of anger or resolutely of forgiveness and moving on. He told only one person his own story, a Korean pharmacist who'd been smashed in the head with bricks but who was saved by a black man, an actor on his way to movement class. The Korean man sat in a chair by the window, wrapped in a white cotton shawl, while his wife brought him tea and wiped the saliva that gathered on his chin. He drifted in and out of lucidity, at one moment delineating the damaged sections of his brain and in the next moment staring into space. But he listened intently to Porter's entire story and at the end said, *"Aigo chukketta."*

Porter turned to the wife, who translated blank-faced and without elaboration: "I could just die."

Porter flew home to Philadelphia and wrote ten thousand words and everyone raved and gushed, everyone except Lee. She said he failed to separate the meaningful political protests that took place from the looting and street violence. "Also, the problem isn't just that these kids who looted are 'locked outside the American Dream,' " she said, taking one of the phrases he had used. "The problem is how deeply they've bought into that dream, which is about consumerism and materialism. They're pissed not only because of the police, but because they don't have more stuff. Society has told them having stuff is what freedom is all about in this country. And so they looted. Get somebody to say that."

"Who?"

"Call bell hooks." And so he did and she gave him an interview, and those few paragraphs, he thought, raised the piece out of the usual mushy-liberal-analytical newspaper swamp and made it snap. He loved that.

Together he and Lee saw the movie *The Crying Game,* which everyone was raving about. Lee said she knew almost immediately the character Dil was a man but, unlike most of America, she found that aspect of the movie less interesting than its exploration of what happens when a person at war humanizes the enemy. They saw the movie *Husbands and Wives* because he liked Woody Allen, but Lee said Allen should get his head out of his ass. "All that sniveling," she said, dismissing Allen. "The unexamined life may not be worth living, but the overly examined life will make you nuts. Not to mention useless to the rest of society." He loved that idea.

He loved how fierce she was, how self-possessed and confident, and he loved how he was able to get inside of that and see her tender side. When he saw her in the cafeteria line, regal and a little aloof—that was her tag already—he'd think of her in his bed. He loved the wet look of her skin against his sheets. He loved how she looked at him dead-on when he took her wrists and held them above her head and kissed her breasts. He would watch her in the newsroom, leaning over the editor's desk, and he'd want to go over and take her hand and lead her into a closet somewhere. Sometimes he'd want her so badly it made him ache.

She dressed conservatively at work, but he knew what lay beneath the jackets and tailored pants and he loved it. He imagined a body like ripe fruit, firm and full of juice. From the waist down Lenora was soft and voluptuous, but she had the broad shoulders and rippled back of an athlete. He loved her hips and her heavy brown breasts with their sable nipples, so different from the shades of pink and rose he was accustomed to. He admired her curves openly and often and loved that she accepted his compliments; a woman who did not in some way despise her body was a revelation to him. Lee was not vain about her looks, but neither did she obsess about them the way so many women he knew did, the way Chira had. She never asked if she looked fat; she seemed to accept her hips and thighs and sweet, round ass as gifts instead of enemies to be defeated. She worked out at a gym three times a week to be healthy, she said, not to lose weight. "This is the way black women are shaped," she said. "It's natural and beautiful and I refuse to let Madison Avenue make me feel otherwise. Besides, most black men like women with a little meat on their bones."

"Not just black guys," he said. "Some white guys too."

She winked at him. "I'll have to take your word on that."

If there was one crimp in his happiness with her, it was her constant references to race. She seemed very nearly obsessed with the color of her skin.

Some days it was barely present, and then some days he felt race as a scrim she kept hanging between them. When he said it didn't matter, the color of her skin didn't matter at all to him, she would laugh or shake her head or just look at him as if he'd asked where babies came from. Race was a constant with her, in thought and in deed. She was a member of the National Association of Black Journalists, contributed to the NAACP and UNCF, bypassed six other gas stations to buy gas at one owned by a black man, looked for black clerks in every store and refused to shop in those with none.

This obsession perplexed and worried him. And, although he understood it on an intellectual level—oppression, racism, a consciousness of being "the other," et cetera—sometimes it just got to be too damn much. Couldn't she just let it go? Did she have to seek out a black doctor? Did she have to count the number of stories about Africa in the paper every Sunday? Did she have to breathe a sigh of relief when it turned out the latest perpetrator of the latest hideous crime was white instead of black? Did she have to see race *everywhere* they went? Once, as they were coming out of an exhibit on Henry Tanner at the Museum of Art, they passed a couple on the steps. The woman was white, the man black. They were holding hands.

"Cute baby," Lee said after the couple had passed. Porter looked back and saw that the man had a small infant strapped to his chest in a baby carrier. He hadn't noticed because of the man's jacket, and because babies, in general, were not on his radar screen.

"Yeah," he said, absentmindedly. "I wonder if we can get into Claudio's for dinner tonight?"

Claudio's was very "hot" and mobbed when they arrived, but they breezed past the line and right to a table because Porter had once done a favor for the manager. He was feeling pretty proud of himself as they sat scanning their menus when Lee said, "So what do you think about biracial children, anyway?"

"Excuse me?"

"Don't freak out—I'm not proposing anything. Just curious."

Porter took a sip of martini. It was cool and tangy and delicious and he was feeling fine. He didn't want to talk about race. "I'm pro any kind of children," he said. "But I don't think they let them in here. No high chairs."

Lee smiled. "But seriously. You ever thought about it?"

"I like children," he said. "I hope to have some someday."

"But what if the children you had were black? Or considered black by society?"

"That would be fine." He had a sinking feeling he was losing his buzz, so he finished his drink and signaled the waiter for another.

"Really? What do you think your mother would say?"

"She'd throw up her hands in joy that I finally got married," he said, though he knew this was a lie. But who cared what his mother thought?

"And how would you feel?" Lee pressed. "How would you feel getting the hairy eyeball from the lady in the grocery store? How would you feel escorting your little mocha daughter to school?"

Across the room a roar of laughter went up from a table full of beautiful young things, Marvin Gaye was playing in the background, and somebody turned it up. Porter took Lee's hand and looked directly into her eyes; he wanted her to get this, to know it the way he did. "I'd feel fine," he declared, trying to lay it to rest. "I'd feel proud."

Some days he felt as if she were condescending to him, or even lecturing. One night three months after they'd begun to date seriously she came to bed wearing a blue silk scarf tied around her head. "Ah, Gypsy Rose Lee," he said, and nuzzled her cheek. "Very sexy."

She laughed. "Well, thank you, sir. But I'm not wearing it to look sexy. It's to keep my hair from breaking as it rubs against the pillowcase. Contrary to the myth, black hair is very fragile. More fragile than white."

"I never noticed you wearing a scarf to bed before."

She shrugged. "I didn't feel . . . comfortable. But finally I decided if you were going to walk out on me over a scarf I should know that now."

He smiled and kissed her passionately to show he wasn't that kind of an asshole, but inside he felt a little hurt.

The whole hair thing, he was discovering, was a thicket. Lee's hair was short and straightened by whatever mysterious, mystical chemical process black women used to transform their hair in that way. It was, moreover, astonishingly dense. For every hair on his head she probably had ten, crowded into more or less the same amount of space. He had never before been so close to a black person's hair, had never touched it, and he was curious, but his curiosity embarrassed him and seemed to alternately amuse and irritate her. When, for example, he asked as casually as he could why she put what appeared to be green petroleum jelly on her hair, she laughed and refused to give him a straight answer. "Mostly to confound white people," she said. But when he tried to stroke Lee's hair she usually found a reason to move away.

"Don't you like me touching your hair?" he finally asked.

"I'm sorry. It's not you. It's just one of those things."

"What things?"

She laughed, embarrassed. "Oh, you know."

"No, I don't."

"It's just hard not to think of those canards. You know, white people rubbing black people's hair for luck, that kind of thing. Haven't you ever heard of that?"

He had, but only dimly. It was, he thought, one of the less violent indignities southern rednecks used to inflict upon black people forty or fifty years ago. Something Joe would know about probably, as ridiculous and outdated as thinking that women were too emotional to drive.

"Don't tell me someone has ever tried to rub your hair for luck?" He didn't believe it.

"Not for luck so much as just to feel the texture. Especially when I used to wear it natural and short, this tiny little Afro. People would just reach out and rub my head, as if I were a toy or a dog. This old white minister I was interviewing once did it. I knew it was coming. I saw him staring at my head and I tried to move away, but he was quick. Zoom! Out came the hand."

Porter was astonished. Did people actually act like that? "What did he say?"

"Oh, I don't remember." Lee rolled her eyes and flicked away the minister with a wave of her hand. "Something like 'Your hair is wonderful. It's so soft.' That's usually what people say. 'It's so soft.' As though they were expecting steel wool."

He was stung. The first time he touched her hair he had, in fact, noted its softness but not because he was expecting steel wool. He hadn't expected anything, although he loved running his hands through a woman's hair when they were making love and he had, he realized now, worried in some dim recess of his mind that this pleasure would be diminished with Lee. As it turned out, he loved the thickness of her hair, the full, springy liveliness of it and the way it seemed to vary in texture from day to day. He loved touching her hair, but here she was relegating him to the same cast as some horny old fart.

"Well, if you don't want me touching your hair, I won't," he said.

She took his hand. "No, no. I didn't mean that. I like that you like touching it."

She was clearly trying to make up, but he was still hurt and so he said, "I'm not 'people.' "

"I know," she said. "I know."

But sometimes it seemed "people" or, rather, "white people" was exactly who he was to her. One Sunday as they sat over bagels and coffee Lee began reading out loud a national story about a California man who had walked into the engineering firm where he used to work, chatted with the receptionist for a few minutes, then pulled out a gun and opened fire, killing her and six other people in the room. Her contention was that black people never committed crimes of that type. "Black people don't go mowing down innocent victims deliberately."

"What about those two gang-bangers last month who killed that six-year-old girl?"

"That wasn't deliberate. She got caught in the cross fire. I'm not saying they're not just as responsible for her death, or just as horrible for being so completely careless of human life. I'm just saying these crazy, random shoot-outs are almost always middle-aged white guys, and yet no one goes around talking about how dangerous and criminally minded middle-aged white guys are. I'm just making a point."

He should have let it drop but he didn't and before he knew it the conversation had ricocheted onto serial killers, the existence of evil, the Holocaust, and finally the big one: slavery. He ended as he always did, feeling defensive, as though he were on trial, as though he should stand up and apologize for all the crazy, festering, gun-toting middle-aged white guys in the world, as if he should apologize for the entire evil, rapacious, limp-dicked, and lustful race.

Political conversations—difficult topics for two journalists in an election year to avoid—were especially dangerous. As he had learned time and time again. Once she asked, "Did you ever see Clinton around a group of black people?"

"I covered a campaign stop at a black church when he was there."

"Did you notice how he seemed?"

"He seemed like any other politician. Working the crowd."

"No, not Clinton. I saw him at a black church too once. He was unlike any white politician I have ever seen, really clapping his hands to the music, not just clacking them together like two chunks of wood. He was completely comfortable. He loved it. He was grinning so much I thought he might get to shouting."

"Why would he shout?"

She'd looked at him and laughed. "Get to shouting—get happy. Start dancing in the aisles. Feel the presence of the Holy Ghost. Anyway, have you ever seen Bush around a bunch of black people?"

"I can't recall."

"I saw him at a White House reception for the NAACP once. He was excruciatingly uncomfortable. He looked like someone had a gun at his back." She laughed again. "It's typical. One or two of us in a room is fine, but put the average white person in a room full of black people and watch how they quiver."

He moved closer to her then, kissing the back of her neck. "Like this?"

"Seriously," she said. "Doesn't matter how 'nice' the black people are, either. I mean what did Bush think—the president of the NAACP was going to jump him in the Rose Garden?"

He put his lips to hers, not to silence her, no, but just to still her for a moment, for a while. Bed was the one place race never came between them, the one place skin was skin. Once, lying spooned to her in bed after making love in the wake of some ridiculous tiff, he kissed the damp base of her neck where her hair always returned first to its wiry, true self.

He whispered, "See? None of that other stuff is important. In the end, there's nobody here but you and me."

Chapter 17

She woke up smiling on Election Day and went to vote hopeful, a sensation so strange and unexpected she barely recognized it. That Bill Clinton, a candidate for whom she would vote, might actually win the White House was strange enough; it had happened in her adult, voting life. That she was really, really rooting for him and not just casting an anybody-but-the-other-guy vote was downright astonishing And she *was* rooting for him, despite all the years of cynicism about politicians and dashed hopes. She found herself willing to take a chance on Clinton, not only with her vote but also with her belief. Maybe this candidate would be different. Maybe this president would deliver, and in delivering would redeem the ones who came before. At six o'clock, when the editors had pizza delivered to the newsroom, she telephoned her brother, Marcus, to make sure he'd gone to vote. "Yeah, yeah I did," he said. "But listen, Lee. I got a tip about Dad. He might be in Sante Fe. What do you think?"

What she thought was there was no earthly reason to believe their father was in Sante Fe and little reason to go out there even if he was. What she was beginning to realize was that Marcus needed to go anyway. "At least make a vacation out of it," she said. "Take your girlfriend. Have a good time."

Marcus hesitated. Then, "Okay, who are you and what have you done with my sister?" Together they laughed.

At eight o'clock, when things looked good, she telephoned her mother from the newsroom, cupping her hand around the telephone to conceal her excitement. Breathlessly Eda informed her that she and her boyfriend, Mr. Carter, had spent the day taking senior citizens to the polls and were now headed to the local Democratic headquarters to watch the returns and celebrate. "Sorry, baby, can't talk!" Eda cried. "We're running out. Don't you work too hard tonight!"

At nine o'clock, when things looked better, she called Pauline. "Girl, if this thing happens I'm going outside and dance in the street," Pauline said. "You can dance with me in spirit, since I know you journalists are apolitical."

At ten o'clock, when the polls closed in California and she was jumping on deadline, Cleo telephoned her squealing with glee. "We did it! We did it!" Cleo cried. "He better not forget us, because it was black people who put his butt over the top!"

At eleven, when it was all over but the shouting, Lee looked across the newsroom at Porter and felt her heart somersault with joy. He looked up from his typing and winked. She winked back, not caring who saw. At midnight they walked out together and drove to her house and drank champagne in bed.

Sunday morning. In bed with Porter after making love. Lee stretched luxuriously, then opened her eyes to the clock. "Oh, shoot. I meant to go to church today." It was the fourth Sunday in a row she'd missed church, unusual for her. "You're a bad influence on me."

Porter lay beside her, flat on his back with his arms behind his head, as though swinging in a hammock on a lazy Saturday afternoon. The reddish brown hair of his armpits stuck out in arrogant little tufts, spiky and adamant, unlike her hair, which in its natural state curled protectively in upon itself.

"What time does church begin?" Porter asked.

"Ten."

He raised his head slightly to view the clock. "It's only nine-fifty. If you hurry, you can still make it."

She ran her hand over his shoulders. "I'm fairly efficient but it does take me longer than ten minutes to get dressed. Plus, it's a fifteen-minute drive from here."

"Can't you be late?"

She could. Her church almost never began worship precisely on time, and even if they did, the first fifteen minutes or so would be spent in singing and raising the Spirit and praising God and testimony, parts of the service she loved but that could be missed. The truth was, she could walk in anytime up until the preacher began his sermon and still reap the spiritual benefits. And she wouldn't be the only one either, slipping in a back pew or sneaking up the aisle, head lowered, hand raised in apology. But it seemed somehow sinful to leap up from having sex and rush to church. And she wasn't going to get into a discussion about CP time with Porter. "I'll go next week."

"Maybe I could go with you."

She started to laugh but choked it off when she realized he was serious. She imagined herself striding into service at Grace Baptist Church, dressed to the nines in her gray woolen suit, trailing Porter who, as far as she could tell, did not own a suit. She tried to imagine what the congregation would think of him. She'd read a story in the *New York Times* about the popularity of Sunday morning Harlem tours among European tourists, who liked to sit in the back of black churches with their cameras and watch the locals perform. Would the mothers and fathers of her church think Porter was like one of those tourists? Would they despise her for bringing him? The people in her church were Christians, of course, and they tried, most of them, to live up to the name. But they were also black people, and they didn't stop being black people when they set foot inside the church. For many of them the church was still the only place they were accorded the dignity and respect they deserved. One Sunday, after the preacher preached a sermon on brotherhood, she overheard Deacon Baxter say, "White man may not be the devil, but he sure took a lot of lessons from him." At that time hearing such words from such a genteel old man had made her smile.

"You want to come to church with me?"

"Sure."

"Why?"

"I think it would be interesting."

At the word "interesting" she sat up. "I thought you were an atheist?"

She had not been surprised to hear this declaration from him. Like many white men, Porter was his own deity. In some ways, she'd been relieved to learn he did not believe in God. It was just another reason they could never be serious.

"More of an agnostic," he said dreamily, still flat on his back, examining her ceiling. "I don't rule out the existence of God."

"But you don't rule it in, either."

"I'd like to believe. The times I've seen you after church, the times I've come over here on Sunday, you always seem so peaceful and happy and stilled. I envy it. And I realize my own questioning is a kind of luxury."

There was something in this that made her itch with irritation. "What do you mean, a luxury?"

"I just mean black people, historically, have needed to believe. They've had precious little else, so it makes sense they'd have to hang on to a sense of faith."

She leaned to search among the clothes on the floor for the T-shirt she slept in. She'd taken it off—or he'd taken it off—while they were making love. "So you're saying the reason I have faith is because my poor, downtrodden ancestors needed to believe in a better life while they were wasting this one picking cotton in Massa's field?"

Porter was still stretched out, eyes half-closed in contemplation, and so must not have heard the tone of her voice. "Even when my mother did drag me to church as a child, for purely social reasons, I never felt anything. Nobody else seemed to either. I think that's the difference between white churches and black churches. White churches are so intellectual."

"And black churches are . . ."

"So much more alive. More passionate, more emotional. More . . . soulful."

She shook her head. "I think you're trying to compliment me, but I think you'd better stop before you compliment us right into a fight."

That woke him up. Sat him up. "What? What did I say?"

"The white church is more intellectual? The black church is more soulful?"

"Yeah?"

"Intellectual meaning intelligent and soulful meaning not. Meaning primitive."

"Don't put words in my mouth."

"Don't sit in my bed and trade in racist stereotypes."

He gasped, sputtered, started to say something, then stopped and took a deep breath. She could tell he was fighting hard to control himself. "Are you saying"—he let out his breath—"you don't think black churches are, in general, more soulful than white churches? That black people don't—by dint of history or tradition or whatever, *not* lack of intellect—worship in a way that is more spiritual than white people?"

"What white people? What about white southern Pentecostals? Don't they stomp and sing?"

"Okay okay!" Porter was up now, looking around for his shorts. It was as though they both needed to be dressed to fight. "I'm speaking in generalities, but that doesn't invalidate anything. Come on, Lee. Can you tell me you don't think white Protestant churches don't distance God? Are you telling me you don't believe black churches are, in general, more soulful than white?"

What could she say? He was right; she did believe exactly those things. How many times had she, attending a white church for work or the wedding of a colleague, rolled her eyes at all that atonal, dispassionate, mumbled singing, those hymns like funeral dirges, the minister reading his sermon from cards, all that standing and sitting on cue, no spontaneity, no spirit, no soul? Still. It was different when he said it, wasn't it? There was something unpleasant in his "luxury of disbelief," something patronizing in his I-wanna-go-so-I-can-stop-thinking-and-feel.

"Let's forget it," she said, standing up.

"I don't want to forget it. I want to talk about it. You're upset."

"I'm not upset. Really." She kissed him to prove her point. She was upset but she wasn't sure she had a right to be. What she wanted most was not to talk about it anymore until she'd figured it out. "Why don't we get dressed and get a paper and go to brunch?"

On Wednesday Pauline called. She was back from Brazil and wanted to drive up for the weekend. But Lee already had plans with Porter, and before she knew it the lie slipped out. "Sorry. I'm working."

"That sucks. I thought you weren't going to have to pull any weekend shifts?"

"Yeah, well, you know. They promise one thing but deliver another."

"See? That's why I told you to get all those promises in writing." Besides being an M.B.A., Pauline held a law degree. She got everything in writing. If the dry cleaner promised to have her clothes ready on Wednesday, she made him write it down. "Then you'd have something to throw in their faces."

"The news business is a little more unpredictable than banking," Lee said, trying to change the subject. This wasn't something she wanted to discuss with Pauline. Pauline was like a hound dog with the truth; if she sniffed around long enough she'd find it eventually. "For one thing, we don't get to leave at three o'clock."

"Please. The last time I left work at three o'clock was 1986. Anyway, this can't be some news emergency. It's only Thursday and they're already telling you they want you to work on Saturday. They have time to find someone else."

Lee scanned the newsroom, trying to catch some editor's eye. Then she looked down at her phone, willing her other line to ring. "It's no big deal."

"It's breach of contract," Pauline said indignantly.

"Forget it, Pauline."

There was a pause, then Pauline said, "Lee, are you okay?"

"What?" She was barely paying attention, focused instead on trying to find a way to end the conversation.

"Are you okay? Is everything all right? You've been acting strange."

Lee's heart did a skid. She'd been about to fake another call to get off the phone but now she decided she'd better give Pauline some time. "Sorry. Just really, really busy. So, how was Brazil? Did you and Andrea have fun? Tell me all about it!"

She was surprised this bald tactic worked. Pauline was not usually so easily distracted, but she must have really wanted to talk about Brazil because she spent the next ten minutes detailing her trip. The beach, the Rio nightlife, the gorgeous men. "And we went on this riverboat cruise," she said.

"Really?" Lee tried to sound interested.

"To this place called the Meeting of the Waters. It's where the Rio Negro, which is so dark it's almost black, meets the Rio Solimões, which is milky brown, the color of coffee with cream. They meet, but they're so different ecologically they don't mix. I have pictures of them: black on one side, light on the other."

"They don't mix?" Lee asked, and now she was interested. This was interesting.

"They just bump up against each other and flow side by side down the riverbank."

"Forever? All the way out to the sea."

"Well, for four miles," Pauline admitted. "Then they finally do mix somehow and become the Amazon. But it's amazing to see. You should have been there."

Pauline was right; Lee should have been there. She imagined Pauline and Andrea standing in the sun aboard some riverboat, watching the two little waterways collide and fight and finally merge to become the mightiest river in the world. It was the kind of thing Pauline loved, the wild, astonishing complexity of nature. Whenever they traveled together, it was Pauline who wanted to hike down the canyon, see the red rocks, visit the waterfall. Lee, who was more interested in museums and jazz clubs, would go along and always be glad. Pauline probably marveled in the Meeting of the Waters, and Lee would have marveled in it with her. She should have been there. She missed her friend.

"I'm sorry I missed the trip," Lee said. And she was. "I'll call you soon, Pauline. I will. Maybe next weekend I can come down."

Hanging up the phone, she knocked over a soda, splashing it all over her desk. It took her two trips to the bathroom and ten minutes of wiping to mop up the mess and even then she didn't feel clean. Her foot kept finding little sticky spots on the floor all afternoon.

That Saturday she and Porter went leaf watching in Bucks County—her idea. Lee loved autumn: loved the air, the trees, the crackling, flaming arrogance of it all. Forty minutes north of the city they hit countryside violent with color. She stared out the window, trying to take in all the beauty, to store it up. They lunched in New Hope at a vegetarian cafe with a terrace overlooking the Delaware River, then spent the afternoon cruising antique stores and picking apples at an orchard.

Back home they decided to stay in for the night and ordered Chinese food. Awaiting delivery, they sat on the couch and kissed—long, hard, feverish kisses, the kind teenagers kissed when kissing was all they were going to accomplish that night. That she actually enjoyed kissing Porter was one of the relationship's little revelations. His bottom lip was fuller than those of most white men (at least of those she'd ever noticed), and although his upper lip was wanting, at least he knew what to do with it. She felt strange when she thought about the times she and Pauline had dismissed white men with their miserly lips and miserly dicks.

The doorbell rang midkiss. "Food," Porter said, pulling back from her with a dazed expression. "Guess we better eat."

"We might need our strength later on."

While Porter went to the door she went upstairs to the bathroom to put in her diaphragm. She didn't much like the diaphragm: it was messy, intrusive, less reliable than the pill even when used properly (and she always used it properly), and when they had sex during the daytime, and they did frequently, she had to walk around for the next six hours with the thing stuck up inside her like a plug. But she'd gone off the pill after Howard to give her body a breathing spell, a chance to reclaim its own rhythm, and though she'd thought about going back on since Porter, she had not, for some reason, gotten around to it. Maybe she needed that little disk of rubber between them, especially now that they'd stopped using condoms. (*How* had that happened? She knew the answer, of course: he'd broken his last one and offered to go out for more but she'd kissed him and said, never mind, and that was that. *But how?*) Maybe the pill lent a relationship an air of permanence she knew this one could not have.

She stuck the pink diaphragm box (why pink?) back into the cabinet, washed her hands, looked into the mirror. Her eyes were bright and her color up, as Eda used to say, her skin burnished and inner lit. And she was smiling again, as though someone had just told her something wonderful. The face of a woman in lust, she guessed, thinking of Porter downstairs waiting. A woman in lust. Though she'd been in lust before and not smiled like this. Okay, the face of a woman in heavy lust. The face of a woman trying to figure out the face of a woman. Lee laughed out loud. Maybe all it was was that she'd had too much to drink. She splashed cold water on her face, applied moisturizer, rubbed Vaseline on her bruised and stinging lips. Then, with a last grin at herself, she opened the door and stepped into the hall.

Porter's voice floated up from downstairs; he was talking to someone. She assumed he was on the telephone, probably talking to the copy desk, although she didn't remember him saying he had a story running the next day. It wasn't until she was about to step back into the living room that she heard another voice. A woman's voice. An instantly familiar voice. Pauline.

"Oh, no," Pauline was saying as Lee entered the room, "she was definitely not expecting us."

They stood, Pauline and Cleo, not ten feet inside the doorway, as though they had advanced that far but dared not take another step. Both clutched overnight bags, and Porter stood next to them, Chinese food in hand, hair ruffled, and shirt untucked. It was quite a tableau.

"You have visitors," Porter said unnecessarily.

She couldn't think of what to do. She had the urge to tuck in Porter's shirt, as though that would make everything all right. Instead she hugged Pauline and Cleo. They both received her hug but neither put down her bag. "Hey! What are you guys doing here?"

"We decided to drive up for the weekend and surprise you," Pauline said dryly. "Surprise."

She was completely unprepared to deal with this. She'd had two glasses of wine, her guard was down, she had no possible way to explain to her two friends what she was doing in her house with this white man alone on a Saturday night. She just smiled idiotically and stared until Cleo said, to the floor, "Maybe we should go."

Yes, please, go, Lee thought. But Pauline dropped her bag onto the floor with a decisive thump and crossed her arms.

"Don't be silly, Cleo." She smiled. "We drove all this way to see Lee and we're going to see her."

"We should have called."

"Actually we did call, remember?" Pauline was headed for the couch. "We left you three messages at work, Lee. Since you said you'd be working, we figured that was the best way to reach you."

"I was working here," Lee said. "At home." Amazing how quickly the saving lie came to lips, though she hated to lie, felt nauseated doing so.

"Oh, well, that explains it," Pauline said, settling onto the couch. She plumped a pillow and placed it behind her back, then crossed her arms. "Boy, that Chinese food smells good."

"Looks like the two of you were just about to eat," Cleo said.

"Eat?" Her tongue felt thick and clumsy, shot through with Novocain, and she couldn't keep the words from tumbling out, nonsensically. "No. I mean, yeah, but, it's only food."

Porter shot her a strange look, then opened the top of the bag, as if to check its contents. "There's plenty," he said. "You're welcome to—"

"Maybe you should put that in the kitchen." The words tumbled out of her and she heard how harsh they sounded, but what could she do? Everything was moving so fast. Everything except her thoughts; her brain seemed to have stalled in its tracks. She wanted Porter to stop talking. She wanted all of them to just be quiet, be still, stop moving, give her a moment to catch up. Porter stopped rummaging in the bag and tried to catch her eye but she avoided his gaze, and after a moment he went into the kitchen without a sound.

"Lee, what the . . . ," Pauline began. But Porter came swinging back into the room, his face hard and white and angry. His eyes, when he turned them on Lee, were flat and wintry. He had a drink in his hand.

"So." He threw himself onto the couch next to Pauline. "You guys are from Baltimore."

"That's right."

"And you drove all the way up here to see Lenora." Porter gulped angrily at his drink and grinned. "You must be good friends to do something like that."

Pauline looked uncomfortable, but Lee knew she would die rather than shift her position on the couch, giving in to Porter's presence there next to her. "Yes, we are, good friends," Pauline said primly. "Isn't that right, Lee?"

Lee wished hard for a disruption: a knock on the door. Earthquake, fire, flood. The sudden appearance of a crack in the walls into which she might disappear—anything to stop what was happening, what was going to happen, what had now, finally, to take place.

"Friends like that must tell each other everything," Porter said. He looked at Lee. It was like an accident happening before her, two cars colliding in the street. She wanted to speak, to yell, to stop it, but her tongue refused the signals from her brain.

"You would think," said Cleo.

"Everything," Porter said again.

There was a moment of silence, then Pauline launched into the breach. Lee couldn't tell whether her friend was defending her from Porter's anger or helping him turn the screw. "You sound like a lawyer, Mr. . . ."

"Stockman. And, no, I'm not an attorney. Just a lowly journalist."

Pauline looked from Porter to Lee. "Oh, so you two work together?"

"That's right. We're coworkers. Right, Lenora?" He dragged out her name.

"What do you cover?" Pauline asked. But Lee could see Porter was beyond polite conversation. He sat forward on the couch.

"We're colleagues. Associates."

From her spot just inside the front door, Cleo hissed at Pauline, "Do we really need to be here for this?"

"Comrades in arms? Fellow seekers of truth?" Porter hurled himself to his feet. "That's what journalists do, right, Lee?"

"Maybe we *should* go." Pauline stood and took a step away from the couch.

"Yes, we work together. That's what we were doing today, in fact, working together, wasn't it, Lee?" He said this with a dangerous quietness, looking directly at her. She could see the freckles on his nose, tiny sprinkles of color from the strong sun of that afternoon. He hadn't shaved, and the faint, reddish brown hairs of his beard shadowed the bottom part of his face. In all the months they'd been dating she'd thought of him simply as blond, a blond, life and nature's fair-haired boy. But she saw now his hair was really a union of colors, of gold and copper and chestnut and sand. "Wasn't it?"

When she didn't answer he turned from her and said, "We've been putting in a lot of time on a project, a very important one. But it looks like it's over now. We're done."

She took the words one by one like body blows. Looks. Like. It's. Over. Now. Suddenly she remembered a childhood habit of counting days, a habit inherited from her father, who used to rise each morning and mark the number of working days left until the emancipation of Saturday. From him she learned that nothing bad or painful lasted forever, and this is how she got through those years of bad times with her mother after their father left. Whenever her mother began staying up all night and cleaning frantically or came home burdened with things they could not afford, Lee would hide the food money, hide the knives, take care of Marcus, call Aunt Alice if necessary, and count the days. Her mother's episodes never lasted longer than a few weeks.

After a while she got into the habit of counting not only the bad times but also the times in between, when her mother cooked for them and went to work and came home every night. When she got older she realized the value of the lesson: everything, good or bad, sad or wonderful, ended. It was necessary to remember this.

And remember it she did now, standing in her living room while the rules of her adulthood and the escape of the past four months collided before her eyes. Four months with Porter. What fun it was, even wonderful. But it had to end.

Cleo lifted her bag. "I'll warm up the car."

They were all moving about the room, all talking at once. She felt dizzy.

"Please don't leave on my account," Porter said. He moved past her, grabbed his jacket, snapped it angrily through the air.

Pauline. "Lee?"

Porter. "If anyone should leave, it should be me."

Cleo. "Come on, Pauline."

Pauline. "Can you just wait a minute, Cleo? Damn!"

Porter. "Right, Lee?"

Cleo. "She wants us to go. Can't you see that?"

Pauline. "Lee."

Porter. "Do you want me to leave?"

He opened the door; the hinges moaned.

She could keep quiet now and let him leave, and find some lie to tell her friends: she'd slept with him once for kicks, he couldn't take rejection, they were not, of course, in the least bit serious. She could keep quiet and resume the life she'd had before him. Without him. "Porter," she said, surprised at the ravaged sound of her voice. "Please."

He stopped but did not turn around. "That's not enough."

No, it wasn't enough. Taking a breath, she turned to Pauline and Cleo. Pauline looked hurt and confused. Cleo looked horrified. She wanted to wrap them all in her arms, move them back to the beginning, do this again. She would do it so much better than this. "Well, you wanted to surprise me. Surprise!" she joked lamely. No one laughed.

"Porter is my boyfriend." The word *boyfriend* sounded juvenile, but she didn't know what else to say. He was her lover? He was her man. "We're together. We've been together for months."

"No shit," muttered Cleo.

Porter crossed the room and kissed her hard, a man making his claim. She returned the kiss, dizzy with relief, not caring, for the moment, about anything else. Then Pauline said, "Guess this is where we came in."

But she could not let them just leave, of course, couldn't send them hurtling back down Interstate 95 on a Saturday night. She insisted they stay for dinner, at least. Pauline said damn straight they were staying, but Cleo almost had to be strapped into her chair. She calmed down, though, when Porter gallantly offered to grab a sandwich on the way back to his apartment, leaving them the house and the food. Now that the truth was out, splashed like wine across the living room floor, he was willing to cede space for the night.

"Are you sure?" Lee asked, not wanting him to feel pushed away. Not now. Not wanting him, either, to leave her alone with Cleo and Pauline, who were in the dining room, probably listening to every word.

"It's okay." He kissed her forehead, her cheek, her lips. He'd been stroking and kissing her steadily since she claimed him and her head was swimming from it all. She felt completely disordered.

"Are you sure?"

"I don't mind. I'll call you tomorrow."

"I'm sorry for what happened."

"You redeemed yourself in the end," he said, kissing her again.

She watched him go off the porch and through the darkness at the foot of the stairs and into the light from the street lamp. She watched him get into his car and drive away. She watched as long as she could, then she turned around and went inside.

In the dining room, Cleo sat whispering fiercely to Pauline but she stopped when Lee walked in. Both women turned their eyes on her. Pauline put down her fork, chewed the last of her moo shu pancake with great deliberation, slowly wiped her mouth. "Well," she said finally. "Well, well, well."

"Pauline," Lee began, but then stopped. She didn't know what to say. Anyway, Pauline didn't want to hear it, whatever it was. That much was clear. Pauline picked up her glass and swirled the wine and put it down again without taking a sip. "Well, well, well," she said again, accenting each word with one sharp tap of her nail against the table-cloth. Then she crossed her arms and smiled. It was a hallmark gesture. It meant she was pissed.

"And imagine, I was actually worried about you!" Pauline's laugh made Lee flinch. "I thought maybe something was wrong. Maybe the girl is sick, maybe that's why she's been acting so strange these past few months. And if she's so sick she doesn't want to tell me—*me*—then it must be bad. It must really, really be bad."

Lee stared at Pauline, astonished. It had never occurred to her Pauline might be worried; she had not allowed herself to realize how strange her actions must have seemed.

"I was so worried I almost called Eda. But I said, no, let me and Cleo go up there this weekend and see our girl before we do anything else. Maybe she's just having a hard time at work and needs some support. Maybe she's just homesick and doesn't want to say."

Pauline stopped, uncrossed her arms, and took a deep breath. Stress management; she'd been taking a class. That she had to apply what she'd learned here, in the home of her best friend, made Lee feel small.

Pauline exhaled in one, long continuous breath. "I can't believe," she said finally, with no expression at all, "that you lied to me over some guy."

"Some white guy," said Cleo. She threw down her napkin and pushed her chair back from the table, scraping the floor. "I can't believe it! Aren't you the woman who's always talking about uplifting the race, the woman who got on my case because I bought my car from a white car dealer."

"I didn't get on your case. I just said you could have gotten the car from Thomas Chevrolet."

"I didn't want a Chevrolet."

"He has other cars."

"He didn't have the color—"

"Are we talking about cars here?" Pauline interrupted.

"No, we're talking about jungle fever here," Cleo muttered.

Lee felt a wave of anger rise up inside her throat, but fought it down. "It's not like that."

"That's what they all say."

She looked at the girl. Cleo had gotten braids since Lee saw her last, and they spilled into her face, making her look more like the teenager she'd been when they first met. Lee remembered that first year, how ghetto-tough Cleo was, how long it took the girl to lower her defenses, how slowly she edged from suspicion to possibility to openness. The people in mentor programs always said not to be surprised if the young person came to idolize you; it was to be expected, even hoped for. That was part of the deal. What they never told you was what that deal might cost you in terms of living your life.

"I'm sorry if I disappointed you, Cleo."

"Not disappointed," Cleo said coldly. "Just surprised."

But that was a lie, and they both knew it. Cleo *was* disappointed. Disappointment leaked from the girl. Disappointment dripped from her side and flooded the floor and fouled the air and Lee felt sticky with it and sick and tired to her bones. She wanted to turn out the lights and slink upstairs into a hot bath. She wanted to stretch out naked and cleansed beneath the quilt of this revelation she'd had, this declaration of love she'd made, because that was what she'd done. Love. For Porter. She wanted a night, just a night between making her choice and having to defend it. She needed a night. But she wasn't going to get it.

"Look, guys—," Lee began, but Cleo cut her off.

"Can we go?" she asked Pauline.

Pauline shook her head. "I'm not getting on the road at this time of night. Not after two glasses of wine."

"I'll drive."

"You had wine too."

"Just a glass."

"You can't even eat a piece of fruitcake without getting drunk!"

"Guys! Stop!" Lee called. They were sniping at each other when everybody knew she was the real target. "Cleo, just stay. You don't have to listen to me, you don't have to talk, but just stay. It's too late to make that drive."

Cleo kept her face averted, but Lee could see the tears standing in her eyes. She was fighting not to cry. "Fine," she said, not looking at Lee. "Where can I sleep?"

Lee led the girl upstairs to the guest room and flipped on the light. "Here it is!" On any other day Cleo would have admired the hunter green paint, the ceiling fan, the safari feel of the room Lee had worked so hard to achieve. But today she was stone.

"I'll get your towels," Lee said, and went out. When she came back Cleo had not moved an inch. She stood in the middle of the room, still gripping her bag, back to the door.

"I'm just trying to live my life," Lee said hopelessly.

"Good night," Cleo said.

Lee went heavily down the stairs. Pauline had moved to the couch in the living room and was sipping a fresh glass of wine. For just the slightest second, Lee hesitated, then collapsed onto the couch beside her. "You don't mind sleeping down here, do you?" she asked.

Pauline shrugged. "You know me: low maintenance."

"And high quality."

Pauline twisted her mouth, twisted her whole body around on the couch to stare Lee straight in the face. "Bullshit, Lee," she said, and her voice quivered again. "Bullshit! Don't bullshit me."

Lee was full of excuses, of reasons, of explanations. They were all there on her tongue, ready to leap up and defend, but then she remembered a spanking her mother had given her once. It was one of the worst spankings she ever received as a child and it was for telling a lie. She couldn't even remember what lie she'd told or why, but she did remember that Eda was in the end stages of a manic phase at the time. When she learned about the lie, she dug her fingernails into Lee's arm and dragged her outside to the crab apple tree in their backyard and made her pick a switch. Then she whipped her right out there in the yard, for all the world to see and hear; that's how manic Eda was. Later that night her mother came into her room with a glass of milk, her face puffy and red. She had cried harder than Lee. "Sometimes you have to lie to save other people," Eda said, still sniffling. "But you should never lie to save yourself."

Now Lee said, "I'm sorry."

When Pauline did not respond, she went on. "I didn't know you were worried about me. These past months have been . . . crazy and I wasn't thinking straight and I screwed up. I don't know what else to say other than I'm sorry."

Pauline kept her chin high, but Lee sensed a crack in the ice. "So, is it serious?"

Lee waved her hand in dismissal. "Oh, who knows?" she said quickly, but then she remembered again her mother's words and she confessed. "Yes, I think it is."

They sat in silence, and Lee wondered if she had lost her best friend forever. But after a long while Pauline sighed and sank back against the couch and Lee knew she had not.

"Tell me," Pauline said.

It all came out: L.A. and Florida, the first date, the first time sleeping together, the first argument, the whole play-by-play of the relationship and all the second-guessing and all the wondering she'd done. And the feeling tonight, the feeling of rightness at claiming and being claimed.

When Lee had finished, Pauline shook her head. "Will wonders never cease."

"I didn't plan this, Pauline," Lee said. "You know me—this is not something I would have planned!"

"Yeah." For a moment Pauline stared off into space, as if lost in thought. Then she said, "So does Eda know?"

"Are you kidding?"

"That's what I thought."

"She'd probably take it about as well as Cleo."

"Yeah. Well. Cleo's young. When you're young, you think life is black and white. Pardon the pun."

Lee smiled. "Still, you think she might have at least faked some happiness. Considering she's sleeping in my house." This was a feeble attempt at a joke, but Pauline answered as if she'd been serious.

"If you're happy, Lee, I'm happy for you," Pauline said. "But don't expect the world to stand up and applaud your relationship with this man. Don't expect them to even sit through the show."

For the first time that evening Lee allowed herself a flicker of irritation at her friend. "I'm not asking the world to applaud. I'm asking my friends to be happy for me."

"Uh-huh," Pauline said. "Can this friend ask you a question?"

She wanted to scream no! But she said, "Of course."

"Why are you with this guy?"

"What?"

"Why are you with him?"

Lee let out an exasperated laugh. Why was she with him? What kind of question was that? That was the lawyer in Pauline, forcing her into the witness stand about the relationship, putting her on trial. Well, it had been a long, long day and she really didn't feel like getting into it. "I don't know," she said with irritation, hoping to end the conversation. But she knew immediately that was the wrong thing to say to Pauline.

"You don't know."

"I'm with him because I'm with him. Okay?"

"Not okay," Pauline said flatly. "Gotta do better than that."

"What do you mean, 'not okay'?" Lee sat up straight. "Why are you even asking me this? You never asked me why I was with Howard."

"It wasn't an issue with Howard, and you know that, Lee. This is different. You need to understand why you're with this man."

"Pauline, please," Lee said. All of a sudden she couldn't sit still anymore. She got up and went into the dining room to start clearing the table. Pauline followed and stood in the doorway, arms crossed. "Answer the question," she said.

Lee grabbed the chopsticks and shoved them into the bag. "Why were you with Anthony for so long? Why did you go out with Gerald?"

"I liked Gerald. I loved Anthony. But—"

"Well, I like Porter," Lee interrupted. "And yes, he's white, but that has nothing to do with it." She heard Porter's words coming out of her mouth. "Not everything is about race."

Pauline raised her eyebrow but remained silent. Another lawyerly trick.

"Look, I like him, I like him. Isn't that enough?" It was a feeble, pleading attempt to end the conversation, and Lee knew Pauline would knock it to the ground.

"No, it's not enough," Pauline said. "Not in America. Because he is white, some things are about race and when you cross the color line, girl, you damn well better know why."

Chapter 18

"Spend Thanksgiving with me. Come to my parents' house."

He tried to make the invitation sound spontaneous and casual, as though he hadn't spent days thinking it over beforehand. He tried not to make it sound like a reward for finally claiming him before her friends Pauline and Cleo. Or like a ratcheting up of the stakes, a one-upmanship, proof he was willing, even eager, to include her in the full span of his life.

It had been a long, long time since Porter introduced a woman to his parents—partly because he didn't like to subject anyone to that particular brand of torture, but also because no relationship in years had reached that stage. Not since Chira. And it was a stage, at least for women. Most women seemed to rank an introduction to family two small steps below little black boxes on the commitment scale. That he was aware of this, and that he invited Lee anyway, was a signal to himself of how deeply he was beginning to want her. And he hoped a signal to her. He thought she'd be pleased.

But she just looked blankly at him and asked, "Why?"

"Why what?"

"Why do you want me to come?"

It was not the response he'd expected and so he was momentarily taken aback. "I suppose I thought it would be nice for you to meet my family and them to meet you. Isn't that the normal reason people invite people to Thanksgiving dinner? That and to risk salmonella from some undercooked bird."

She reached across the table to squeeze his hand. "Thank you. Really. But I don't think it's a good idea."

They were having dinner at what had become their favorite Vietnamese restaurant. It was far from plush—eight tables, Formica-topped and wobbly, with plastic roses in the bud vases and a picture of a waterfall that actually seemed to cascade above the door and mirrors all around to give the illusion of space, but the food was delicious. Porter watched Lee use her chopsticks to pluck a chunk of spring roll from her bowl and waited for the rest of the joke. But it was clear Lee had no plans to elaborate.

Finally he said, "Okay, I give. Why is it a bad idea? Have I made my parents look that bad? They usually hold it together for company."

Lee smiled. "I'm sure your parents are very nice people. There's just no reason to get them all riled up."

He exhaled, but quietly. He knew where this was going: back to the same worn slice of territory, that same beaten-down path. Didn't she ever get tired of it? "If they're very nice people," he said, "they won't get all riled up. Will they?"

"I don't know. Will they?"

"No. They won't." He spoke without hesitation, as though he were absolutely certain, confident his parents were open-minded, right-thinking people who would look at Lee and see only her beauty and elegance. And he was fairly sure about his father. His father was full of such self-contempt, he had no room left over for disliking anyone else (except his mother, of course). Porter had never heard his father say a word one way or the other about black people. Or Jews or Hispanics or Asians. Besides, Porter could bring home a gorilla and his father wouldn't care, as long as it did not interfere with his drink.

His mother, though. His mother was less open-minded. Not a racist by any means, just limited. She was, after all, from Mississippi originally. Race was rarely discussed in the house when he was a boy; there were no black families in their neighborhood, no black kids in his school until junior high. His mother had absolutely no interaction with black people, zippo. Still, when the issue arose, his mother stated that although Negroes (she persisted in calling them that until the 1970s) were not their kind of people, they were people and should be left alone. Harassing them or bothering them in any way was ignorant, calling them names was common, denying them fair treatment simply wrong. He remembered dimly once watching television at a friend's house (his mother hated television, called it common) when he saw, on the news, a group of black people being attacked with whips and dogs by state troopers for trying to march somewhere. What was most clear to him was that the troopers, the people behaving so horribly, were southern. He went home and asked his mother if all southerners were like that. She seemed upset by the question. "That's trash acting that way," she said insistently. "White trash. Your people do not come from that." Then she left the room. He heard no more about it.

Now he said to Lee, "My parents will be fine. And I'd very much like to spend the day with you."

"I have to go home to Baltimore," she said. "If I don't, my mother will be . . . upset."

"Tell her you have to work."

"You want me to lie to my mother?"

"Okay. Tell her your boyfriend wants you to spend Turkey Day with him."

He knew she hadn't told her mother about him. She knew he knew it. It was something they hadn't talked about until now and he knew she wanted to keep it that way. Lee smiled a capitulating smile.

"Maybe I can figure out a way to do both. Go to Baltimore Wednesday night, have Thanksgiving breakfast, and make it up here in time for dinner. What time do you eat?"

He still wondered what she was going to tell her family but he wasn't going to push it when he'd won. "I'll meet you at your house around three?"

"One condition: you better tell them first. I don't want to show up on the doorstep and be responsible for somebody's heart attack."

He kissed her, assured her neither his mother nor his father was prone to passing out at the sight of black people. But later on, alone in his apartment, he decided telephoning beforehand was probably a good idea. "I'm bringing someone to Thanksgiving," he said as soon as he heard his mother's voice. "Someone special."

"How wonderful, dear. Who is she?"

"She's a reporter. She works with me. Her name is Lenora Page."

"Page? There are Pages in Haverford, is she one of them? A lovely—"

He cut her off. "She's from Baltimore. She's beautiful, intelligent, a wonderful writer, very brave. She saved someone's life while covering the riots in L.A." He decided to leave the details of that particular incident out of the story. One shock a day would be enough for his mother to absorb.

"Really? How brave."

"She's the most amazing woman I've ever met in my life."

"She certainly seems to have impressed you."

"She's very impressive," he said. And there was nothing left to say except that Lee was black, but now that the moment had arrived he was uncertain how exactly to break the news without it sounding like either an apology or a declaration of war. Irritation at his mother buzzed like a mosquito around his head. If she had a problem with Lee's race, she'd just have to deal with it. Making his voice casual he said, "Also, just so you know: she's black."

In the ensuing silence Porter listened hard for some sound to indicate his mother was still present and alive. After a moment he heard a scraping sound, a chair being pulled over the floor, and then a loud and crashing thud. "Mom?" He imagined his mother's smoothly coiffed head meeting the smoothly polished living room floor. "Mom? Are you there?"

"Yes." She cleared her throat, something she always told him never to do. It ruined the vocal cords and was impolite. "Yes," she said again.

"I'm only telling you because she seemed to think it was important that you know. Her color doesn't matter to me."

"No," she answered, as if she'd been shocked into monosyllables.

"I hope it doesn't matter to you, either, Mother."

"No."

"I care about this woman. Very much. Do you understand?"

"Yes."

"Are you sure you're all right?"

"Yes."

"Okay, then. We'll see you Thursday." He started to hang up but heard his mother calling his name. She seemed to have sprung back to life.

"Sorry, dear," she said, laughing a little. "I was so . . . interested in your news I forgot to tell you mine. We'll have someone else for Thanksgiving. Your sister is coming home."

It was pouring rain and the drive to his parents' house took longer than usual. The traffic announcer on the radio said the heavy rains had sent a small landslide of rocks down the embankment near Gulph Mills and into the right lane of the highway's eastbound side, smashing through the windshield of one woman's car, missing her physically but so terrifying the poor driver she slammed on the brakes and caused a four-car pileup. Porter and Lee were headed west, away from the city; the incident should not have affected them, but some imbecile up ahead had slowed to gawk and others followed and so both sides were obstructed. The radio traffic announcer called it "Turkey Day gaper delay."

"So," Lee asked. "How'd they take it?"

"It's not going to be an issue."

Lee shrugged and switched stations on the radio. Porter's hands were moist. He wanted to wipe them on his pants, but he didn't want Lee to take it as a sign of nervousness, so instead he focused on the road ahead and prayed to whoever might be in charge of these things. *Don't let it be an issue. Don't let it be.* He was suddenly uncertain why he had arranged this whole event. What exactly was he trying to prove—that his parents were open-minded people? That he didn't care what they thought? The potential for disaster seemed ten times the potential for any kind of gain. But it was too late to back out now. He had to count on his mother's heightened sense of decorum to keep her polite and on booze to take care of his dad. And at least his sister would be there—the only other reasonable member of the family. He was excited about seeing Peg again; it had been nearly two years since he saw her last. He wondered briefly why she had called his parents instead of him to say she was returning to town, but that was a minor point. She would buffer whatever behavior his mother chose to demonstrate. They would, all three of them, eat dinner and get the hell out.

At his parents' house Porter pushed the doorbell, and chimes rang through the hall. He reached for Lee's hand, squeezed it. "Here we go."

The door flew open and his mother stood before them, hand outstretched, mouth drawn wide into a smile. She was dressed in a suit the color of a robin's egg with little pearl buttons running up the front and matching blue shoes. All that was missing were white gloves and a pillbox hat. "You must be Lenora!" she said, beaming at Lee. "Welcome! Welcome, my dear. Please come in."

Porter watched his mother suspiciously. Beside him Lee seemed frozen in surprise. His mother had to take Lee's arm and tug to get her moving across the doorway.

"Come in, come in! Join the party. Today seems to be a day for delightful surprises!"

On closer inspection his mother seemed not beaming but almost feverish, as if her response to Lee was to become physically sick. Porter took Lee's hand, gave his mother a significant look. *Calm down*, it said. *Any nonsense from you and we hit the street!* His mother simply blinked and kept smiling for all she was worth.

"Where's Peg?"

"Upstairs, freshening up. They arrived not thirty minutes ago, though due this morning. Some manner of plane delay in Chicago. High winds, if you can imagine. Isn't Chicago the Windy City? Haven't the authorities come up with a way to deal with that? Apparently not. They spent three hours on the runway, waiting to take off!"

It wasn't until his mother's second use of "they" that Porter registered the plural pronoun. "Who's they?" he began, but then their little group entered the living room and the answer stood with his father near the liquor cabinet.

His first thought was: ex-marine. Or retired marine—wasn't that how they put it? Once a marine always a marine? At any rate this guy had that look: buzz-cut hair, square jaw, chest like a support beam, blue oxford shirt buttoned up to his neck and tucked tightly into jeans that, despite three hours on the ground at O'Hare, were as fresh and wrinkle free as a baby's tush. Over it all a brown, corduroy sports jacket which would probably not be removed.

He stood at parade rest, apparently conversing with Porter's father but in reality scanning the room for a nest of enemy Vietcong. Then Porter and Lee entered the room and the guy turned and saw them and blinked: enemy located.

But no, probably he was just startled. And he was too young for Vietnam, younger than Porter, actually. Peg's age.

"Francis," his mother drawled. Her accent grew more pronounced when she was excited or wanting to be charming or under stress. "Francis, this is my son, Porter, and his friend Lenora Page. Porter, Lenora, this is Francis McGrath. Margaret's fiancé."

"Call me Frank," Francis said, shooting out his hand toward Porter, then, more tentatively, to Lee. "Your sister says all kinds of great things about you, Porter."

"Does she?" he squeaked, and everyone laughed with relief at the note of surprise in his voice, including Porter. It seemed to break the ice. But that Peg had said nice things about him was the only thing about which he was not surprised.

His father introduced himself to Lee. "I'm John Stockman, Miss Page. What can I get you to drink?"

"I'd love a glass of wine," Lee said, indicating an ice bucket on the server of the liquor cabinet. She smiled at his father. She seemed to have recovered herself.

"White wine it is. Porter?"

Clearly he was going to need a glass of something to get through this. "Bourbon," he said. "Neat." His father smiled.

His mother fluttered over to the couch and lit on the edge, a glass of white wine somehow in hand. "Francis is a police detective in the city of Chicago," she said. "Isn't that something?"

"A detective," Lee said politely. "Great."

"Actually I'm still working on my detective shield," Frank corrected. "I took the test, but right now I'm still in uniform."

So, not only a marine but a cop. Porter could not have been any more amazed if his sister had shown up and announced she was marrying a leprechaun. He himself had nothing against police officers; he'd covered the cop beat enough to know their merits as well as their foibles. But Peg? The last time he'd spoken to her on the subject—which, admittedly, was probably four or five years ago—she'd brought up Move, Frank Rizzo, the Philadelphia cops' reputation for harassing black kids, and labeled all cops thickheaded, trigger-fingered bullies in uniform. And now she was going to marry one. Porter sipped his drink.

Delicious smells crept out of the kitchen and crowded the living room: roasting turkey, sweet sautéing onions, even a hint of what might be the nutty-sweet scent of pumpkin pie. But his mother was a careless and indifferent cook. When it was just family, she made little attempt at putting on a grand spread, even on holidays. Porter assumed she must have had the meal catered. Or hired someone.

"Is Camellia cooking?" he asked. As far as he knew, Camellia was a once-a-week maid and not especially adept at cooking. But somebody had to be producing those smells.

"Oh no, dear. Camellia left us. We have someone new now." His mother smiled. "Esther! Please bring the appetizers in!"

A large black woman squeezed into a too-small uniform came through the swinging door from the kitchen balancing a tray in her pink-and-brown hands. Porter's stomach shrunk to a knot at the sight of her and he had to fight to breathe. What the hell was his mother thinking? The woman, wearing ridiculously high heels, teetered over to him and lowered the tray. It bore bone-white crackers with thin slices of pink salmon atop. He could hear the woman's labored breathing as she bent. He shook his head. "No, thank you," he said. He couldn't have choked one of the crackers down if his life depended upon it.

"Where is that Peg?" he asked no one in particular, and stood. "Maybe I should go check on her."

But just then a voice said, "Here I am." He turned. His sister stood in the doorway, beaming at the room. She was wearing a green jumper over a long-sleeved white blouse, the kind of thing a kindergarten teacher might wear. Her hair was shorter than the last time he'd seen her; it made her look surprisingly young.

"Hey, you," he said, and went to hug his sister. She smelled of lilies and jasmine, a garden at dusk. His mother's perfume. "Big news I hear. Congratulations."

"Thanks." She hugged him back, then disengaged herself and went to stand beside her man. "We're very happy. Now, Porter, introduce me to your friend."

It was Thanksgiving as fun-house mirror, both familiar and bizarre. His mother chirped and twittered, never allowing the conversation to stall. His father drank. Francis sat stoically, speaking mostly when spoken to. Peg hung from his arm and chatted up Lee, who seemed to be taking the whole bizarre scene in stride, though, in truth, Porter had no idea what was going on inside her head. Was she upset about Esther? What did she think of Peg's silent cop? Was she really being taken in by all this gracious living crap? He couldn't tell, but whenever he looked at her she was smiling and whenever he squeezed her hand beneath the table, she squeezed back.

And so with the bourbon sailing in his bloodstream and the first bites of moist turkey and creamy potatoes singing in his mouth—Esther was a great cook—Porter allowed himself to relax just a bit. Then somebody brought up the Los Angeles riots.

"Porter covered those events for his newspaper," his mother informed the table. "Did you know that, Francis?"

"No, I didn't," Francis said, eyeing Porter. It was clear he bore the cop's inherent distrust and dislike of journalists, especially journalists who covered events in which the police might be made to look bad. Porter eyed back to show he understood.

"And I believe you did also, Lenora. Is that right?"

"Yes," Lee said. "For the Baltimore newspaper."

"Terrible, terrible events, weren't they?" his mother asked, shaking her head. "We watched on television. Such ugliness."

"It was worse in person." Lee glanced at Porter. "A lot of people got hurt."

The turkey he'd been only recently enjoying lost all taste. This conversation was a minefield, in many ways. Lee knew he had not told his parents about the incident; she said she understood. But what was that look? Was she having second thoughts? Did she plan to spill? And any discussion of the riots had, ultimately, to include some discussion of Rodney King. Porter knew Lee's views on that topic. Very unlikely they aligned with those of Francis-the-cop.

And, as it turned out, this was where the biggest mine lay: beneath Francis-the-cop. Swallowing a bite he looked directly at Porter—not at Lee; he had not, in fact, looked at or spoken much to Lee all evening— and said, "What bothered me the most about it was how afterward people were calling it a rebellion. It wasn't a rebellion. It was a bunch of thugs and gang members running around beating up innocent people and threatening police officers. Then when they get caught they bitch and moan—excuse me, Mrs. Stockman—and blame everybody but themselves. Makes me sick."

Lee put down her fork. His father got up for another bottle of wine. "Anyone?" Heads shook all around.

"And what do you think about this Roger King?" his mother asked.

"Rodney," his father contributed. He was enjoying the spectacle. "Rodney King."

Porter, trying to turn the conversation, said, "What I find most interesting about southern California is how people keep flocking there even though they know a big earthquake is bound to happen sometime." A tiny bone, tossed out in desperation. Francis-the-cop did not bite.

"I think King got exactly what he deserved," he said stubbornly. "I know it's not politically correct to say it, but he resisted arrest. He threatened those officers. They did what they had to do."

"They *had* to stun him with a stun gun?" Lee said. Porter could feel the anger coming off her in waves. He tried to squeeze her hand beneath the table but she pulled away. "They had to keep clubbing him even when he was flat on his face in the street? Just like they have to stop and frisk any and every black kid they see walking down the street?"

"Oh, come on! What you're talking about has nothing to do with King!" Francis-the-cop said. "And King had nothing to do with the riots, if you ask me. He was just an excuse for those people to get out there and run wild!"

Dead silence. Then, Lee's voice, a block of ice. "Those people?"

Porter too was seething now. Who the hell did this guy think he was? "Listen, Francis—," he began, but his mother cut him off. "Looks as though everyone has finished eating," she trilled, ever the gracious hostess. "Why don't we all go into the living room for pie?"

Everyone stood in a burst of idle conversation, relieved at having been saved from witnessing a head-on collision. Still, Porter knew damn well Lee wasn't going to stick around for coffee and pie with Francis-the-cop. "I'm sorry," he whispered. "I had no idea. Let's go."

"Yes."

His mother pleaded daintily, but Porter was firm. They had to go. Lee wasn't feeling well and neither was he. He kissed his mother's cheek, shook his father's hand, nodded toward Francis-the-cop, and considered that gracious; what he wanted to do was slug the guy. He told Peg he would telephone her later that night. He definitely needed to talk to her. But they were in such a hurry to leave they got to the car and discovered Lee had forgotten her scarf. He left her in the car with the motor running, the heater turning warm, and ran back inside. Peg was in the hallway, alone, retrieving something from her bag.

Porter couldn't stop himself. "Nice boyfriend," he said.

"Fiancé," Peg corrected. "I'm going to marry him, Porter."

"Why? He seems . . . not at all who I would have expected for you, Peg. Do you really think you can be happy with a guy who thinks like that?"

She brushed at her hair with the back of her hand. It must have been only recently cut, because she still had the mannerisms of someone with longer hair. "He just gets upset about the King thing. About the way the cops were blamed for doing their job. About how they're being tried again, in federal court this time. It's double jeopardy."

"He's . . ." Porter paused. He didn't want to accuse his sister's future husband of racism; that was a big stick. He changed tactics. "It's a hard life, being married to a cop. Not just the danger. Cops are very insular, almost to the point of paranoia. I know—I've interviewed enough of them. Believe me, Peg. It's a weird little world."

But his sister crossed her arms over her chest and shook her head. "He's a good man," she insisted. "I know his heart. He's a good man and I love him."

Porter understood. This wasn't Peg talking, this was the blinding quality of love, the hands over the eyes. She and Francis-the-cop probably hadn't even known each other that long—why else hadn't Porter heard about him?—and were still in the gooey-eyed stage of infatuation. Porter felt relieved on that score at least. Peg hadn't changed, she was just in love.

But then she said, "He's not completely wrong, you know."

"What?"

"About what happened in L.A. About what's happening in cities all across this country. I know, I know—the correct thing is to lament the situation of these poor, oppressed inner-city kids. How terrible life is for them. But you know what? From the inside it's not so simple a story. I worked there, I know. Welfare has created a subculture, a violent, vulgar subculture with a sense of entitlement. Boys who think they deserve hundred-dollar sneakers. Fifteen-, sixteen-year-old girls planning to get pregnant so they can start 'getting their checks.' And if you say anything they curse you out, or call you a racist, or threaten to meet you after school and slash your face." Peg shook her head. "Frank's right: a lot of these kids, they're looking for an excuse to run wild."

"I can't believe this is you talking, Peg."

She twisted her mouth into a funny frown, waved her hand at him, laughed. "Oh, don't be so dramatic! I'm not talking about your friend out there—"

His heart was sinking. "Her name is Lee. She has a name."

"Okay, Lee. I'm not talking about Lee. She seems very nice. Although, to be honest, I'm not sure what you're doing with her."

"Doing with her?" he repeated dumbly. He suddenly felt close to tears. He felt like a kid whose idolized older sister has just been exposed as the school slut. "I'm dating her, Peg. The same way I dated Chira. The same way I've dated a dozen women in my life. I'm not *doing* anything with her, Peg. She is not an object, she's a woman."

"All right, all right. Calm down."

He stared helplessly at his sister. "What happened to you?"

"Nothing happened to me!" She laughed again, moved toward him for a quick hug. "Or maybe something did. Maybe I just grew up, Porter. You know one day I was sitting in my classroom having just broken up the third fight of the day. Two girls, going at it with box cutters. We had so much violence in our school, we had to have cops. That's how I met Frank. And sometimes I wondered if they were there to protect the kids or protect the outside world from them. Sometimes it felt more like a prison than a school."

Peg shook her head again, as if amazed by it all. "And this one day I just started wondering what I was doing there. I didn't like it. I don't even particularly enjoy teaching. I started wondering if I was just there, in some warped sense, to get back at Mom. I started wondering if most of what I've done in my life has been out of . . . out of anger or resentment at her, you know? And I just realized what a stupid way that was to live."

He didn't know what to say. His sister was a stranger to him. He found the scarf, moved toward the door. "I have to get back to Lee."

When he got to the car, Lee had turned the radio on and the heater up full blast, creating a cozy little world of steel and glass. "I'm sorry," he said. "That was awful. I apologize."

She kissed him, then leaned back against her headrest, eyes closed. "Not your fault. You're not responsible for some jerk your sister brings home."

No, he wasn't responsible for Francis-the-cop. And he wasn't responsible for Peg, either, even if she was blood. Still, the turkey and stuffing sat like concrete in his gut, and he felt like he could not eat for a week. How could his sister have changed so terribly? And she must have changed, because she was never like that before. He had never seen that side of her, not even a hint. Or maybe what Peg said was true: she'd spent her entire life rebelling against their mother. Maybe the change was that she'd stopped rebelling, had, in fact, reverted to her true self. That was a frightening thought. Frightening too that he hadn't seen it, that he'd been so deceived. If he didn't know Peg, who did he know?

When his mother called the next day to deconstruct the dinner, Porter told her to leave him alone. He didn't want to hear her thoughts about Lee or about Peg. And when Peg herself called a week later, all chatty and chipper, it was all he could do not to hang up the telephone.

Chapter 19

People stared at them. Not all the time, certainly, but enough. Enough. He didn't notice at first, but Lee did and she insisted always on pointing it out to him. Did he see that glare from the cashier? Did he catch the way those two guys at the corner table stared? Did he notice, did he notice, did he see?

The way she saw disapproval everywhere irritated him. "I didn't notice," he would answer. "Anyway, so what? Why do you care what some gum-smacking, big-haired salesgirl thinks?"

"I don't," Lee said.

"Then why do you notice it all the time?"

She looked at him. "Because not noticing can be dangerous. But if it bothers you so much, I won't mention it next time."

And she did not. She was true to her word; she did not raise the subject again. But it was too late. Too late because he'd been infected by her sensitivity, and he began noticing himself. He noticed guys who gazed at Lee and then turned to him with greasy, smirking smiles. He told himself this was just typical guy behavior. Lee was a beautiful woman after all, and hadn't he done his share of discreet leering in his life? But there was something hot-eyed and offensive in the way these guys looked at Lee, something infuriating in the way they sought to involve him in their thoughts. One sweaty, fat asshole in white socks and black shoes on the subway actually winked. Porter was stunned, then so furious he began to shake. "What's wrong?" Lee asked. "Nothing," Porter said, then glared at the guy until he shrugged and turned away.

He noticed women, waitresses and ticket sellers, who flirted with him as though Lee were invisible. He noticed too young black men who glared with unconcealed hostility as he and Lee walked hand in hand down the crowded Center City streets. It was by turns infuriating and frightening; as much as he tried not to he connected their faces with those guys in L.A. Once, when he and Lee were on their way to a movie, a black guy passed breathlessly close to Lee and hissed something into her ear. She stiffened against his arm but kept walking until Porter forced her to stop.

"What did he say?" he demanded.

"Nothing." Lee tugged at his arm. "Come on. We'll miss the movie."

"Tell me what he said." He was shaking with fury. Suddenly it seemed the whole world was involved in their relationship. He couldn't even walk down the street with his girlfriend without some idiot having something to say. Porter turned around, yelled, "What the fuck did you say?" but the black guy was gone.

Other people turned and stared at them. "Porter. Porter," Lee whispered. "Please. Let it go."

"Tell me."

"The movie is starting."

"Damn it, tell me!"

She looked at the sidewalk. "He called me a whore."

"What?" A stunned and joyless sound escaped from his throat. "Because you're with me?" Lee didn't answer, just stared into space. "That asshole! That prick! I ought to kick his ass! That's so ridiculous! That is so . . . obscene!"

She turned to him then, her face flushed and darkened, and he could see she was upset. He reached for her hand, but she pulled away. "How do you feel when you see a black guy with a white woman?" she demanded.

"What?"

"How do you feel when you see a white woman walking down the street with a black guy? Doesn't it piss you off?"

"No!"

"Are you sure? Doesn't your gut turn a bit, before your brain takes over and tells you not to feel that way?"

People were stepping into the street to pass them, unwilling to be caught up in the path of their argument. "Come on, Porter!" Lee cried. "It's only natural—a member of your tribe being stolen by the enemy."

"I don't see it that way."

"All men do. And black guys have a lot more reason to resent it than white men."

He threw up his hands in frustration. Somehow, someway, she had managed to turn the whole thing around, to make him the enemy and forgive the asshole who called her a whore in the middle of the street! "So if some white guy stares at us in a restaurant he's a racist bastard, but that asshole who just called you a whore, he's just protecting his tribe? What a bunch of bullshit! My God, Lee! Do you feel that bad about being with me?"

She was crying now, slapping away tears with the back of her hands. "No. No, I don't."

He pulled her against his chest. People were passing closer now, watching, staring. One old woman even smiled and Porter wondered why.

"I'm sorry," she said.

He had to restrain himself from holding her too tight. He wanted to squeeze her into himself, to mesh their tissues, to dilute her race-obsessed blood with his own. "White or black, it's their problem, not ours," he whispered into her ear. "Remember that, for God's sake, remember that. Not our problem. We don't feel that way."

They were out in the newsroom, their relationship finally and widely known. Not because he talked or she talked but because Nancy Norrington saw them together one Sunday at brunch and by Monday at noon had spread the news so effectively even the editors knew. Lee said she was glad, she wanted people to know. He said he was glad too. Those who gave a shit, he said, would probably be happy for them.

A few of the women caught him one by one in the cafeteria or hallway and trilled and cooed all over themselves about what a cute couple he and Lee made. A few of the guys, his closest buddies, elbowed him and winked broadly in tongue-in-cheek imitation of what guys did when they found out one of their own was seeing a woman. Porter thought maybe Nathaniel, a black sports reporter with whom he'd had a joking, score-related, talk-in-the-elevator relationship for several years, looked at him differently, but he could not be sure. The vast majority of people in the newsroom chewed over the gossip for a minute, then returned to a state of neurotic self-obsession. Just as he knew they would.

The only sour note came from Karl, the transportation reporter, who cornered Porter in the bathroom one afternoon. Karl was the kind of moron who wanted to hold a conversation at the urinal, ignoring the unspoken rule that a guy did not speak to another guy when they were standing next to each other with their dicks exposed. Unless you were on the same football team.

"So, you and Page, huh?" Karl said, unzipping himself and grinning across at Porter at the same time. After years of trial and error, Porter had learned the best way to deal with Karl was to ignore him, and so he did.

"She's quite a woman," Karl said. Porter said nothing.

"I remember the first time she walked into the newsroom," Karl said. Porter said nothing.

"I got a woody the size of Chicago," Karl said. "I mean, wow!"

"Shut up, Karl."

"No offense! I'm just saying I wish I was in your shoes." Karl stuck out his tongue and waggled it around, jiggling his entire body in his enthusiasm.

"Try to keep your piss off my shoes." Porter zipped himself, flushed, and tried to escape to the sink. But Karl followed him, grinning like a fool.

"You know what my father used to say to me?" Karl leaned close, smelling foully of onions and peppers and greasy sweat. "He used to say you're not really a man until you've split a black oak."

"What?" Porter blinked. It wasn't that he hadn't heard, but that his brain refused to take the words in. Not even Karl could be idiot enough to utter something so crude about a woman Porter was dating, a woman they both knew? Not even Karl could be stupid enough to repeat it, so if he just asked him again Karl would say something silly but not offensive, and they could both get out of that echoing bathroom without damage being done.

"You're not really a man until you've split a black oak!" Karl elbowed Porter in the side and laughed. "So now you've joined the club, eh? The black oak club!"

So strong was the urge to punch Karl's leering face Porter had to shove his hands into his pockets to keep from giving in to it. He'd noticed, since Los Angeles, his own increased attraction to violence, how the idea of physical attack came to him sooner, and stayed longer, when someone cut him off in traffic or hung up the telephone in his face. He'd never been a fighter, not even in school. His size and wits and words and the world in which he lived kept him safely removed from violence most of the time. Until Los Angeles. And now he wondered if a blow to the head wasn't really the best way to deal with certain kinds of people. People who attacked a man because of the color of his skin. People like Karl.

But of course he couldn't do that. So instead he stepped on Karl's foot. Karl yelped in surprise.

"Hey!" With his free foot Karl pawed at the ground like a horse. "Hey! My foot! My foot!"

"Excuse me?"

"Get off! Get off! You're breaking my toes!"

"Oh, sorry." Porter stepped away, feigning regret. "Didn't see it. I thought it was in your mouth."

Back in the newsroom Porter threw himself into his chair, waiting for Karl to emerge. After a few minutes he did, white-faced and shaking, beads of water clinging to his bushy eyebrows. Porter glared him across the newsroom, daring the little skunk to head for the managing editor's office to complain. Like anybody would care. Karl was deadweight, a piece of driftwood they kept on the staff because it was too much trouble to fight the union in trying to fire him. Nobody respected him and nobody liked him and no one would give a damn if Porter crushed all ten of his toes. Karl must have known this too because he just slunk back to his desk, grabbed his jacket and a notebook, and disappeared. Porter didn't see him the rest of the afternoon.

How could Karl have said such a thing? It was not surprising he would think it; Karl was, after all, an idiot. But what astonished Porter was that even someone as moronic as Karl would think he could get away with *saying* what he did, that he would think Porter would not be offended by his words. Karl was forever panting over women and imagining, out loud, Porter's bachelorhood, but he had never spoken so bluntly, so crudely about a woman Porter was dating. What made him think he could get away with it now?

Porter seethed all afternoon. He couldn't write, couldn't think straight, couldn't read through his notes for a story he was writing for the weekend without hearing Karl's lecherous voice in his head. He was still seething that evening when he met his buddy Charlie for a drink. When Charlie heard the story he shook his head.

"Where's Karl from again?"

"Missouri."

"Remind me never to go to Missouri," Charlie said, swirling his bourbon. "Must be one hell of a scary place."

"I should have punched his fat face in. I don't know what stopped me; some ridiculous sense of refined maturity, I guess."

"Maybe you were afraid you couldn't take him."

"If I can't take Karl I need to turn in my balls," Porter said.

"Karl's an idiot."

"Clearly. But just the fact he felt he had the right to say something like that to me."

"He's just jealous. You've seen his wife."

"There's no use playing on my pity."

Charlie laughed. "Just ignore him. He's just pissed because he never got to try it like everybody else, you know? He and his wife got married when they were eighteen, I think. He got her pregnant and her father came over with the shotgun."

Charlie laughed and, after the slightest hesitation, Porter laughed too. They laughed a lot when they were out together. It was one of the things Porter liked most about Charlie, how his friend's biting, cynical sense of humor neatly matched his own. They'd been friends for years, through dozens of girlfriends, two newsroom overhauls, and hundreds of Phillies games, and they very often saw things in the same light. Which is why Porter could ask Charlie what he meant by saying Karl never got to try it like everybody else. Because he knew Charlie didn't mean anything.

"I didn't mean anything," Charlie said. "I just meant he never got to, you know, date outside his experience before he settled down."

" 'Date outside his experience'? " Porter laughed. "Who are you, Phil Donahue?"

"Give me a break. I'm trying to be politically correct here, okay?"

"And you think that's what I'm doing? Dating outside my experience?"

Charlie laughed nervously and made punching gestures in the air. "Down, boy! I didn't mean anything by it. Lee is great. I'm happy for you. Don't get defensive."

"I'm not defensive."

"Because you could take Karl but you couldn't take me."

"I could take you asleep," Porter said. "I could take you with two broken arms and arthritis in my left knee."

They laughed. The bartender refreshed their drinks.

After a moment Porter, trying to hit a light note, asked, "Have you ever dated a black woman?"

"Nope. Haven't had the good fortune."

"But you would." It was a statement, not a question, because he knew what Charlie would say. This man had been his friend for years. He knew what Charlie would say. "You'd date a black woman, given the chance, right?"

"You know," Charlie began, and for some reason, hearing him, Porter felt a sharp pain in his gut.

"When I was younger I would have, no question," Charlie said. "I've seen some beautiful black women I wouldn't have minded taking out. Like Lee. You're a lucky man."

"When you were younger."

"Yeah."

"But not now."

Charlie shrugged. "Now, I guess I'm getting a little older and I'm ready to start thinking about settling down. Now when I take a woman out I'm looking at her in a different way. I'm wondering if it might lead to something permanent, to a house and kids and a station wagon and all the mundane rest of it."

"And it couldn't with a black woman?" Porter asked. He asked it gently, forgivingly, because he knew now what Charlie was going to say and he felt bad for him having to say it. Porter felt bad for Charlie and bad for himself and bad for the whole damn world.

"Not for me, no," Charlie confessed, looking down at the bar. "I just don't see it." There was a pause. "I hope that doesn't upset you."

"No, no, of course not," Porter said. What else could he say? This man had been his friend for seven or eight years, had seen him through overzealous editors and overzealous women and everything in between. What else could he say?

"I'm not a racist."

"Of course not."

Charlie's grin was sheepish. "It's just that we get these images of ourselves, of our lives, you know? I guess I always kinda saw myself out in the backyard, rolling around on the grass with my three, towheaded tykes."

"Gerber babies," Porter said, trying to grin. "Campbell kids." He finished his drink and signaled the bartender for the check.

"Yeah, I guess so." Charlie shrugged. "I mean, children are pretty much the point of being married, aren't they? And I just don't see myself having . . . you know . . ."

There was silence for a moment. Then Charlie said, "But that's just me. You know how it is."

Porter nodded. He didn't know how it was. But maybe he was beginning to find out.

There was going to be a newsroom party at the home of Porter's friend Elena, a send-off for the foreign editor who was departing to greener pastures up north. Charlie would be there. Karl, the transportation reporter, would be there. Porter would have just as soon skipped the festivities, but Lee, to his surprise, wanted to go. "Why not?" she teased. "Now that we're out of the closet, let's party."

He hadn't told her about his conversations with Charlie or Karl. What was the point? She would have taken both as more evidence of the world's disapproval, of the long-term impossibility of their relationship. He didn't want to have to argue that question anymore because he was tired of it. And because, on certain days, for certain brief moments, a part of him wondered if she wasn't right.

Elena greeted them at the door of her house wearing a grin and a diaphanous, burgundy silk pantsuit that perfectly matched the tint of her hair this season. By nature, Elena was a pale and freckled strawberry blonde but nature had long ago lost that war. When he first met Elena her hair was the color of pumpkin pie, but as she climbed the advertising ladder she graduated to darker, richer, plummy shades that highlighted the paleness of her skin without the glow-in-the-dark quality.

"Greetings!" Elena kissed him on the cheek, whispered, "By the way, Rachel's here."

This bit of news was a little static electricity zap. Rachel. He hadn't seen her in nearly a year, not since their whirlwind monthlong romance which ended when he went to Chicago for work and came back to find she'd telephoned all his female friends in a paranoid and jealous fit. The breakup was awkward, as breakups always are, but they hadn't dated long enough for her to carry a grudge; he had no reason for nervousness. Then again, they hadn't dated long enough for her to act the crazy way she had, either. So, just something else to make the party fun.

Elena took their arms and pulled them through the doorway into the living room, an area nearly as big as his entire apartment. Porter had been there before, of course, but he watched Lee take in the massive oak furniture, the floor-to-ceiling windows looking out over the terraced yard, the Oriental rug, the antique leather sidesaddle Elena kept to remind herself of her prize-winning riding days.

"You have a beautiful home," Lee said.

"Thank you! And you have beautiful cheekbones!" Elena's mossy green eyes were bright and her face flushed, the way it always became when she drank or exercised or made love. He used to tease her about that, back when they were a couple. "You should be a model."

"Thank you." Lee smiled. Porter couldn't tell whether she was genuinely flattered or just being gracious. But Elena seemed fascinated. "Porter," she said, "why don't you go get drinks? We'll stay here and chat."

This meant Elena wanted to separate them so she could grill Lee about their relationship. He glanced at Lee to see if she minded. She winked and so he left, making his way across the increasingly crowded living room toward a table that had been set up as a bar. It was a popular destination and he had to stand in a long line. While waiting he chatted with a prosecutor in the attorney general's office, a woman who seemed to turn up at every newsroom party there was. She was a journalism groupie. She thought journalists were so much more interesting than lawyers and proved it by sleeping her way through the newsroom staff. She began telling Porter how she was thinking of going back to school to become a reporter, but he cut her off as graciously as he could and made his escape.

Lee and Elena had disappeared from their spot. He was searching for them when someone tapped him on the shoulder.

"Hello, stranger."

He turned and it was Rachel. "Hi," he said, not knowing, for a moment what else to say.

"Hi."

"Elena said you'd be here."

"Did she?" Rachel laughed. "And you came anyway?"

"You look great," he said. It was true. She'd gained weight since he last saw her, just enough to fill out the hollows in her cheeks and smooth the lines in her face and make her lose that anorexic look. Her dark hair hung loose and shiny down her back, and the black eyeliner she'd smudged around her eyes made her look like a Gypsy queen.

"Here alone?" she asked.

He couldn't tell how she meant the question. "No. I'm with someone now. She's over there, talking to Elena."

"Which one?" Rachel craned her head over the crowd.

"The tall woman with short hair."

"The one next to the doors?"

"No, the one in the red shirt."

"You mean the black woman?"

"Yes." He was embarrassed. He should have said that, "the black woman." It was a much more efficient description, a much more definitive naming of Lee who was, after all, the only black woman in the room, was, in fact, the only black woman at the party as far as he could see. Why hadn't he just said that? What did Rachel think, that he couldn't? That he was too busy pretending Lee wasn't black? Or that he was embarrassed?

"The black woman."

"She's beautiful," Rachel said, smiling up at him. Her pale, pale face glowed under the soft light of the room. He had always liked that, the contrast of her white skin and dark hair. She looked wonderful. "How about that? I'm here with someone too."

"Great," he said, as enthusiastically as he could. "Where is he."

"Over there." She pointed to a group of six people, two guys and four women, all clustered around a black man. Porter was scanning the faces of the two guys in the group, trying to decide which one Rachel could mean when she added, in a smiling, ironic tone, "The black guy."

Porter nodded and smiled. She was watching him closely, and he did not want his face to give off anything but casual interest. Certainly not surprise. The black guy was tall and athletic and bald in the way Michael Jordan was bald, expensively dressed in caramel-colored slacks, camel hair jacket, and one of those kente cloth vests. He had the height, the hulk, and the arrogant mass of a guy who'd played football in college, maybe even gone on to the pros as some second-string linebacker.

"He looks familiar," Porter said, then wondered if that was a mistake. Was he just assuming the guy had to be a jock because he was black?

"He played defensive end for the Eagles. His name is Walter Daniel Brooks."

"Oh yeah. Babbling Brooks." So named because he talked so much trash in the huddle and to reporters. "I remember him. He didn't last very long."

Rachel looked at him, amused. "He injured his knee."

"Of course." Did that sound sincere? He was trying.

"He says now it was the best thing that ever happened to him. If he hadn't been injured he might have wasted another ten years playing football, sacrificing his body for other people's idle entertainment instead of developing his mind and challenging himself and giving back to his community."

Idle entertainment? Porter wanted to laugh. This was bullshit of the highest degree. He'd never known any professional athlete who considered his sport anything less than a divine calling, and the only reason this guy was pissing on football now was because he hadn't been able to make the grade. He couldn't believe Rachel had swallowed this line.

"So what's he doing now?"

"He owns his own dry-cleaning business. Eight stores."

"That is important work."

Rachel smiled. "He's also pursuing a doctorate in education at Penn and plans to open a school for underprivileged boys in North Philadelphia next year."

Not *underprivileged,* he thought. No one uses that word anymore. "Inner-city" and "at-risk" were the preferred, inoffensive terms. But this was just jealousy speaking. "Sounds like quite a guy," he said with as much genuine admiration as he could muster.

"Yes," Rachel said. "He is."

Just then Mr. Magnanimous looked across the room at them and with a finger as thick as a cucumber beckoned Rachel to his side. "It was good seeing you again, Porter," she said, twitching like a puppy. "I'm glad you've found someone." He watched as she trotted across the room, face beaming, and inserted herself neatly under her master's massive arm. Amazing. The guy really had her hooked. He tried to imagine how Lee would react to being summoned like that. He tried to imagine how Rachel would have reacted to being summoned like that when they were dating. He imagined both women would tell him to go screw himself, but then he wasn't a living, breathing combination of Albert Schweitzer and Mandingo.

Mandingo? Where the hell had that come from?

He spent the rest of the evening avoiding Charlie, who seemed embarrassed and apologetic, and Karl, who seemed terrified, and trying not to watch Rachel and her boyfriend. They seemed always to place themselves in his line of vision, laughing, caressing, holding each other's hands. They were like a splinter in his heel, just slightly tender but ever present, though he told himself he didn't care. He'd liked Rachel for a few weeks a year ago and had not given her a thought since. Still, he couldn't relax until they left—though he tried, with repeated trips to the bar—and they didn't leave until just before the party broke up for good.

When it was time to go Lee took one look at him and said she would drive. He didn't argue; when he rose from the armchair where he'd hunkered most of the evening while Elena paraded Lee around, the room tilted. He was drunk, no doubt about that.

On the way home Lee dissected the evening the way women always did. This man was an arrogant asshole, that guy a sad and insecure little jerk, this woman more thoughtful and decent than Lee had known. Charlie she liked a lot; she said this with a big smile, clearly thinking he'd be pleased. He grunted his assent. Then she mentioned Rachel's name and his heart thudded guiltily, but she was only talking about how strange it was for her to still dislike seeing black men with white women, even though she was dating a white guy. He'd heard all that before. She moved on to Elena, saying she liked her well enough but found her chatty, touchy, instant familiarity a little much.

"She just wants to be friends." He leaned his head against the seat. With his eyes closed it felt as though they weren't so much driving as bobbing down one of those amusement park log rides, sloshing through the water, thudding from side to side. He couldn't even tell when they were moving and when they had stopped for a light. He opened his eyes.

"Don't think it's going to happen," Lee said. "Not in the way she wants."

He knew he should drop it. What did he care, after all? Still he asked, "Why not?"

Lee shrugged. "She's not my type."

"You have a type for friends?"

"Don't you?"

The question irritated him. "Let me guess: your type is black."

She didn't rise to the sarcasm in his voice. "There are too many things I have to explain to a white woman."

He sighed exaggeratedly. He had thought they were beyond all this. "That's ridiculous."

"It's not ridiculous. What do women talk about? Men, our families, our hair, our bodies, how we get along with other people at work, what movies we like. It sounds innocent enough, but all those things are, for me, affected by my being black. I could meet a black woman tonight and talk to her about those things and she'd understand my perspective immediately. It wouldn't be like meeting a stranger, it would be like meeting a distant relative. All we'd have to do is catch up."

"And you couldn't catch up with Elena."

"Maybe. Eventually, if I explained everything to her. But it's too much work. She might even be worth it. I used to think no white person was." She looked over at him. "Now I see she might be. But it's usually still too much work."

"That's sad."

"Yes. It is."

They reached Germantown Avenue in silence. The car bucked like a horse over the cobblestoned street, dizzying him. He rolled down his window for air. Lee reached out her hand, touched his forehead. "You okay?"

The gesture disarmed him. He took her hand, kissed it. "I think Elena slipped me a Mickey. She wanted me to get drunk and put a lamp-

shade on my head." He said this all as distinctly as he could, testing himself for slurred words. It had been a long time since he was this drunk.

Lee laughed. "Well, I think she was hoping for some kind of show.
You and your new girlfriend, who happens to be black, and your old
girlfriend, who happens to be dating a black guy. No wonder you spent
the night in a corner of the room."

Damn Elena and her fat mouth. He couldn't believe she'd told Lee
about Rachel. Now Lee would attribute his actions at the party to his
seeing an old girlfriend there. "I didn't spend the night in a corner," he
said. "I was . . . just letting the party come to me."

"So you weren't upset about seeing Rachel with someone else?"

"No!" He tried to sound indignant at the idea.

"It wouldn't be surprising if you were." Lee laughed again and this
time he noticed it was a nervous sound. "Especially if you loved her."

His irritation and weariness melted at the softness in her voice. It
was rare that Lee allowed herself to be vulnerable. He stroked the back
of her neck, wanting her suddenly. Bad. He had the urge to paw at her
clothes, to tear them away. He turned toward her in the seat, stroking
her neck. She arched against his hand like a cat.

"I don't love Rachel. I never did." As he said it he knew it was true.
So what was it? Why had he been so disturbed at seeing Rachel slobber
over Mr. Big? He had liked her for a while, before she went nuts with his
appointment book. That was a long time ago, and he hadn't thought
about her since. So why now? His sister once told him men were like
toddlers: they might have zero interest in a particular toy but let some
other toddler pick it up, and stand back. Was he just being a two-year-
old here? Protecting his sandbox from all the other boys? And what was
that Mandingo crack? He stroked Lee's neck, thinking how much he
didn't even want to think about that.

Chapter 20

By the time they got inside her front door he was nearly frantic. He panted and puffed and clawed at her silk blouse so urgently she worried he'd rip a hole. "Calm down," she said, pulling his hands away so she could unbutton the blouse herself.

"Lee," he moaned, mouth mashed against hers. "Lee." When she was naked, he knelt before her on the wooden floor and, moaning, took her breast into his mouth. "Let's go upstairs," she said, but he didn't move.

"Oh. Oh." He sounded almost pained.

"Calm down."

"I love you," he said.

She stroked his hair, feeling the thinness of it, the silken insubstantiality. What was hair for, really? A covering of the head, protection from the sun. His was no help at all.

"I love you," he said, seeking her eyes. "I mean it, Lee. I see a future for us. I love you. I do."

It was the first time the word had passed between them in that way, the first time in six months, and Lee's heart stood up and clapped at the sound like a trained seal. Love. Her heart clapped but her brain had learned a long time ago, and painfully, not to believe the things a man said when he had his face buried in your breasts, his body inside your own. To do so was a good way to get hurt. But Porter was saying it again, and looking into her face as if he expected an answer.

"I love you, Lee. Do you love me?"

Did she? Did she love him? She felt, at the moment, a kind of wild irrational anger toward him, as if he were her enemy and they were struggling against each other there in her living room on the naked floor. She had the urge to plow her fingernails deep into his scalp and, at the same time, to collapse against his chest, to surrender.

"Let's go upstairs," she said. It would be safer in bed.

There had developed between them a routine to sex, variable enough for excitement but always within a certain norm, only what he was doing to her now—all prodding tongue and belligerent knees, sharp fingertips—wasn't it. Something was different, something had shifted. He knelt above her, his breath hot and boozy against her face. She had to break from his kiss, pull back, turn her head to breathe.

He was drunker than he'd been in a long time; just sober enough to realize it but drunk enough not to care. Drunk enough to let go of rational thought. Struggling up the stairs behind her, he was overcome with the feeling she was trying to get away from him. And in bed he kissed her and buried his face between her breasts, wanting to drown in her, to merge with her. But she kept slipping away. She hadn't answered when he asked if she loved him. She was slipping away, tilting up, up into the gusty wind like a woman in a cartoon. *Wheeeeeeee!* He had to do something to hold her down. "Let's try something," he said against her skin.

"What?" Her voice was coquettish, he thought. Willing.

Still he asked, "You want to?"

"That depends," she said, but she was smiling. He could hear it. So he got off the bed, went to her dresser, to the drawer where she kept the long, silk scarves she tied stylishly around her head some Saturday mornings, mornings she called "black hair days."

"What you got there?" Her voice came at him from far away.

"These." He held up the scarves, coming back to her. "What do you think?"

Her first inclination was to laugh. She flashed on a story that had dominated the Baltimore papers a few years before, the story of a city councilman found dead in his bedroom, dressed up like a Roman slave and tied with red silk scarves to the four posters of his bed. Heart attack, the coroner ruled. The police finally found the frightened and tearful black prostitute who told the whole sordid tale. It was ruled an accident. She and Pauline had laughed about it—cruelly she guessed—but that was the kind of crazy, freaky shit white people were into: paying a prostitute to tie you up and beat you, in this case to death. She and Pauline had laughed and shaken their heads, seeing in the tale one more reason to never get involved with a white man.

So when Porter came toward her, his face glistening with lust and hope, she laughed, out of nervousness and disbelief and even a kind of lingering white-folks-is-crazy amusement. *Unbelievable!* He was going to ask her to tie him up. She'd heard about that before, white men wanting to be beaten by black women, wanting to be dominated, overwhelmed, overcome. Once, a long time ago, a white man she knew from work had gotten drunk at an office party and whispered in her ear, "I want you to tie me up and do things to me!" Meaning nasty, funky, freaky *black* things. And now here came Porter, his face mottled, his eyes glowing and wet. He climbed back onto the bed and kissed her gently, then squinted one eye and raised the opposite eyebrow in mocking, dastardly lust. "I have you now, my pretty," he said.

"What are you doing?"

"Why, I'm going to rape you, dear." And, looking into her eyes, took her arm and pulled it above her head.

It was Chira who'd taught him how to tie the knots: tight enough so she could writhe and fight and really pull against them but not so tight as to leave any marks. He hadn't done this with any woman since, had not missed it, he thought. But something surged in him at the sight of Lee's long cocoa arm stretched helplessly upward against the white sheet. A furious energy. A wave, blinding. He dove in, wanting to be submerged, and trembling, grabbed the other wrist. Lee mumbled something he could not understand. Then, moments later, "Stop."

He thought she was playing along and it excited him. "I won't."

"Stop, I said."

"Stop. Please."

He could barely breathe and his hands trembled against the silk. He laughed.

"I want you to stop!" she cried. The urgency in her voice sounded so real it shook him.

"What's wrong? Is the knot too tight?"

"I don't want to do this."

Placate, he thought. Reassure. "It's okay. I'll be gentle."

"No. Untie me."

"Lee—"

"Now!"

"Okay, okay!" He fumbled at the knots, addled and surprised and shaking from the pain of having to pull away from her. He nearly wept in frustration.

"Hurry!" She sounded as though she might be getting hysterical.

"Okay!" After an eternity he managed to untie the knots and toss the scarves onto the floor. He grabbed her slim wrists, searched for bruises—"Did I hurt you?"—kissed them gently. But she pulled away.

"What's wrong?" He was still raw from wanting her; his penis still throbbed with pain, and he had to fight not to take her hand and place it there. *God, if only she would.* But she lay with her back to him, no longer answering, and he felt some emotion—surprise? anger?—cascade from her body, soaking through the mattress and racing, racing to his side of the bed. That she hadn't liked the game was clear. Perhaps he'd moved too fast and startled her. Had he gone more slowly, had he prepared her better . . . And it was stupid, just plain stupid, to use the word *rape*. Chira had loved it, but of course some women might be offended. Some women took that word very seriously.

"Are you okay?"

"Fine."

After a moment he asked again, "What's wrong? Did I hurt you?"

"No," she said. Then, quietly she asked, "I'm just wondering what made you think I'd want to do that?" There was a quality to her voice he could not identify. It wasn't anger and it wasn't fear.

"I thought it would be exciting."

"Exciting."

"Yes," he said. Then added, "I'm sorry. I thought you wanted to."

She ignored this. "Have you done it before?"

"Yes."

"With a white woman?"

Too late, he saw the ground opening before him, the familiar chasm looming up ahead.

"You've never done that with your white girlfriends," she said, not asking but accusing. And although he knew he'd screwed up, his anger began to rise.

"As a matter of fact, it was a white woman who initiated me," he said.

"Really?" Disbelieving.

"She loved it."

"Did she? So I guess you thought that if she enjoyed it, naturally so would I. Even more so, right?" she said, with such turnaround logic it nearly took his breath away. First she was pissed because she thought he'd never done that with a white woman and now she was pissed because he had? A throbbing began at the back of his neck and raced to his forehead. Through the window he heard voices, two people, laughing. Then doors slammed and a car pulled away. He closed his eyes and opened them again, testing to see if the ceiling would spin, which it did. Holding his head, holding his breath, Porter climbed out of bed.

"Going home," he said. "I don't have the energy for this tonight." But they hadn't turned the lamp on, were operating by light from the window and the hallway, and he stumbled getting out of bed.

"You can't drive like that," she said from the dimness of the bed. He couldn't see her face but her voice sounded worried, a little. Apparently she did not want him dead.

"I'll call a cab."

"You won't get a cab here this time of night. Sleep on the couch."

"Very kind," he said, not knowing himself whether he meant to be sarcastic or not.

He stopped in the bathroom on the way downstairs but the medicine cabinet was clogged with fingernail polish, eyedrops, tweezers, everything but pain relief. He went downstairs, stabbing pain with every step, and into the kitchen, where he remembered seeing a bottle of ibuprofen on the windowsill. He swallowed four of the little white pills along with enough water to make a sloshing sound whenever he moved. The old college cure. It had been years since he'd been drunk enough to need it. Porter thought of his father and wondered, like father like son? He went into the living room and turned on the television. An old episode of *Charlie's Angels* was on, Farrah Fawcett cat-footing around a yacht in a blue bikini, solving some devious crime. Porter bet Farrah never accused anyone of whatever it was he'd just been accused of. Farrah simply strapped on a backless dress and beamed her welcoming, megawatt smile. The sexual simplicity of his youth. What he wouldn't give right now to be at home, alone, dreaming of a luxuriantly blond Farrah happy beside him in bed.

Hard to make sense of what had happened. Didn't help that he was tipsy, but even sober he probably would still not have understood. What, exactly, did he do that was so horrible? Get carried away? Tried to introduce some variety? No, what he'd done was what he'd been doing since the beginning of this thing, namely, being himself. His real crime was being white.

For the first time in his life he considered himself not as Porter, as an individual, good and bad, but as a member of that most vile and hated group: the white men. Rapacious and lustful, greedy and mean, the twentieth century's bogeyman. It pissed him off.

He was neither so naive nor so disingenuous as to deny the obvious benefits. But there were disadvantages too, one being having to sit back and listen while a universe of righteously indignant women and blacks and Latinos and gays cataloged your failings and made malicious fun. If you were a white man you couldn't play basketball, couldn't jump, couldn't appreciate jazz or the blues, couldn't *feel* anything, ever, other than avarice and gall. You couldn't dance and certainly you could not fuck, not you with your thin-lipped, limp-dicked self. *Don't make us laugh!* If you were a white man and you listened to Muddy Waters you were a leech preying on the cultural munificence of a people you gleefully oppressed. If you worried out loud about the possibility of being jumped by a murderous thug some late, dark night you were a racist using code words to spread hate. If you wanted to love a black woman, everybody assumed it was only because you wanted her to do all the things you couldn't get your uptight, flat-assed white girlfriends to do in bed. It was deviant and it was shameful and it was certainly not love. Everybody assumed that. Especially her.

Porter was damn certain he hadn't been thinking about black or white or race just now, upstairs. In bed. He had not been thinking anything at all, his brain too muddled by beer and craving for the musky sweet scent of her, the salty taste of skin between her breasts. (But women never stopped thinking, not completely. Their brains clicked and whirred continuously, impossible to shut down.) Hadn't anyone else Lee had slept with ever looked down on all that coiled energy, at her body, taut and glistening like a porpoise about to slip back into the sea, at her huge, dark laughing eyes and wanted to capture all that, to harness, to hold? Didn't black men crave these things, didn't they too sometimes get swept up in the vastness of a woman, carried tossing and clawing on her waves?

Upstairs Lee dialed the phone number, hung up, looked at the clock, dialed again. Three rings and a groggy voice answering, "Hello?"

"Pauline it's me. Sorry I woke you."

"Lee?" Across the line she heard Pauline click into disaster preparedness mode. "What happened? What's wrong?"

"Nothing, nothing. Calm down. Everything's fine."

"Everything's fine? Then why are you ringing my phone at . . . one-forty-five A.M.?"

Now she felt like an idiot. "I'm sorry, Pauline. I shouldn't have. It was stupid. I just . . ." Lee stumbled, then burst into tears, feeling even more idiotic.

"It's okay. Calm down. Take a breath," Pauline instructed. "Don't worry about it. I don't really need to sleep more than one or two hours a night anyway. Now, tell me what's going on."

Steadying herself, Lee related the story in full color, nothing left out. It seemed less egregious in the retelling, less earth-shattering. By the time she finished telling it all, she wondered if she hadn't overreacted.

"Hell no!" said Pauline. "If some whiteboy wanted to tie me up? And started talking about rape?"

"I know: he'd have to kill you first. But what if he had asked me to tie him up? To dominate him? Would that have been better or worse?" It was dawning on her that things weren't so simple. She'd reacted out of habit with Porter, suspicious to the end. But was she right?

"What if he wanted me to pretend to be a French maid or to wear high heels or cowboy boots or swing from the chandelier? I mean, be honest, Pauline. Hasn't some man, some brother, ever asked you to do something unusual in bed? What about Marvin? I remember you telling me something about him."

Pauline chuckled, as if remembering. "Oh, yes. Marvin. Marvin had this thing about breathing during sex, as in, he didn't think I should have to do so. The first time we were together we were going along fine when the next thing I know there's a pillow over my face, and I don't mean gently either. I had to fight to get it off."

"You're kidding!"

"He said he was only trying to heighten my pleasure. I told him breathing was one of the most pleasurable activities I knew."

"That's not kinky, that's dangerous."

"Apparently some women like that stuff." Pauline yawned into the phone. "And you? What about Howard?"

"Howard? No!" Howard was as straight an arrow in bed as humanly possible. He made love as though he'd learned it from an army manual. Even turning the light on was big doings for him. "But there was this one guy, come to think of it. Right after college. His name was Alvin."

"A chipmunk?"

"Hardly. This brother was, shall we say, ample. But he didn't like me to use the equipment much. Mostly he wanted me to sprinkle baby powder on him while he jerked off."

"And you didn't think this was strange?"

"I was twenty-two at the time. What did I know?"

"Men!" Pauline sighed. "Still, Marvin and your chipmunk aside, most brothers I've known liked it straight. That's the irony. White folks think we're doing something freaky-deaky in bed and really it's them with all the kinky shit."

"So Marvin is an exception?"

"Yes."

"But not Porter? Couldn't Porter be an exception to the rule that white men just think of us as whores?" Lee pressed, as though she were the prosecutor and Pauline the stubborn witness who would not give the truth.

"I suppose it's possible."

"But you don't think so."

"Look. Even if Marvin was a freak, it's . . . different."

"Why?"

"Because it is. Because history is alive."

"But—"

"But nothing," Pauline said. "The past is present. He can't escape it and neither can you." Pauline paused. "You know that, Lee."

Did she? She fell back against the headboard, feeling as though her bones had melted and could no longer offer the requisite support. History was alive; that she believed. But should the present be discounted? Porter was a good man. He was.

But good white people were sometimes the most dangerous.

Maybe this was why more people did not cross the color line to love—not the taboo or fear but the confusion. The never-knowing of it. If a black man said or did something to her, something hurtful or kinky, it was just him. He was just an asshole; there were no generalizations to be read into it. But when Porter spoke or acted, it was the entire white race acting upon her—*the devil race*, Malcolm called it, though he softened in the end. Still. History. How would she ever know whether

Porter wanting to tie her up was simply a part of his own sexual bag or something else? He said he'd tied up white girlfriends before, but was that the truth? And even if it was, was it the same thing? Even if he thought it was?

"Go back to sleep, Pauline. I'll talk to you tomorrow."

"What are you going to do?"

"I don't know. But thanks. Thanks for being there."

She hung up the phone, shook her head to clear it. Was she making this all too complicated? Porter was smart, funny, kind. He understood her job and appreciated her talent. He didn't make her feel anxious or unworthy. She believed he would not leave. He was nearly everything she wanted, and Lee was old enough to know nearly was usually as close as you got in the real world. She'd decided long ago, while dating a man whose laugh was high and girlish, that the *fear* of settling she saw tormenting her friends was worse than the act itself. It was a fallacy that settling was somehow wrong. Everyone settled, everyone tempered their childish expectations of the world; everyone happy and everyone sane. She settled for department store clothes instead of designer originals because she didn't want to spend that much money dressing herself. She settled for a sedan instead of a foreign sports car because although sports cars were nice, they were also dangerous and expensive. And yet she loved her car. It had nearly everything she wanted. And nearly, if you were smart, was good enough.

She remembered a day, just after Thanksgiving, when she and Porter drove to Atlantic City, not to gamble but to walk along the beach. They both loved the beach in the fall, loved the slanting gray light and the comforting loneliness of sea and sky. But almost as soon as they arrived a storm rolled in, the sky opened up, and they had to race back to the car. It was the drive back to Philadelphia she remembered now: the two of them cocooned together by the silky rain and the voice of Sarah Vaughan, herself warm and drowsy in the passenger seat, Porter humming as he steered the car home.

She'd looked over at him and noticed, for the first time, a scar at the outer edge of his right eyebrow. It was tiny, half an inch perhaps, a small but obvious crescent of discolored flesh. Perfectly clear if you were paying attention, but she had never noticed it. All these months of staring at Porter and she had missed it. It was amazing how you could love some- one without seeing him. She had allowed herself to love—cautiously to be sure, but love nonetheless—this man before her while all the time still thinking of him, relating to him, not as a person but as an archetype. It was just the kind of thing she would have accused men of, and white people. She would not have thought it possible of herself.

The couch was uncomfortable. After much tossing and fluffing of pil- lows he finally gave up and curled up on the floor beneath his overcoat. It was there she found him in the morning. He woke to the feel of her fingers in his hair.

"Hey," she said.

"Hey."

"I'm sorry about last night."

"Me too." He struggled to sit up; the water and ibuprofen had dulled his hangover, but his back hurt like hell. "You need a new couch."

"I'll get right on it." She helped him to the couch, made coffee, brought it out. "Listen, I'm serious about what I said. I'm sorry about last night. I'm sorry about all of it, all the suspicions and challenges and crap I've given you since the beginning."

"Wow" was all he could say. His head wasn't pounding but that didn't mean the synapses were firing right. "Think we might need to have this conversation later."

"Good idea." She put down her cup, then took his from his hands. Pushing him backward on the couch she said, "I just want you to know I know I haven't been easy."

"No," he admitted.

She unbuttoned his shirt, began caressing his chest. "I'm not sure why you've put up with it. But I'm glad you did."

"Yeah," he said, still muddled, no longer trying to work it through. "Me too."

Chapter 21

But it was different.

They made up, forgave and tried to forget, put the misunderstanding aside. He was old enough to know a relationship required this kind of mapping early on, this kind of settling in, settling down. It meant only that they were two intelligent, strong-willed, and independently minded people, trying to carve between them a space where they could meet. And wasn't that the good part? Wasn't that part of what excited him—her independence, her originality?

Plus, if anything, Lee seemed more settled, more trusting of him, more willing to picture a future for them. Less eager to delineate by race. "We are the world," she joked, lying naked and warm beside him in bed, her dark legs wrapped around his own.

"We are the children," he joked back, taking her hand.

But it was different. He felt it. As much as he tried not to.

Lee invited him to Baltimore for Christmas. This was, he knew, no idle request; it was a signal of her seriousness, her willingness to claim and be claimed. He'd long since stopped asking her when she was going to let him meet the folks, had stopped asking if her folks even knew about him yet.

But he'd drawn the weekend rotation and had to work Christmas Eve, a Saturday, while Lee had taken it off so she could head down to Baltimore a day early; she wanted to get on the road. After tossing around various scenarios he finally suggested, with what he hoped was appropriate regret, that maybe they should just celebrate early, by themselves, then spend the day itself with their respective families. His sister, Peg, was staying in Chicago and his parents would be alone, et cetera, et cetera, et cetera. Lee said she understood.

They exchanged gifts over dinner Thursday night. She gave him a beautiful wool sweater, a gift certificate for a massage, and two tickets to the Sixers when the Chicago Bulls were in town. He gave jewelry: pearl earrings and a long necklace of freshwater pearls, pearls being Lee's birthstone. The earrings were expensive. The necklace was fairly cheap, but he included it so the jeweler could wrap them together in a big box instead of a small one. He didn't want any raised expectations. Even for the minute it took to open a gift.

She planned to leave Friday after work but got stuck on a story until nine and decided to go home and leave early Saturday. He offered to come over, but she said no, she was just going to bed. So he stayed home that evening, luxuriating in the just-right feel of his apartment after so much time in Lee's rambling house. He bought a six-pack of beer and ordered up the Playboy Channel. On Saturday morning he slept in, then rose and cleaned house in a domestic frenzy, sweeping out cobwebs, vacuuming dust, changing sheets that had not been changed in months because he so rarely slept on them. He threw out the living organisms in his refrigerator, wiped the inch of dust from the top of the television, laid to rest three brown and withered houseplants, and went to the local nursery for more. On the way home he decided to stop at the grocery store for flour and milk and eggs and other essentials. He was going, reluctantly, to his parents' for Christmas dinner, but the rest of the weekend he'd be eating at home. He couldn't remember the last time he'd cooked. He and Lee ate most of their meals at restaurants, and when they did eat at home it was at Lee's house, not his, with Lee cooking up pork chops or fried chicken and candied yams. All of which he liked. All of which he had, in fact, encouraged her to make. But now he craved something else, something cozy and homespun. Something like the meals he used to wish his mother would make.

He was thumping cantaloupes when he noticed, a few feet away at the potato stack, a woman. She had black eyes, pouty pink lips, and short, black hair tucked behind the most delicate seashell ears he'd ever seen and, most important, she was looking at him. At least he thought she was.

Be cool, he told himself, and glanced nonchalantly over his shoulder to make sure Mel Gibson had not wandered into the store. The coast was clear. No Mel Gibson, no Randall Cunningham or other local sports star (that had happened to him once), nobody. He turned back, and met the woman's eyes dead-on.

Snap. Crackle. Pop. The woman flushed and smiled and dropped the glance. Porter flushed and smiled and felt, below his belt, a quickening, a surge. Suddenly, he was juiced. The woman was still fondling potatoes, and so he took the moment to allow his eyes to roam. She wore jeans over her slender hips and a tight, pale-green sweater made out of something soft and cushiony, like cashmere. He stared at the sweater. He wanted to walk over to the woman and drive his head into the pillow of her chest and root around like a pig. The idea of it excited him so much he could barely stand. He felt, suddenly, like a drained battery being jump-started back to life and he hadn't even realized he was drained. He hadn't gone blind during his months with Lee, but his acknowledgment of pretty women, his seeing of them, had become—he realized now— more about distant appreciation and less about possibility. The desire for possibility. It was an amazing thing, tantalizing and sharp, like fresh-squeezed lemon juice. He had missed it so.

"Good-looking cantaloupes," said the woman.

"Yes," he said back. He was about to ask if she knew how to tell when one was ripe when the woman pulled a potato from the stack and sent the rest thudding to the floor. "Yikes!" she yelped. Very prettily, he thought.

"Spudslide!" he cried, for want of anything better to say and, amazingly, she laughed.

"That's pretty good!" she said. She had a surprisingly deep, sexy voice.

"Not really, but thank you for saying so."

Together they scrambled for the potatoes, dodging carts and chasing runaway spuds beneath the shelves. A frantic stockboy came to help and accidentally scored a goal with one potato in the onion bin, which made the woman toss back her head and laugh again.

"Not that I should be laughing," she said. "I'm the idiot who started this all."

"It could happen to anybody."

"Yeah. Right."

"It happened to me once."

"Really?"

"No. But you felt better for a second there, didn't you?"

She laughed again; it was so easy and so nice he felt like thumping his chest. He liked the way her hair fell into her face and he liked her laugh, liked that she laughed so easily and openly and well. She seemed utterly unburdened, though he knew that was unlikely. Still.

They retrieved most of the potatoes and stood side by side trying to re-form the stack. She smelled fresh and pink and faintly damp, like a baby after a bath. "It's not your fault," he said. "This bin is way too small for this many potatoes."

"I could have been hurt!"

"You could sue."

He wanted to ask her for coffee, not because he hoped it would lead to something but just for fun. Was that too much? Was that misrepresenting himself? He was still toying with the idea when he heard a child's voice say, "Mommy?"

The woman, still smiling, turned her eyes from him and looked around.

"Mommy, can we get this?"

Porter turned around and was surprised to see a little black girl looking up at the woman and clutching a bright orange box of tooth-decaying cereal. He was surprised that she was black, since Mommy clearly was not, but he reasoned that she must be adopted. He had once done a story on cross-racial adoption and he knew all the perils it entailed. He knew how some black people and most black social workers were against it, because they believed it distanced the child from her community and stripped her of her cultural identity. His heart went out to the girl, poor and black and cross-racially adopted and, truth be told, unattractive too. It was low to call a child ugly, but there was no getting around the truth with this girl. She had dull copper skin, a face splotched with brown freckles, wild, frizzy, cinnamon-colored hair. He looked back at the mother—who stood hands on hips, shaking her head against the cereal—and wondered what she saw when she looked at the girl. And then, with a jolt, he realized the two of them shared the same eyes.

He looked back at the girl. Same eyes, same tender ears. No question, she was the woman's daughter. The girl was biracial, not black.

He'd seen biracial children before, of course. This was Philadelphia, not some backwater, redneck southern town; if not exactly crawling with mixed families, the city certainly had its share. He'd seen biracial children in the months he and Lee had been together, hadn't he? He must have. God knows, they'd talked about it enough. *Yes, but how will you feel, escorting your little mocha daughter to school?*

I'll feel fine. I'll feel proud.

So it wasn't, it could not have been, the girl's biracialness now roiling his gut. It wasn't that race—race!—had once again shoved itself into what was a pleasant little scene. It was the child's ugliness that bothered him. Before she'd been simply an unattractive little black girl, and that had been okay—some black people were pretty and some were not, just as some white people were pretty and some were not, and he was clearly able to see beauty in black people because he thought Lee astonishing.

But now she was an ugly biracial child. She was a biracial child *he found ugly*, and he didn't know why or what that said. He looked at the girl, trying hard to discern what about her repelled him. Was it that stain of freckles? The dull, murky tone of her skin? Were her features simply skewed or was it, in fact, her very biracialness which telegraphed *ugly* to his brain? He thought about Charlie. Charlie who saw himself someday being a father, playing in his backyard with his three beautiful, tow-headed tykes. His pink-cheeked, blue-eyed Gerber babies. Picture perfect before the world.

"Is there a problem?" the mother asked. She was no longer smiling. She had seen him staring at her daughter and probably taken it for disapproval. She must be used to disapproving looks.

"No, no, of course not." He stuttered and flushed. "You have a very pretty daughter."

"Yes," she said, cold now as January. "I do."

He tried to think of something nice to say to the girl, hoping to God she had not somehow managed to read his mind. "I used to love that cereal when I was a kid," he said. "My mother said it would rot my teeth."

The child ignored him, focused solely on pleading her case. "Mommy, please? We never get to eat anything good!"

"Come on, honey."

"Mommy, please? Please? Please?"

"I said no. Let's go." The mother wrapped her arm protectively about her daughter's shoulder and marched off toward the deli counter.

"Merry Christmas," he called to their retreating backs, but was ignored. He grabbed a few supplies and left the store, not wanting to run into them again. In the car he dug around in the glove compartment until he found an antacid and popped it in his mouth. Calm down, he told himself. Get a grip. He was making far too much of this. The child was ugly. He didn't make her ugly. Being half-black didn't make her ugly. If she'd been white and looked the same she still would have been ugly and that would have been the end of it.

But if she were white she would not have been the daughter he might someday have with Lee. That's where this thing with Lee was leading, wasn't it? Marriage, children. The reality hit him like a snowplow. It was as though he'd been driving down the road with Lee and she'd been telling him where they were going and he'd been nodding, but now, suddenly and for the first time, he could really see the end. That girl in the store could be his daughter. Being half-black didn't make her ugly, but maybe he did. Maybe he made her ugly because she was half-black. And maybe one day he would look down into the face of his child and make her ugly too.

He drove around the city for an hour, unable to go home. He felt infected, and going home would contaminate everything in his apartment and he would never be able to get it all out. He tried to tell himself he was being silly, overreacting. He would love any kid of his, no matter how she looked. Mother Nature, in her wisdom, would take care of that. Didn't that woman in the store think her daughter was beautiful?

He drove around the great, gray hulk of City Hall and down the broad expanse of Franklin Parkway, all decorated with plastic wreaths and giant swaying Christmas balls, and beneath the Museum of Art up on the hill and past the Schuylkill and up Lincoln Drive and into Germantown. He drove over cobblestones and into Mt. Airy and out of Mt. Airy and into leafy Chestnut Hill. He drove past a park full of bundled, laughing children and their mothers, and he noticed how cute they were and he noticed that all of them were white.

He had not thought the girl in the store beautiful, and neither would the world. That was the real problem. The world. That little girl had to live in the world and the world was cruel. That girl, no matter where she went, would always stand out. And standing out was hard, standing out was painful. Standing out was a lot to ask of a child, just so that you could prove how ding-damn liberal you were. Hadn't that woman in the store thought of that? Wasn't it more important to think of the child?

He drove on through Chestnut Hill and got on the highway and made his way back into the city, knowing as he drove that he was completely full of shit.

Was this him? Porter wondered. Was this really who he was? The taste in his mouth lay thick and foul, like curdled milk. He rolled down the window and spat, but he wasn't moving fast enough or he didn't spit hard enough because the saliva caught on his lip and splashed onto his cheek, which was exactly what he deserved. Was this who he really was? *Think of the children.* What a crock of shit. His mother would be so proud; they could be her words. He could picture her with her hands neatly clasped, he could hear the words coming from her mouth.

He was too tired to drive anymore so he went home. When he got back to his apartment the telephone was ringing. He picked it up and heard Lee's voice, sexy, candy sweet, on the other end of the line and his heart lurched.

"So I was driving through Wilmington and the strangest thing happened," she said.

"What was that?"

"I was suddenly overcome with longing for you. Do you think it's something they pump into the air?"

A block of ice had wedged in his gut since the grocery store but now it began to melt. "Probably. You know I'm wanted all over Wilmington, by every man, woman, and child."

"I don't doubt it," she said. "But you want me, right?"

The bad taste in his mouth went away, replaced by the flavor of her lips, her honeyed nipples, the confectionery between her thighs. He did want her. He wanted her because she was smart and because she made him think. And he wanted her because she was tough and damn near impenetrable sometimes and at other times, like this, she would suddenly open to him, as welcome and tender and vulnerable as the first buds of spring. He imagined her now, leaning into the telephone booth, clasping the handset with her long, brown fingers, the back of her lovely neck exposed. He imagined the guy in the next booth glancing over in admiration, tracing with his eyes the heartbreaking outline of her hips. He imagined himself coming in from the outside, seeing her there, this exquisite black beauty in a room full of lard-assed suburban travelers in their sneakers and stirrup pants and fat, Michelin Man coats, seeing her there and going to her, past the mouth-breather in the next booth, and knowing she was his. She was his and she was amazing and he was insanely lucky and all that nonsense earlier, all that frantic mind shucking and jiving was just small-minded, panicky crap, the cold, tenacious grip of his suburban breeding trying to rise up from the dead and claw him in the back. She was an amazing woman and she was his and if he lost her, if he screwed this up, he would regret it. He would kick himself, he would. If he screwed up this thing somebody should just take a two-by-four to the side of his head.

"Where are you?"

"First rest stop in the lovely state of Maryland. Got a later start than planned."

"When are you coming back?"

She laughed and it seemed to him the most seductive laugh he had ever heard. "I'm not even there yet!"

"So turn around."

"You know I can't. My mother expects me for Christmas. I'll be back Monday. We can have dinner if you want."

"What I want is to hang up the phone and go into my bedroom and find you there on the bed. Right now."

"I'd like that too."

"I love you," he said. He felt an almost frantic anxiety, as though she were going someplace dangerous and he needed to arm her, to make sure she would come back safe.

"I know," she said, very softly. He panicked. Why didn't she say I love you too? Probably just because she didn't want to declare herself for all the world to hear. Still he panicked.

"Come back," he said.

"I can't, Porter. They're expecting me."

"Okay, okay. But get back as soon as you can. We'll do something."

She laughed coyly. "Like what?" He could hear, among the noise in the background of the line, children running and shouting and a woman's voice calling, "Cut that out!"

"Like get married. I want to marry you."

He held his breath, awaiting not only her response but his own. "Lee?"

"What?"

"Did you hear me?"

"I heard. I just don't know what to say."

"You don't have to say anything now. Just think about it. I'm serious, Lee. I love you and we're not children." He flinched at the word *children* but kept going, there wasn't time to stop. "We're not children, far from it, and suddenly I don't know what we've been waiting for. Let's get married. Let's start our lives and stop this half-assed bullshit. Let's get off the pot! Let's close our eyes and jump in with both feet! Let's do every other cliché you can think of!" He didn't want to stop talking but his heart was pounding and he needed to find a chair.

For a minute neither one of them spoke. Then, finally, when he could breathe easily again, Porter said, "Lee?"

"Here," she said.

Her voice was so small it made him ache. "What are you thinking?"

"I . . . I guess I'm thinking. . . . I'm thinking we'll have to tell our children how their daddy proposed to their mommy Christmas Eve while she was standing in a rest stop off I-95 watching some woman yell at her kid. It will make a great story."

"Is that a yes?"

"It's a yes."

He exhaled a great, ecstatic gust into the telephone. He felt light-headed and woozy with love.

"This'll be good! This'll be great!"

She laughed. "Man! Now I guess I really do have to tell my mother. Believe it or not, I planned to do it this weekend."

"Tell her about me?"

"Yes, baby."

It was out of his mouth before he knew he was going to say it. "Don't tell her about us getting married. Not yet."

"Why not?" Lee asked lightly. He could hear the smile in her voice.

Porter hesitated. Why not? He didn't know why not. He didn't know why he'd said it; his brain was spitting sparks all over the place but none of them were catching fire. "I want to get you a ring," he said, and it sounded right, so he went with it. "I want people to know I'm serious."

He hoped he didn't sound like he was convincing himself, because he wasn't. He was sure. On the other end of the line, somewhere in Maryland, Lee laughed into the phone. "Well, one thing I'll say for you, Porter. You certainly know how to surprise a girl!"

Chapter 22

On the front door of Marcus's condo hung an enormous wreath, bedecked with ribbons and glass balls and bits of real holly. Lee figured the wreath must have been put there by the girlfriend, since Marcus was hardly the decorating type.

Her brother came to the door yawning and rubbing his eyes. Lee tapped on her watch teasingly. "Hm, still in bed at eleven in the morning? Late night?"

"Sherry and I were up until four."

"Ah, youth." She pecked her brother's cheek, then led the way into his kitchen and began making coffee. "I remember those days, dancing until dawn."

"We weren't dancing." Marcus collapsed into a chair. "We were talking."

"Uh-oh. That doesn't sound good. Breaking up?"

"Actually just the opposite. We're getting married."

She nearly dropped the eggs in her hand. "You're kidding?"

"We even set a date. Middle of June."

She could not have been more surprised if Marcus had announced he was taking up cricket and moving to Bangladesh. It wasn't only the coincidence of having Porter propose to her that very morning; it was also the idea of Marcus getting married at all. Her brother believed in serial monogamy, but his serials rarely lasted longer than a few weeks; two months for him was an eternity. He'd always told her he did not plan to marry until age forty, if at all. "If I get married I'm having kids. And if I have kids I will not leave them, no matter what happens," he told her. "So before I get married I want to be damn sure. It's way too easy to make a mistake."

Apparently this Sherry had found some way to reach him, had succeeded where many, many other women had failed. "Are you sure, Marcus?"

If he'd answered with a grin or a blush or some other expression of loopy, head-over-heels love, she would have worried. But he looked her straight in the eye and said somberly, "I'm sure, Lee. And I'm sure I'll work hard to stay this sure." And so she knew he'd be all right.

"Then stand up so I can hug you!" She had to stand on her toes to reach his shoulders, and her tears stained the front of his shirt. "Where is Sherry. Is she upstairs?"

"She's at her place. We were there. I came home because I knew you were coming down this morning."

"Have you told Mom yet?"

"We just decided five hours ago, Lee. I'll go over this afternoon."

"Amazing. This is really amazing!" She shook her head and began searching the cabinets for flour and baking powder. She would make biscuits from scratch, the way she used to on Saturday mornings when they were children. Marcus and her, stretched out on the floor before the television watching cartoons and crumbling the dense biscuits, soaked with butter and jelly, into their mouths. The memory made her smile. Her baby brother had grown up.

"You won't believe this," she began. But Marcus wasn't listening or didn't understand because he said, "Just a second, Lee. That wasn't the news I called you about. There's something else."

She knew, from the tone of his voice, it had to be about their father and it had to be bad. She felt a stab of panic, which was surprising. Even with updates from Marcus on his eternal search, she'd thought about her father less and less since Porter came into her life. Since she'd decided Porter really should be in her life. Her father would hate Porter, would loathe the very idea of him. Wasn't that the main reason she'd resisted Porter so long? Couldn't she admit that to herself? It was amazing how hardwired people were to need the approval of their parents, even when they thought they no longer did, even when they were grown. She wondered—would her father blame himself for Porter? Would he see, in her love for a white man, some kind of subconscious rejection of him? Or wasn't he that kind of man—introspective, self-analytical, open to self-doubt. The truth was, she had no idea.

"Did you find him?"

"Yes. I did." Marcus rose and took a piece of paper from a drawer. He handed it to her. "I got this in the mail Thursday."

It was a death certificate, or a copy of one, from Gary, Indiana, twenty-eight miles, she happened to know, from the city of Chicago, of which their father had always dreamed. The copy was crooked on the paper, blurred, done in a hurry by someone careless and unconcerned. But it had an official seal and it had a name: Clayton Page.

"How did you . . . ?"

"A total fluke." Marcus's smile was pained. "After all the time and money I've spent on this search I finally find what I'm looking for through a total fluke."

All of a sudden she was breathless. She lurched toward the kitchen table, needing to sit down. Marcus looked at her with alarm. "You okay?"

"Fine," she said, and pulled her mug to her lips, feigning a sudden desire to savor it while they spoke. She held the cup and let the heated liquid scorch her lips. "I didn't even know you were checking death records."

"I wasn't. I mean, I resisted that for the longest time. I just couldn't believe he was dead. You know that."

Yes, she did. Every time she'd suggested the idea—gently or otherwise—to her brother he'd gotten upset, refusing to hear.

"But over these past few months, as Sherry and I have gotten closer,

I don't know, I've started to realize I had to let this thing go. It was keep-ing me from moving on with my life. I realized that. And so I decided, no more searching. I decided it coming home one day in the car. But they were playing that Jackson Five song, the one we used to love?"

Lee tried a smile. "Which one?" She'd loved every song the Jackson Five ever recorded.

" 'Going Back to Indiana,' " Marcus said. "It made me think about how close Gary, Indiana, is to Chicago. If somebody, for whatever rea-son, couldn't make it in Chicago, they might end up there. So I decided I would check there before I gave up. It would be my last city, the end of my search. And I wasn't going to spend any more money. I wasn't going to hire anyone to check things out. I was just going to write the depart-ment of records and see what they had for Clayton Page."

"And this is what they had." She was still holding the death certifi-cate but only because she couldn't think what to do with it. Clutch it to her chest? Tear it up? Thirty years and all that remained of her father was his name on a cheap piece of wood pulp.

"That's what they had," Marcus said. For the first time in the con-versation his voice cracked a little and he sounded like a child, a boy try-ing hard to be a man. It was this sound from her baritone-voiced brother, this note of pain and loss, that brought her father back to her. Not his face—she was startled to realize she couldn't remember his face—but she could remember his voice, the amber sweet sound of him singing. Only this time it wasn't "Change Gonna Come" but "Lift Every Voice and Sing"—a song that always made her teary-eyed, though until this moment she hadn't realized why.

> Lift ev'ry voice and sing
> Till earth and heaven ring
> Ring with the harmony of Liberty
> Let our rejoicing rise high as the listening skies
> Let it resound loud as the roaring seas

"Maybe it's not him," she said.
Marcus shook his head. "It's him."

"How do we know it was him? There must be a thousand Clayton Pages in the world."

She tried to control the shaking in her voice, but Marcus must have heard it because he put his hand over hers and squeezed it. It was a strange thing, being comforted by her baby brother. She wanted to put her head on his shoulder and cry.

"Even if it's not him, it doesn't matter. He's been dead to us since the day he left. Isn't that what you've always said? That son of a bitch left us and so good riddance and good-bye."

Regret, regret; she was steeping in regret. As though she'd been the one to walk away and not look back. As though she'd been the one to desert, to abandon. But the alternative to regret was anger, and she'd been angry at her father for so long. She hadn't fully realized the burden of that anger, the heaviness of it, not until this moment, watching her brother pick it up and shoulder it.

"Don't hate him, Marcus," she said.

"Why not? He deserves it."

"Maybe so. But you don't. It's not worth it, believe me."

Marcus looked carefully at her for a moment, then he handed her the envelope without a word. He went back to his cooking. He scooped the dough onto the floured board, kneaded it deftly and lightly, then patted out the dough and cut the biscuits with a quick turn of his hand. That he knew how to cook was amazing enough to her. That he owned a biscuit cutter was beyond belief.

"Are you sure you want to give up?" she asked.

"If he is still alive, he knows where to find us. If he ever comes . . ." Marcus let his voice trail off. "But I'm through."

"I'm so sorry, Marcus," she said. "I'm so sorry for you."

"Yeah." Marcus shrugged and smiled, as though he'd lost a parking space or a quarter down a sewer grate. Not a father. "Life is tough. What can you do?"

It was the shrug that broke her. Suddenly she was crying, her shoulders swaying back and forth and Marcus was holding her, his floury hands wrapped protectively around her back. "It's okay," he said.

"It's not okay," she choked out between sobs. "Don't pretend it is. You've spent your whole life wanting this. How can you just give it up?"

"All right, it's not okay," Marcus said. He stepped back, handed her a tissue. "It sucks, right? And, yeah, I'm pissed and hurt and there's a hole in me and there always will be. Okay? But I'm moving on."

Lee wiped her face and sat down. Marcus pulled out a cookie sheet, lay the biscuits gently atop it one by one. "I'm growing up. People are allowed to grow up, aren't they?"

They ate the biscuits hot from the oven, slathered with butter and raspberry jam. Lee was impressed at how light they were and how good; they tasted of good mornings with their mother, of Christmas and Easter and long ago. Lee demolished two, then cracked a third and told her brother about Porter without nervousness.

"I figured you were seeing someone since you weren't coming down here nearly as much as when you first moved to Philadelphia," Marcus said. "And knowing you, I figured it was serious."

He was, he said, surprised she would marry a white man. But he did not disapprove. "Hey, it's your life, and I'm not trying to run it. It's hard enough work running my own."

"Don't worry: Sherry will run it for you," Lee joked.

"Oh no," Marcus said. He reached for his fifth biscuit. The boy could eat. "We're not like that. We're partners. I hope you and this guy will be too. As long as you're happy, I'm happy."

"I am," she said, and she couldn't help smiling. "I love him."

"Good."

Lee got up to refresh her coffee from the pot, relieved at how easy it had been telling Marcus about her love. But there was something else, still hanging out there in the distance. She sat down. "Of course, Pauline says I better know *why* I love him. She says the fact that he's smart and kind and stable and passionate about me is not enough."

Marcus shrugged and wiped his mouth with a paper napkin. "Maybe you just got tired. Maybe you just got tired of being suspicious and contemptuous of men and this guy was the one hanging around when you did."

Lee put down her cup. "I am not contemptuous of men!"

Marcus laughed. "Please! I'm your brother, remember? Anyway, I didn't mean it in a bad way."

"There's no good way you could mean it." She crossed her arms and leaned back into her chair. She was a little hurt that her brother could think such a thing.

Marcus reached across the table and punched her arm playfully, the way he used to when they were children. "Come on, Lee."

She turned her face away.

"All I'm saying is you had a hard time with guys, letting yourself be loved. You can admit that?"

Could she? That's what Howard said. Lee thought back over the short string of men who had infiltrated her life, the ones who'd left her and the ones she'd left. Was that the common string, an unwillingness to let herself be loved? She didn't know. But apparently Marcus thought he did. Had he been watching *Oprah* too?

"It's because of Dad, of course," Marcus said. "No one blames you for that. And maybe you just got tired of holding people at arm's length and this guy . . ."

Marcus was smiling, leaning toward her, reaching for a name and for détente. She softened. "Porter," she offered.

"Porter." Marcus smiled. "Maybe Porter is the one who made you realize how tired you were."

She stared at Marcus, astonished at such wisdom from the mouth that used to call her "butthead." Had Marcus, of all people, somehow figured things out? "And that's a good thing?" she asked. "That's a good reason to marry somebody?"

"As good as any," he said. "Better than a lot."

Her mother cried at the news of Marcus's engagement, cried and threw up her hands to praise the Lord. "What a wonderful surprise!" Eda cried.

"It's a day full of surprises," Marcus said, eyeing Lee. He telephoned Sherry and invited her to dinner, then left to pick her up. Lee knew he was leaving her alone with Eda so that she could tell her own news. There was no guarantee her mother was going to be as happy about that.

When Marcus was gone, Eda actually danced around the living room, executing a deft little soft shoe while Lee sat on the couch drinking tea and trying to pretend her eyes were red from tears of joy.

"The amazing thing is I actually like that girl," Eda said when she got winded and collapsed on the couch. "Got more sense than his last ten girlfriends combined. So I'm happy. One down and one to go." She looked at Lee. "Got any news for me in that department, baby?"

"Actually, yes," she began, before she realized her mother already knew. Eda was looking at her, mouth pursed and eyebrows raised. Perfectly plucked eyebrows raised when Lee could remember a time when getting her to comb her hair was a major accomplishment. But now . . . it was hard to imagine she had ever known her mother as weak.

"Who told you?"

"Nellie Hampton."

"Of course." Nellie Hampton was Cleo's mother and the biggest gossip in Baltimore. Lee should have known the news would filter down to Eda eventually.

"I ran into her at a community meeting on the police a few weeks ago," Eda said. "She came at me like a locomotive. 'So, I hear Lee is dating a white gentleman?' Obviously hoping I didn't know."

"I'm sorry, Mom."

"I pretended I did. She tried to be nasty about it but she could only go so far because the truth is, she was jealous. That's how backward Nellie is. Told me, 'Well, at least if they get married you'll get some pretty grandbabies out of it. They'll have that good hair.' "

Lee sighed. There was no sense being angry with Cleo. Cleo was young and righteous and unforgiving; she believed she knew herself and understood the world. She would learn. And there was no use being angry with Nellie Hampton, who was old and confused and beyond hope. *Pretty grandbabies. Good hair.* It broke Lee's heart to imagine people still carried such shattering nonsense inside their souls, but she knew they did. And not only old people. And now that she was with Porter some people would assume she did too. And if they had children, if, if, those children would have to confront the furious jealousy and confusion and self-loathing from which that nonsense sprang, she would have to lead them through. She would lead them through.

She looked her mother in the eyes. "His name is Porter Stockman. We work together. He's a good man." She wasn't trying to be challenging and she hoped her mother did not hear it that way. Eda did not answer for a moment. Then she asked, "Is it serious?"

"I love him and he loves me."

Eda smiled. "Those are words, baby. Words are not serious."

"He asked me to marry him. Is that serious enough?" She knew she sounded fourteen years old, but what could she do? Eda looked at Lee's hand and twisted her face skeptically. Just as Porter had predicted, no one took you seriously without a ring.

"He just asked this morning. It wasn't a planned thing. But he is serious and so am I. Mom, I'm going to marry him."

Eda pushed herself from the couch and began turning on lights. Outside the sun was setting in the blue-gray winter sky. "I don't know this man. If you say he's good I have to believe it." She'd turned on every light in the living room, not only the overhead but every lamp as well. Then she stood before Lee like a schoolmarm, hands clasped in front.

"But most of them I've met have been sick. Sick at heart, sick in their souls from so much hatred and fear all of their lives. And what they've wanted from me, what they want from all black people, is somebody to save them, to bring them back to life. Somebody to bend over and suck all the poison from their souls. And they don't care if you suck that poison into your own bloodstream and die. That's your problem. They just want what they want."

Lee stood. Her hands were trembling but her voice was not. "I can't tell you not to feel that way, Mom. Lord knows, I can't even tell you I don't sometimes still feel that way myself. But I can tell you Porter is not like that, that he sees me in a way no man, white or black, ever has. He makes me feel loved and safe and happy. And I have to go with that."

"But baby, it's going to be so hard. Why would you want to make your life that hard?"

Lee smiled. "Life *is* hard, Mom. You of all people know that."

"That's right, I do! I know how hard it is to make it with a man no matter what. Why complicate it by bringing race into the mix."

"Because I love him."

Eda scoffed. "Love does not conquer all, believe me."

"No, it doesn't." Lee put her arms around her mother. "But don't you think sometimes it conquers enough?"

Eda sighed and gave in to the embrace. "I'm scared for you, Lee. But if this is what you want, I'll support it. Bring Mr. Stockman down and let's see his face."

Lee laughed. "Maybe we can have a double wedding. Save you a few bucks."

"What makes you think I'm paying for this?" Eda pulled away and straightened her skirt. "Isn't Mr. Stockman rich? Don't tell me you're marrying a white man and he's not even rich. What's the point?"

They went into the kitchen together to make dinner for Marcus and his blushing fiancée. Eda already had a chicken roasting in the oven, sizzling and popping and smelling delicious. Eda handed Lee a bowl of potatoes and a peeler and sat down herself with a huge bowl of snap beans, enough to feed an army. The kitchen was warm and snug, and it was nice sitting there with her mother, both of them content. The scene did not remind her of her childhood because her childhood had been nothing like that. But it helped her imagine a future with her own daughter someday.

"Is Marcus still looking for your father?"

Lee fumbled a potato and nicked her forefinger with the scraper tip. It was a good thing her mother hadn't handed her a knife.

"Oh, don't look at me like that," Eda said. "I'm not a mind reader. One of his little girlfriends let it slip. She felt horrible about it, asked me to promise not to tell."

"How long?"

"Oh, I don't know." Eda shrugged in a way that showed she remembered the exact moment she found out her children were searching for their father. "Not long. I'm not upset, if that's what you're worried about. I admit I was a little hurt at first, but Mr. Carter helped me realize it was only natural for you both to want to know your father. It has nothing to do with me."

Mr. Carter. Living proof that God never forgot you, even when you thought He had. Lee wished he'd been around twenty-five years earlier, for Eda and for her. What a difference a man like that would have made.

"Is he still looking for Clayton?"

"No," Lee said without hesitation. She and Marcus had already agreed never to tell their mother and she saw no reason to change that now. "He gave up."

Eda nodded, her hands moving like a machine through the great bowl of beans. "I'm sorry," she said after a moment. "I'm sorry you grew up without a father around."

"It wasn't your fault."

"When you're a mother, it's always your fault."

"You weren't the one who left us. You weren't the one who walked out."

Eda stopped snapping beans. She looked at Lee, licked her lips. "Your father didn't walk out on you, Lee."

"It's too late to try to protect him now. Way too late."

"I kicked him out. I made him go."

It took a moment to make sense of her mother's words. And then they began to pry up layer upon layer of memory and belief. Her father singing to her mother across the dinner table. Her father stumbling into the bathroom and slamming the door. Her father walking down the steps, suitcase in hand, not looking back. Her mother slumped on the floor in the kitchen, crying and calling his name. Herself glancing through the small window in the front door thousands of times over the years, always half hoping to see him standing there on the porch, about to knock. Herself at her high school graduation, willing him to appear out of the smiling crowds so she could throw her diploma in his face.

"I just couldn't take it anymore," Eda was saying. "He was drinking more and more. He couldn't keep a job. Or he wouldn't keep a job—he hated the white men who ran the companies. He couldn't stand working for them, and so he'd get himself fired or just up and quit. And then he'd get drunk and come home late at night and be sick as a dog the next day and I had to take care of him and you and Marcus too. I felt like I was losing my mind. I told him he was useless and we didn't need him and to get out."

There was a long pause. Then Lee asked, "Why did you tell us he left us?"

Eda didn't answer, just shook her head.

"Why did you lie?" Lee nearly reeled from the force of her sudden fury. "All these years you let us think he abandoned us!"

Eda leapt from her chair, sending the bowl of beans crashing to the floor. "He did abandon you! Just because I kicked him out of the house didn't mean he had to leave Baltimore. He could have stayed around, could have gotten a job and sent you a few dollars now and then! He did abandon you! He abandoned all of us and don't you forget it!"

Lee looked up and saw, in her mother's weathered face, the terrified young woman she must have been back then. Despairing, drowning, struggling desperately to stay afloat as she pried her husband from her back and then watched in horror as he floated away. Lee had always believed she knew what her mother went through all those years. She'd been there too, going through it beside Eda, sometimes pulling her along. But now she realized she had no idea what truly her mother had suffered. No idea at all. She put the potatoes on the table and got down on her knees to pick up the beans. After a long while Eda wiped her face with a paper towel and got down on her knees too.

"I guess." She sighed. "I was so, so angry at him for so long for what happened to us, for all the hard times we had to go through. And I was jealous. I didn't want you and your brother growing up worshipping him. Children always worship the absent parent."

"That's not true."

"Yes it is, baby. They worship the absent parent and blame the one left behind."

Lee pulled her mother to her feet and made her sit down in a chair while she picked up the remaining beans. "We don't blame you, Mom. You sacrificed yourself to save us. We know what you did."

While Eda rinsed the beans, Lee filled a pot with water and put the potatoes on the stove to boil. She thought about the death certificate, about their decision not to tell their mother because they would also have to tell her they'd been searching for him in the first place. It seemed now beside the point. And she was tired of lying; it was time to stop. "I didn't tell you the whole truth earlier. About Marcus not searching for Dad anymore."

"So he is still searching? Good. I have something that might help."

"It's too late. Marcus found a death certificate. From Gary, Indiana. He's dead."

She wasn't sure what reaction to expect, but the one she received surprised her. Eda shook her head and laughed. "He's not dead."

"How do you know?"

"Because I have just checked with the Social Security office last week and they don't have him listed as dead. I used to do it every year, half hoping he was dead. I haven't done it in a while."

"How can you check with the office?"

"Because I'm still his wife," Eda said. "And I have his Social Security number."

Eda wiped her hands on a towel and wrote nine numbers on a piece of paper. She handed it to Lee. "Here's your father. Maybe this will help Marcus with his search. I should have given it to him a long time ago."

Lee put the paper in her pocket and together they finished making the meal.

Chapter 23

His Christmas gift to himself was not breaking the news of his engagement to his parents over duck à l'orange. He made the decision on the drive out. Why rush? The engagement was only a few hours old; it would keep. He would get through the holidays, get Lee a ring, make it official before announcing their upcoming nuptials to the world. When his mother asked about Lee—and he could see it cost her to do so—he said only that she had gone home to Baltimore to spend the holiday.

"How nice," his mother said.

In the end, it was February before Porter finally got around to shopping for the ring. The week after Christmas was out—forget it—as were the first two weeks of January; he just couldn't brave the wild-eyed mobs of bargain seekers and gift returners at the stores. Then work got busy: there was a new administration in Washington and everyone wanted to know what that meant for Philadelphia's fortunes. And then he realized he'd better do some research first, go to the bookstore and find a book on diamond buying before running off to the mall. He'd decided on a Saturday morning trip to the bookstore, but on Wednesday night in bed

Lee teasingly waved her naked hand before his face and said something about Valentine's Day bearing down.

So that Saturday he pulled himself from bed. It was bitterly cold in his apartment. When he called the superintendent to complain, the man answered with a frazzled "I'm on it!" and slammed down the phone. Porter wrapped himself in sweaters, brewed coffee, and headed out the door. He drove to a strip mall near King of Prussia, to a store owned by a guy named Louie Flexner. Louie had sold him Lee's pearl earrings and the emerald necklace he once gave Chira and every other piece of significant jewelry Porter had ever bought. It wasn't a glamorous store, and Porter always felt a little silly buying jewelry next to a Pack-And-Save, but he trusted Louie, and that was important. Especially with this. He would need Louie to get him through this one.

But Louie wasn't there. A sign on the door said he was ill. Since it was a one-man store, the shop was closed. Porter didn't know what to do. He stood with his hand on the doorknob for a full five minutes, trying to figure out if this was a bad omen or just bad luck and whether he should give up and go home. He'd almost made up his mind to do just that, but then he saw Lee on Valentine's Day, waiting expectantly by the door.

Porter tried to shake off his stupor. He could do this. Louie wasn't the only jeweler in the world. He got back into his car and headed to Center City, to jewelers' row.

The first store he went into seemed to specialize in gold: earrings, pendants, and especially the thick, ropy chains so popular among people of a certain age. The store was crowded with young men, mostly black but also a few white, and behind the counter two Indian men scurried about. The engagement rings were limited to a single, tiny case on the far right-hand side of the store, and even to his untrained eye they looked more like bubble gum machine prizes than something to win a woman's heart. He turned and left.

The next store was bigger, brighter, and less crowded. Frank Sinatra played softly in the background, and there seemed to be only one salesperson on duty, a woman of about fifty, with silver hair pulled back into a bun and jeweled, cat-eye glasses hanging from a string around her neck. She looked downright grandmotherly, and he relaxed. She was chatting with a customer, a young woman, but she must have smelled "engagement ring" because she quickly excused herself and made a beeline for him.

"Good morning!" she chirped. "Beautiful day out, isn't it?"

He smiled and agreed. They made pleasant chitchat for a moment; she seemed to have all the time in the world to talk to him.

"Well," he said finally, "guess we should get to the business at hand."

"Oh, you're right. I'm such a blabbermouth! What can I help you with today?"

"I'm looking for an engagement ring."

The woman clapped her hands in delight. "Oh, how wonderful! Congratulations!"

"Thank you."

"Marriage is the foundation of civilized society, I always say. My own dear husband and I were married for thirty-two years before he passed on." She lifted her eyes heavenward and sighed.

"I'm sorry," Porter said, hoping that was the correct thing to say.

She shrugged. "What can you do? I told him not to go fishing in a thunderstorm. Now you, come right over here!" She grabbed his arm and dragged him across the shop floor to a display counter. "Maybe we should start with you telling me how much you want to spend? I'm sure you know the standard is two months' salary."

He tried not to look stunned. Two months' salary was a lot of money: more than ten grand. He'd expected to spend maybe half that amount. "Is that before or after taxes?"

"Oh, that's a good one!" she cackled, still clawing his arm. "Oh, that's rich! I'll have to remember that!"

Porter smiled weakly.

"Of course," the woman said, abruptly serious, "that's just a baseline. Many men spend more. You have to remember this is an investment in your love. You want it to be as special as she is to you."

She squeezed his arm and began a long, breathless rant about carat size. Size mattered. He wanted the woman of his dreams to be proud of her ring, didn't he? He wanted her to be able to flash it before all her friends and to have them look at it without a magnifying glass? One carat was the minimum he should consider, and if he really wanted to impress his girl, how about two?

She pulled a tray from the case and began plucking rings and shoving them under his nose. "This one's a real beauty, the best in our collection. One-point-five total carat weight. It's a bargain at eight thousand, seven hundred and seventy-five dollars. This one is very Tiffany but, of course, without the Tiffany price. This one is my favorite. If I were getting a ring for myself, this is the one I'd buy."

A dull throbbing began at the back of his head and his nerves began to twitch and strain. He faked a yawn so he could raise his hand and shake the woman off. It worked, and he even managed to step back a bit, but as soon as he stopped yawning she pressed right back into his space.

"Look at this one," she said. "Your fiancée would flip over this, I guarantee." Porter glanced at the price tag: $9,500. His head began to throb. Ten thousand dollars? How could he be expected to plunk down ten grand for a scrap of pressurized carbon no bigger than a sunflower seed? Ten thousand dollars was a lot of money. Ten thousand dollars was the down payment on a house, only a house was a lot more stable, a lot more predictable. You knew what you were getting with a house.

"What shape does your fiancée like?"

"Shape?"

"You know: round, oval, square? Pear-shaped diamonds are nice, my favorite. How about marquis?"

She picked up rings one by one to demonstrate, but all Porter could do was shake his head. "I don't know."

"Oh, that's not unusual." The woman waved off his apparently superficial knowledge of the woman he was going to marry. "What about gold, though. Does she like white gold or yellow? Or platinum?"

"I don't know," he admitted again. He and Lee had never discussed gold. They had never discussed jewelry at all.

"Better get platinum to be safe," the saleswoman suggested. "Every girl loves platinum."

But by now Porter's head was clanging like a fire bell and the only thing he wanted to do was escape. It was ridiculous anyway. What the hell was he doing, about to hand over thousands of his hard-earned dollars to some woman just because she reminded him of someone's grandmother? Not even his own grandmother, not even close. It was crazy to just walk in off the street and buy a diamond ring. It was crazy to get yourself into something without knowing what it was.

"You've been very helpful," he told the woman as he began his retreat. "I'll come back later and decide."

She didn't want to let him go. The rings might not be there later, she said. If financing was an issue . . . a diamond spoke volumes to a woman, don't put it off! He backed out of the store, hands up as if to hold her off, nodding and mumbling empty promises to return as he went.

That night, Lee cooked dinner at her place. She was in a good mood, humming along to Marvin Gaye and swaying her hips as she cooked. He watched her with a strange, gnawing sensation in his gut he could not name. He loved her, he did. He was pretty sure of that. But . . . something. Something. That night in bed, he felt his coming not as sweet release but as a hollowing.

On Monday, in desperation, he drove back to Louie's place and was relieved to find the door open and the lights on. "It was nothing," Louie said. "A little gas. What can I do for you?"

"I need an engagement ring," Porter said. "I have five thousand to spend. Well, maybe six thousand."

"No problem," Louie said, moving behind his counter. But Porter waved him off.

"You do it," he said. "I mean, I trust you. Pick me something nice. I have to get back to work. I'll come back on Thursday."

Louie smiled and nodded, as if it was perfectly normal for a man to delegate complete responsibility for his future wife's engagement ring. Maybe it happened all the time.

Four days later, on the day before Valentine's Day, Porter went to the little strip mall. Louie opened the little velvet box with a flourish: inside was a ring of white gold with a small but clear white diamond in the middle and two much smaller diamonds on either side.

"That's a nice diamond. That's the key: buy the diamond loose, then put it in the ring," Louie said. "You take that anywhere in the city and get it appraised. If it's not worth at least seven thousand, I'll take it back."

Porter closed the box. He didn't want to take the ring someplace. He didn't want to get it appraised. He didn't want to think about it anymore. He wrote Louie a check, put the ring in his pocket. On Valentine's Day he took Lee out to dinner and put the ring on her butter plate. She cried. He shoved down his mounting trepidation and took her hand. They set October 16 as the date.

He left work and drove west along the highway, leaving the city behind, headed toward the suburb of his youth. It was a warm spring evening, fervent and fresh scrubbed, and the old neighborhood was vibrant with the squeals of children playing tag, with the laughter of women pushing strollers around the block, with the smell of warming earth and the sight of great, sunshiny bursts of forsythia everywhere.

His father was napping when he arrived. "Exhausted from a hard day of nonachievement," his mother said, greeting Porter at the door with a peck upon the cheek. "This is a nice surprise, Porter. We don't usually see you twice in one month."

They went together into the living room, which had been stripped of its three-year-old wallpaper and painted white since the last time he was there. The overstuffed floral couch and matching loveseat had been replaced by two elegant, cream-colored couches with Queen Anne legs and wooden arms. The Sunday paper, purchased but unread, sat perfectly displayed on a new walnut coffee table.

"The room looks nice," he said.

His mother glanced around the room with disinterest before sitting on one of the couches. Porter sat across from her and said, "I have some news. Maybe I should go wake Dad so I can tell you both at the same time."

His mother crossed her legs. "No," she said. "Tell me first."

"Okay." He sat down opposite his mother and met her eyes. "I've asked Lee to marry me. She said yes."

He had expected disappointment, disapproval, perhaps even a barrage of anger and recrimination. But his mother's face remained expressionless.

"I see," she said.

"You don't seem surprised."

She smiled at this, a formal, ladies' luncheon kind of smile. "Is that why you're getting married? To surprise me?"

He felt himself flush. "This has nothing to do with you."

"Doesn't it?"

Her calmness infuriated him. He stood, wanting to be on his feet. "Lee and I are getting married," he said, looking down on her from his full height. "It would be nice if you could act like a normal mother and be happy for me."

"A normal mother?"

"You know, one who supports her children?" He hated the way he sounded, whiny, petulant. He didn't want to get dragged down to her level in this argument; he didn't want to argue at all. "The point is this," he said, making his voice cold and condescending. "Lee is an amazing woman. If you could overlook the color of her skin you'd recognize that."

Finally, her composure broke. "Overlook? Overlook!" His mother inhaled sharply, lifted her manicured hands, tossed back her head as if appealing such idiocy to the gods. "You make it sound as though her race were crooked teeth or a bad haircut! A preference for beer over wine! Something unimportant."

"It is unimportant."

She turned on him eyes brimmed with disdain, and he was so startled he let out a gasp. He was accustomed to seeing ambitiousness on his mother's face when she looked at him and frustrated pride and even disappointment but never disdain. "I thought you were supposed to be so smart," she said coldly.

"Meaning?"

"Meaning race is important. Class is important! Background is important, whether you like it or not. People are who they are and they always revert to that, no matter what, and if you don't know who a person is before you marry him you're a fool!"

"I guess that's something you should know about, huh?" he said angrily. "Were you a fool, Mother?"

She smiled, that mirthless upturn of the corners of her mouth he knew so well. "The biggest fool there ever was."

In the silence, Porter sat, defeated by the fathomless bitterness in his mother's voice. What was the point in lashing out at someone who was already dead? And his mother was dead, killed long ago by something, by thwarted ambition or greed or desire or just plain arrogance. He didn't know what it was, but he did know her hatred and cold contempt were the sources of all the misery in that marriage, the misery which, even when he and his sister were children, had been like a fifth person in the house. An unwanted guest who came vile and stinking to the dinner table day and evening and ruined every meal. He looked across the room at his mother and asked the question he'd waited all his life to ask: "If you hate my father so much, if you despise him so, why did you ever marry him?"

His mother didn't answer right away. Instead she rose and walked to the fireplace, the only part of the room to remain unchanged by the redecorating. On the mantel, carefully arranged, stood the obligatory family photographs: Peg and Porter in various school pictures and in their high school graduation gowns; his father in his official company portrait; his mother in a studio shot taken right after Porter was born when she was at the height of her beauty and probably knew it. Porter had long ago noticed there were photographs of the entire family, but now, for the first time, he noticed there were no candid shots, no pictures of them tossing fall leaves or walking on the beach. No captured moments, only pose and artifice.

His mother picked up the portrait of his father, taken maybe twenty years before, when he was still a rising young insurance executive. "I married him because I loved him."

He wanted to laugh at this statement it was so ridiculous, so painfully, horribly ridiculous. "That's love? From where I've been sitting all these years it's looked like war."

"It was love in the beginning. Your father was my shining knight. That's really the way I thought of him. He was the first man who ever looked at me without . . ." She let the thought trail off, then gathered herself. "He courted me as though I was a princess. He brought me flowers and candy and took me to dinner and told me all about New England where he grew up, about rocky beaches and the leaves in the fall. He made me so happy. He showed up in White Haven and laughed at it, laughed at the big people and showed me I could laugh at them too. He rescued me."

"Rescued you?" He was bewildered. "Rescued you from what?"

But his mother just said, "I loved him for that."

He waited to ask his next question, wanting to know so desperately and not wanting to hear. Finally, when it was clear she wasn't going to volunteer the information, he prodded, "What happened?"

His mother, still holding his father's photograph, said, "You never really knew your grandmother, did you? She died when you were three, but I think we have a picture of her somewhere. Your father used to keep one on his bureau but it has long since disappeared."

He didn't know what this had to do with anything, but he knew if he just kept quiet and waited, the connection would be revealed. He was a good reporter, and a good reporter knew no secret could remain forever hidden. You could always, if you waited long enough, get someone's story out of them.

"She was . . . a very difficult woman. Your father was her firstborn. She had certain expectations of him. Which he resisted. I didn't know all this, of course. We married without me ever meeting her. You know your father was stationed at Fort Sand and we met and got married and lived there for six months before he was discharged. And then we moved back here, back north, and I met her for the first time. It was winter, I remember that because it was bitterly cold and I didn't have the right shoes and my feet were freezing. We walked into her house and she looked at me with her lip curled. She was a big woman, huge, and her voice was like somebody scraping out the inside of a can. And she said, 'My son has married you to throw it in my face.' I was nineteen. Hundreds of miles away from home for the first time in my life. Up north for the first time in my life. I didn't know what to say. The only thing I could do was look over at your father. He was sitting in a chair in the corner, legs crossed, picking at the lint on his pants. And I heard his mother tell me that and I looked at him. He had the faintest little smile on his face. I looked into his eyes and I saw that it was true."

Porter looked past his mother to her photograph on the mantel. It was one of those hand-painted black-and-white pictures. She was wearing a pale blue jacket with a Peter Pan collar, and her hair was pulled back and her face shone and she was beautiful, so golden and blossoming and young. The fairest flower in the Delta state. He imagined that face wilting under an old woman's bitter attack, that face turning toward his father, reading his father's eyes. He imagined the scene and it was painful, so painful he shut his eyes against it. Because to imagine such a tableau required a reversal of all he thought he knew about his parents and their relationship. It required a recasting of the roles he had long ago assigned them—mother as cold and embittered harridan, as driving fury, as lost southern gentry desperate to regain her way of life; father as sweetly ineffectual, weakly ball-busted, wanting only to be loved, and failing that, finding solace in his glass. It required a revolution, upheaval, and it flung an orderly world into disarray. Everything was tipsy. People and things he thought he knew were now rolling off mark. He felt unmoored, adrift.

"Why didn't you leave? Why didn't you just walk out?"

"I was already carrying you."

A wave of nausea swept over him, as though he were the one pregnant, abused, and alone. "What about your family? Couldn't you have gone back to them?"

His mother put down the photograph and turned around. "My family?" There was something in her voice he could not read, something dangerous. He felt a fine layer of sweat break out on his forehead. It was his duty to ask, to push ahead and get the whole story, even though he wasn't sure he wanted to hear it. Finally, though, he managed to ask, "Wouldn't they have taken you in? Didn't you want to go back there?"

But his mother just smiled, and he saw she had regained herself. She clapped her hands together as if smacking off dirt, and when she spoke, her voice had reverted to its usual cool containment. "Families can be perplexing, can't they? Have you met her family yet?"

So apparently that was as much of the story as he was going to get. He was ashamed of his relief. "No," he said. "But she's told them and they are not opposed."

"Well." His mother walked back to the couch and sat across from him. "Then I suppose you're all set."

"Yes."

"All is cleared."

"I suppose it is."

"Of course it is," his mother said firmly. "Her family shall not oppose the marriage. Neither shall I." She paused for a second, then smiled that unhappy smile. "And your father, I am quite sure, will be the first to raise his glass."

Chapter 24

They went through five stores before finding the right dress; even then, at first sight, Lee was unsure. She pulled it off the rack only at the saleswoman's insistence, already shaking her head. She'd envisioned herself in a fairly traditional gown with long, slender sleeves, a fitted bodice, and miles of satin below the waist. This dress was cream colored and mermaid-style, form-fitting to the floor with an ankle flare. She thought it would make her look hippy, but Pauline said, "Might as well try it on."

And so she did. She pulled up the zipper, turned toward the mirror, and fell in love.

"*That* is your dress." Pauline sat in a chair in the dressing room, beaming like somebody's mother. "It's beautiful!"

"It's sleeveless, though. Does that work for an October wedding?"

"It works if you want it to work," Pauline said. "You think somebody's going to stand up in church and yell, 'Hey! That's a summer dress!'"

The price tag said $500: cheap enough. But the dress must have been last year's style because the saleswoman was clearly eager to sell it. Lee feigned ambivalence and got the price knocked down to $450 with the matching hat and a pair of short lace gloves tossed in. "Now all we have to do is find *your* dress," she said, hugging Pauline as they left the store.

"If you make me buy something with mutton sleeves, I'll shoot you."

"No mutton sleeves. But I saw this gorgeous dress the other day, pink with big, fat peonies all over it. What do you think?"

Pauline rolled her eyes. "You are buying me lunch."

It was a bright, beautiful day, falsely warm for February, a day to deceive coats into slipping from backs. But away from the sun there was a bite to the air. Pauline and Lee strolled for a while, enjoying the sun, but when they finally chose a restaurant and went inside, they discovered their hands and feet were cold. At the table they ordered hot tea to warm themselves and then a bottle of champagne. Their waiter, a beautiful young brother with baby dreadlocks all over his head, popped the cork with a flourish. "You sisters must be celebrating something?"

Pauline took Lee's left hand and held it up for inspection. "Behold the rock," she said.

The waiter squinted his eyes as if blinded. "Very nice."

Lee took back her hand and rolled her eyes at Pauline, feigning embarrassment, though the truth was she loved it, loved the whole, silly, superficial magic of "being engaged." She loved showing people her rock and she loved being urged to talk about her wedding plans. She loved how some women, the most unexpected women, sighed moonily, and she loved how men, the most unexpected men, teased and flirted outrageously, as if the ring itself emanated sex appeal. She loved buying *Bride* magazine. She loved, she had to admit, the whole princess-for-a-day fantasy of it all. Which, of course, Pauline knew perfectly well. "That's platinum, by the way," Pauline pointed out to the waiter. "Some people think it's silver."

"Pauline!"

"Very nice," the waiter repeated. "Congratulations, sister."

"Thank you."

"Or am I supposed to say, 'Best wishes'? " The waiter popped the champagne cork and poured. "You congratulate the man?"

"It doesn't matter," Lee said graciously.

"Well, either way, the brother who got you is a very lucky man."

For a moment she didn't know what to do. Should she nod and let the waiter go on thinking her fiancé was black? Or was that a betrayal of Porter? Should she speak up, correct his assumption, claim her man? Then the waiter finished pouring their champagne and stood back, flashing them a smile, and she realized he was only charming them for a tip. He didn't give a tinker's damn whether she was marrying a brother or a white man or an Eskimo. Lee smiled. "Thanks."

As he walked away Pauline raised her glass. "To a long and happy marriage."

"To good friends and their happiness."

The champagne was dry and tangy. Lee held it on her tongue, wanting to savor it. Pauline opened her menu. "Speaking of friends, heard from Cleo?"

"No. I sent her an invitation but no response."

Pauline shrugged. "She's young. She'll come around."

"I hope so. I miss her," Lee said. She missed Cleo's earnestness, her sincerity. And yes, she missed having someone look up to her in that way. "I can't tell you how many times I've started to call her. I keep thinking if I could just sit down with her and talk, she'd get it. But like you said, I have to accept that not everyone is going to be happy. I have to make myself happy. To thine own self be true."

"Yes," Pauline said. "Except the author of that particular little saying neglected to mention how much being true can cost."

"Listen," Lee said, opening her menu. "It's well worth the price."

Chapter 25

It was March, almost a year since the riots, and the four cops who started the whole mess were again on trial, this time in federal court for violating Rodney King's civil rights. The national editor asked Porter if he wanted to fly out to California and help cover the trial and its aftermath. Everyone was dreading the aftermath if the cops were again found not guilty; everyone but the national editor.

"We're sending three people with three more on standby," he said, a gleam in his eye. "If that town blows again the Pulitzer is mine!"

Porter declined the offer, having decided if he never saw L.A. again it would be too soon. He could decline without fear of career damage because he'd already earned his stripes. "Sure, buddy, I understand," the national editor said, slapping him on the back. "Been there, done that."

"Exactly," Porter said.

Lee also managed to escape conscription; she was busy covering the local version of racial malevolence: two concurrent murder trials between warring ethnic groups. She was so busy they rarely saw each other, and when they did she was cranky and out of sorts. "I'm sorry," she apologized. "This stuff is making me nuts." He read her articles every day and wasn't surprised; the anger and violence of the two killings was ugly and common as dirt. Some days Porter woke up and wondered if "us versus them" wasn't the axis on which the world tilted and spun and he'd simply been too blind to notice it before.

Each evening while Lee stayed late in the newsroom writing on deadline he went home to watch coverage of the events in Los Angeles. This time the trial was being held in the city. This time the jury was not all-white and suburban and fearful of a rising tide of crime. This time Porter found himself strangely sympathetic toward the cops.

Watching them enter and leave court each day, their heads held high against the protesting crowds, he wondered if they were the demons they'd been made out to be? Maybe, as they claimed, King was a terrifying monster, high on PCP and as strong and dangerous as ten men. At any rate, the cops had been found innocent in the state trial. No matter what you thought of the first verdict, wasn't this double jeopardy? Weren't they just sacrificial lambs to racial peace—or not even peace, but the absence of racial war?

He didn't mention his feelings to Lee.

And then, on the day the defense rested after calling to the stand only one of the four cops, Porter thought he saw, in the crowds outside the federal courthouse, a familiar face. The reporter, an Asian woman with sultry eyes and bee-stung lips, was explaining defense strategy in front of a barricaded crowd when a skinny black kid of eighteen or twenty, wearing thick, black glasses and a black stocking cap, stuck his head into view and grinned at the camera. He had astonishingly white teeth.

Porter gaped at the television, electrified.

A street corner. A fusillade of bricks. The shattering of glass. Burning rubber acrid in the air. I'm talking to you, bitch! A glob of spit. What the fuck you looking at? Better take off, whiteboy! I will kick your ass.

The woman ended her report. "Back to you, Tom," she said. The camera cut back to the studio, where a white-haired anchor looked stern and shook his head. Porter felt a sting in his left forearm and realized he'd been clenching his fist. He opened his hands and wiped his sweaty palms on his pant leg. On television the meteorologist was wearing sunglasses and a white beach hat and gesturing with a stick. The face was gone, but Porter knew it had been him.

He remembered going to a police station in L.A. two days after his attack and filing a report. He had gone only at the national editor's insistence, and when he walked into the station and saw the chaos churning there, he almost walked back out. But then a sergeant, red-faced and potbellied, spotted him. Easy enough to do, since, aside from the cops, his was the only white face in the crowd. The sergeant took him to a desk, got him coffee, nodded grimly as he filled out the report. He was all gruff sympathy until he learned Porter was a journalist; after that he was cold contempt. *We'll try our best to apprehend the suspect. Tell you what—if we catch him, we'll take him down to the Ritz until you can get there and make sure we don't violate his civil rights.*

Porter left the station without hope for his assailant's arrest. And for the past year he had assumed he was still out there on the streets of Los Angeles, causing trouble and squandering his useless life. But to believe the man who beat him was free was one thing; to see him clowning for the cameras in the California sun was another.

When Lee called he barely let her finish saying hello before he launched into it. And that asshole was standing there, grinning at the camera! Can you believe it? He had the nerve to go down there to the federal court and protest them beating King! As if what he did wasn't just as bad! Wasn't worse! What the hell are we coming to in this country? What the hell is wrong with somebody like that?"

He could tell Lee was taken aback by his outburst. She spoke in a low, quiet voice, as though he were an animal that needed to be calmed. "I'm sorry, baby. I know that must have been a shock to see him there."

"Damn right! He ought to be in jail."

"I know, I know. But there's nothing you can do about it."

"I can call the cops! Tell them to look for his skinny ass out there tomorrow!"

To her credit, Lee didn't point out the hopeless improbability of this idea. "Maybe I should come over."

"No. You're tired. Go home and go to bed."

"Are you sure?"

He took a deep breath, tried to even his voice. "I'm fine. Really. It was just a surprise. I'll see you tomorrow at work. I'm going to bed too."

But he slept fitfully. In his dreams he wrestled the spitter, grinning still, until morning light. He grumped into the deserted newsroom at seven and counted the hours until noon—9 A.M. on the West Coast—when he telephoned the Los Angeles district attorney's office. Some assistant to an assistant tried to give him the runaround; he reminded her he was a journalist for a major Philadelphia newspaper and had been in L.A. on assignment when he was attacked. She promised someone would call him back that afternoon.

It was after five when the telephone rang. He was writing a brief about a legislative vote on green space, but he stopped typing when the woman on the line identified herself. "Porter Stockman? Beverly Soo from the Los Angeles district attorney's office."

Beverly Sue? Beverly Sue what? Did even the lawyers in L.A. go only by their first names? Porter shook his head; this was a crazy line of thought. "You have some information for me?"

"Good news, actually. We made an arrest in your case three months ago. Dwayne Jefferson, twenty-three years of age, 456 Sunrise Avenue. Currently residing at the Los Angeles County Jail."

He stared at his computer screen in amazement. All around him in the newsroom reporters were typing, shouting into telephones, dashing back and forth between desks. It was the contained chaos of approaching deadline and beneath the hurry and the anxiety was a sense of smug satisfaction at accomplishing something so difficult. Writing on deadline, editing on deadline, putting out a newspaper. Shaping the world!

"He must have been released on bail," he said.

More papers flipping. "Couldn't make bail. He's been in lockup since 12-20-92."

Since Christmas, Porter thought. Dwayne Jefferson spent Christmas in jail. Couldn't happen to a nicer guy. But then if Dwayne Jefferson was the man who attacked him, and Dwayne Jefferson was in jail, who was the guy dancing on TV? "Are you sure you have the right guy?"

Beverly Sue's voice took on a sheen of irritation. "Excuse me?"

But he realized how absurd it would sound. *I saw the guy who beat me on television last night. He was in a crowd, he was out of focus, I saw him only for a moment.* Beverly Sue would ask if he was certain it was the same man and he would have to say no. "I'm just surprised you caught him without me having to look at a lineup or anything. Given how many crimes you had during the riots."

More rustling of papers. "Looks like Mr. Jefferson has a big mouth. He bragged about beating up a white reporter near the intersection where you were attacked. He bragged, somebody else squealed, et cetera. If he'd kept his mouth shut we probably never would have apprehended him. You'd think some of these guys would figure that out."

"Not the sharpest knives in the drawer, I guess," he said. He felt suddenly energized, ready to join in a laugh at Dwayne Jefferson's expense. That son of a bitch—they caught him! He wanted to stand up and applaud. He wanted to take back every snide and nasty thing he'd ever said about cops. He wanted to fly out to Los Angeles and put his fist in Dwayne Jefferson's face.

"So you want me to come out and testify?" he asked, feeling a surge of energy at the idea. He saw himself striding into the courtroom past a cowed and frightened Dwayne Jefferson and climbing onto the witness stand. He'd finger the asshole, stare him down, and send him to jail, no hesitation, no doubt.

But Beverly Sue said, "That won't be necessary. We've made a deal. In exchange for his confession and some assistance with other cases, we've offered a reduced sentence."

"How much?"

More papers rattling. "Twelve to eighteen."

"Years?" Surprised, Porter did a quick mental calculation: Dwayne Jefferson would be thirty-five when he got out, not old, certainly, but older. His youth squandered. Good.

"Months," said Beverly Sue.

Twelve months. A year, maybe less with parole. A year was no time at all. It had been almost a year already; had Dwayne Jefferson been caught immediately he'd be getting ready to reenter society. Porter glanced up from his desk. The national editor was staring across the room at him and pointing at his watch. That meant: get the story in, now. Porter wanted to flip him the bird.

"I want a trial."

"Excuse me?"

"I want a trial," he sputtered. "I demand a trial. Don't I have the right to demand a trial?"

"I'm afraid not," Beverly Sue cooed sympathetically. Which he knew, he knew, he knew.

"At least he will do some time," Beverly Sue continued. "Do you know how many crimes we had during the riots? Thousands! We're lucky if we caught a quarter of the participants."

"That makes me feel so much better."

"How about this, then: do you know how many people died? Fifty-four. Most of them were people like you, in the wrong place at the wrong time."

"You're telling me I was lucky," he said, not believing it.

"It could have been worse."

Yes, it could have been worse; he could have been beaten to death. Instead he was saved by Lee and the rest was history. A fairy-tale romance born out of the civil disturbance of the decade. He bet even Beverly Sue would get a kick out of the thrill of it all if he told her, but the national editor was bearing down on him and his other line began to ring.

"Okay, okay."

"We'll try to make sure he serves his full sentence."

"Yeah, whatever." Fatigue washed over him. He wanted to finish his story and go home. "Thanks for calling."

She said, "We in the Los Angeles district attorney's office believe the public has a right to know."

Chapter 26

He made the obligatory trip to Baltimore to meet Lee's family. Mrs. Page was nothing like he'd imagined her; she looked very little like Lee. She was shorter and more stout, and her skin had a lighter, more yellowish tone. She wore her hair processed and marcelled around her head in tight, little waves. Had he passed her walking down the street he wouldn't have given her a second look, would not, in fact, have registered at all. And now she was going to be his mother-in-law. The thought reverberated all evening in his mind. Mother-in-law. He tried to imagine her with his mother, together with their beige grandchildren at the zoo.

The brother, Marcus, was young and strapping and approachable. They exchanged career information and then talked sports, the universal language of men. His fiancée, a pretty black girl with dark, dark skin and a tiny Afro, smiled a lot and gave him computer tips.

Lee had promised everyone would be nice. She said her mother was the only one who'd expressed hesitation, and that was out of fear more than anything else. "You have to understand who she is, a black woman who lived through Jim Crow, Bull Connor, the assassination of Dr. King.

It's hard for her really to believe black people and white people can love each other across the line and live in peace in this country. But she's behind us all the way."

Still he'd braced himself for an underlying hostility from her or from the brother or from both. The only tense moment came when Mrs. Page asked about his family.

"I'm sure your parents are pleased you're finally settling down," she said. They were at the dinner table, making their way through an astonishing amount of food: roast pork, mashed potatoes, macaroni and cheese, biscuits, cornbread, homemade applesauce, green beans, corn, and lima beans. The tone in his future mother-in-law's voice was unreadable and her look was pleasantly suspicious, like someone listening to a used-car salesman. He didn't know how to respond to this obviously loaded question. What did she mean? What did she suspect?

He glanced at Lee, who was smiling warmly. He'd told her his mother wasn't thrilled with their being married—she wouldn't have believed him otherwise—but that she was reconciling herself to the idea and wanted to make the best of it. He didn't mention his grandmother, his father, the rest of the story and the scene. He didn't mention anything else.

"Yes, they are," he said. "They were beginning to think I had designs on the priesthood."

"Which might be okay if you were Catholic," Lee joked.

"So your parents are looking forward to the wedding, then?" Mrs. Page persisted. "And your sister too?"

He felt a flash of irritation at her questioning. Who did she think she was, pushing him like that? What was with this family—did they always look for the worst in people? Still, he managed to smile his response. "Why wouldn't they?"

That did the trick. Mrs. Page deepened her suspicious look, but what could she say? After a split second of silence the conversation rolled over this little rock in the road and moved on.

The future mother-in-law had offered in advance to put them up for the night, but Lee said no, they would spend the night in a hotel. "No one should be expected to face their future mother-in-law over break-fast," she said. He was relieved when she suggested it and even more relieved when it was actually time to go.

"Thanks for a lovely dinner," he said. He wasn't sure whether he was supposed to shake his future mother-in-law's hand or peck her on the cheek, and she wasn't giving him any help; she just stood there watching him, as though he were some kind of lab rat. In the end he wrapped her hand in both of his, giving it what he hoped was a warm squeeze. "Welcome to the family," she said, and seemed to him to be smothering a laugh.

"I'll call you tomorrow," Lee said. He stood by while hugs were exchanged, and then they were out of there.

In the car, Lee was ecstatic. "I think that went pretty well, don't you?"

"Sure." He thought it was horrible, but what did he know?

"Let's go somewhere and have a drink and celebrate!"

They tried to get into a jazz club Lee knew, but the place was packed and a line snaked around the corner. The doorman smiled at Lee in recognition but shook his head: there was nothing he could do. Porter wondered if Lee had been with a black man whether she would have been granted entrance. "Never mind," she said. "Let's find someplace I don't know."

After two more failures—one sold out, one so desolate they were both afraid to go inside—they ended up back at the hotel, downstairs in a newly opened "performance space" that had clearly served time as a conference room in another life. Some designer had tried to mask the room's bland vastness by painting sand dune murals on the walls and scattering potted plants and rattan chairs everywhere, but it didn't work. The crowd was middle-aged, middle-brow, and white, people trying to be young and hip but who ended up listening to a jazz harpist in a conference room, and Porter saw with a start how much he resembled them. Same clothes, same age more or less; only Lee was different. Heads turned as the hostess led them to a booth, a few eyes caught Porter's and flicked away. He glared these people down, but Lee seemed strangely oblivious to it all. She pulled him into the booth and ordered a bottle of champagne.

"I'm very happy," she said, taking his hand.

"Me too." He said this as brightly as he could and held her hand until the singer retook the stage and the lights went down. Then he gently disengaged to wipe the moistness from his palms.

He had always loved spring, but this year it rained and rained and the world was more soggy than renewed. Porter woke each morning with a low-grade sense of unease. It had to do with his upcoming wedding, of course; that much he knew. What he didn't know was whether it was just normal, premarriage jitters or something else.

Lee said she needed to spend part of the weekend in Baltimore, picking out a bridesmaid's dress and doing heaven knew what else. Although the wedding was going to be in Philadelphia, Lee's mother was organizing much of it from Maryland.

"I'm sure you're all torn up about having to spend this weekend by yourself," Lee joked as they stood at his apartment door on Saturday morning.

"I'll miss you." This was duty talking, but as soon as he said the words they were true. He pulled her into his arms and kissed her hard.

"Wow," she said. "I'll have to go to Baltimore more often."

But then she was gone and he felt relief like a pocket of fresh air in the stale atmosphere enclosing him. What a mess he was: up and down, in love and out. He didn't know what the hell was going on. He called Joe and asked if he wanted to meet for a drink later. He cleaned the bathroom, hauled his clothes downstairs to the laundry room and put them in the wash, watching a movie on television. But by then it was still only four and he wasn't meeting Joe until eight. He couldn't sit in his apartment any longer. What was needed was movement. He decided to go for a drive.

For the first time that week the rains had ceased. It was a lovely afternoon, soft and warm and feverish with spring, and Porter realized March had gone away and April slipped in without him noticing. April.

One year since he first saw Lee on that Los Angeles street. People always said time sped up as you aged, and it was true. Time was racing; his life was speeding by.

He got on Interstate 95 headed north, no destination in mind. Maybe he'd drive up to Bucks County and look at the countryside bursting with green before heading back down to meet with Joe. Or maybe he'd keep driving till he reached Canada. He turned on the radio loud and rolled down the window to let the warm air caress his face.

He drove to New Hope, walked along the quaint streets for a while, looked at the river, then ducked into a bar for a hamburger and a beer. When he came out it was getting dark and he decided to head back. In the car, a Bruce Springsteen song came on the radio and he began singing along. He'd achieved nearly the perfect state of movement and void when he noticed something bright flashing behind him. He glanced in the rearview mirror; some asshole was riding his tail and blinking his headlights at him, trying to get him to move out of the way. Except Porter was not in the passing lane. He was in the middle lane, the traveling lane, doing five miles above the speed limit—he was in the right and this prick, if he wanted to go faster, should go around. Of course there were trucks in the fast lane, eighteen-wheelers pulling their loads down I-95, and this asshole behind him didn't want to get out there and play with the big boys, he wanted to run Porter off the road. Porter took his foot off the accelerator; the car slowed; the guy behind him blinked his lights furiously. Porter slowed more, his hands gripping the wheel. "Fuck you, asshole!" he cried aloud. "Fuck you!" They played this game for another mile, then, suddenly, the guy found an opening on the right, slashed into it, sped up. In that brief second when they were hurtling along the highway together Porter looked into the asshole's face. He was black, young, grinning. He gave Porter the finger, then sped up and swung back into the middle lane right in front of Porter, forcing him to hit his brakes for a second to avoid an accident. Behind him another car blew its horn and raced past. Nearly rigid with fury and fear, Porter regained his speed and watched the asshole's red lights recede into the distance.

He was beyond thought. He focused on those lights, felt them like two hot coals in his gut. He didn't even glance at the climbing speedometer, only at those lights. They came closer and closer, he wanted to take this roaring machine beneath him and stab it between those lights like a knife. He followed those lights off the highway and onto a city street. He had no idea where he was and didn't care. It was a blink of time and all he wanted was those lights.

The lights pulled into the bright orange glare of a gas station and became again a red sports car. Porter followed. He heard the screech of the parking brake as the guy yanked it into place, then leapt from his car, engine still running. "What the fuck is your problem, man?" he screamed, coming toward Porter's car. "Are you crazy? I will kick your ass!"

A street corner. A fusillade of bricks. The shattering of glass. Burning rubber acrid in the air. I'm talking to you, bitch! A glob of spit. What the fuck you looking at? Better take off, whiteboy! I will kick your ass.

The guy was moving closer, yelling, "Get out! Get out!" Abruptly, Porter began trembling. What the hell was he doing? This was insane, he could be killed. He slammed his car into reverse and backed up, tires squealing. The guy followed on foot, gesturing furiously and grunting and leaping around. He looked like a fucking ape.

"You better run!" the guy screamed. "You better run!"

"Fuck you!" Porter screamed as he swung around toward the street. He felt the scream like a birth, like a bursting inside him, and he pushed it out with every ounce of breath, with every muscle and every vein and every pore. He screamed like he wanted to rip his throat into shreds. "Fuck you, asshole! Fuck you, nigger!!!"

The next thing he knew he was back on the highway, headed south again, panting and checking his rearview mirror for signs of pursuit. Cars came up behind him and passed, their drivers looking straight ahead, oblivious to his existence.

He got off at the Center City exit and parked on the street near the Franklin Museum in the first space he could find. The word. The word. It sloshed in his gut, rose like bile in his throat. He thought he might throw up; he wanted to throw up. He opened the car door and leaned into the street, but nothing came, and when a police car cruised past he pulled his body back inside. *Nigger!* He saw Lee's face, not horrified but glistening with triumph. *See? It lies within you too, the beast, slumbering but lightly. All it needs is a tap to awaken and roar.* Through the windshield, blurry with rain, he saw couples scurrying through the drizzly evening, on their way to dinner and companionship. He was sweating, his hands trembled. He turned off the radio and wiped his forehead with his sleeve.

"Do you think I'm a racist?"

Joe was in the midst of some witty comment about the wrestling match on the television above them, but he stopped talking and turned to Porter. "Come again?"

"Do you think I'm a racist?"

They were at a bar on the edge of South Philadelphia, a workingman's hangout, one of the many Joe frequented when he felt the need to "rub his toes in the raw and splendid muck of life." There was a long, scarred bar, the television, a dartboard, a few booths, and not much else. The bartender, when he wasn't pouring, leaned against the cash register flipping through a *Car and Driver* magazine. There were no black people in the bar. That was the first thing Porter noticed and he noticed himself noticing it.

"Hmmm." Joe put down his drink and crossed his arms. "So, you call up your best man six months before your wedding to a lovely African-American woman and invite him for a drink to ask if he thinks you're a racist? Is this some kind of test? Do I get the best party favor if I get it right?"

"This is no joke, Joe. This is serious."

"Serious." Joe put one leg on the floor and pulled his stool closer to the bar so he could lean on it. "Okay, I'll play. Do I think you're a racist? No, I do not."

It was the answer he'd expected, but it was oddly disquieting. Porter finished his drink, feeling the bourbon warm his blood. He signaled the bartender for another round.

"Of course, what I think is irrelevant," Joe was saying. "The question is, do you think you're a racist?"

The bartender refreshed the ice and poured the booze in a long, brown stream, his face an impassive mask. Maybe he had not heard Joe in the noise of the bar or maybe he thought it was a stupid question or maybe he just didn't care. Still, Porter waited until he'd finished and gone back down the bar before he answered. He took a sip of his drink and whispered, "I don't know."

Joe said, "I see."

Haltingly then, Porter recounted the evening's events. Putting the incident into words gave it a distanced, movielike quality. That was good. "And then I called him an asshole. And then I called him . . ." Porter lowered his voice, though they sat at the end of the bar, away from all the other men, who, at any rate, probably would not have objected to hearing the term. But Porter could not bring himself to say the word again; just the thought of it in his mouth made his stomach lurch. "I called him that word."

"You're not a racist," Joe said. "You're an idiot. You're the most astonishing idiot who ever walked. You're lucky he didn't kill you."

"Maybe he should have," Porter said miserably.

"Oh, don't be so dramatic!" Joe cried in exasperation. "All right, so you got mad and lost your temper because some asshole cut you off on the highway and you said a bad word. So what?"

"You make it sound as though I'm some kid who called his brother a doo-doo head," Porter said bitterly. He should have known better than to come to Joe with this. Joe was a pontificating, southern smart-ass. "This is a little more serious."

"No, what's serious is that you're sitting there acting so shocked and horrified that your pure, unsullied I'd-like-to-teach-the-world-to-sing little brain could even maintain an imprint of the word! Horrors! Porter has prejudices! Banish the thought!"

Porter flushed angrily. "I see. You're in touch with your inner racist. That makes you better than me."

"Yes, it does," Joe said with a smile. "My esteemed grandfather used to say it's easier to pull a weed when it's young but you got to get out there and face it. Can't hide in the house."

Porter gulped his drink. "Please, no folksy southern crap tonight. I can't take it."

"All right, how's this: if it had been a woman who cut you off, wouldn't you have thought, at least for a second, 'Bitch!' Does that mean you want to keep them all barefoot and pregnant?" Joe stopped, seemed to consider for a moment, then went on. "Well, maybe that's not the best analogy, but you know what I mean. The point is, grow up! Of course you harbor some stereotypes, some prejudiced beliefs. We all do! You're only a racist if you don't struggle against them. Or don't admit they're there."

Porter shook his head, signaled the bartender again. The booze in this place must be watered down; it was doing nothing to melt the giant block of ice sitting in his gut. He looked at Joe. What he was saying sounded all well and good, all very diversity-workshop and politically correct but it was really bullshit. Bullshit that didn't help him now, not in the least.

"But if those beliefs are there, I shouldn't be marrying Lee. Right?"

Joe didn't answer.

"Didn't you once ask me why I liked her? Maybe you saw something, something I didn't see."

"Maybe I was drunk."

"Maybe I'm with her for the wrong reasons."

"And what, pray tell, would be the right reason? She reminded you of your mother? She didn't remind you of your mother? She giggled at your jokes? She was the first woman to suck your cock?"

Joe was working himself into one of his rants, and when he got going, he liked nothing better than an audience. Porter looked around the bar to see if anyone was paying attention to them. "Perhaps you'd feel better if you were marrying her because of the way her blond hair glinted in the sun, as if you were both starring in a shampoo commercial," Joe said, but some of the air had gone out of him. He lowered his voice and signaled the bartender for a refill of his drink.

"Yeah, okay. People are attracted to each other for all kinds of stupid reasons, and that doesn't matter when you're just screwing around. But we're getting serious, and when you get serious, you should know why. And it should be for real, shouldn't it?"

"For real?"

"You should want the other person for herself. The foundation should be love."

Joe flapped his arms through the air. "Ah, love. I'm running through a field of daisies and buttercups."

"Screw you," Porter said. "I'm glad you find my life so amusing."

Joe sighed. "Look, I know what you're asking. But my esteemed grandfather used to say if you want scrambled eggs you can't expect the hen to crack the shells."

Porter started to protest but Joe held up his hand. "It's not a perfect analogy but it means this: if you want out of this wedding you have to do it yourself. I am not handing you the key."

Outside the drizzle continued but a warm front had come through, heating the air and making it unpleasantly muggy. It pressed in on Porter as he prowled his way back toward Center City, too restless to go home. He stopped at the Pen & Pencil club for a drink, but Karl, the transportation reporter, was there, tomcatting it up while his wife was away visiting the in-laws. Porter couldn't stand being in the same physical space with such an asshole, so he swigged his bourbon and left. He went into another bar and sat down without looking at anyone, but when the bartender appeared he was black. He had the broad shoulders, the wide chest and thickening gut of a former football player and his skin was so dark as to be nearly purple.

"What can I get you?"

Porter hesitated, then said, "Bourbon. On the rocks."

The bartender poured Porter's drink and went back to the other end of the bar where a cluster of three or four black guys stood laughing and drinking. None of them even glanced Porter's way but he felt, across the long space of the bar, a subtle stiffening of backs and necks, their awareness of his presence. He thought it must show like a stain on his face and he was afraid. So, with only one sip of his drink, he left.

What a crazy night, what a crazy world. He walked on, feeling caged even as he covered blocks and blocks of city streets. He was passing a bookstore-café when he stumbled over a crack in the sidewalk and realized he was very close to being drunk. He thought a bottle of water and a cup of coffee would sober him up enough to walk home—who knew where his car was—and maybe he could even find something to read, something to occupy his racing mind.

He was wandering the science fiction aisles when someone came up behind him.

"Hello, sailor. Come here often?"

It took him a minute to place her. "Janine. How are you?"

She smiled. "Very good. You remembered."

"Hard to forget a face like yours."

"A person could take that one of two ways."

"Take it as a compliment." He watched himself flirt with a kind of appalled fascination; apparently this was who he was, the real Porter Stockman. "You look great."

She did too. Her hair was longer than he remembered, her waist smaller, the bones of her face more delicate. He expected at least a little passive hostility; he'd left a message on her machine after their only date, thanking her for dinner but he'd never telephoned again. But Janine was all smiles as she asked about his job.

"I always look for your byline now," she said. "That series you did on the appointment of judges was amazing. I read every word and then sat down and wrote a letter to my state representative."

He laughed. "Oh, so you were the one."

They talked for a while about the local judicial scene, then about other stories he had written. Porter felt the familiar excitement of a new woman, a woman whose body he had not yet seen. A man with glasses came down the aisle where they were standing and Janine moved closer to him to get out of the way. She smelled fresh, like lemons.

"So what are you doing here?" she asked. "Searching for something particular or just browsing?"

"Browsing. Looking for something to occupy my mind on a lonely Saturday night."

She smiled. "Lonely? You?"

"Happens to the best of us."

She was holding a book called *Getting the Love You Want*. Easy enough to guess from the title what that was about. She saw him noticing the book and blushed. "It's for my sister," she said. "She saw it on *Oprah*."

He didn't believe her but found her embarrassed lie surprisingly sexy. Everything about her was sexy: her blue eyes, the smallness of her wrists, her long, honey hair. He imagined her above him, bending over, his face drowning in the silkiness of all that hair. Somebody else came down the aisle and he stepped toward Janine to clear the path. He noticed they were standing in the fiction section, near the *M*s. He saw that Toni Morrison book Lee had given him at the beginning of their relationship and which he still had not gotten around to.

He looked at Janine. "Have you eaten?" he asked.

Chapter 27

He awoke to the pressure of lips against his own and reached out, expecting to feel Lee's soft, springy, animated hair. Instead his hand encountered silk, gossamer strands. For one long moment he was lost. Then he managed with great effort to pry open his eyes.

"Good morning," said Janine. "How did you sleep?"

The night before rose like stale cigarette smoke from the pile of clothes beside the bed and floated back to him: dinner with two bottles of wine, fifty dollars' worth of drinks at some overcrowded, overpriced yuppie meat market, the cab ride to his apartment, the driver scowling in the mirror at them, fumbling for his keys, bed.

"Morning," Porter mumbled. He tried to move his head; it felt as though his brain had hardened into rock. He moaned.

"Little hungover?"

"Either that or you played hockey with my head last night."

Janine laughed and kissed him again. "I'll help you with that." She bounded out of bed and strolled naked toward the bedroom door. Though it hurt his eyes to follow so much movement, he watched her. Her body was nothing like Lee's. She had more boyish hips, firmer but

smaller breasts. Her stomach was flat from a million sit-ups, almost con-
cave, whereas Lee's stomach had a gentle roundness to it. Janine's shoulders were thin, her arms firm but without Lee's effortless brown
musculature. It had been more than a year since he last saw rose-colored
nipples, a triangle of honey-colored hair. He watched Janine's flat, rosy
ass disappear through the door and wondered how long it would be
before he saw them again.

Not long, if that's what he wanted. He could have Janine—that
much was clear—and free himself of Lee in one, calculating, repugnant
swoop. If that's what he wanted, and wasn't that what this was all about?
Waking up six months before his wedding with another woman in his
bed. It was so cliché. And all Lee had to do was find out. And there were
many ways she could find out. And then he would be free.

He closed his eyes against the rebellion in his gut and in his heart.

After a few minutes Janine returned from the kitchen bringing with
her a pitcher of water, a box of baking soda, aspirin, and a plate of what
Porter knew must be stale crackers if they came from his cupboard, all
on a cookie sheet. A picture of domesticity. "I couldn't find a tray," she
said, settling on the bed. "Here we go: just what the doctor ordered. A
teaspoon of baking soda in a glass of water, then two aspirin and more
water. Then some crackers and more water. Picking up on a theme?"

He performed as instructed, moving slowly so as not to restart the
clashing in his head. "What time is it anyway?" he asked.

"About ten-thirty," Janine said.

He choked down two of the crackers, which were indeed stale. Ten-
thirty. Sunday morning. Lee was probably on her way to worship, down
there in Baltimore, probably already alight with that gentle radiance she
always got from church.

Lee.

Lee glanced in the rearview mirror and hit the gas. Traffic on Interstate
95 was flying as usual, and she had to floor it to get back into the stream.
She pushed a gospel tape into the tape player and sang along, feeling
good. God would understand why she'd skipped church that morning:
she was in love and she missed her man.

She'd woken up too happy to stay in Baltimore. Maybe it was seeing Howard the night before. She was having dinner out with Pauline and in he walked, a woman no older than twenty-five on his arm. Pauline said, "Lookee, lookee, lookee," while Lee tried to hide behind the menu. But Howard spotted them. He came over, smiled.

"It's good to see you," he said, and his voice sounded so sincere, the ice block that had formed in Lee's gut at the sight of him began to melt. He introduced his friend. Pauline pointed out Lee's rock. Howard congratulated her and wished her well. Then he and the woman took their seats on the other side of the restaurant, thankfully out of sight. Pauline cracked on the woman's youthfulness and Lee laughed along, but she was happy to see Howard happy. It made everything okay.

Now Lee changed lanes and inched the speedometer up to sixty-five. She'd be in Porter's bed in thirty minutes or less.

"Actually, ten-thirty isn't bad, considering how late we got in," Janine said. "Shall I make breakfast?"

Porter closed his eyes. *Shall I make breakfast?* He knew the subtext of the question had nothing to do with orange juice and toast. Janine was asking if the night before had been merely a mutual gratification, pleasing but meaningless, in which case he should make up some excuse about work or a sick relative and send her on her way. But if the night before had been something more, a possible start to a possible something else, he should lie back against his pillow and let her conquer his kitchen and cook for him, feed him. Janine was really asking: What now?

"I think I saw all the stuff for pancakes in there. And eggs. You've got plenty of eggs."

"Those eggs are probably old enough to bury."

"I'll check the expiration date."

"I'm afraid of what might happen if I saw food."

"Have some toast, at least," she wheedled.

"I couldn't swallow."

"It'll make you feel better."

"I don't want anything to eat," he said, then, afraid he'd hurt her, lightened his tone. "I mean, I've been here before and the only thing that really helps is water, aspirin, and sleep."

"Maybe I should go," she said, uncurling from the bed. "I've got a million things to do and you'll recover faster alone."

He smiled gratefully; she was so easy. Janine returned his smile and disappeared into the bathroom. He heard water running, splashing, the clicking of a purse. After ten minutes or so she emerged looking remarkably refreshed. He dragged himself from bed, pulled on his jeans. At the door they chatted awkwardly for a minute and then he kissed her, on the lips but lightly, because a kiss on the cheek or the forehead was callous but an open mouth and tongue was a promise he did not want to make. It was all so depressing, these mating games. He remembered how much he'd hated it, how glad he'd been to be done with it with Lee.

"I had a wonderful time last night," she said.

"Me too." Then, because something else was expected, "Thanks." But that was wrong, that was degrading. It was insulting to thank a woman for sex, as though she'd done a favor or performed some service for him. He remembered once, early in his relationship with Lee, thanking her in a rush of aftersex enchantment and new love. She took his hand, shook it briskly, and said, "That'll be one million, cash."

But Janine just smiled and said, "You're welcome. We should do it again sometime soon."

Back in his court. He was supposed to name a time, set a date, promise believably to telephone. Instead he heard himself say "I should tell you . . . I'm involved with someone. Or I was, until yesterday. Or I am but it's a mess." He didn't know if he was doing the right thing, the hard but morally responsible thing or just salving his own conscience. Getting out clean. Just being a prick. He didn't know. He didn't seem to know much anymore.

Janine was still smiling but the look in her eyes had sharpened. "Oh!" she said brightly. "Well!"

"I'm sorry. You're an incredible woman. When I ran into you last night—"

"Hey! I'm a big girl!" She was shaking her head, still smiling hard and backing out the door. "I really have to run."

"I'll give you a call," he said.

"Sure, sure! Nice seeing you, Porter. Bye!" She fled past the elevator to the stairwell and was gone. He closed his door and leaned his head against it.

He'd always considered himself a decent guy where women were concerned. The kind of man who treated women with consideration and fairness, never lying, never promising more than he could deliver, getting out when it was clear things would not work. He never consciously used a woman; he'd thought himself wholly incapable of it.

So much for knowing thyself.

He crawled back into bed, pulling the sheet over his throbbing cranium, but it was no good. Whenever he closed his eyes he saw spinning images of Janine, of Lee's beaming face, of Dwayne Jackson and the guy in the red sports car coming at him with a gun. He saw himself, wild-eyed and ugly, leaning from his car window and screaming that word. It was too much.

He rose, crawled into the shower, turned the water past hot to scalding, and forced himself not to flinch. Afterward he stood naked and dripping for a long time before the bathroom mirror, trying to discern his face through the fog.

Then the front door opened and closed. He assumed it must be Janine, she must have forgotten something. But then he heard Lee's voice. "Porter?"

He pulled on his robe and went into the living room. Lee was standing just inside the doorway, smiling and holding a bag. "Looks like somebody had an interesting night."

She came to him and pressed her lips on his, and for a moment he didn't think, just clung dumbly to her. She was wearing a sleeveless pale blue cotton dress with tiny white flowers, which fit at the waist and fell down to her ankles. It was one of the more feminine items in her wardrobe, and he loved seeing her in it. She called it her "girlie dress."

"You still have a few months of bachelorhood, you know." She pulled back from him, swept her hand across his forehead. He felt blistered by her touch. "Joe doesn't have to pack it all into one night."

He disengaged himself, moved to check the thermostat. "I didn't expect you until later. I thought you'd stay in Baltimore for church."

Lee kicked off her shoes. "I missed you. Wanted to get back."

He smiled weakly. "Want a bagel?" she asked. She went into the kitchen and he realized he was holding his breath. He hadn't been in there all morning and didn't know how Janine had left it. He couldn't even remember what they'd done when they got back to his apartment last night. Had they had something to drink before stumbling into bed? Was there a lipstick-stained glass in the kitchen, waiting to slice into Lee? He checked the thermostat again. It was set at sixty-five and he could feel the cool air pumping from the baseboard, but he was sweating and his stomach reeled and lurched. He thought he might throw up.

But Lee came out of the kitchen humming and smiling. She put the cream cheese and toasted bagels on his little dining room table and kissed him again. "You look like a hurting puppy. Did you take anything?"

His head was pounding. He rubbed his temples. "Aspirin, but that was a few hours ago."

"Let me get you some more."

She went into the bathroom and he collapsed on the couch, head in hand. What a fucking coward he was. If he wanted to end it, why didn't he just open his mouth? Why drag this on and on? He felt as if someone was slowly peeling away skin from his body, piece by piece. It was agony and the only way to end it was to rip it all away at once.

"What's this?"

He looked up. Lee was standing above him, aspirin bottle in one hand, a makeup compact in the other. Her voice was light; she might have been asking about a new kind of soap. He could lie. He could make something up—his sister had visited, the maid was here, a friend from work. He could lie and she would probably believe him because she wanted to. But he knew he'd seen the compact in the bathroom earlier and left it there for her find. And so what was the sense in lying now?

"Porter?" This time her voice wasn't casual. He didn't respond and she said again, "Porter? What's this?"

"It," he began, faltered, then went on. "It belongs to someone who was here last night."

"Someone?"

"A woman I dated once. Before we met."

"And she was here." She seemed to be trying to get the facts straight.

"Yes."

"Last night."

"Yes."

For what seemed the longest time, she felt nothing. It was as if what was happening hadn't registered with her brain, and yet another part of her brain knew it was coming, coming soon, like a locomotive down the tracks. Brace yourself, her brain was saying. Brace yourself. And then it hit.

She felt dizzy, so she sat down, but something about the pressure and the texture of the couch against her thighs made her stomach threaten revolt and so she stood up again. She looked toward the bathroom, as if going back in could reverse what had occurred. She looked at the dirty window, at the bare floor, at the bookshelf. Then she looked at him. "Say it."

He was looking at the floor. He didn't speak.

"Say it."

He looked up. "Lee."

"Say it, you bastard." She heard her voice climbing and she was glad. "Don't you even have the guts for that?"

He looked away. "I slept with her."

Besides insects, Porter had killed only one living creature in his life. When he was eleven he heard his mother screaming and rushed into the kitchen to find her cowered atop a chair, pointing at a squirrel. The animal was staggering around, clearly rabid. He picked up a cast-iron pan and swung with all his eleven-year-old might. He never forgot the sound of that tiny skull against the pan, the sick feeling of crushing into death what before had been alive. He felt that same feeling now, watching Lee. What he'd done was as violent and irreversible as killing the squirrel. He had taken what they had and clubbed it to death.

For a long time neither of them spoke, but he was conscious of the astonishing noise of his body. His gut churned, his heart thrashed, his blood drubbed. He could hear sweat squeezing from his pores, and although he had just showered, he could smell himself, smell his own, foul odor. He smelled like something you wouldn't want in the house.

"You son of a bitch," she finally whispered. Then, louder: "You son of a bitch! You son of a bitch!" She hurled the compact across the room and it smashed against the bookshelf, breaking in half. "What the hell is wrong with you?"

"It . . . just happened," he said. But that was a lie and he was immediately even more disgusted with himself. The urge to justify, to self-defend was so strong.

"Bullshit!" She came at him, hands up, and he stood to take the punishment. But a foot away from him she stopped so suddenly her body swayed and she stood there, panting. They faced each other across the room like gunslingers, knowing both might be killed, none might survive. He was waiting for her to ask about Janine. He was waiting for her to ask if Janine was white, and that would be his ammunition, that question would be his release. See? See! *She* was the one who started it all, the one who first sewed those mustard seeds of doubt. *He* never wanted to believe race was an issue between them, was an issue at all. She poisoned his mind.

But Lee didn't ask about Janine. "Bullshit. You don't just sleep with someone six months before you get married," she said with great venom. "You can do better than that."

She was right, of course, the way she often was, and it both pained and infuriated him. "Okay, you got me," he said. "It didn't just happen. I made it happen. I wanted it to and I wanted you to find that compact too. How's that for true confessions?"

She looked slapped. Then fury and tears flooded into her eyes and her face stormed and twisted and she ripped his engagement ring from her finger and hurled it at his face. He ducked and heard it thud somewhere on the couch and disappear. Neither looked to see where it had gone.

"I guess you wanted that to happen too!" She threw back her head sharply, fighting tears. She seemed to be complaining to the gods. "I can't believe this. I cannot believe it! You're turning out to be—"

"Turning out to be what? Another white guy who only wanted to get in your pants after all? Turning out to be exactly what your friends and your mother warned you about?"

"Don't try to turn this on me." She glared at him.

"It is on you!" Yelling made his head pound harder, but he kept going, part of him enjoying the pain. "It's on both of us!"

"Both of us didn't fuck somebody else last night," she said, but everything had gone out of her voice. Tears spilled down her face. "Bastard."

He said nothing; he could not disagree.

She backed away from him. On the other side of the room she bumped against a bookcase, sending books onto the floor.

"I'm sorry," he said. But even to his own ears he sounded insincere.

"Fuck that," she said. "Tell me why."

His head hammered and his stomach heaved; the last thing he wanted was to splash breakfast all over the floor in front of her. But he didn't have the strength to head toward the bathroom. He was exhausted, his knees too weak to move. He felt like a swimmer, pounded by the surf and going down.

"I don't know," he said, sinking into the couch.

She mimicked him. "*I don't know!* How pathetic."

He was grateful for her scorn. It was like a match, lighting his own anger, and for a moment he could pack his heart with hate. "Don't you see that's the problem? I don't know what I'm turning out to be. I don't know who I am anymore and I can't stand it! Everything's unraveled and I can't stand it and all I do know is that it began unraveling with you."

She wiped her face with the back of her hand. "What a bunch of nonsensical crap!"

He tried again. "How many times, in how many ways, have you asked me why I'm with you? When we first started, you asked all the time. You were convinced there was something there, something hidden and ugly. You told me it was inevitable, that society had stained us all and would keep staining us and that there was no escape. You told me either I was lying or I just hadn't faced it."

"And you told me I was wrong! You told me you wanted me because of who I am. Nothing more, nothing less." She laughed bitterly. "I guess that was a lie, huh?"

"It wasn't a lie! I believed it then."

"But you don't now," she said. It wasn't a question.

He thought of the little girl in the supermarket and of Charlie and his Gerber babies and of Dwayne Jackson and of the guy in the red sports car and the word spilling hideously from his mouth. *Nigger!* Porter rubbed his hands roughly over his face. "I don't know."

She flared up. "What do you mean you don't know?" she exclaimed. "You know! You know, you just don't want to admit it, you damn coward. Fuck you!"

She grabbed her purse from the table. His heart splintered as she stalked toward the front door. This was it, this was it. What he'd wanted. Mission accomplished, relationship smashed. He was turned away from her, unable to watch the final act, but she must have hesitated at the door because there was a split second of silence, a snapping absence of sound. He held his breath.

"Good-bye, Porter."

His first action as a newly freed man was to run into the bathroom and puke.

Chapter 28

Somehow, she made it to the car, climbed in, locked the door. Wailed until her belly hurt. Until her throat ached. Until it came back to her that she was sitting in broad daylight on a public street, losing her heart and her mind for all the world to see.

She struggled to calm herself. "Breathe!" Lee said aloud. "Breathe! Come on, calm down, get a grip." But she couldn't stop her thoughts from racing and where they raced was excruciating: Porter with someone else. Porter in bed with another woman last night, in bed with her that very morning. If Lee had gotten up an hour earlier, if she hadn't made pancakes for Eda but gotten right on the road . . .

No, the image was too ugly. She threw back her head to shake it away and ended up whacking the back of her neck against the headrest. "Shit!" she screamed. "Shit, shit, shit!" That amoral asshole, that selfish prick, that cowardly bastard. She hated him. Lee rubbed the back of her neck gingerly. The pain waned and she felt infinitesimally better. The body protecting itself from a major pain with a minor one.

"Miss? You okay?" A black man of about sixty-five was knocking at her window. He held the Sunday paper in one hand and a cigar and a walking stick in the other and he had a fedora perched atop his head. "You need some help?" he asked.

She wiped her face with her hands and rolled down the window. "No, no, I'm fine."

He eyeballed her skeptically. "Somebody hurt you, gal?"

She thought about her father, who used to call her "gal" when he was teasing her. *What's wrong with you, gal? Cat got your tongue?*

"Somebody hurt you?" the old man repeated.

"I'm fine," she said again, sniffling. "Thanks, though. Thanks."

She started the car, waiting for him to back away. But he just stood there, watching her with his ancient eyes. Finally he put his cigar in his mouth and said, "Life is too short, gal. Remember that. Life is too short." She sat in her car and watched him strut off down the street.

She drove without thinking and found herself on the interstate headed south, as if some magnetic force were pulling her back to Baltimore. And why not? Might as well run back home. Back to her mother and brother and Pauline, back to the person she used to be and the risk-free life she had lived for so long. Maybe this was the punishment for leaving in the first place. Maybe this was what she got for stepping outside her circle. What was that saying the Japanese had: the nail which stands above the rest gets hammered down? Something like that.

And then the tears were back. She drove half-blinded to the next rest area and pulled off, steering her car as far away as possible from the young couples in their two-seaters and the child-packed family vans. There, on the outskirts of the parking lot, she pushed back her seat and gave into it.

She couldn't face Pauline, not today. Eda, too, would open her arms thinking, "I told you so." Lee wasn't up for that right now. But maybe Marcus. Maybe Marcus would know what to say. He had shown surprising wisdom that day in his kitchen, suggesting she chose Porter because he made her see how tired she was of holding love at arm's length.

What he didn't suggest, and should have, was that the choice was wrong. Rotten. Of course, she couldn't blame Marcus for that. He hadn't even met Porter at that point. Maybe if she'd introduced them earlier, Marcus would have seen what kind of man Porter really was. He could have warned her.

"Bring 'em home before you marry 'em," her Aunt Alice used to say. "The way your grandfather carried on, you might be related!" The point being: families know things. Shut them out at your own risk. That's why you told your brother when a bully was harassing you. That's why you asked your mother if you should complain about the teacher or not. That's why you brought the guy you loved home to meet Dad.

Lee sat up and rooted around in the glove box for tissues. A station wagon rolled past and parked two spots away. A man got out and walked around to help his daughter from the backseat. Together they opened the back and a dog leapt out. They were going to walk it along the narrow strip of grass at the edge of the parking lot.

All at once time slipped and she was five years old, walking hand in hand with her father into a pet store. He was recently returned from one of his jaunts; the usual fight with her mother was over and he was feeling magnanimous. "Pick out something for yourself," her father said, sweeping his arm through the air like a game show hostess. "Anything at all."

She glanced longingly at the puppies. They looked so cute and fun. But as she and her father were leaving the house her mother had warned, "Don't come back here with something I have to walk or clean up after. Get her a fish or something like that."

Lee knew her father would buy her a dog anyway, if she asked. But it would lead to a fight and then he might leave again and it would be her fault. So she walked to the aquarium section and pointed out a small, purple fish swimming in a bowl by himself. "That one. I want him."

Her father tapped on the glass. The fish didn't move. "That fish looks sick," he said. "If you want a fish pick another one."

But something about the little purple fish had captured Lee's heart. She wanted it. She begged her father and pleaded with him. The store owner swore up and down the fish was sound.

Finally, her father gave in. "Okay, but when that fish gets sick and dies, don't come crying to me."

All that afternoon she felt deliriously happy. Her father helped her set up the bowl, then took her mother into the bedroom and closed the door. Lee spent hours talking to the fish, whom she named Vivian after a girl in school she desperately wanted to befriend. She sang songs to the fish, showed it a picture book, blew her twenty kisses good night.

The next morning Vivian was dead, floating like a soggy cracker atop the water. Lee cried inconsolably, not only because her friend was dead but because she was terrified her father would be angry. But after flushing Vivian down the toilet, he came into Lee's room and took her on his lap.

"Stop crying," he ordered, but his voice was gentle. "You had fun with that fish yesterday, didn't you?"

She nodded, too afraid to speak.

"Crying won't bring that fish back and it won't take you back to yesterday and make you choose another fish," her father said, stroking her hair. "Crying just makes you feel worse, so you ought to stop it."

But she couldn't. "Daddy, I'm so sorry!" she sobbed.

"Don't sit here feeling sorry for yourself, gal!" he cried. "And don't apologize. Makes you look weak. You ought to pick up your chin and say, 'Daddy, I picked that fish and I'm glad, no matter what!' "

Remembering that day now, Lee looked again out her window. The father and daughter and dog were gone. Lee started her engine, wiped her face, got back on the highway behind them, but at the next exit she got off and turned around.

Thinking about Porter hurt, like somebody took a rake and was slowly scraping back and forth across her heart. So instead, she thought about her father. She thought about him all the way home.

He spent the rest of the afternoon cleaning up his own vomit. It was a nasty, foul-smelling job, and he made himself take his time with it, wipe out every crevice in the bathroom tile, clean under the toilet, swab the bottom of the bowl. He stretched it out as long as he could, then he had a glass of water and climbed into bed and didn't get out again the rest of the day.

He woke at five Monday morning with his heart in his mouth and a sledgehammer in his gut. He considered calling in sick, but that was cowardly and he knew he'd stockpiled enough cowardly actions to last awhile, thank you very much. So he made himself shower and dress and then he drank coffee until it was time to go.

On the drive in, it occurred to him that she might not be there that day, that she might call in sick. The image of Lee curled up in her bed crying stabbed him. But no, she was tougher than that. She'd been hurt, that was true, but she'd get over it quickly. Unlike Chira, she was the kind who could bounce back without apparent damage. She was probably getting over it the minute she left his apartment, and it wouldn't take her long to find someone else, not as amazing as she was. Guys would be lining up around the block. She'd probably forget all about him in no time.

As it turned out, he didn't see Lee that day. Whether she had called in sick or was at her desk high above on the fifth floor, whether she lay prostrate with grief or was already flashing those eyes at another man, he would never know. He didn't go up to look and he didn't telephone and he avoided the cafeteria and the elevator and the halls. At lunchtime, he snuck down the back stairs and bought a sandwich from Jesse, the vendor at the corner, then ate it in his car. Or tried to eat it. Two bites in, he lost his appetite.

Back at his desk that afternoon, Porter sank low in his chair and willed the clock to move. Twice, from the corner of his eye he thought he saw her and twice his heart thrashed and bucked so furiously he thought it must certainly explode from his chest. Both times it was someone else, and both times he sank back into his chair, palms sweaty, stars swimming before his eyes. He felt drunk, badly drunk, though he hadn't touched a drink since Saturday night.

"What the hell's the matter with you?" asked Karl, the transportation reporter. "You look like crap warmed over."

Normally he would have asked Karl whether he routinely heated up crap but this time he didn't have the energy. "Shut up, Karl."

He happened to be looking directly at Karl when he delivered this line and so he saw, for a split second, the injured look fly across his face. Then Karl twisted his mouth and said, "Well, excuse me. Sit over there and have a heart attack. See if I care."

"Karl . . ."

"Fuck you." Karl got up and stormed across the newsroom. Porter sighed. Maybe, if he really tried, he could hurt a couple more people that week.

He put on his tape player headphones and stared at his computer screen as though he were listening to the next Watergate tapes. How in the hell was he ever going to get through this? What were they going to do—take separate entrances? Divide up the elevators? You take elevator one on Mondays, Wednesdays, and Fridays. Twice before he had dated a woman in the building and twice before when it ended he'd made sure to have the I-admire-you-and-I-hope-we-can-still-work-together conversation very soon after the split. But he couldn't imagine having that conversation with Lee; he wouldn't insult her with it. Besides, the idea of talking to her at all was terrifying.

By four-thirty, three other people had come over to ask if he was okay. "He's fine," said Karl. "Happy as a clam."

Porter tried again to apologize. "I'm sorry I snapped, Karl. I'm not feeling well."

But Karl was having none of it. "Why don't you go home, then, instead of sitting up there breathing your germs into the air? What makes you think anybody here wants what you've got?"

Good point, Porter thought. He gathered his things and went on home.

A week passed, then two, then three, and Porter waited for the gloom to lift, or, at least, to stir. He did all the things he normally did with a broken heart. He spent a couple of school nights hanging out at bars and drinking too much. He avoided places he knew, and scouted out dark, narrow, sweaty places, preferably Irish, where the dartboard was in constant use and the most-requested mixer was ice. He loved it, loved the gritty, real, workingman feel of it all, and if anyone asked, he was a printer down at the newspaper, just like his father before. This worked well for the first week, until one night in one bar the conversation turned to "smokes" and their general stupidity and uselessness and he was so drunk it took him ten minutes to realize what they were talking about. When he did, he lurched up in horror and called them all a bunch of beer-swilling, knuckle-dragging racists. He had to run eight blocks to the subway and hop over the turnstile and through the closing doors of a train to keep from getting beat up. That was the end of that.

The next week he became a teetotaler and took up jogging along the Schuylkill. The weather was beautiful, the adrenaline nice, and if he pushed himself hard enough to cause pain, he might actually stop thinking about Lee for a while. But Porter hated running. Short of a marathon, it seemed like such a silly, yuppie, boring thing to do, and he was almost glad the day he stepped in a hole (because he'd seen a car like Lee's drive past and was turning his neck to follow it) and twisted his ankle. That was the end of that.

Work had always proved the most reliable distraction in the past, but this time just walking into the building every morning filled him with dread. He finally saw her for the first time eight days after she walked out of his apartment. He was coming back into the building after an interminable lunch with Lou, when he saw her step off the elevator. She was with two other reporters from the features department, a man and a woman, both black. They were laughing at something; not loudly, but with meaning and what he imagined were these knowing nods among themselves.

Lou, oblivious, rattled on and on about something, but Porter ignored him. He was focused on the freight train of terror and longing roaring through his head; he couldn't hear anything else.

Except her voice. One of the other reporters, the guy, said something, and she turned toward him and smiled and said, "All right, now," with this warm, teasing thing and her voice and those words came to him like his own name over the loudspeaker at Grand Central. *All right now.* Then she saw him. Looked him dead in the eye as she passed not three feet from him, looked at him dead-on without blinking or changing expression. Then she and the other reporters went out.

He saw her several more times after that. Three, to be precise; but each of those times was from a distance. Lee getting onto an elevator at the end of the hall. Lee passing through the newsroom. Lee going out the door.

His friends were no help at all. Joe called him an idiot and refused to discuss it further. Elena rolled her eyes and told him to grow up, but when she saw how miserable he was, softened and offered to fix him up with someone else. "A friend of mine, a sweet girl."

"I don't think I'm ready to jump back in just yet," he said.

"Oh, she's on the rebound too, doesn't want anything serious. That ought to be just your speed."

His friend Charlie was the only one who seemed to take his agony seriously. They met during his teetotaling week, and so Porter sat at a bar sipping cranberry juice and told Charlie the whole, sad story while Charlie had a beer. Charlie listened with such somber sympathy Porter wanted to give him a hug.

"That's rough, man," Charlie said. "I feel for you."

"Thanks."

"I mean, I've been there before, believe me. You're with this woman and things are wonderful. Then they aren't so wonderful. Then you start to have this feeling in the pit of your stomach and you don't know whether it's indigestion or your instinct telling you to get out." Charlie shook his head woefully. "It's not the feeling that's so terrible, not really. It's the not knowing."

Porter knocked back the last of his cranberry juice. Charlie had just moved in with a woman he'd been dating for five years. Clearly something was amiss.

"That's the bitch of it," Charlie repeated to his dwindling beer. "The not knowing. That's the bitch of it."

That *was* the bitch of it. The piercing, sleep-stealing, ball-twisting bitch of it was Porter didn't know whether he'd done the right thing or screwed up his happiness for life. He'd suffered various degrees of heartbreak in the past, the worst with Chira. But each time he had believed, deeply, that if he could just survive the breakup he would be infinitely better off. This time he didn't know, and it ate at him. It ate at him but it wasn't surprising. Hell, he didn't seem to know much anymore.

Twice he caught himself, receiver in hand, about to dial her phone number. The first time it happened he was drunk, having just been dropped off at his apartment by Joe. The second time he was as sober as a saint. It was a Sunday morning, in fact, one of those crystalline late spring days when the air was like something pumped down from God. He was feeling less horrible, for a change, and reading the paper when a story caught his eye and he thought, with a kind of horny excitement and pride, *Lee's going to have a fit with this one,* and picked up the telephone. But then he remembered. And he was still tempted to call, but then he remembered Lee, early in the relationship, saying something about white people. *White people this, white people that.* And he remembered his mother telling him about what his grandmother said. And he hung up.

He knew he was desperate when he telephoned his father and invited him to lunch.

Porter offered to meet out in the burbs but his father said no, he'd be in the city on business anyway. They met at an Italian place in South Philadelphia. Porter arrived twenty minutes early and found his father at the bar, working his way through a bourbon neat.

"You going back to work?" Porter asked.

"Insurance never rests," his father joked. Then, following Porter's glance, he added, "Oh, this?" He laughed. "I always thought journalists understood the world."

"So did I," Porter said.

The host sat them with menus, and they chatted for a while, exchanging pleasantries like any other father and son. Their waiter appeared. He was a man in his fifties, slightly stooped, who walked with a limp and rasped through the daily specials in a ruined voice. Porter's father ordered calamari to start, followed by fettuccine Alfredo. "Ballast," he said. Porter ordered a Caesar salad, knowing he'd never be able to eat even that. After the waiter left with their orders, he took a long, long breath.

"Lee and I broke up," he said in a rush. "A few weeks ago, now. The wedding is off."

He wasn't sure what reaction he'd expected. Dismay? Outrage? Certainly surprise. But what he got was the practiced spiel of an insurance salesman. "What unfortunate news," his father said. "You must be quite upset."

"Actually, I am, yes," Porter said.

"Of course." The waiter appeared with a heaping plate of fried cala-mari. His father tucked the red-and-white-checked napkin in his collar and dug in without breaking stride. "But you know, life is unpredictable. When these things happen, the best thing to do is move ahead."

Porter put a tiny little octopus on his plate but he didn't have the heart to eat it. "Is that all you have to say?"

The surprised look Porter had expected earlier now appeared on his father's face, and Porter realized he'd spoken more sharply than he intended. "I'm not sure what else you expect me to say?"

"I don't know." Porter shoved his plate aside. "Tell me I did the right thing! Tell me I made a terrible mistake. Tell me something."

His father shrugged and said, "How the hell do I know whether you did the right thing or not?"

The waiter came with their plates. Porter's father tucked into the fet-tuccine as though he had not just consumed half a sea monster fried in fat. Porter took a bite of his salad and tried to chew.

"All in good time," his father said.

Porter put down his fork, exasperated. "What does that mean?"

"Hell if I know," his father said. "I'm just trying to give you what you want."

He had come there seeking help, guidance, direction, for once in his life and instead his father was handing him platitudes, bad platitudes, platitudes that didn't even make sense given the context of the situation. He was so furious he wanted to stand up and slug his father in the face, and so disappointed he wanted to curl up beneath the table and cry. Instead, he pushed his salad around on the plate. He would just get through the lunch and leave, because nothing of value was going to be learned here. Not today.

But then his father lifted his head from his fettuccine and he had the faintest little smile on his face. He looked like he was trying to be seri-ous, but he had the faintest little smile. Seeing it made Porter's heart sink, though he couldn't figure out why. Then he remembered. His mother, his grandmother, the faintest little smile.

"Didn't you ever love my mother?" Porter asked. "Didn't you ever love her at all?"

His father looked up and said, "Ah." As though he'd been waiting for the question a long, long time. Still, he did not answer right away. He took another mouthful of fettuccine, wiped his lip, stared at the bread-basket, as though his answer were written on a roll. He seemed like a man who had many, many speeches prepared but didn't know which one to give.

Finally, he cleared his throat. He said, "I don't know."

"You don't know?" Porter didn't try to hide his disgust. "That's it? You don't know? That's all you have to say?"

"Might not be the answer you wanted," his father said. "But at least I'm honest."

"Honest!"

"Yes, honest," his father insisted. "Those are the three most honest words in the world."

"And they're so extremely helpful too." Porter knew he was being petulant but he couldn't help it. He felt like a kid alone on a corner on a hot August day, watching his scoop of ice cream fall into the gutter and melt. "You've been a regular font of wisdom today, Dad."

"I don't like your tone."

But Porter didn't care. He was rolling now. "In fact, I don't know why I didn't call you sooner. You could have saved me a lot of headaches. Why try to figure anything out? Just throw up your hands! Say, I don't know! That's the best way to go through life, huh? That and carrying a fifth."

His father slapped his hands on the table with a loud pop. A woman at the next table glanced over, examined Porter, examined his father, turned away. "You want advice, Porter? Is that what you want?" His father leaned so far across the table his tie fell onto the oily calamari plate. In a kind of nauseated trance, Porter watched it slowly, slowly soak up the grease. "Okay, here goes," said his father. "Here's the sum total of wisdom I've collected in my sixty years. I can reduce it to a sentence: the world is unknowable and so is man. We like to think we're so smart, so self-aware. We like to think our big brains lift us above the animals. What a crock of shit! The truth is, we don't have a clue. Nobody knows why they do anything, not really! We're all running around like mice in a maze and then using a lot of words, words, words to justify it to ourselves. We're all talking through out hats."

His father fell back in his chair, his face red, his forehead glistening, his mouth twisted and ugly. Porter sat in stunned silence, not knowing what to say. The waiter limped up and pointed a finger accusingly at Porter's plate. "Something wrong with the salad?" he rasped.

Porter shook his head and tried to smile; it was the best he could manage. He felt dangerously close to weeping and was afraid what might spill if he opened his mouth.

"It's great," his father said, grinning now and giving the waiter a wink. It was amazing how quickly he could turn it on and off. "He's just watching his girlish figure, you know!"

You wouldn't know this was the man who had just misanthropically reduced the human race to a bunch of scurrying rats. Looking at Porter's father as he joked with the waiter, you would think he was a happy guy.

"I, on the other hand, have no pretensions," his father cried, tapping his gut. The waiter smiled a smile that said: Just leave the tip.

"I'm sorry for you," Porter said. "I really am."

His father eyed him speculatively. "You think I'm a bitter old man, don't you? Well, maybe I am, maybe I am. But that doesn't mean what I've said isn't true."

"It's not true."

"Oh really? Go ahead—tell me one thing you know, Porter. One thing you really, really know."

Porter thought: *I know I don't want to be like you.* But he kept the words to himself; to say them aloud might have felt good but it would have been cruel. And cruelty begets only cruelty. If he'd learned anything from his parents, it was that.

Porter heard himself say, "I know I love Lee."

And in saying it, he knew it was true.

His father sneered. "Oh really? Then why'd you dump her?"

"Because I was afraid. Because I thought I loved her for the wrong reasons."

"So you didn't know why you love her," his father said. But he seemed suddenly bored with the conversation. He glanced around the restaurant and settled his eyes on the ass of a waitress retreating through the swinging kitchen door. "I rest my case."

She wouldn't see him. He called her house three times a night, every night, for almost a week. She either didn't answer at all or, as soon as she heard his voice, just hung up the phone. "If you keep it up," she said finally, "I'm going to have to call the police."

He had left her alone at work, trying to hang on to some measure of propriety. But after a week he was so desperate he began sending her messages across the office computer system. "Please. Can we just talk?"

"No," she messaged back. "Leave me alone."

Finally one evening he left work early and drove to her house to wait. At first he sat in his car. Then, fearing how that might look, he got out and sat on her front step, trying to look casual and at ease. It was a warm June evening and the cries of children playing up the block filtered down to him. He felt a headache coming on. Across the street a curtain moved. He smiled and waved. The curtain fell back. He felt like a stalker, one of those crazed ex-boyfriends they were always writing about. He hoped nobody called the police.

She saw him right away, before she even got out of the car. For a moment she sat there, as if she were trying to decide what to do, and he was afraid she would just drive away again. What would he do then? Sit there all night?

But then she turned off the engine and got out, slamming the door. She was wearing black slacks that outlined the curve of her ass and a simple man-tailored white shirt made of silk. She looked painfully good.

"What are you doing here?" she yelled from the sidewalk, keeping her distance.

"I just want to talk."

"Get off my step."

He stood up. "Lee. Please."

"All I have to do is scream," she said. "People would be out here in a minute."

"I know," he said softly. Just looking at her made him ache; he had to sit down. From his position on the step he looked up at her, feeling himself at her mercy. Again. "They'd probably be only to happy to beat me to death."

For a long time she said nothing.

"At this minute, I'd be only too happy to let them," he said. It was getting dark and the streetlights came on and he couldn't see her eyes.

Finally she moved. "Five minutes."

He followed her inside. She turned on the lights, took off her jacket. Then she crossed her arms over her chest. "Talk."

But now the moment had arrived he was paralyzed. His brain went blank. "Um."

"Four minutes," she said.

He took a breath. "Come on, Lee. This isn't easy."

"Time's up," she said, and reached for the door handle. He stepped in front of her to cut her off.

"All right, damn it! You want me to talk? You want to know why I did what I did? You want the whole, ugly truth? Okay."

He stepped away, moved into the living room, his thoughts racing. He was lost because it wasn't going to go the way he'd planned. It wasn't going to go the way he'd planned because he wasn't going to tell her about the driver guy on the highway, about the word he'd used. He would confess everything else, but not that because if he confessed that, she would never come back to him. And looking at her, he knew if he lost her a second time, he would surely die.

"Okay. I think it started with just the normal jitters. You know. And it started with you always talking about race, race, race, race."

"You slept with another woman because I was talking about race?"

"No, no. Just listen. Please. All I'm saying is when you're white, you don't spend your life thinking about race. And all of a sudden, there it was, like a tree that had sprung up in the middle of my driveway in the middle of the night. I had to deal with it. And so I started thinking . . . I don't know. Crazy things. And then, one day, I saw this little girl, this little biracial girl. In the grocery store. And she was ugly. I thought to myself, that's one ugly kid. And then I realized she was biracial and it scared me because I didn't know if that was why I thought she was ugly. Do you see how terrifying that was? She could have been my child. Our child."

He didn't listen to himself; if he listened he might stop talking and it all had to come out. Lee stood with her arms crossed, protecting herself.

"And then, I found out my father married my mother out of spite. He wanted to get back at his mother and so he went down to Mississippi and found this poor, country girl and dragged her home. And when my grandmother called him on it, with my mother standing right there in the room, he didn't say a word. Just stood there and watched his wife get devastated."

"What?" She must have been so surprised that for a moment she forgot she hated him, because her voice was soft. It made his knees wobble. It took everything he had not to fling himself at her like some maniac.

"Oh, it's an ugly story. I don't want to bore you with it. And I'm not trying to excuse myself. There is no excuse. And it has nothing to do with us. Except . . ."

She looked at him dead-on and finished the thought. "Except you wondered if history weren't repeating itself?"

What a woman. "Yes," he admitted. "And once that ball started rolling there was no way to get out of its path. Maybe I just wanted to prove something to her. Maybe I just wanted to prove to the world how cool and unconventional I am, how open-minded. How willing I was to look beyond your color."

"Mighty big of you," she said.

"Please. I know." His head was throbbing now. He looked longingly at her purse, where he knew she carried a bottle of aspirin. "Do you think you could spare me some aspirin? My head is really killing me."

She got him the aspirin and a glass of water, then went into the living room and collapsed into a chair. He heard, outside, an ambulance race past, sirens blaring. On its way to the scene of human destructiveness.

"So you got scared and ran out and slept with somebody to get you out of things," she said wearily. "Old story."

He was stung by her easy dismissal of his agony. "This was a struggle for me. I was trying to save us both from a big mistake."

She sat up, exasperated. "Struggle? Don't you know what I had to go through to love you, Porter? Where have you been all these months?"

Where indeed? He had no idea.

"I had to decide if loving you meant hating me," Lee said. "I had to decide if you were for real. I had to decide if I could really do this."

"And you did? Just like that?"

She looked at him. "That's what grown-ups do."

She was putting it to him: Was he an adult or not? Was he a man? Decide. He felt panic rise up in his throat.

"Here's the question, Porter," she said. "It's a simple one. Please don't lie to keep from hurting my feelings because I assure you they are already very badly hurt."

He held his breath, waiting.

"Here's the question," she said. "Do you love me? Yes or no."

She'd been remarkably steady to this point, but at the end her voice betrayed her by trembling. Still, her eyes held steady on his face. He thought of the first time he had ever seen her, arriving on that Los Angeles street like an avenging angel, taking his arm. He was astonished again at the depth of her bravery and of her passion and her soul and he wondered if it wouldn't have been better for them to meet under less dramatic circumstances, say, watching clothes spin at the Laundromat.

But, then, would he have noticed her at all?

He looked at Lee and was assailed by the ferocity of his love. "So much it's killing me," he said. "But I don't know how you can trust that. I don't know how I can trust it."

For a long time she studied his face. He held it out there for her examination, his throat closing, his heart suspended in his chest. He thought of his mother, turning toward his father in the corner and seeing in his face her future collapse. He tried to keep his face as open as possible. He wanted Lee to see. He prayed that look was absent from his face, but if it was there, he wanted Lee to see. He wanted her to see and save herself.

After an eternity, she sighed and came to the couch. "What now?" she asked.

He pulled her into his arms. The aspirin had done its job; his headache was gone. He buried his face in Lee's hair and felt the elation that arrives with the absence of pain. After a few moments, he dug around in his pocket for the little black box he'd brought along. His fingers trembled as he took her left hand into his own, and he noticed she was quivering too.

"Somebody has to do something," he said.

They were both shaky, there on the couch, fumbling with the engagement ring. They were shaky but together they managed to slip the damn thing on.